'An epic love story'
Clare Pooley

'This gorgeous, unusual love story manages
to be both heartbreaking and hopeful'
Good Housekeeping

'Utterly moving, this heartfelt read
will capture your imagination'
Woman's Own

what
might
have
been

Holly Miller grew up in Bedfordshire. Since university she has worked as a marketer, editor and copywriter. Holly currently lives in Norfolk with her partner.

Also by Holly Miller

The Sight of You

HOLLY MILLER

what might have been

HODDER &
STOUGHTON

First published in Great Britain in 2022 by Hodder & Stoughton
An Hachette UK company

1

Copyright © Holly Miller 2022

A CIP catalogue record for this title is available from the British Library

Hardback ISBN 978 1 529 32440 2
Trade Paperback ISBN 978 1 529 32441 9
eBook ISBN 978 1 529 32442 6

Typeset in Plantin Light by Hewer Text UK Ltd, Edinburgh
Printed and bound in Great Britain by Clays Ltd, Elcograf S.p.A.

Hodder & Stoughton policy is to use papers that are natural, renewable
and recyclable products and made from wood grown in sustainable
forests. The logging and manufacturing processes are expected to
conform to the environmental regulations of the country of origin.

Hodder & Stoughton Ltd
Carmelite House
50 Victoria Embankment
London EC4Y 0DZ

www.hodder.co.uk

1

'You did what?'

I pause next to the pub's chalkboard craft beer menu, phone pressed to my ear. 'I quit,' I repeat. 'Just now. I mean, ten minutes ago.'

'You handed in your notice?'

'More like . . . stormed out.'

My sister yogic-breathes for a couple of seconds. 'Wow. Okay . . .'

'I couldn't take it any more, Tash. It was one time too many.'

I picture her nodding, trying her best to understand.

'Something will turn up,' I say, with a confidence I definitely don't feel.

'Let me guess: the universe has got your back?'

I manage a smile, but it wobbles a bit. 'Here's hoping.'

The bus back to Tash's isn't due for an hour, so I've taken cover in The Smugglers with a Virgin Mary. I stay sitting at the bar after my drink comes. The Smugglers is something of a Shoreley institution: it's the first place I ever got served, heard live music, met boys who weren't school friends.

I'm starting to feel conscious of just staring into space, so I tap absent-mindedly into the horoscope app on my phone. Checking my horoscope has become my latest guilty pleasure, like watching trashy TV, or eating crumpets in bed. The kind of thing you'd never admit to in front of someone you fancied. But it is slightly addictive. A bit like playing the lottery. *Maybe this time . . .*

I read today's prediction, and my heart does a little tap dance through my chest.

> *Today will see you head off on a new career path. If you're single, this could also be the day you bump into your soulmate.*

And then, as if in slow motion, it happens. As I'm lifting a hand to catch the barman's attention for another, the person next to me gets up, letting someone new slide in. 'Pint of Guinness please, mate.'

The barman hesitates, then glances at me. My new companion turns, and our eyes meet.

'Ah, sorry.' He smiles broadly, the friendliest apology ever. 'Didn't see you there.'

It's the oddest thing: I feel as though I know him. That we have met before. But I can't place my finger on when, or how.

He's the type of good-looking favoured by knitwear adverts – all dark stubble and ruffled hair and dewy eyes. His expression as he looks at me – amused and intense all at once – combined with the sweet haze of his aftershave, makes me draw breath.

'Hi. No. You go,' I say.

'What are you having?'

'Oh, you really don't need to—'

'No, I insist.'

'Well. A Virgin Mary, then. Thank you.'

To his credit and my relief, he doesn't attempt to tack a vodka shot onto my order, or crack a lame joke about pubs traditionally being for boozing in.

When the drinks arrive, he glances around the room, then shrugs and stays where he is on the stool next to me. 'Do you mind? It's packed tonight.' He raises his glass to mine. 'I'm Caleb, by the way.'

I don't recognise the name.

'Lucy.' I smooth back my beachy mess of hair, wishing I'd at least thought to glance into a mirror before storming out of the office earlier. It's super-stuffy in here, swarming with bodies between the thick walls and low ceiling, and I suspect it's only a matter of time before I start wilting in the warmth.

I imagine Tash face-palming at this, despairing at my unkempt mane, my crumpled dress. I've always thought of my sister as the slightly more polished version of me: she has three extra inches on my average height, hair a shade or two blonder, skin with a few more lumens' worth of gleam. Still, Caleb seems relaxed, like he probably doesn't care too much about smooth hair, or lumens, which is just as well.

'I remember when this was a proper spit-and-sawdust place,' he's saying, sipping from his pint, his gaze alighting on the dazzling wall of gin bottles behind the bar. 'Now it's all craft ales and signature cocktails and wood-fired pizzas.'

'And perfectly-staged Instagram posts.'

'And ridiculous bar snacks.' He slides a bowl across the bar towards me. 'Wasabi pea?'

I laugh and shake my head, trying to ignore the fluttering in my chest. 'I'm more of a Scampi Fries kind of girl.'

Smiling, he raises a fist and we bump knuckles, his hand dwarfing mine.

'So, you're local?' I ask, wondering if I might be able to find out whether we know each other, somehow.

He nods. 'You?'

I nod back.

'This your Friday night haunt?'

'Not exactly.' I hesitate, but then the words start spilling into the space between us. 'I actually . . . just quit my job.'

His eyes widen. 'Wow. Okay. So you're in here . . . drowning your sorrows?'

'No. I mean, it was a good thing, quitting. A point of principle.'

'Well, then, congratulations.' He lifts his glass, and then – for just a millisecond – we are looking right into each other's eyes. I feel my breath flex in my chest, a spread of warmth across my skin. 'Good for you.'

'Thank you,' I manage, and then – possibly to distract either him or me from my fluster, which must surely be visible – I say, 'So, how about you – are you gainfully employed?'

He nods. 'I'm a photographer.'

'Really? For a living?'

He laughs. 'Believe it or not, we do exist.'

'Sorry,' I say, mortified. 'I just meant . . . there are a lot of people who dream of doing that, so . . . I'm impressed.'

He smiles and nods a thank-you. 'Well, you're free now . . . so what do you dream of doing?'

I hesitate. I could tell him – *I've always really wanted to write a novel* – but that would turn me into the kind of person people try to escape at parties. 'Actually, I'm not sure yet.'

'What did you do before you quit?' He's swivelled round on his stool to face me now, his eyes attentive and bright.

'I worked for an ad agency.'

He sips from his pint, eyebrows elevated. 'We have those in Shoreley?'

I laugh. 'Just the one, actually. We liked to think of ourselves as small but mighty.'

'And you quit because . . . ?'

I hesitate, and just as I'm thinking of the best way to explain it, I freeze.

No. It can't be.

I blink rapidly, trying to make out if what I'm seeing is real.

Because, from out of nowhere, on the section of street visible from where I'm sitting, I spot the last person on earth I'd have expected to see.

Halfway across the window, he's paused to look at something on his phone. As I watch on in shock, I feel my heart start to beat a little faster.

It's definitely him.

Max. Max Gardner.

'Excuse me,' I murmur, pushing back my stool with a scrape, so hard it almost falls over. I abandon Caleb and

5

my drink, elbowing my way through the crowd and finally out onto the street. The coldness of the air after the warmth of the pub draws a gasp from my mouth that feels like my heart leaping to my throat.

'Max,' is all I say.

He looks up, and I take him in – black woollen coat, pinstriped suit, same gleam to his gaze, same sharp jawline, no trace of ageing on his handsome face. Tall, fair, gravitas just standing still. Briefly, he is motionless. The moment has cast its spell.

I rummage in my stomach for my voice. 'Hi.'

He smiles gently, steps towards me. 'Oh my God. It's really you. Hi.'

2

We air-kiss, which is ridiculous, because Max and I used to laugh at people who did that, and then stand back to take each other in. For the second time tonight, I curse the fact I'm looking decidedly less than sharp, that particular kind of frazzled you become when you've had way too much on your mind.

Max and I aren't connected on social media, and like any good lawyer, he keeps his Facebook and Instagram private. I've never been able to bring myself to friend or follow him, but I do check his LinkedIn from time to time. It never changes: Real Estate Litigation Lawyer at Heyford West White, or HWW if you're into acronyms, an American law firm with its UK offices in the City.

His profile picture – professionally-shot and classic Max – matches up pretty well to the man standing in front of me. Killer jawline, sandy hair, devilish gaze. The kind of expression that confirms he'll take your case seriously, but with a glint that hints he'll be celebrating hard when he wins.

The person you were meant to be with, my heart whispers without permission. *The one that got away.*

'What . . .' I say eventually, because one of us has got to start speaking. 'What are you doing here?'

'Work. Well, sort of.' He rubs his jaw, looks uncharacteristically sheepish. 'I had a meeting just off the M2, then I
thought ... might as well carry on, take a trip down
memory lane.'

Memory lane. You were thinking about me.

'I was actually debating trying to get in touch with you,
but ...' He trails off. 'Wasn't sure if you lived here any
more, or if you'd even want to see me, or ...'

'No, it's ... Of course I'd want to see you.' I smile,
emotions quick-stepping around inside me. 'What was the
work thing? Anything fun?'

He laughs. 'Not even slightly. Just a site visit. High-rise
office development. Allegedly stealing light from neigh-
bouring buildings. All very dull.'

I smile at the *allegedly*. 'You achieved your dream, then.
To be a lawyer.'

As he smiles and nods, I catch a glimmer of pride in his
eyes, which is more than merited. I feel oddly gratified by
the sight of lawyer Max, in his smooth white shirt and
charcoal-grey tie, thriving and smart, everything he ever
wanted to be.

We catch up for a few minutes, about his life in London,
and the strange turn my professional life has taken today,
before it starts to feel a bit ridiculous that we're having this
conversation standing out on the pavement, a Friday-night
tide of people forced to part around us.

I clear my throat. 'Listen, do you fancy getting a drink,
or ... ?'

'Actually,' he says, checking his watch and grimacing
gently, 'I have to get back to London. I've got a flight at

stupid o'clock tomorrow, and I've not even packed. This was all a bit . . . spur-of-the-moment.'

The thrill in my chest subsides. Maybe his old urge to escape me still lingers. But I make myself smile. 'Lucky you. Anywhere nice?'

'Seychelles. Two weeks.'

'By yourself?' It's out of my mouth before I can help it.

He shakes his head. 'Diving. It's a group thing.'

'That sounds amazing,' I say, privately relieved – though of course it's not my right to be – that it's not a romantic getaway for two. 'Well, maybe when you get back we can—'

'Definitely,' he says, looking right into my eyes, making my stomach twitch with pleasure. 'We've got nearly ten years to catch up on.'

For a moment our gazes clamp together, and I find it hard to look away.

'This is kind of crazy,' I say, eventually. 'How many people are there in Shoreley on any given day?'

'Hundreds? Thousands?' he says, smiling. He must be thinking what I am – how could he not? 'And yet . . . here we are.'

We swap numbers, and then I watch him walk off along the cobblestones, a squall of thoughts inside my head. Could it be possible that my stupid app was right – have I just bumped into my soulmate? I've so often thought that, for me, Max was simply the right guy at the wrong time.

3

'**Y**ou did the right thing,' Jools assures me, when I tell her I walked out of my job yesterday. 'They've been stringing you along for long enough.'

I'm still in bed, video-chatting with my oldest friend, the person who's been by my side since primary school, who never fails to reassure me in times of uncertainty.

'Thanks,' I say, biting my lip. 'Feels a bit hasty in the cold light of day, though.' I'm not, as a rule, someone who makes rash decisions. I might occasionally drink coffee late at night, try a bold shade of lipstick or pick an item at random off a takeaway menu, but that's generally as risky as I get.

Jools sips her tea. Like me, she's not been awake long. Her hair is falling loose from its knot, and she pushes it away from her face. 'So, what did Georgia say, when you told her you were quitting?'

'Not much, actually. I think she was in shock.'

When I first started at Figaro nine years ago, it seemed like luck I didn't fully deserve – a role at Shoreley's only creative agency mere months after dropping out of university. I originally applied for a writing job, but Georgia employed me as a planner, because she had a vague idea her fledgling agency wouldn't get very far without one. I

10

said yes straight away – I was so grateful to be offered a job at all – and vowed I'd mention a writing role again once I was settled and had proved myself. There were just six of us at the start, and together we grew the business to the forty-strong outfit it is today. And for most of those years, it was good. Fulfilling on many levels. But deep down, I wasn't a planner: I'd always wanted to write. It was in my blood. The whole time I was researching products and industries, liaising with clients or composing briefs, I knew my heart really lay in writing. I'd scribble down headlines, feed creative angles to the team, sometimes draft copy to help the writers out.

It all came to a head yesterday afternoon, when I discovered Georgia had recruited an external copywriter. She'd promised the job to me on five separate occasions over the years, and now she'd given it to someone else.

I stormed into her office to demand an explanation, whereupon she informed me weakly that the timing wasn't right, that she couldn't afford to lose me from planning. So – surprising myself as much as anyone else – I simply walked out.

'So, what now?' Jools says, biting into a slice of toast. 'Are you going to move to London?'

'London?' I echo, like she's just said, *The moon.*

'Yeah. Didn't that big-time agency contact you a couple of weeks ago?'

I nod. 'Only because they're looking for a planner.'

As it happens, a recruiter for the crème de la crème of creative agencies, Supernova Agency of Soho, did message me a fortnight or so ago. Its staff is like a roll call of the industry's hottest talent, and it regularly competes for the biggest accounts in the country, winning pitch after pitch, award after award. Famously ruthless, Supernova has a fierce reputation: for poaching staff, demanding regular all-nighters and refusing to acknowledge weekends. But the pay is eye-watering and the office has its own bar, gym and nail station. Plus there are the legendary all-expenses-paid staff away trips.

I've received similar messages from various recruiters over the years, but they all seemed to coincide with reasons why I shouldn't leave Figaro – another promise from Georgia about making me a writer, a pay rise, Shoreley being voted the best place to live in the UK, a *Guardian* article about Londoners fleeing the city in droves. And to be honest, I've been pretty happy in Shoreley, living with Tash and her husband and my nephew. I've never seriously considered moving to the capital.

'This is perfect timing, Luce,' Jools is saying. 'We've got a room going free. Literally, today. Cara's moving out.'

Jools left Shoreley for London nearly twelve years ago to study nursing, and never came home. For the past three years she's lived in a house-share in Tooting. Like me, she's been saving to buy her own place, and in the interim a house-share's cheaper than a one-bed flat. Plus it's just a street away from the hospital where she works.

She's had various housemates and flatmates over the years – all too often a source of amusement for us – but her current lot seem pretty decent. I've met them a handful of times. Cara in particular was warm and sharp-witted, with a guttural laugh and a penchant for making cheese-on-toast in the middle of the night.

And Jools' house is nice. Yes, it's scruffy and well-worn, with peeling wallpaper and over-trodden carpets and a permanent symphony of drips and leaks. But there's a warm and homely vibe there, too. And it's always full of people. It's a place I can imagine feeling safe.

Jools tells me Cara's going travelling. South-East Asia, then Australia.

My stomach swings as my gaze flicks to my bedroom window. An instinctive search for air, an escape route.

I take a couple of steadying breaths, then look back at my phone. 'Are you serious?'

'Yes! Get that high-flying agency job and move in with me.'

'But . . . I don't think I want to be a planner in London any more than I do in Shoreley.'

'Become a copywriter, then. I mean, you might have to start in a more junior role – but look at all the industry experience you've got.'

And a portfolio, I think, cautiously. Ads I've sketched out in my spare time, copy I've written when the team has been up against it, scamps I've worked up with designers, just for fun.

'Plus, you know who else lives in London,' says Jools, meaningfully.

'Who?' I say innocently, even as my mind is whispering, *Max*.

'Max.'

★　　★　　★

'*Max?*' my sister says a few minutes later as I'm downstairs getting breakfast, her eyes going wide as a deer's in a torch beam.

Tash has never been a Max fan, ever since he broke my heart.

'I know, I know. But he was lovely, last night. He seemed . . . pleased to see me.'

'What was he doing in Shoreley?'

'Just passing. A work thing,' I say, opting not to fill her in on Max's self-confessed trip down memory lane.

Tash hands me a coffee. While I'm shovelling Coco Pops at her immaculate kitchen breakfast bar, she's prepping for a gym session, head to toe in Sweaty Betty, a giant canister of water in one hand.

I moved in with Tash and her husband Simon two years ago. It was part of a big idea – hers more than mine, at the start – to help me save money and eventually get on the property ladder. As it happens, I hate living on my own, and I was craving the company anyway after splitting up with my ex, so it worked out pretty well.

It's not as much of a sacrifice on Tash and Simon's part as it sounds. Their converted farmhouse has six bedrooms and two actual wings, plus I'm live-in unofficial babysitter. It's about ten miles inland, surrounded by nothing but vast arable fields, with no near neighbours. The depth of the quietness here can sometimes feel eerie, making me crave the agitation of crashing waves or the commotion of enthusing tourists roaming Shoreley's cobblestone streets.

'Jools thinks I should move to London,' I say, through a mouthful of cereal while Tash bounces up and down from her ankles. 'There's a room going spare at her place.'

The furrow on Tash's forehead deepens. She stops bouncing. 'Luce, just because you've bumped into Max, you can't just up and—'

'It's not that,' I say, because really, it isn't. I mean, yes – my horoscope did happen to mention bumping into my soulmate yesterday, and it does seem ridiculous to think it could have been referring to anyone other than Max. But it did also hint I was about to embark on a new career path. Jools has a free room, and I *have* had that message from the ad agency recruiter: maybe all the signs are pointing in the direction of London.

'I've got a better idea,' says Tash.

'Go on,' I say, suspiciously, because – let's face it – I am talking to a person who enjoys a pre-breakfast workout.

'Why don't you use the opportunity to write? That's always been your dream.'

'Yeah, that's sort of what I was thinking – trying to get a writing job at an ad agency.'

'No, I meant . . .' Tash hesitates, then breaks into a smile. 'Look what I came across at the deli yesterday.' She leans over to the fruit bowl, slides a flyer out from underneath it.

WRITE THAT NOVEL! ALL LEVELS WELCOME.
WEEKLY WORKSHOPS. £5 A SESSION.
RUN BY PUBLISHED NOVELIST
RYAN CARWELL.

I look up at her. 'Write a novel?'

She reaches across the breakfast bar, takes my hand. 'You know, just before you went travelling, you read me that short story you'd written, and I was . . . blown away. Honestly, Luce. I've been thinking ever since that you should do something with your writing. Well, maybe this is your chance. To get back to doing what you really love. Didn't you say you'd had an idea for a novel?'

I swallow. In many ways, she's right: writing fiction *is* what I love to do. It was born out of being a voracious childhood bookworm, I think: I would always turn to books in times of uncertainty or when I needed an escape, or to lose myself for a while – like when Dad was made redundant, or there was that spate of burglaries in our street, or our beloved grandmother eventually succumbed to stomach cancer. And the books I sought solace in were, almost without exception, stories about love. The kind of books my parents had always had lying around the house, timeless old romantics that they were. So during holidays and weekends, and on school nights by torchlight beneath my bedsheets, I lost myself in *Wuthering Heights* and *Pride and Prejudice*, *Anna Karenina* and *Dr Zhivago*. The stories were not always cheerful, of course, and love didn't always prevail. But I liked what they had in common: that they put love centre stage, that universal, all-encompassing emotion with the power to either complete or destroy us.

As I got older – and especially at moments of disappointment, heartache, or trauma – my passion for reading turned into a desire to write, a longing to see if I could make other people feel the way I felt when I read: moved to tears, inspired, comforted.

So I began to write the kind of fiction I understood best: love stories. At uni, I joined a creative writing group, entered competitions, even had a couple of short stories published in the student magazine. Writing became my form of self-expression, a way to try to make sense of life. Even when I dropped out of my English literature degree, I told everyone it would be okay, because I was off to become a writer as I travelled the globe. And at that point, I'd had an idea for a novel – I had the premise, characters and rough chapter plan sketched out, had filled half a notebook.

But then came Australia, when the world stopped making sense to me entirely. And I no longer wanted to express how I felt. I simply shut down. Back then, merely glancing at my own words on the page was enough to bring bile to my throat.

I've not so much as looked at that novel again since.

My sister's eyes are lighting up with possibility. 'That was the plan when you left uni, Lucy, wasn't it – to write a novel? But after you came back from travelling ...' She trails off, and I know what she really wants to say: that on my return, I wasn't quite the same person as I was before.

'I need money,' I say. 'I can't just ... not work.'

'So get a part-time job, to tide you over. The cost of living's so much cheaper here – you could get by on something casual.'

I can't deny I do have it easy, living in Shoreley. The outrageous cost of renting even a single room in Jools' house-share has already given me mild palpitations.

'Actually,' Tash says, blinking rapidly like she's just had a light-bulb moment, 'Ivan's looking for someone to help run the shop.'

I stare at her, blankly. 'Who's Ivan? What shop?'

'You know Ivan. Luke's dad.'

'I don't know Luke, or his dad.' Tash does this a lot – name-drop other kids and their parents from my nephew Dylan's school, most of whom I've never met or heard of before.

'Luke's in Dylan's class. His dad owns the gift shop in town. Pebbles & Paper.'

'The place that sells candles for thirty quid a pop?'

Tash smiles. 'Come on – you're into signs from the universe, or whatever. I pick up this flyer, Ivan's looking for someone to help in the shop . . . This is an *opportunity*. To finish that novel and do what you've always dreamed of.'

Once, at uni, a group of us were lounging about in my bedroom in halls when we started discussing our biggest fears. We agreed on the usual things – losing a loved one, or illness, or being in this much debt for the rest of our lives – but there was one thought that kept ringing through my mind like a bell: missing my calling. I couldn't imagine anything worse than overlooking the chances – however big, or small – life might send my way. I still can't, as it happens, even all these years later.

I feel something stir in my stomach at the thought of reacquainting myself with the person I used to be.

'So?' My sister, my best friend, my long-time confidante, is looking at me, her eyes alive with expectation. 'What are you going to do, Luce? Stay, or go?'

4

Stay

'So, your sister said you're a writer.'

Only six short days since that morning in Tash's kitchen, when I made my decision to stay in Shoreley, and she's already telling the world that I write for a living, which really couldn't be further from the truth.

I'm meeting Dylan's friend's dad Ivan at Pebbles & Paper before it opens for the day. According to Ivan's spiel, it's an award-winning gift shop that's featured in numerous magazines – though it's unclear exactly what award a gift shop might win, and I don't believe for one moment his claim that Kate Winslet stopped by last summer to buy fifty quid's worth of vegan soap. His outfit is kind of setting the tone – he's wearing off-white chinos, loafers and a striped shirt of the kind most often seen at Henley Regatta.

The shop's interior is all very beach chic, making liberal use of bunting, seashells and nautical stripes. I've popped in here just a couple of times before, only to baulk at the prices before legging it empty-handed. I don't tell Ivan this, of course, a man who's spent the last five minutes bragging about his profit margins.

'Sort of,' I say meekly, in reply to his half-question, as I breathe in the fug of essential oils, scented candles and handmade drawer fresheners. 'I mean, that's the plan.'

Ivan frowns, like my life goals could do with some serious unpacking right here among the inspirational driftwood signs. 'Well, anyway, we're expanding next year,' he says. 'Lining up a couple of little premises in Suffolk and West London.' He pushes his fringe out of his eyes. 'So, look, we'd mainly need you to do weekday mornings. Me or my wife, Clarissa, will take over in the afternoons. But we would need you to work all day on alternate Saturdays.'

'Perfect,' I say.

'All right. Let's go over how the till works, shall we?'

I nod and follow him to the counter, where there's a computer screen, a goldfish bowl full of artisan soap and a complicated assortment of tissue paper and ribbons that I sincerely hope I won't be expected to touch. It's long been my opinion that gift bags were invented for a reason.

'So, what's your novel about?' Ivan says, logging in to the till on the touchscreen.

I hesitate. 'Well, it's sort of . . . a love story, I suppose.'

'Ah,' he says, knowingly. 'One of those books, is it?'

'One of what books?'

I can tell he's trying to resist waggling his eyebrows. 'Racy.'

I clear my throat. 'Not exactly. It's loosely based on my parents, actually.'

He looks faintly disappointed and not at all convinced. 'So, what were you doing before this? Tash said something about advertising.'

'Figaro,' I say, the word sticking unexpectedly in my throat as I try not to picture the expression on Georgia's face as I told her I was leaving. No matter what had gone down between us, I'd always considered her a friend. 'Do you know it?'

'Sorry, never heard of it. Right. Punch in this code here to log in. And then we'll do a few dummy scans using the alpaca-wool bedsocks.'

When I get back to Tash's around lunchtime, the house is empty and utterly still, shrouded in the type of silence I've only ever really encountered this deep in the countryside. If the house is full, I'm usually able to tune it out, but whenever I'm alone, it hits me like a waterfall. At new year, when Tash, Simon and Dylan went skiing to Chamonix for a week, I had to turn the sound system on in every room – exactly as I'm doing now – just to feel a bit less like an apocalypse survivor. To drown out that all-too-familiar drumming in my chest.

The job at Pebbles & Paper looks like it will work out. Ivan seems okay, if a bit ridiculous. He's asked me to start a week on Saturday. But for the whole bus ride home, I couldn't stop wondering if I've made the right decision, staying in Shoreley.

I mean, really – who do I think I am? I'm actually nothing more than a wannabe writer who's never even had so much as a paragraph of fiction published professionally. Maybe I should have gone to London, moved in with Jools, got a job at that Soho agency. Maybe I still can.

But as I'm tipping Worcester sauce all over my cheese-on-toast, a message from Jools flashes up on my phone. She says Cara's room has been taken by someone called Nigel, who works in financial auditing. Apparently, he brought an actual *basket of muffins* with him when he turned up to view it.

Well, I could never have competed with that.

I look again at the flyer Tash showed me last week, pinned up now on the kitchen corkboard, and feel a fresh and unfamiliar rush of conviction. *Come on. You can make this work.*

I just need to take a breath, and put my trust in the universe. It's an approach that's worked pretty well for me in the past: I got the job at Figaro because Georgia happened to drop a bag full of shopping in front of me on the street and, as I helped her pick it up, I cracked a joke about the poorly written pack copy on her box of granola. A mere twenty-four hours before I met Max for the first time, I opened a fortune cookie that said *Love is on its way.* I have an excellent track record with four-leaf clovers, and double-yolk eggs.

My faith in all this stuff is partly hereditary – my mum and dad met on holiday when they were twenty, after the travel agent messed up and sent my dad to Menorca not Mallorca. They even have the words *What's meant for you won't pass you by* stencilled onto the wall of their kitchen. I'm willing to let the cringe factor slide, because I'm so on-board with the sentiment.

Once I've finished eating, I head up to my bedroom and take another look at the only item I brought home from my travels nine winters ago. A single notebook, bound in leather. I'd bought it specially before I left the UK, intending to fill it and return with at least something to show for the disaster that had been the preceding three months.

Flipping through it again now, I'm transported back to every place I was sitting while I was scribbling across its pages – a beachside café in Morocco, a park in Singapore, a bar in Kuala Lumpur. And then I'm confronted once more with what happened in Australia, the sour and uncomfortable reality that just a few hours after writing this last paragraph – I finger the page now in regret – a man would flash a double-take smile at me in a bar, and tell me his name was Nate.

And what about Max? Reacquainting myself with this book has reminded me just how much I loved him back then, how he hovered in my mind as I wrote. I remember how long it took me to get over him. How many times I've thought of him in the intervening years, wondering if I've missed out on being with my soulmate.

Have I been monumentally stupid in opting to stay here? Should I message him – or is the fact he's now on holiday a sign to forget him? Might I have missed a second shot at lifelong happiness?

As I'm shutting the notebook with a sigh, my gaze alights on something else, something that startled me when I happened across it this morning.

A beer mat, with Caleb's number scribbled on it.

Unsurprisingly, he hadn't hung around in The Smugglers last week, after I sprinted off to chase after

Max. I felt bad about it – just upping and leaving, abandoning our conversation like that – but I never got the chance to apologise.

It was only today, as I got ready to meet Ivan and put my work coat on for the first time since quitting, that I discovered Caleb had slipped a beer mat with his number into the pocket.

I flip the beer mat now between my fingers a couple of times, recalling with a smile the gentle probe of his eyes, his friendliness, how his laughter made my stomach fizz. And before I've even really thought about what I'm doing, I find myself dialling his number.

He takes me by surprise when he answers, somewhat curtly. I'd assumed he'd let an unknown caller go to voicemail. 'Yep?'

I feel my stomach plunge. 'It's . . . It's Lucy. From the pub. The Smugglers, last week? You wrote your number on a beer mat?'

His gruffness turns instantly to brightness. 'Lucy. Hello. I did. Nice to hear from you.'

'I only found it this morning. The beer mat,' I falter, wondering if perhaps I should have messaged him instead of calling. Nobody calls anybody these days, unless they're the wrong side of fifty, or a member of the emergency services.

'Yeah, sorry about that,' he says, with a hint of abashment. 'I think that might be just about the cheesiest thing I've ever done.'

Oh, God. He's changed his mind. He regrets giving me his number. I knew I shouldn't have called.

'I'm really pleased you called,' he continues.

'You . . . You are?'

He laughs. 'Yeah. I was starting to think I might have to go back to The Smugglers tonight on the off chance you'd be at the bar again.'

A little eddy of pleasure rushes through me. I smile. 'Well, as it happens, I am free tonight.'

I can hear him smiling too. 'Excellent.'

Caleb was at work when I called, so he suggested we meet at his studio, in town. It's inside a converted terraced house, one of those old whitewashed ones tucked down a cobbled side street, all sloping walls and creaking floorboards and beams low enough to headbutt.

After he buzzes me in I climb a narrow, winding staircase and pop my head around the door marked with his name.

I don't know what I was expecting – lots of lights and tripods, maybe, and some of those weird white umbrellas – but the studio is in fact just a small room, with stripped wooden floorboards, white walls and white furniture, along with a pot plant, coffee machine and massive Mac computer. I can't even see Caleb at first, until he pokes his head out from behind the monitor, which is about the size of your average cinema screen.

Smiling, he gets to his feet. 'Hello again.'

He's even more handsome than I remember, casual in a pair of dark jeans and faded navy-blue sweater.

'Nice studio,' I say, feeling slightly shy suddenly.

He laughs. 'Thank you. Although I do realise I must have come across like a bit of a tosser, suggesting we "meet at my studio".'

I laugh too. 'Honestly, I didn't even think about it.'

We both pause for a couple of moments, taking each other in.

'You look nice,' Caleb says.

God, so do you, I want to say. *Where did you spring from?*

I agonised this afternoon over what to wear (is this a date? Isn't it?) before eventually aiming for the mid-point between comfort and style in a grey cotton smock dress, sheer tights and heeled boots. And some bright red earrings, for a pop of colour.

'Thank you,' I say.

'Um, I got you something.' He passes me a paper carrier bag.

I peer inside, and laugh. The bag is filled with packets of Scampi Fries. He must have gone out specially this afternoon to buy them.

'Wow. Thank you. That is a truly superior gift.'

'You're welcome. Hey, have a seat. Just need to press "send" on one email, then I'm all yours.'

The nearest chair is one of those wire-basket-type affairs of the kind that frequently feature in interiors magazines. I'm slightly worried it's going to have a sausage-factory effect on my backside, but I flip down the cushion propped up against the back of it, whereupon it becomes much comfier than it looks.

'So, Lucy,' Caleb says, showing no interest at all in attending to his email. 'You were in the middle of telling me why you quit your job, when I saw you.'

I wince, recalling the way I sprinted out of the pub to chase after Max. 'Listen, about that—'

'You really don't need to explain.'

'But I want to.'

I meet his gaze. His brown eyes are kind. 'Okay,' he says.

'The guy I saw . . . was an old friend. I hadn't seen him in years. I was really enjoying talking to you, but—'

'Likewise.'

'I just had to . . . run out and say hi. Sorry, though. You must have thought I was pretty rude.'

He laughs, affects agreement. 'Oh, absolutely. But weirdly . . . I still wanted you to have my number.'

I smile. 'Well. Thank you.'

'I would have waited for you to come back actually, but I had to meet someone.'

I hesitate for a moment, confused.

'I was waiting for a mate when I saw you,' he explains, 'but I'd got the wrong pub.'

Serendipitous, I think but don't say.

'Anyway. Your job . . .'

'Oh. Well, essentially, they promised me a certain role, then hired someone else for it.'

'Ouch. So, what's your plan now?'

I release a breath. 'You know how you said suggesting we meet here might make you seem like a bit of a tosser?'

He laughs. 'Yep.'

'Well, I can probably top that.'

'Go for it.'

'I've decided to . . . write a novel.'

'What are you talking about? That's cool.'

27

I bite my lip. 'Thanks. Have no idea if I can even do it, though.'

He leans back in his chair. 'How long are you giving yourself?'

'Not sure,' I say, realising as I'm speaking how little of a plan I actually have. 'I've got a part-time job at that gift shop to tide me over. Pebbles & Paper.'

Caleb's face lights up when I say this, and all at once he looks like he's struggling to hold back a laugh.

My eyes widen. 'What?'

'I'm barred from that place.'

'How can you be barred from a gift shop in Shoreley?'

'I had a sort of . . . heated debate with the owner.'

'Ivan? About what?'

'Oh, he was selling these wooden trinkets that he claimed were handmade by a local carpenter. Unique, bespoke, all that bollocks.' Caleb makes liberal use of air quotes as he speaks. 'So I bought my mum a couple of bits for her birthday. Came to seventy quid. Except it turned out my stepsister had a load of stuff from the *exact same range*. Bear in mind she lives in Newcastle and has never set foot in Shoreley.'

I smile. 'Oh no. What did you do?'

'Well, I went down there and politely suggested he stop lying to his customers. And I *might* have mentioned Trading Standards, which was when he got all sweaty and defensive and barred me.' He laughs. 'I mean, it's not even like I've been barred from a pub or a cool nightclub. It's Pebbles & Paper.'

I shake my head, start laughing too.

'Sorry. Being a bit tactless, aren't I?'

'Not at all. It's good to be prepared.'

'So.' He's still not touched that email. 'What kind of novel are you writing?'

I hesitate, wondering if I should even really be describing what I've written as a novel at this point. Over the past week, I've managed to inch my way through a sum total of fourteen pages. A few thousand words. But as for being able to call it a novel quite yet . . . well, that feels like a bit of a leap.

My shyness notches up a touch. 'Oh, just girl-meets-boy stuff. Fairly standard.'

'Since when was girl-meets-boy ever standard?' Caleb says, and then my eyes meet his, and for a moment we are just looking at each other, and it feels weirdly lovely and comfortable in a way I can't quite define.

I clear my throat. 'So, how long have you been a photographer?'

'Um, over a decade now. Eleven years.'

'Nice.'

'Dropped out of art college,' he says quickly – I'm not sure why at first. Maybe he thinks the numbers have made him sound older than he is.

I smile. By my calculation, we must be nearly the same age, give or take a couple of years. 'Rarely meet fellow dropouts.'

'You too?'

I nod. 'English literature.'

'What'd you do instead?'

I swallow, skirt the full truth. 'Went travelling.'

'Really?' He leans forward. 'Where did you go?'

'Oh, just the usual gap-year kind of places. Europe, Morocco, Australia.' I keep talking, before he can ask me more. 'How about you – why did you drop out of college?'

He laughs. 'Impatience.'

'What kind of photography do you do?' I get to my feet and wander over to the back wall, where there's a tiny, stiff-looking sofa and a large black folder on top of a small coffee table. 'May I?'

Caleb nods, so I lift the cover and peek inside.

'That all needs updating,' he says, as I start to turn the pages. 'But . . . lifestyle and portrait, mainly. A lot of corporate work. Weddings, occasionally. Whatever comes my way, really.'

The photos are incredible: some striking images of a red-haired girl sipping coffee in a café, dogs whirling on a beach, a couple walking beneath an umbrella on a grey, wet day that Caleb's managed to make look spectacular, the rain like glitter in the air. 'These are amazing.'

'Thanks,' he says, sounding as self-conscious as I did when he asked about my writing. 'I've been meaning to frame a few. Jazz this place up a bit.'

I look up. 'You've not been here long?'

'Well, long enough. Six months.'

'Where were you before?'

'London. I moved back here when I separated from my wife. I grew up in Shoreley, so . . .'

Separated, I think. *That's not quite divorced, is it?*

I feel him watching me. 'That was my clumsy way of telling you I've been married.'

I shut the folder carefully. 'Happens all the time.'

He lets loose a breath. 'I was hoping you'd say that.'

Go

Just a week after walking out of Figaro and making my decision to give London a go, I find myself moving in with Jools.

The house is on a quiet street in Tooting – or at least, quiet for London. It's just off the high street, bookended by the hospital at one end, and a pub at the other. I happen to know from previous visits that the pub excels in the three essential criteria of any decent public house: quality quizzes, live music and a cracking Sunday roast. Jools and her housemate Sal, who's a midwife, go there for food if they can't be bothered to cook.

I've had a knot in my chest for the past few days, wondering if I'm doing the right thing, moving to London; if I should have taken some time out to think before jumping straight back into another job. If staying with Tash and working in that gift shop and writing a novel might actually have been a better way to go.

It would have been a lot less stressful, for a start.

Earlier this week, I called the Supernova recruiter and explained my situation, and I've been invited for an interview, a week on Friday. Not that I have the faintest clue how to persuade them I'm a talented writer – other than my makeshift portfolio, I don't have an awful lot going for me. Hardly any real-world writing experience. A degree I dropped out of, six months before graduation. I mean, this is Supernova – solar systems apart from anywhere else I've worked.

At the house, Jools shows me up to the double room Cara's vacated. It's identical to Jools', only this one looks over the street at the front – plus it lacks the stylish artwork and hip furnishings, of course. The space is bare except for a bed and chest of drawers, but it feels pleasingly blank-canvas. Somewhere I can make my own. It's roomy and high-ceilinged, with a bright wash of April daylight spilling in through a large bay window. I'm weird about light, can't stand gloomy rooms.

I look out over the street, my ears adjusting to the background hum of buses and cars and reversing ve-hicles. So different to Tash's place and its canyon-grade silence. Here there's always something moving, someone nearby. I find it comforting, but it still feels a little like culture shock.

Jools loops her arms over my shoulders from behind. She's freshly showered after her shift, the familiar scent of her body lotion comforting as cashmere. 'Welcome home,' she whispers, and I feel the tightness in my chest loosen slightly.

It's going to be okay. Jools is here. You have an interview for your dream job. This is a clean slate, a fresh start. Time to make the most of it.

Sal and Reuben, Jools' housemates, are out, so Jools and I head to the pub to celebrate my first night.

'This is definitely the best place you've ever lived, Jools,'

What Might Have Been

I remark, as we settle down in a corner – white wine for Jools, sparkling elderflower for me. The pub's busy, and the air is laced with that strangely comforting scent of hops and frying food. It's a proper pub, albeit with a slightly gastro vibe, reminding me a bit of The Smugglers.

'Oh God, by a *mile*. Remember Camden?'

I smile at my friend, her hair still damp from the shower. She never blow-dries it – she doesn't even own a hairdryer – and in about thirty minutes' time it will have magically lifted into thick, glossy waves. She's completely make-up free, the day scrubbed clean from her face. Jools is a natural beauty, the type of girl who wakes up with whipped-butter skin, her molasses-brown eyes newly brightened by sleep.

It would be easy to resent her for this. But Jools is the best person I know. Always has been.

'You mean the garage,' I say. It actually *was* a converted garage, and not a very good one at that.

'And that landlord in Bethnal Green.'

'Yeah, Mr Don't-Mind-Me.' Her landlord would let himself in unannounced with alarming frequency, until Jools reported him, whereupon she was instantly evicted.

'I'm sure I heard someone say he was arrested recently,' Jools says.

I shudder, think of Nate. 'Oh, don't.'

Jools sips her wine. 'Yeah, I'll definitely look back fondly on this place.'

'How's the saving going?'

'Slowly. Be another couple of years at least. Hey – I forgot to tell you,' she says, setting down her glass. 'When

Cara said she was leaving, Reuben arranged for a friend-of-a-friend to come over and see the room. Without telling us, of course. But he forgot to let him know you'd got it. So this poor guy turned up on the doorstep with a *basket of muffins*, to view the room.' She clutches a hand to her chest. 'Can you imagine?'

'Oh God. What did you do?'

'Well, Reuben was out, and me and Sal were mortified, obviously. And bless him – he tried to give us the muffins, but we felt too *awful* about it. So now I've just got this image of him walking off down our front path with his little muffin basket swinging from his hand . . .'

'Now I feel guilty.'

Jools shakes her head. 'Please. It was Reuben's fault. You know what he's like.'

'He doesn't mind me moving in, then?'

'Reuben? Of course not. Actually, if he didn't have a girlfriend, I'm pretty sure you'd be his type.'

I laugh. 'Why's that?'

She looks thoughtful. 'His last two girlfriends have reminded me a bit of you. But I'd never recommend him. He's too much like my ex. I'm pretty sure he's on something more often than he's not.'

Jools would know: she's from a family of loving but self-declared, permanently wasted hippies. Her childhood was somewhat chaotic, so her approach to adolescence essentially involved pedalling as far and hard in the opposite direction as she could – becoming the neat, organised and fashionable adult she is today, with a penchant for stylish interiors involving no tie-dye or dreamcatchers whatsoever.

What Might Have Been

She says it's why she's drawn to 'normal' and 'sensible' men, the ones with steady jobs and minimum baggage. Her most recent boyfriend was shaping up to tick all the boxes – banker, mortgage, no significant exes – until one night he confessed to moonlighting as a naked waiter and a growing reliance on class A drugs.

But every now and then, I am treated to a delicious glimmer of the person Jools used to be, before she became a fan of practicality and pragmatism. A person who believes in fate, trusts in gifts from the universe, and loves to indulge the idea of meant-to-be.

She puts a hand over mine now. Given the amount of handwashing involved in her job, I'm always struck by how staggeringly smooth her skin is. 'So. When do we mention the elephant in the room?'

I blink at her. 'What elephant?'

'What elephant. Max, of course.'

Max. We met on the first day of moving into university halls in Norwich. I was studying English literature, Max was studying law, and we bumped into each other in our shared kitchen. Neither of us was in there for a specific purpose – like making tea or filling up the fridge – but we were the first to arrive, and Max seemed as eager as I was to start making friends, to not be left behind.

If love at first sight exists, I'm sure I felt it right then. Max said afterwards he felt it too. When my eyes met his, for a few delicious moments, instead of either of us speaking, our gazes simply danced.

'Hello,' he said eventually, like he'd had to remind himself how to speak. 'I'm Max.'

'Lucy.'

He smiled. Casual in jeans and T-shirt, he looked as though he'd had a good summer. He was broad and tall, with skin that was deeply suntanned, and blond hair grown out enough to carry a kink.

I'd put a lot of thought into my moving-in outfit, eventually opting for a green dress that showed off my own tan, the likes of which I haven't achieved since.

'What are you studying?' he asked, leaning back against the sink.

For a few ludicrous seconds, I couldn't remember. *What am I studying?*

At my hesitation, Max laughed. I can still conjure up the sound of it, all these years later: easy and loose, as though he was the happiest person in the world. Straight away, it put me at ease.

'Sorry. English literature. I'm a bit nervous.'

'Me too,' he said. He must have been being kind, because he didn't seem nervous at all. 'Hey, would a drink help? Got beers in my room.'

'Sounds good,' I said gratefully.

We decamped to his room, just down the corridor from mine – me on the single bed and Max sitting on the floor, his back against the wall. He'd already tacked up some pictures – friends, I noticed, he had lots of friends – and he'd had the foresight to bring a little fridge with him, so the beers were already cold. Over the next few hours, we got through all six of them.

What Might Have Been

Beyond Max's closed door, we could hear other students moving in, parents leaving, the pump of music. The growing swell of conversation and the clinking of bottles. But neither of us suggested venturing out of his room to join in. Right then it was just us, and Max's bedroom was the whole world. It felt beautifully illicit, hiding away in there together when we were supposed to be mingling and being our most outgoing, gregarious selves.

He was relieved to have finally left his hometown of Cambridge behind, he told me. He'd never known his dad, wasn't close with his mum, had no siblings.

I decided it would be insensitive to regale him with the story of my parents' fairy-tale romance, once he'd said that. But then he asked.

'It's kind of a crazy story,' I said, fingering the label of my beer bottle.

Max leant his head back against the wall, but kept his eyes on me. I was enjoying the feeling of it – him watching me. Intense, but in a good way. 'Aren't the crazy stories always the best?'

'Well, they met on holiday when they were twenty. Dad was supposed to be going to Mallorca, but the travel agent messed up and sent him to Menorca instead. So my parents ended up in apartments next door to each other.'

Max smiled.

'Long story short, it was love at first sight, and my mum fell pregnant with my sister on that holiday.'

Max straightened up a little. 'Seriously?'

'Yep. Classic holiday romance.'

He caught my eye. 'Not *quite* classic . . .'

I laughed. 'Okay, maybe not quite. But they were head-over-heels.'

'Did they . . . I mean, was the pregnancy planned?'

'No. But they just . . . knew how they felt about each other. So they came home, got married, had Tash – my sister – then a couple of years later, I came along.'

'That's amazing. They're still together now?'

'Married twenty-two years and counting.'

Max ran a hand through his hair. 'That is nuts.'

I beamed. I loved telling that story, subverting expectations. I would relate it as proudly as if it were my own.

'I mean, that's setting . . . a ridiculously high bar,' Max said then.

'For whom?'

'Only anyone you ever meet.'

Our eyes locked, and I felt a blush of heat spread over my cheeks.

But Max hadn't seemed to notice. 'Do you ever wonder what would have happened if they *hadn't* got pregnant on that holiday?'

'You mean, would they still be together?'

'Yeah. I guess I just . . . What if they'd each gone home, and lost touch, then met other people, and . . . ?'

'I know. I might not even exist.'

He winced. 'Sorry. Haven't offended you, have I?'

I knew already that nothing Max said could offend me. Or if it did, it wouldn't have been intentional. He seemed too nice for that. I shook my head. 'Not at all. Actually, my mum and dad have talked about that loads. The what-ifs.'

38

'I mean . . . if they were each other's first loves . . . how do they *know*? That there's no one else—'

'They just do.'

Our eyes met again then, but this time, Max got up to fetch us each another beer. 'So, what do you want to be, Lucy? When you graduate.' He passed me a bottle then sat next to me on the bed, our shoulders touching like we'd known each other for years.

I thanked him and swigged. 'A writer.'

'What kind of writer?'

'I want to write novels.' I smiled. 'Do you know what kind of lawyer you want to be?'

'Commercial,' he said, without hesitation.

I tried to look as though I understood, then gave up and laughed. 'Sorry. That means absolutely nothing to me.'

'Let's just say,' he said, 'commercial law pays well.'

I nodded. 'Is that why you're doing it? For the money?'

'Kind of.' He shrugged. 'My mum never had much, so—'

'Sorry, it wasn't a criticism.'

'No, I know.' He waved my apology away.

By now the light had more or less vanished from the room, and we were sitting in the gloom.

'Do you want to go out and join the others?' I asked him. 'Sounds like it's getting rowdy out there.'

'Actually,' Max said, 'I'm really enjoying just sitting here with you.'

I'm enjoying sitting here with you, too, I thought.

Eventually, we fell asleep together on his single bed. I woke up several hours later in the middle of the night. Our bodies were curled up against each other, big spoon and little spoon. We hadn't kissed, we hadn't even really touched, but I had the strangest feeling, as I crept back to my room at three in the morning, that I'd met the man I was destined to be with.

5

Stay

I n the week since our – what would I even call it – date?
– I've been indulging in some light virtual stalking of
Caleb. There's not much in the way of personal stuff online
– his social media is all set to private – but I do learn he's
won a lot of accolades for his photography.

I unearthed a photo of him at some awards ceremony
last year, his arm around the waist of a dazzling, sylph-like
woman with olive skin and glistening dark hair. *Magazine
editor Helen Jones joined her husband Caleb on the red carpet,*
the caption said.

Of course, this then kicked off a frenzied search for
'Helen Jones + magazine editor', which revealed she
edits an achingly cool interiors magazine called *Four
Walls*, based in London. It's one of those inexplicable
coffee-table bibles exclusively for cutting-edge people
– more book than magazine – which recommends things
like concrete floors and replacing all your internal walls
with glass. Google Images also confirms that Helen
Jones does not take a bad photo. This is unsurprising,
really, for a woman who's been with a man as handsome

as Caleb, with whose own image I am now worryingly familiar.

'Maybe him being recently separated is a bad sign,' I said to Tash, as we watched Dylan go berserk at soft play on Sunday morning, two days after Caleb and I met up again.

Tash rolled her eyes. 'Please, will you just stop with your signs? People are allowed to be married and then separate, Lucy. It's really old-fashioned to think that means he's damaged goods.'

'Who said anything about damaged goods?'

'You, with that expression on your face. Listen, half the dads at Dylan's school are divorced, or separated. And most of them are really nice.'

'Everybody has to be nice at school. It's hardly the done thing to air all your deep-seated commitment issues at PTA meetings, is it?'

Tash smiled and sipped her green tea. 'I'm only saying, just because his marriage didn't work out doesn't mean he's fundamentally dysfunctional.'

I sipped my coffee and trained my eyes on Dylan, who was currently wrestling his way heroically through a ball pool.

She turned to face me, eyes suddenly greedy for juicy details. 'So, come on. What happened the other night? Did you kiss? Did you—'

'No,' I said, shaking my head. 'We just hung out at his studio, then we went for a drink, then he pecked me on the cheek and I got the bus.'

'Oh,' she said, crestfallen. 'So, what – you don't think there's any chemistry?'

Oh, there was definitely chemistry. I could feel my stomach leap whenever I so much as pictured Caleb's face. 'There is,' I said slowly. 'It's just . . . he walked me to the bus stop, and there was a big queue, and it didn't seem quite right to start snogging in front of it like teenagers. You know?'

She looked relieved. 'Oh, yeah. Makes sense.'

A beat passed.

'You're sure you don't recognise his name?' I asked, even though we'd already been over this. 'You didn't go to school with anyone called Caleb?'

She shook her head slowly. 'Nope. Definitely not.'

'Weird. I could swear I know him from somewhere.'

'So, are you seeing him again?'

I nodded. 'He's got a few things on this week, so we said Friday.'

I caught Dylan's eye as he beamed at us, clapping enthusiastically against my thigh with my free hand.

'I've got a good feeling about this one,' Tash said warmly. 'I mean, he wrote down his number on the only thing he could find and slipped it into your coat. I think that's so romantic.'

I smiled. I suspected there was another reason why Tash was so keen on Caleb: because she was even more keen for me to forget about Max Gardner. I could tell it had been playing on her mind ever since I told her I'd run into him outside The Smugglers; she'd even idly asked me a couple of times if I'd heard from him since.

But I haven't, and I'm increasingly thinking about that moment outside the pub as nothing more than a brief flashback in time. That maybe the person I was meant to meet that night was Caleb, who I can already tell is so different to Max. I'm excited to see where it goes, and determined to keep anything to do with Max Gardner firmly in the past.

On Friday morning, Caleb messages to ask what I fancy doing later. I suggest making the most of the warm evening with a walk on the beach and fish and chips, which we can eat on the wall of the promenade overlooking the sea.

It's sort of a Shoreley tradition, to get chips from Dave at the Shoreley Fryer and then eat them on the wall, legs swinging, watching the waves sneak up to kiss the shingle. We all did it as kids with our families, then as teenagers with our friends, and now we're doing it as adults with our dates.

We share a can of Fanta, and a large cod and chips between us, because Dave's portions are famously grotesque. We sit on the wall, our feet dangling above the beach. Caleb's height means that, side by side, my feet only reach halfway down his calves.

'Do you mind if I ask why you split up with your wife?' I ask, once we've talked about school, and our childhood homes, and the best place to get good coffee in town. In front of us on the beach, couples are walking arm in arm, kids and dogs careering across the pebbles, grasping kites and footballs and strings of seaweed. The hue of the evening sky is slowly softening from blue to lilac, the clotted-cream clouds gradually blushing pink.

Caleb prongs a chip from the tray we've balanced on the wall between us. 'Not sure I can really boil it down.'

'Did you marry young?'

He waits for a couple of moments, then nods. 'She was my second-ever girlfriend. We met when I was twenty-one, married two years later. But by last year, we were fundamentally just . . . different people.'

I nod, take a swig from the Fanta can.

'Actually, you know, I'm making it sound a lot simpler than it was. When we met, we had this five-year plan to move back here, to Shoreley.'

'Is Helen from Shoreley too?' I say without thinking, before feeling myself swiftly turn purple with embarrassment.

Caleb enjoys the moment, which I can't really blame him for. 'Well stalked,' he says, laughing.

I dab a chip fiercely into ketchup. 'Okay, okay. I *might* have had a quick look for you online.'

'Just teasing. I'd definitely have stalked you if I'd known your surname.' He pauses. 'Which is?'

'Lambert,' I say, coyly.

'Okay, Lucy Lambert. No, Helen's not from round here, but she is a country girl. She's from Dorset. Anyway, we had this plan to spend a couple of years travelling, then move back to Shoreley, buy a cottage, and . . . I don't know, grow our own potatoes, or something. Get a goat and some chickens. After "finding ourselves" halfway up Machu Picchu, obviously.'

'Obviously.'

He smiles, but it cracks a little, and I suddenly wonder if it's a bit insensitive of me, asking him to rake over all this a mere six months after it ended.

45

We stare out at the view. The tide is low now, the shingle a pale flurry of pebbles hemmed by a shimmering stripe of sea. As the sun sinks through ribbons of cloud and sky, long shadows spring from beneath the feet of the beach-goers, and for a few minutes, everything appears dipped in liquid gold.

Caleb starts talking again. 'Anyway, I guess . . . just as I was starting to feel uncomfortable in London, Helen was settling in. She'd made lots of friends, she had this big high-powered magazine job, and she was getting a bit obsessed with . . . you know, status and stuff like that.'

'Which you're not?'

Caleb laughs and rubs a hand through his hair. 'Do I look like I worry about status? Please say no.'

'You're doing well for yourself.'

'I get by. I don't drive a Mercedes, I can tell you that much.'

Unexpectedly, an image of Max in his crisp suit jetting off to the Seychelles floats into my mind. And – not for the first time since spending time with Caleb – I feel sure I'm enjoying myself more with him than I might have done seeing Max again.

'We were just different people, in the end,' Caleb concludes.

'Was it amicable? When you separated.'

He looks across at me. 'Not really.'

'And are you . . . ?' I break off, the words 'planning to divorce' dissolving in my throat. Because really, is that any of my business? 'Sorry. It's probably a bit weird to be talk-ing about this stuff on a—'

'On a what?' he whispers, but before I can reply, he is leaning across and kissing me. It's a kiss so good it makes my heart thump – full and intense, undercut by the sea breeze and the tang of salt and vinegar. A kiss that makes me forget everything else, that makes the whole world drop away, until there's just the two of us, getting lost in each other, set on fire by this incredible sunset.

As dusk descends, Caleb invites me back to the fisherman's cottage he rents a couple of streets back from the seafront. We walk there along the cobblestones, our hands and shoulders occasionally colliding and sending a tingle of anticipation all the way to my toes.

It's been a long while since I went back to someone's house, and I'm trying very hard not to over-think the idea of being in an unfamiliar space with a man I barely know.

But as Jools often reminds me, I can't let my history hold me back for ever. And despite the belly-deep anxiety threatening to override my craving to kiss Caleb again, what we're doing feels strangely right.

As we walk, I distract myself by telling him about my sister, that I was saving up to buy my own place before I walked out of my job.

'Why?' he says.

I inhale the scent of salt and seaweed for a couple of seconds. The coast always feels so much more alive than Tash's farmland fortress in the middle of nowhere. 'Why what?'

'Why do you want to buy somewhere?'

I glance across at him. 'That's just . . . what everybody does, isn't it? Renting's a nightmare.'

'Depends on the landlord, I suppose. I kind of like the idea that I can just up and leave whenever I like.'

'Did you own your place in London?'

'Sort of. I mean, Helen did. She inherited it. Which meant . . . it never felt fully mine, I guess.'

'Whereabouts in London did you live?'

'Islington.' He smiles. 'It was nice and everything, life-style-wise . . . but that doesn't really mean anything, if there's more important stuff missing.'

'True,' I say, thoughtfully.

We come to a pause outside Spyglass Cottage, a narrow-fronted whitewashed end-of-terrace, where the air is perfumed by a blush-pink clematis winding skyward up the wall facing the street. All the houses on the row have things propped up against them, like buoys and ancient lifebelts and old crabbing pots. The evening has cooled now, and there's a coastal quickness to the breeze.

As Caleb lifts his key to the bright-blue front door, he hesitates. 'You know, we don't have to . . . I mean, we can just talk. This doesn't have to be . . .'

He trails off then, but I know what he means, so I just nod and say, 'I know. Thanks.'

Inside there is a tiny living room, with only just enough space for a two-seater sofa and single armchair. A wood burner is set into the chimney breast, and there's a faint lingering smell of essential oils, or perhaps it's scented candles.

He cranks open the living-room window, the one that looks directly onto the street. We're so close to the beach, I can hear the gentle crush of waves on the shoreline as the tide rolls in.

'Can I get you a coffee?' he asks.

I say yes, then follow him over to the doorway to the kitchen. He fetches mugs from a cupboard, starts boiling the water on an Aga which looks like it's seen better days. I realise I am trying not to stare too hard at his hand gripping the kettle, the broad set of his shoulders.

'How do you take it?' he asks, once he's poured out the hot water.

'Just a splash of milk, thanks.'

As he retrieves the milk from the fridge, he starts talking about his love affair with the Aga, which came with the cottage. I tell him I've always wanted one, ever since my parents got theirs, and he says, 'Me too. My kitchen in London was horrible. Like, properly space-age. You couldn't tell where any of the cupboards were. There wasn't a single handle in there. I had to push in ten different places just to get to my cereal in the morning.'

I glance at the design on the mug Caleb's handed me. It's faded, like it's been through a dishwasher a few too many times, but I can still just about make out the 'I HEART LONDON' motif on the front.

He notices me looking. 'Stocking filler from Helen, once she'd worked out I was itching to leave.'

'Ouch.'

'That's what I said.'

We head back into the living room. It's pretty sparsely

49

decorated, with walls in that shade of magnolia that nudges towards peach, and a well-trodden beige carpet. There's hardly anything personal in the room, aside from a few framed photographs, a pot plant, a tripod with some lenses, and a handful of books. One's a *National Geographic* publication; another's about the natural wonders of the world. There are some crime novels too with creased spines, a Nick Hornby, a Ben Elton.

We cosy up together on the tiny sofa, which smells very faintly musty – but in the sense of being cherished and well-used, like a beloved grandmother's armchair, or the perfect find in an antiques shop.

'So,' Caleb says, sipping his coffee. 'Tell me more about your novel. I mean, I know you said girl-meets-boy . . . but what girl? And what boy? And how do they meet?'

I've fully drafted the novel's opening now – a loose reimagining of my parents' meeting, but with an interwar twist, in that my two protagonists fall for each other on holiday in Margate, in the fabulous roaring twenties. I've decided that their subsequent marriage should be cut cruelly short by war – though everything will come together to give them a happy ending eventually. Beyond this vague plot, though, I still have no real idea what I'm doing. I haven't a clue about structure, or pacing, or characterisation, or anything, really. I'm just writing what I feel. What's in my heart.

The *Shoreley Gazette* once ran a story about my parents for its Valentine's Day edition – a splashy feature about the serendipity of Mum and Dad's meeting, their whirlwind romance, their happy-ever-after. Dad had it framed – it still hangs in their spare room, albeit in a tongue-in-cheek kind of way. I remember being so starstruck, seeing my parents' love story making the paper – *the actual newspaper!* – and perhaps that's where it started, the idea that I might one day immortalise their fairy tale even further. That maybe I could do even more for it than a spread in the *Shoreley Gazette.*

Because while my school friends' parents were divorcing and bickering and slinging pints of cider at each other at summer barbecues, mine were taking ballroom dancing lessons and learning Italian together and holding hands on the sofa in front of *Blind Date.* They fully bought into Valentine's Days, and loved nothing better than big romantic gestures – like the hot-air balloon ride Mum bought Dad for his fortieth, or that trip to Paris Dad arranged to celebrate their twenty-fifth wedding anniversary.

Anyway. Over the past week I've spent my days immersed in all things 1920s, lost in P.G. Wodehouse and Nancy Mitford, absorbed by images of flapper dresses and cigarette holders and women showing off newly bobbed hair, of Coco Chanel and Marlene Dietrich, of cocktail bars ringing out with ragtime and jazz. I've become happily reacquainted with all the great love stories I admire too, dipping into them as I go. And I've already found myself tearing up at the prospect of sending Jack, my main character, off to war.

I explain all this to Caleb, describing my parents and how the way they met has loosely inspired what I'm writing.

'So why the twenties?' he asks me, leaning forward, his expression attentive and keen. 'Why not the present day?'

I hesitate. 'I think it was just such an intoxicating time on some levels, you know? I like stories about hope, and the start of the twenties were so optimistic, and glamorous, and even frivolous.'

'Sort of *Great Gatsby*-esque?'

'Yes,' I say, getting more animated now. 'Like, there was that mood of escapism and hedonism and empowerment . . .'

'Before it all came crashing down.'

'Well, that's sort of the point. I want what's happening in society to mirror what's going on in their marriage, with the Depression and then the war, and everything.'

'It sounds brilliant,' he says, sipping his coffee again. 'I'd read it.'

'You would? Do you read much?'

'When I get the time.'

'What kind of thing?'

'Whatever catches my eye. I'm a sucker for a decent cover. Couple of times a month I go into a charity shop and just buy whatever looks good.'

I smile. 'Incredible.'

'What?'

'You've not even tried to pretend you're reading *Ulysses*.'

A bark of laughter slips free. 'Should I?'

'Definitely not.' I tell him about the two guys on my course at uni – one of whom was nicknamed Ulysses and the other War and Peace, on account of the answers they gave when our tutor asked everyone to name their favourite books in our very first seminar.

'So, will you let me read it? Your novel, I mean.'

'Oh,' I say, feeling briefly flustered.

Caleb waits for a couple of moments, which is fair enough, given I haven't actually answered his question. Then: 'I'd love to take a look. If it doesn't feel too personal to show me.'

A few seconds' silence. It's not that it feels too personal – more that I'd like to get to know Caleb better, and if he hates my writing . . . might that change what he thinks of me? What if he reads it and he decides I'm a talentless fantasist?

'I mean, I've only written about thirty pages,' I confess, half-expecting him to laugh and say, *Hardly a novel.*

He leans back against the sofa, his eyes steady against me. 'So . . . tease me with ten.'

I laugh. 'Fine. Okay. All right. Ten pages.'

'You'll email them to me?'

I nod.

'Promise?'

I tilt my head playfully. 'Why are you so keen to see them, anyway?'

He shrugs softly. 'Because I have a sneaky feeling they're going to be really good.'

His gaze sweeps over me now, lighting up little touch-points inside me I didn't know I had, making me draw breath. We're sitting pretty close together – near enough for me to detect citrusy drifts of his shampoo whenever he turns his head, to see every dip and crease of his skin when he smiles, to count his crow's feet when he laughs. I can't deny I've been hoping he might make a move, because the memory of our kiss on the wall earlier is like a glitterball in my mind, beautiful and glorious and impossible to ignore.

I feel a sudden urge to lean forward and press my lips against his. So I do, and he responds instantly, his hands on each side of my face. I am suddenly flushed with heat and hunger and urgency.

And it would be easy, I know, to turn the kiss into more, into something frantic and fast. But as the moment lengthens, there seems to be a hesitancy in both of us to do more. We seem to be saying, without saying it at all, that we'd both like to linger here for just a little while longer, because it would be a shame not to drink in every last second of something that tastes so good.

Go

It turns out that Supernova Agency of Soho, London, England, is one of those places where the recruitment approach is less interview, more ritual humiliation. They ask me to name ten uses for a brown carpet tile (they have one to hand) and what the name of my debut album would be (I panic and say *Lucy Lambert Goes Pop*, which gets a laugh, at least). They give me fifteen minutes to design my own ad agency (what?), then another twenty to write a pitch for their team introducing staff uniforms (thankfully, this one's easy – I just tell them they're all going to be the next Matilda Kahl).

I'm given an office tour by a spindly lad called Kris, who seems overly keen to impress on me that his name starts with a K. The premises are a striking mix of steel, bricks and concrete spread over three floors; oversized, retro-style signage; and long, open-plan areas filled with low seating, rugs and cushions matched to employees' preferred Pantones. There's a vast canteen with its famous free snacks and drinks, plus a bar, gym and salon, as well as the 'Supernova' itself – a cavernous room lit up to imitate, according to Kris, the nucleus of a stellar explosion. It's warm and sound-proofed, the walls and ceiling like a fire-work in freeze-frame, reportedly designed to tap into certain areas of the brain. Or maybe Kris is just getting a little free and easy with the brand story.

Anyway, it's a world apart from Figaro, where the trend-iest office feature was a boiling water tap in the kitchen so encrusted with limescale that it spat like a snake in fifteen different directions whenever anyone tried to use it.

But the most surreal part of the whole experience is being called back in to see the head of creative, creative director and senior copywriter before I leave, whereupon they offer me the job of junior copywriter, with a salary I could only have dreamed of and unfathomable perks. I start in just over a week.

Stunned, I exit the offices, stumbling into the heart of Soho at midday. I look around and blink like I've just fallen out of a time machine, before getting shouldered into a parking meter by a tutting suit-and-tie.

I tip back my head, letting my eyes settle on the slice of sky between the building tops. It looks like an upturned swimming pool, prophetically blue. I draw in a breath.

I'm going to be a writer. An actual, paid writer. Someone who earns their living from what they can do with words.

It's all I've ever wanted my whole life, and now – unbelievably – I'm actually going to be doing it.

Later that night, Jools looks me up and down, shakes her head. 'Don't suppose there's any point me telling you to be careful, is there?'

'This is Max we're talking about.'

My oldest friend's expression turns almost pitying, like she's lost me already. 'I meant your heart, not your . . .'

I finish her sentence in my head. *Personal safety.*

It's Friday night, exactly two weeks since I bumped into Max outside the pub in Shoreley. After talking to Jools and Tash the following morning, and making my decision to move to London, I spent the afternoon coming down from the chemical rush of having seen him again, growing increasingly dejected at the idea that he was currently en route to the Seychelles, where surely he'd spend his time hanging out with a lithe, long-haired diving instructor named Celeste, who'd look good in a wetsuit and know how to flirt underwater. I was convinced he'd return to London shagged-out and refreshed, wondering what that moment of madness revisiting Shoreley was all about, when he thought it would be a good idea to raise the hopes of an ex-girlfriend he'd long since left in the past.

But after a few days, I started to think about the fortuity of having seen him on the street that night. I mean, what were the chances? Didn't it signify *something*? Wasn't it a nudge from fate, one that shouldn't be ignored?

What Might Have Been

So I sent him a message. Just a couple of sentences, casual and light. And if he didn't want to reply, then so be it.

> Was so nice bumping into you the other day. Hope you're having a great time. L.

He replied almost instantly.

> Was nice bumping into you too.

A pause. *Typing.*

> I'm thinking about you way more than I should.

My stomach flipped, and a familiar longing began to churn inside me.

> Why shouldn't you be thinking about me?

The pause between my message and Max's reply was mere moments.

> Because I know I don't deserve a second chance.

And now, he's back. So we're meeting for dinner at a posh restaurant near his flat in Clapham Old Town. I looked up the restaurant online first, was horrified to discover it's the kind of place with tablecloths and taster menus and a sommelier for pairing the wine.

I haven't gone as far as to buy a new outfit for the occasion, but I have unearthed the most beautiful dress I own – wrap-style in blue and gold, with a pair of midnight-blue suede Jimmy Choos (Reuben, of course, launched into an Elvis impression when I entered the living room earlier). Jools did my hair and make-up, and we decided I should get a cab, whereupon I started to panic we were turning this into far more of an event than it actually was. But then we looked at the restaurant website again, and decided it was definitely worth the effort, all Max-related complications aside.

The nicest place Max and I ever went while we were dating was a mid-range pasta chain, where three courses and two glasses of wine apiece always felt highly indulgent. I dwell again on how much time has passed, the different worlds we're now inhabiting. The idea that maybe Max isn't the person he was before. That maybe I'm not, either.

Still. I guess there's only one way to find out.

I spot him straight away – is he really that striking, or is my mind just sharp with lust? – already at our table, eyes on the door, waiting for me. My stomach spins. He has the radiant demeanour of the recently holidayed, his skin a couple of shades browner than it was two weeks ago.

The restaurant is warm and mood-lit, the decor mostly charcoal, but accented with bright colours by the art on the walls. The waiters are in black, the linen is starch-white, and I can just make out the trickle of piano music beneath the ringing of glassware and cutlery.

What Might Have Been

I swallow as I cross the room, trying not to think of that imaginary – though real to me – long-limbed diving instructor. After our initial exchange of messages, he was in contact every day, and I almost felt bad that he was thinking of me while he was on holiday somewhere so magical. But as Sal pointed out, we were indulging in some A-grade flirting, and what could be more magical than that?

He stands up when I reach the table. 'You look incredible.' Leaning forward, he kisses me on the cheek, and I peck him politely back, which feels so weirdly formal.

We sit, and for a moment I just enjoy the sight of him across the table from me, newly tanned, fair hair brightened by the sun. He's wearing a shirt in a flattering shade of blue, and has that particular kind of watch on his wrist most commonly seen advertised by Hollywood actors. I suddenly worry that this man I once loved has soared completely out of my league.

'You look great,' I say. 'Very . . . relaxed.'

He laughs. 'Thank you. Though that really only lasted till I checked my emails.'

'When did you get back?'

'Last night.'

'You're not jet-lagged? What's the flight time?'

'Ten hours. I've been asleep most of today.'

I smile. 'So that's why you look so ridiculously—' I break off, feel my face warm a little.

Max smiles too, lifts an eyebrow. 'So ridiculously . . . ?'

'*Well-rested.*'

As he laughs, I remember how much I love the sound of it: completely natural and unaffected, the kind of laugh that slips free while you're watching live comedy, or your favourite sitcom.

'Champagne?' he asks, nodding down at the drinks menu, and I notice a waiter approaching.

We've never drunk champagne together before. The most we could ever stretch to as students was bargain bin cava.

'Actually,' I say (I've practised this bit), 'I'm kind of taking a break from alcohol at the moment.'

He looks surprised for a split-second before blinking it away. 'No worries. What do you fancy instead?'

We don't talk too much more until our mocktails have arrived and we've ordered courses one to three of a total five. And then Max lifts his glass and says, 'I loved getting messages from you. I've missed you being in my life, Luce.'

The abbreviation of my name feels flattering and intimate – like we're right back in his room at halls, making out on his single bed, sharing a bottle of red wine so cheap it made us wince. Half-undressed, laughing into each other's necks as friends knocked on his door, trying to track us down. We did a lot of that, at uni: sneaking off together, hiding in darkened lecture theatres, behind buildings, in bathrooms with the lights off. *I love you, Luce*, he'd whisper, his mouth on mine, and I'd feel so frenzied I could barely say it back.

I smile and sip from my glass, hoping my face isn't flushing with nostalgia.

'Hey, how was your interview?' he asks.

I fill him in, tell him I got the job.

'That's incredible, Luce. Congratulations.' Max locks eyes with me, shaking his head, because he knows – he knows what this means to me, the chance to get to write for a living. It's all I ever talked about, the whole time I knew him at uni.

'Thank you.' I realise I'm fighting the urge to well up.

He raises his glass to mine. 'Well, here's to you. And your new life in London.' We both take a sip. 'How are you finding it so far? Must feel pretty different to Shoreley.'

I lied a little when he called, told him my move had been in the works for a while. I couldn't bear for him to think our meeting had influenced my decision at all.

Max visited me back home in Shoreley on just three occasions during university holidays, because the rest of the time he was either studying or doing internships. Max's degree was one of those where the breaks were really just another form of study leave.

'I think different is what I need right now.' I mean, Max is right – London *is* a world away from Shoreley and particularly Tash's place, where the stillness was so loud it sometimes buzzed. Here, silence is only a concept – it can't be found, I've learnt, because the rumble of the city is a stereo you can't switch off, even at night. Rattling train tracks, sharp blasts of music, the commotion of voices. The city is a restless creature, but I've taken pleasure from its fitfulness. It has stirred me up, switched me on.

'Luce.' Max meets my eye. 'Did you ever make it back to uni, to finish your degree?'

I shake my head. And then I find myself hesitating, because – despite everything – I want to tell him all about what happened after I left, including what went on with Nate. I feel as though he would understand, because he was always compassionate to a fault. It was Max who'd insist we demonstrate in support of good causes at uni, who volunteered to make peace with our unreasonable neighbours in Dover Street, who stood up for someone in a law seminar if they expressed an unpopular opinion.

But as quickly as the right moment comes, it passes. And now, across the table, Max is grabbing my free hand with his.

I don't flinch, trying not to let my mind travel back to that Friday night nearly a decade ago, when we were standing on the bridge over the river next to the railway station in Norwich. Max was heading home to Cambridge for the weekend. I can still picture him so clearly, in his favourite jeans with the scuffed knees, and oversized woollen coat. Our final autumn term had only recently begun, and it was pouring with rain.

'Please don't go.' I was too numb at that point to even cry.

'I'm going to miss my train,' was all he said, his voice vague and watery.

I didn't want to beg. I couldn't. So I just watched him walk away, over the bridge and out of my life.

I take in his face now – those grey, searchlight eyes, the gentle beckon of his lips – and I am filled with sadness. For all the years we lost. For all we might have been. For everything that happened after our abrupt, inexplicable end.

'I know this is coming about ten years too late . . . but I'm so sorry, Lucy,' Max says, squeezing my hand like it's the most natural thing in the world to do. In this moment, it would be easy to imagine we never broke up, because we're carrying on pretty much where we left off. Which is enjoyable and confusing all at once – like reading a brilliant book with some of the pages missing. Or arriving at the cinema halfway through a really good film. 'I wish things hadn't ended the way they did.'

He loved me back then, and I knew it. Just the way my parents – only a year older than Max and I had been, when they met – felt it. They still feel it today. They'll have been married thirty-four years this September.

Max was unlike any guy I'd known at school, or our other friends at uni. Effusive and expressive, he was vocal in his adoration of me, and eager for everyone to know it. He would flick bar snacks at the people who teased us – *Married already?* – before gripping my hand even tighter; would make a big show of kissing me in the middle of wherever we were. Pubs, roads, university corridors. We talked about our future all the time: moving in together, marriage, kids. We were bold enough – and sure enough – to want it all. It didn't even feel fanciful. It just felt like . . . fact. We were meant to have met in that kitchen on our first day at uni, and we were destined not to leave each other's side.

Until the night he ended it. Just like that.

I blamed myself at first – thought I'd demanded too much of him – but he kept saying it wasn't that, that it wasn't my fault.

Of course, it crossed my mind he'd met someone. Not at uni – I was fairly confident about that – but perhaps at the law firm he'd interned with over the summer. Maybe some-one who'd be heading to London the following year too, to complete the LPC, the next step in qualification for aspir-ing lawyers.

And yet, despite everything, none of that really made sense. Max wasn't a cheat, a liar. If he'd met someone else, he would have just told me. Wouldn't he?

I look into his grey eyes now, heart drumming in my chest. I want to ask him again what was going through his mind when he broke it off that day in September nearly ten years ago. Was it just the classic fear of commitment he kept denying? But we're in the middle of a nice restaurant – hardly the right setting for turning your heart inside out. Feeling tears crowd my eyes, I slide my hand out from beneath his as our starters arrive.

'Let's talk about something else,' I say, swallowing my emotion away. 'Tell me about your holiday.'

So between bites of his rabbit dish, Max describes the world-class diving, the plush resort, the beaches, the heat.

'Did you know the group?' I ask. 'I mean, beforehand?'

He shakes his head. 'I've been diving with the same company before – Egypt, Israel – but the group's always different.'

'And did you . . . meet anyone interesting?'

Smiling, he hesitates. 'Are you asking what I think you're asking?'

'What do you think I'm asking?'

'Whether I was messaging you one minute then . . . doing something else the next.'

I smile too. The rhubarb from my pickled mackerel starter is tart on my tongue. 'I mean, I wouldn't judge. You were on holiday.'

He sets down his fork and takes my hand. 'No. I meant what I said. I was thinking about you the whole time I was there.'

I'm inclined to believe him. Max was always so straight-up, so honest – the kind of guy who would never copy anyone else's coursework, or take even a single penny in miscalculated change.

I swallow. 'So, come on. Tell me about your life here. Your friends, your job. I want to know everything.'

Because actually, right now, I just want to hear Max talk, so I can simply sit back and quietly love the sound of his voice again, after all these years.

We stay in the restaurant till late. The minutes melt into hours. Time becomes a river – long and beautiful and begging to be swum through. We finish our drinks, then order more. We discuss his work, and I fill him in on my years at Figaro. He describes his flat in Clapham, and I tell him about moving in with Jools.

I'm vaguely aware that outside, dusk has become dark. I'm trying to pretend our little corner of the restaurant isn't hot with electricity. That his hand doesn't keep nudging mine. That beneath the table, our knees aren't bumping.

'So, Luce. Tell me. Are you . . . with anyone?' Max's glass is raised to his lips, his eyes glimmering above the rim.

'Nope. Been single for about two years.' I make a face, exhale. 'God, that sounds like a lifetime. You?'

'Actually, about the same. I broke up with my last girl-friend a couple of summers ago.'

I swallow. It's still an odd and uncomfortable feeling, picturing Max with someone else. I guess when someone leaves and you're not ready, a part of your heart will always go with them.

'And since?' I ask.

He tells me tactfully that he's been concentrating on work. I find myself daring to wonder what he's like in bed these days, nearly a decade on.

Once we've finished eating and drunk coffee, we're almost the last people in the restaurant, so I reluctantly suggest getting the bill.

'That's already taken care of,' Max says.

'What? When?'

'Don't worry about it.'

'Max, *no*. It's too much.'

'Forget it. Really.'

'No. This place is . . .' *That's irrelevant, really.* 'I want to pay my half.'

'Well, how about you pick up the bill next time?' His eyes brim with amusement. He's enjoying teasing me, I realise.

I tip my head, deliberately evade the suggestion. 'You don't have to be all smooth moves, you know.'

He raises both hands. 'What? I wasn't.'

'Don't forget . . . I know you.' Yes – the old Max, with the scruffy clothes and Pot Noodle fetish and terrible time-keeping and secret affection for Take That.

A *busted* smile spreads over his face. 'Oh, yeah.'

'I'll transfer you the money. Just ping me your details.'

He feigns taking me seriously with a frown. 'Okay. I will.'

I kick him beneath the table with my foot. 'I mean it.'

'Absolutely.'

I smile and shake my head, glance around the virtually empty restaurant. 'Okay. Well, I should probably get a cab.'

Endearingly, his self-confidence sways momentarily. I watch him swallow. 'Unless . . . you fancy coming back to mine? Strictly for coffee, of course.'

'Of course.'

Max's flat is less than a five-minute walk from the restaurant. *Handy for seductions*, I think, before scolding myself. He's been nothing but a gentleman tonight.

It's a two-bed place, which I'm guessing puts it at about three-quarters of a million. Inside, it's beautifully done out – immaculate paintwork, all the period features not only intact but gracefully showcased. Stylish prints hang in sleek frames from the picture rails – the French Riviera, a Hockney reproduction – and there are polished copper light fittings, cushions in bold geometrics and pot plants exploding from various corners. The kitchen-diner we're standing in smells of furniture polish and anti-bac, and I can't spot a single item out of place. Even the tea towels look as though they were pressed prior to hanging.

'This is . . . like a show home.' I think about my scruffy bedroom back in Tooting and make a mental note to not invite Max back there for as long as I possibly can. Either that, or I'll have to fly quickly up the ranks at Supernova so I can afford to rent somewhere as swanky as this.

'Can't take the credit really,' he says. 'I had someone come in and help with the furnishings and stuff, when I moved in.'

I sit down on the sofa I've been standing next to. 'You mean, an interior designer?'

He wrinkles his nose, clearly slightly self-conscious about it. 'Not exactly. It was just a favour really, from a friend of a friend.'

He presses a button on his coffee machine, then retrieves a bottle from an art deco-style walnut drinks cabinet. 'Mind if I have a nightcap on the side?'

'Of course not.'

He twists the cap from the bottle. 'I've been really getting into vintage cognac lately.'

I laugh. I can't help it. 'Did you just say, "I've been really getting into vintage cognac"?'

He turns to face me, clocks my expression and smiles. 'This is what you meant earlier, isn't it?'

'About you being all smooth moves? Picking up the bill, rhapsodising about cognac? Absolutely.'

He crosses the room, then – making his voice deep and husky – instructs Alexa to play jazz over his shoulder.

I laugh, and he laughs too, like he's enjoying trying – and failing – to impress me. I suspect it's probably been a while since he's had to work very hard at the seduction game.

'Well,' he says, his eyes tracking mine as he sits down next to me, 'maybe I'm just trying to win you over.'

What Might Have Been

The air seems to thicken then, the levity dropping from the room. Our gazes lock, and I reach for Max's hand. There is a single moment in which our eyes are asking the same question, and in the next, his lips are on mine. We slide our arms around each other, and now he's pressing against me, and in the next moment we're horizontal on the sofa, a tangle of tongues and hands and limbs, tugging at each other's clothes and making up for that lost decade like both our lives depend on it.

6

Stay

On my first day at Pebbles & Paper, I spot my old boss
Georgia as I'm heading from the bus stop to the shop.

I stiffen for a moment before diving down the side street
to my right. I can't face her, not after the way we left it –
with me accusing her of betrayal and her begging me to
stay. Because the truth is, there was a lot to love about working at Figaro. That feeling of knowing we'd built something
pretty great between us. The family vibe, the banter.

I walk a little too swiftly in the opposite direction to
Georgia, my ankles wriggling as I navigate the cobblestones. It's a warm day, and I've broken out a cotton skirt
and sandals for the occasion. Above my head the sky is a
faultless blue, still as a lagoon.

The morning passes as smoothly as I'd hoped – there's a
steady stream of browsers, a few purchasers, but nowhere
near enough people to overwhelm me at any point. Ivan's
here anyway, in case I have any teething problems on my
first shift. He takes great pleasure in pointing out just how
many of the items in stock are unique and handmade. I
think about Caleb's story from last week and smile.

What Might Have Been

So far, I've sold some birthstone jewellery, a few toiletries, a handmade silk scarf, several greetings cards, a pair of bookends and a box of artisan chocolates. Ivan seems to think that's a decent morning's takings, and for a moment I wonder how he ever manages to break even, before reflecting on the staggering markup there is on most of the items I've sold.

Things pick up a bit over the course of the afternoon, and by the time I next look up, it's five o'clock. Checking my phone as I get ready to leave, I smile as I see a message from Caleb.

> Thoughts on Shakespeare?

> I'm his biggest fan.

I respond.

We meet at dusk outside the walled garden of Shoreley Hall, where Caleb's bought tickets for an open-air production of *Romeo and Juliet*.

'You can translate,' he says, handing our tickets to the steward. He's brought a rug with him, plus a picnic in a carrier bag.

'Me?'

'Yeah – you know, being a writer. And apparently Shakespeare's biggest fan.'

I laugh, prod him gently in the small of his back with my fingertips as we enter the garden and search the grass for a place to sit.

The walled garden looks magical, like something out of a fairy tale. Long lines of bulbs loop between the branches of the trees, the air full with the scent of late-spring dew and thickening grass. The flower borders are resplendent, bursting with tangerine-toned tulips and wallflowers, blossom blazing from the plum, cherry and apple trees.

Beyond the red-brick wall, the sky is suspended indigo, those last rich minutes before it fades to black and a galaxy of stars erupts above our heads. The space is warm, packed tight with bodies and humming with conversation, dappled with laughter.

'This is inspired,' I say, as Caleb lays out the picnic rug.

'Well, I was trying to think of how to persuade you to see me again. And an old friend of mine mentioned he was in this, so . . .' He spreads his hands to finish the sentence.

I laugh. 'Yep, it was Shakespeare that swung it. Would definitely have turned you down otherwise.'

We share a loaded glance, and I wonder if he's picturing last night, too – the minutes melting away as we kissed, that feeling of having stumbled across something special.

'That's what I thought,' he says, deadpan.

'So, what part's your friend playing?'

He flicks through a copy of the programme. 'Count Paris.'

'Oof.'

'What? Is that bad?'

I keep my face straight. 'Couldn't possibly say.'

He laughs and starts unpacking the food. 'Knew there was a reason I should have paid attention in English. Speaking of which, you haven't sent me your pages.'

I grimace a little. I'd been wavering over hitting 'send' first thing this morning, before being flooded with self-doubt. 'I know.'

He smiles. 'I probably shouldn't have asked.'

'No, I want to, I just . . . I might polish them up a bit first.'

He nods. 'If you change your mind, it's cool. Really. Right – are you hungry? Had to guess what you'd like.'

'Talk me through it.'

'Well, I am trying to impress you, so most of it's posh. But I did throw in some Scotch eggs and cocktail sausages. Plus . . .' He lifts up a bag. 'Couldn't go without Scampi Fries.'

I shake my head. 'This is amazing. You guessed *so* well.' I survey the feast of garlic-stuffed olives, vegetable samosas, four-cheese focaccia, smoked ham and chicken salad spread out on the rug. 'You succeeded – I'm seriously impressed.'

'Wasn't sure what you'd want to drink, so I bought prosecco, and' – he examines the bottle – 'rhubarb pressé.'

'I'll go for some pressé, please.'

He takes the bottle and starts to unscrew the lid before hesitating, then swearing softly.

'What's up?'

'Forgot glasses,' he says, laughing. 'We're going to have to swig from the bottle.'

'That might lower the tone,' I joke, nodding at the people surrounding us, who are all equipped with plastic champagne flutes.

'Okay,' he whispers. 'We'll have to wait till the lights go down.'

As if on cue, a drum strikes on stage, the lights in the garden fall and a hush descends over the murmuring crowd. Moths flit through the air as the stage becomes illuminated.

An actor steps forward into the spotlight. 'Two households, both alike in dignity,' he bellows. 'In fair Verona, where we lay our scene . . .'

Across the rug, Caleb reaches out, takes my hand and squeezes it. 'Okay, we're safe. Swig away,' he whispers. And as I smile, I feel an overwhelming swell of relief that I decided to call him last week, rather than hold out for the memory of a man nearly ten years in my past.

Though today's been warm – weather more suited to summer than late spring – neither of us was prepared for how sharply the air temperature would dip as the Capulets' and Montagues' feud wore on. By the time the actors are lined up on stage taking their bows, I am shivering and my teeth are chattering, despite drowning in the jumper Caleb draped over me during the half-time interval.

Caleb's friend, who was playing the doomed Count Paris, was very good, but there's a large crowd around him at the end, and we decide it's too cold to wait to say hi.

'God, sorry,' Caleb says, once we've gathered up our things and have joined the queue to exit the walled garden. 'Didn't think it would be quite this Baltic.' We're surrounded by people who clearly do this sort of thing all the time and have come prepared in layers, hats and thick coats. My

skirt and emergency jumper are clearly marking me out as
a first-time outdoor-theatre fan.

Once we've made it outside, we both hesitate. I'm pretty
sure neither of us wants the night to end, but we're still at
that point of getting to know each other where we need to
discuss what we're going to do next.

'Fancy coming back to mine?' Caleb asks, slipping an
arm around my shoulders. I like the feeling of being held
close by him, of our bodies pressed together, of his warm,
unflinching frame.

I look up at him and smile. 'Sounds good.'

We walk briskly back in the direction of his cottage, hand
in hand. He didn't say anything as he wrapped his fingers
around mine, and I didn't pass comment. It felt the most
natural thing in the world for him to do.

The night sky is lustrous with stars now, the coastal air
sharp and salt-filled. Above the rows of rooftops, the moon
hangs low, like a candlewax disc stamped into the
blackness.

'So, shall we mark it out of ten?' Caleb asks, as we pass
the town's little art gallery, a display of seascapes illuminated in its window.

'The play or the date?' I say, then catch myself. I mean,
this *was* a date, wasn't it?

Caleb doesn't appear to pick up on this split-second of
self-doubt. 'Let's go with the play. Not sure I'm quite up to
being scored yet.'

'Of course. Sorry. Okay – I'm giving it a firm nine. You?'

'I'm going with . . . seven.'

'*Seven?*'

'Sorry. But I do like my plays to have a happy ending.'

'Even the Shakespearean tragedies?'

He laughs, then winks. 'See, I always just thought it was a love story.'

In his kitchen back at the cottage, Caleb offers me a nightcap, and when I decline, says, 'Do you mind me asking . . . ?'

'Booze just doesn't really . . . agree with me.'

'So, do you drink at all, or . . . ?'

I shake my head. 'Not any more.'

He nods, apparently entirely unfazed by this. 'Well, I can offer you an impressive array of hot drinks.'

'You can?'

He rubs his chin. 'Yeah, I seem to collect – don't you do this? – random boxes of herbal teas, about five different types of coffee . . . I've got hot chocolate, and Horlicks, and . . .' He starts rummaging in a cupboard.

'Coffee's fine,' I say with a laugh.

So he makes us both coffee, and while the water's boiling I wander back into the living room and over to a row of photos on one of the walls, all bearing Caleb's pencilled signature on their mounts. There's a windswept vista of the dunes at the far end of Shoreley beach; a deer mid-leap above a five-bar gate; a shot of a bride and groom on their wedding day with the flare of a setting sun behind them; a black-and-white shot of an older woman laughing, who looks strangely familiar.

I feel him at my shoulder, watching me looking.

'These are insanely good,' I say, feeling almost intimidated by his talent.

'Thank you,' he says modestly. He is standing delectably close. I can smell the scent of his washing powder, the faint trace of aftershave lingering on his skin. 'That was my stepsister's wedding day. And that last one's my mum.'

'She's beautiful,' I say, realising now why she'd looked familiar.

Caleb heads back into the kitchen to finish making the coffee. I move over to two more framed pictures on the mantelpiece above the wood burner. One is of Caleb standing on a bridge with two other men about his age and an older man and woman. In the other, he's sitting around a dinner table with his mum, stepsister, another younger woman and a younger lad.

He appears at my shoulder again, hands me a mug. 'My parents divorced when I was ten, so I have about a million step-siblings.' His smile as he says this doesn't quite reach his eyes, in a way that reminds me of Jools whenever she talks about her family.

I sit down on the sofa, tuck my legs up beneath me. 'Do you get on?'

Caleb draws the curtains, then passes me a blanket before switching on an ancient-looking lamp that flickers and fizzes in protest.

'We do,' he says, sitting down next to me. 'It's more that . . . I don't know. I was an only child, but my parents have both had new families for getting on twenty years now. So I sometimes wonder . . . where I fit in. If that makes sense.'

It does, and I feel a sting of sadness for him. 'Do they live close?'

He shakes his head. 'Dad's in Devon, Mum's in Newcastle. Like, as far from each other as they could possibly be. And me, come to that.' He smiles. 'How about your folks?'

'Oh,' I say, with an irrational onrush of guilt, which I get whenever I talk to anyone whose family background isn't entirely happy. 'Well, my parents are sort of . . . this crazy fairy tale.'

'Yeah?'

I sip my coffee. 'Yeah, they met on holiday when they were twenty, fell pregnant with my sister and have been stupidly in love ever since.'

He smiles. 'Nice. What's their secret?'

'I guess . . . they always saw themselves as soulmates.'

His smile falters slightly. 'My dad used to say that about every woman he met after my mum.' I catch the faintest of eye-rolls as he speaks.

I wrinkle my nose in sympathy. 'That must have been weird.'

'Let's just say, it definitely killed that old-fashioned idea of the fates aligning, love being written in the stars . . . that sort of thing.' His smile returns. 'Must have been nice for you though, to see living proof of the real deal.' To his credit, he says this without a shred of cynicism.

'Are you and your dad close now?'

He sips his coffee. 'To my shame, yes. I've always kind of idolised him.' He laughs. 'Really wish I didn't, actually. He's just . . . infuriatingly cool.'

'What does he do?'

'Wildlife cameraman. You know, for documentaries and stuff. So, yeah – I basically just wanted to *be* him, my whole life.'

'That's where you got your wanderlust?'

He nods. 'I guess after Helen and I broke up, I was like . . . *Yes. That's what I need to do next.*'

I feel my chest clench with trepidation. 'So . . . will that be . . . soon?'

He holds my gaze for a moment or two, then releases a breath. 'No. I mean . . . no. It's not like I'm taking off next week, or anything. I've got nothing planned, not yet.'

I force myself to smile, but inside, I'm catastrophising. *Of course* someone as lovely as Caleb wouldn't just turn up in my life, catch-free. Men like him don't actually exist. *Of course* he's about to up and leave for the other side of the world – that's why he's more than happy to rent. He doesn't want to put down roots. And maybe for that reason he's not interested in starting anything serious, romantically speaking, either.

'You mentioned you went away, after uni?' Caleb says.

'Um, not for long. Just three months.'

Eyes eager, he leans forward and asks me more, but it's hard to match his enthusiasm when I talk about it, and eventually his questions peter out.

'I had to cut the trip short,' I conclude, lamely.

He nods. 'How come?'

'Oh, you know. Just . . . wasn't meant to be.'

He doesn't know, of course, but thankfully he doesn't probe any further, and then we sit in silence for a little while, finishing our coffees. I feel horribly guilty suddenly – like I've spoilt the night by ending on such a low note. But then he sets down his mug before turning to brush the hair from my face. 'Warmed up yet?'

I smile, shake my head. 'Nope. Not yet.'

'Well, maybe I can help with that,' he whispers, leaning forward to kiss me.

'I mean, I'm literally freezing,' I whisper back, as his lips move to my neck. On the wall, our shadows loom large in the lamplight.

This time, as we kiss, I venture a hand beneath his T-shirt, running my fingers over his skin, skimming his ribs, the ridges of his muscles.

Please don't go anywhere, I think, as he groans softly. *This has barely even started, but already I don't want it to end.*

Go

Sunday night, forty-eight hours after my date at the restaurant with Max.

We're in bed, trying to muster up the energy to order in some sushi, which basically sums up exactly how decadent this weekend has been. We've left the flat just once since our date, popping out yesterday morning for sustenance, which essentially involved shoving half of Waitrose into a trolley. Now we're nose-to-nose on the mattress, a breeze from the open window stroking my hot, bare shoulders, the gossamer kiss of pillows against my face.

Max's bedroom is pale and clean, high-ceilinged with sash windows. Lots of light. The iron bed frame is set against a rugged wall of exposed brickwork and piled with white bed linen the texture of marshmallows. There's just a smattering of other items in here – a cornflower-coloured rug on the floorboards, mounted speaker in one corner, blond-wood chest of drawers, and full-length mirror propped near the window. I keep catching myself glancing around, trying to spot things I recognise, little trinkets from our past, but there is nothing.

The flat is calm and peaceful, like we're in a village rather than London, with windows so well glazed you can't really hear much traffic. Occasionally there is the muted thump of feet above our heads, but it's nothing like sitting in the living room in Tooting, where even the light crossing of a room upstairs resembles a stampede. Max told me last night he chose this flat partly for the neighbours, doing extensive research on them before he signed the contract.

'Is that legal?' I laughed.

'You think journalists have to dig for a living, try doing what I do. You wouldn't believe the things I find out about people.'

I reach out now to touch his face. His skin is bright and damp with exertion. 'You know, the night I saw you in Shoreley . . . I'd just started chatting to this guy, in the pub.'

He props himself up onto one elbow, raises an eyebrow. '*Chatting* chatting?'

I smile and shrug. 'Kind of. But then I saw you out the window, and I just . . . abandoned him at the bar. Anyway, he wrote his number on a beer mat and put it in my coat pocket. I found it last week.'

Max laughs. 'Wow. And you say *I'm* smooth?'

'I know. Who'd have thought you'd have competition on that front?'

'So, are you going to call him?'

I found the beer mat while I was packing up the last of my things for the move, and it fell out of my coat pocket. I turned it over in my hands and smiled, then placed it gently into the box of stuff that would be staying in Tash's loft.

I feign deliberation. 'Yeah, maybe. Just to hedge my bets, you know.'

'Oh, absolutely. Very wise.'

I shuffle forward on the mattress and kiss him – a kiss that's long and full and intense, so he can be in no doubt at all I'm just teasing.

'In all seriousness,' I whisper, 'you should know, I don't make a habit of this.'

His eyes crease at the corners, a tiny spray of crow's feet. 'Of what?'

My heart is cartwheeling in my chest. 'Sleeping with guys on the first date.'

'First date.' He pretends to think about this. 'But isn't this technically like ... our four hundredth date, or something?'

I smile. It's what I wanted him to say. 'Maybe.'

Beneath the covers, he runs a hand across my hip. 'It doesn't count, Luce. We're exes.' Then he catches my eye, rolls onto his back. 'That came out wrong. What I mean is, it's you and me. We're past all that.'

'Yeah. We can just skip straight to the good stuff.'

'Exactly.'

'Pick up where we left off.'

He rolls back towards me, fixing me with smoke-grey eyes. 'Yep.'

But . . . where *was* that? I mean, where did we leave off?

I've been burning to ask him since Friday night. Since our kiss, and that spark that turned into dynamite right there on his sofa. Since yesterday morning, when we returned from the shops with coffees from the Italian deli that ended up going cold and untasted in the kitchen. Since yesterday afternoon, when he eventually left the bed and invited me into the shower. I've spent the past forty-eight hours in a kind of daze, suspended in dreamy disbelief, but so far I've been unable to break the spell by saying the words I'm saying now.

'Why . . . did you end it, Max?' I whisper. The question's almost too hard to ask.

His gaze tracks back and forth across my face, like he's trying to pin down the right answer. 'I had to,' he says, eventually.

I trace a shape against his left pectoral with a single finger. His skin is still beach-brown, muscles undulating beneath it, his body – nearly a decade on – seemingly an even better version of how it was before. He's always been a runner, into sport, but now his physique looks more attended-to, like he might lift a few weights from time to time, too. I feel briefly self-conscious, wonder whether he's been comparing the me of today to the girl he loved back then.

I don't think I've changed, much. I haven't got the baller-ina physique of my sister, or Jools' natural beauty – but when I compare myself to old photos, I don't see a lot of difference, except maybe an easing of the youth from my face.

'Were you . . . scared of the commitment?' Our plan had been to move to London after graduating, and we'd already talked about finding a place there together, until a conversation with his friend Rob made me think I'd got that wrong. We argued about it one afternoon – about whether he was going to live with me, or with Rob and his other friend Dean – just a week before he broke things off. So I convinced myself that was why – but he kept saying it wasn't.

'No,' he says again now, but doesn't elaborate.

'Did you meet someone else?' I asked him this back then, of course. But maybe some things are easier to admit in retrospect.

He shakes his head. 'I was single for two years after we split up.'

We're still facing each other, so close our lips are almost touching, fingers gliding over skin. It's as though we're having the most intimate discussion of our lives, rather than getting stuck along a succession of conversational dead ends.

His forehead gathers into a frown. 'Have you ever . . . had to walk away from something because you knew it was the right decision – even though it broke your heart?'

'No,' I say truthfully. *It was you who broke my heart that day.*

To my surprise, his eyes begin to brim with tears. I've barely had time to register them before they're spilling down his cheeks, striking the pillow like raindrops.

What Might Have Been

Swearing softly, he sits up, then climbs out of bed and heads into the en suite. I sit up too, a little stunned. I've never seen Max properly cry before. Not even when he was facing me on that bridge in Norwich, rain-soaked and stricken, just before he walked away.

You were the one who left, Max. I thought it was what you wanted. How can you still be hurting this much?

I hear the splashing of water before, a minute or so later, he comes over to the bed again, seemingly now composed. He sits on the mattress next to me, takes my hand, works my fingers in his. 'I know I owe you more than this, Luce, but . . . all I can tell you is that it felt like the right thing to do, back then.' He shakes his head. 'That isn't to say I don't have massive regrets. I've spent so much time . . . thinking about where we might be now, if we hadn't broken up.'

To hear him say all this now feels like watching a rocket soar into the sky, only to crash back down to earth moments later. Because while it's comforting to know I'm not the only one with regrets, doesn't that mean parting was pointless, if we've both been feeling this way?

I revisit my all-too-familiar fantasy of what Max and I would be doing now, if he'd never ended it. We'd be living together in a beautiful flat – or maybe even a house. We'd have lots of friends, hundreds of shared experiences to cherish. We'd have seen the world, hosted the wedding of the century. We'd be cat people, definitely. And we'd be planning a family. A noisy, colourful tribe to fill our hearts with love all over again. My life would have taken an upwards trajectory, rather than failing to ever really get started.

But worse than that, perhaps, is that I would undoubt-edly have stayed at university for that final year, been awarded my degree. And then I would have moved to London with Max, found a proper job. By now, I'd be years into my career. I would never have gone to Australia, I wouldn't have met Nate and I wouldn't have lost everything.

'Lucy?'

I shake my head. An unwelcome vision of Nate – his leering face – has lodged in my mind. 'Sorry?'

'I was asking what you want,' Max says, gently.

'What I want?'

He nods. 'I feel like enough time has passed to maybe . . . And I know I don't deserve you, Lucy, but—'

My heart rushing forward, I lean over, smother his words with a kiss.

It doesn't even occur to me to wonder why it would be important for time to have passed.

Max has to catch an early train to Leeds on Monday morning. He says he'll be there until late Thursday, in meetings and on site visits to a high-end mixed-use devel-opment in the city centre – the subject of a dispute his firm is working on, with millions at stake, apparently. But we arrange to meet on Friday night, as soon as he returns to London.

Back in Tooting, the house feels gloomy and lonely, rattling with street noise and the sound of intermittent gunfire from next door's TV. I quite like noise, normally – I find it comforting – but after a weekend cocooned in the smooth, gleaming sanctuary of Max's flat, it's easier to see this place for the unloved rental it is. Grimy corners and stark surfaces, peeling paint and zero water pressure, the faintest scent of damp.

I'm aching to talk to someone, but Jools and Sal are still on the night shift, and Reuben is at his girlfriend's place in Leyton.

I make a cup of tea, head upstairs, check my phone. Just one message, from Max.

> The best weekend ever. You're amazing. Until Friday xx

I call my sister. Predictably, she's already in her office at work – she's head of business development at a digital marketing agency – sipping a green juice, which I guess she'd call breakfast. She's dressed for the warm weather in a cream blouse with capped sleeves, her bobbed blond hair immaculate as spun gold. My heart flexes when I see her, mostly because I know how much she'll worry when she finds out why I'm calling.

'I've got something to tell you.'

She peers at the screen, like she's searching for clues in the murky backdrop of my bedroom. 'What? What is it? Is everything okay?'

I release a breath. The reassuring little speech I've prepared vanishes from my head completely. 'I'm . . . Me and Max . . .'

Her face tightens. 'You and Max what?'

'I think . . . we're going to give it another shot.'

Her face crumples within a second. I hadn't expected her reaction to be so immediate. 'No, Luce. Please not him.'

'Tash, it's okay—'

'No, it's not. It's not okay.' For a moment, I think she's about to start hyperventilating.

'He feels awful about how it ended, before.'

She shakes her head, like that's irrelevant. I watch her try to compose herself. 'I just think you could do . . . *so* much better. There must be so many good guys out there. Why don't you wait until you start work, see if there's anyone nice at your new place?'

'Because,' I say weakly, 'it's *Max*. He was always my one that got away. The person I was meant to be with. You know?'

'Except he wasn't, was he?' she says, her voice softening slightly like she's breaking bad news. 'You split up, and then didn't speak for nearly a decade.'

'But now . . . we've found each other again.'

It feels weird to be discussing Max like this. We've rarely done so in the intervening years – Tash never forgave him for what he did to me, plus he was evidently long gone. There never seemed to be very much point in talking about him.

'Lucy,' Tash says, her voice more urgent now, 'it's just nostalgia. You know that, don't you?'

'Or maybe he's my soulmate.' I decide against mentioning what my horoscope said, the day I bumped into Max, since I'm pretty sure that would be enough to tip her over the edge completely.

Tash's forehead pinches together. 'You know, I was read-ing this article the other day about how people think they've met their soulmate when it's actually . . . just lust. That all the fireworks and the love at first sight is just a bunch of chemicals shooting around. That it's the slow-burn connec-tions that actually mean the most.' The way she says this implies she suspects Max and I would be at the lighter-fuel end of the emotional depth spectrum.

'What about Mum and Dad? They're definitely soul-mates. Or you and Simon.'

She pauses for a moment, staring at the screen like she no longer recognises the person looking back at her. 'I just don't want you to get hurt again, Lucy,' she says, eventu-ally, like she knows she's losing the argument – and almost, by extension, me. 'After you broke up, when you came back from travelling, you were like . . . a different person.'

She assumes Max did that to me, but I don't tell her it was actually nothing to do with Max – or at least, a lot less to do with him than she thinks. I never confided in her about what happened in Australia. And so much time has passed now, I doubt I ever will.

Back then, she used to say I'd forgotten how to take risks, be spontaneous. Well, what is agreeing to see Max again if not a risk, proof I've rediscovered my sense of adventure?

'Please, please just promise me you'll think about this, before rushing into anything,' Tash says.

It's a bit late for that now, I think. But her heart looks almost as if it's breaking, so I nod, tell her yes. 'He's away with work this week. I promise I'll think it through prop-erly before the weekend.'

I know what she's thinking: *Max went on holiday for a fortnight, and now he's 'away with work' for a week?* She probably suspects he ran off with someone else back then. If nothing else, I know she thinks I'm making a big mistake.

But how can that be true, when being with Max never felt anything but right?

By the time Christmas rolled around at the end of our first term at uni, we'd been friends for three months. Friends who flirted a lot, whom everyone assumed were already together. Who messaged all day then decamped to each other's rooms at night. Who met for coffee on campus, sat together in the pub, saved seats for each other in the cinema.

I'm still surprised we held back from taking it further for so long: we were both single, frequently uninhibited by booze, fully intimate with the details of each other's lives. But Max said afterwards he was afraid of messing up our friendship, and I was probably too filled with self-doubt to make the first move. After all, this was *Max* – so popular on campus, so handsome, the kind of guy people gravitated towards – and I'd never even had a boyfriend before, not a serious one.

I knew he'd had a girlfriend back home in Cambridge. They'd broken up over the summer – she was staying on there, to go to actual Cambridge University. I'd stalked her a bit on social media, which didn't help my confidence issues – she was gorgeous in a sunny, carefree way that made me convinced Max would be compelled to seek her out again at some point.

What Might Have Been

So three months passed, and then it was December and I was packing to go home to Shoreley at the same time that Max was due to catch the bus back to Cambridge.

He walked into my room early afternoon on our last day on campus, holding up a hoodie. His hair was damp, and he smelled faintly of that herby shower gel all the guys I knew seemed to like, so I assumed he'd just been for a run.

'Found this under my bed,' he said.

'You star.' I smiled. 'I've been looking for that.'

He hesitated then, seeming disoriented suddenly, which was very unlike Max. He always knew what to say, was never lost for words. His success in the law student mooting competitions was testament to that.

Appearing to recover, he smiled, continued to hover by my bed. It was stripped bare, the sheets in a bin bag ready to be shoved straight into my parents' washing machine back in Shoreley. 'Hey, I bumped into Anna at the canteen earlier. Finally got the balls to tell her my name isn't Matt.'

I smiled. One of Max's tutors, who'd been getting his name wrong all term – even though she was reportedly already convinced he had the potential to be a top barrister. 'Was she embarrassed?'

'Yeah. So much so, she bought me a mince pie and a coffee.'

'Worth it, then.'

'Ha,' he said, because it was a running joke between us that the canteen coffee was little more than tepid, discoloured water. And then, suddenly, 'You should come to Cambridge.'

'Sorry?' I lowered the T-shirt I'd been folding.

'Come to Cambridge. Stay for a bit. Feels weird I won't see you for three weeks.'

I nodded. 'I know. I'll miss you.'

He looked down at the floor. 'I nicked something earlier, too. From the canteen.'

'Did you?' I was confused for a moment. What did he mean? Max was far too honest to steal.

He nodded, then reached into the back pocket of his jeans and produced a sprig of green plastic, slightly bent.

Mistletoe.

A smile spread through me, and my heart started to spin, instantly out of control on an axis I didn't know it had.

Max lifted the mistletoe with one hand, his other arm behind his back, grey eyes steady against mine. 'I needed an excuse, Luce. To do something I've been wanting to do since we met.'

My blood got hot then and my heart became wild, every part of me rushing with wanting. And so I stepped forward, put my lips to his, and then we were kissing, hard and warm and fast, Max's arm firm across my shoulders as the gap between us closed. And soon the mistletoe was somewhere on the carpet, kicked under the bed as we toppled onto it.

Somewhere along the corridor, someone was playing Christmas music, a jingling tambourine-heavy melody. Doors were squeaking and banging, there were footsteps and voices, laughter and whooping, the ever-present scent of browning toast in the air. We were surrounded by people, and yet – just as I had felt on our very first night in halls

– their presence only seemed to heighten the privacy between us, hidden away behind my closed door.

I wanted to sleep with him. It didn't seem to matter that this was our first kiss, let alone anything else. I knew Max and I had something special, even though we hadn't explored what that was yet. I felt a future with him. I *sensed* it. Some inexplicable knowing that we were destined for each other.

'Lucy,' he breathed, as we began to tug at each other's clothes, 'have you . . . Have you . . . ?'

'No,' I breathed back. 'But it's okay. I want to.'

'Are you sure? Because it's fine if . . .' The words were muffled, but I knew he meant them.

'Yes,' I gasped, kissing him harder, more insistently. I didn't even care that I was wearing my scruffiest jeans, and a T-shirt so old the logo had faded right off it, or that I was completely free of make-up. I could only think of Max – the deep press of his kiss, the damp warmth of his newly clean skin. 'Yes, I'm sure.'

So Max was my first, on that bright, chilly December afternoon in my university bedroom. And it was nothing like the way my sister or friends had described it – not awkward, or painful, or just a little bit *lacking*. It was full-hearted and special, tender and memorable. Everything I'd hoped it would be.

7

Stay

It's early evening, and I'm on one of the sofas in Tash and Simon's living room. Dylan's curled up in an armchair with Tash's iPad, already bathed and in his pyjamas. He's supposed to be playing a times-table app, but I know he's really watching kids unwrap pricey toys on YouTube. He announced he wanted to make his own videos last week, and my heart kind of broke for him, because I know that deep down, he doesn't understand why other boys get to play with all these awesome toys on tap, and he doesn't. Tash and Simon might be well off, but Dylan's never spoiled.

Tash and Simon have cracked open a bottle of wine from their basement – or as I like to think of it, lower-ground floor, given the basement is roughly the size of your average bungalow. I'm trying out a margarita made with non-alcoholic spirits: I was sceptical at first, but Tash is one of those people for whom my not drinking is a bigger deal than it is for me, who feels guilty about drinking herself unless I've got a non-alcoholic alternative in my hand. So I let her faff about with limes and ice and agave syrup, and the result is actually not bad.

What Might Have Been

It's been a peach-warm afternoon, and the brocade curtains are still parted at the French windows, which are open to entice a breeze. The sound of bleating lambs drifts through the gap. Beyond the boundary of the vast lawned garden, the landscape undulates, giving way to a tapestry of fields and hedgerows that leads, eventually, all the way to the sea.

'So, we read your pages,' Tash says, tucking her feet up beneath her on the other sofa.

Tash and Simon have been pestering me to let them have a sneak-peek of my novel, so a couple of days ago, I emailed Tash the first ten pages or so for them both to read. And then, before I could change my mind, I emailed the same to Caleb, with a note that said, One condition: you can't say it's good if you think it's terrible x

He emailed back within thirty seconds. Pretty sure that's not going to happen. But of course – I promise x

'So . . . what did you think?' I ask Tash, tentatively.

'We thought it was lovely,' she says brightly, like she's reporting back on a wedding that secretly bored her stiff.

Next to her, Simon nods with an enthusiasm that hints at rehearsal. 'Really, really good.'

Simon's what I guess you might describe as classically handsome. He keeps his dark hair short – it's little more than a neat shadow, really – and there's a crisp line of stubble along his jaw. He's a mortgage broker, which seems to involve a lot of golfing, and attending a never-ending series of niche mid-week awards dos.

Dylan clambers down from his armchair and runs up to Simon with the iPad, bellowing something incoherent about a scooter.

'Okay,' I say, uncertainly. 'Anything more specific than "lovely" and "really good"?'

'*Atmospheric*,' Simon declares triumphantly, after a pause, in the manner of a gameshow contestant having a brainwave. He holds open his arms, letting Dylan climb onto his lap.

'Come on,' I say, impatiently. 'What did you really think?'

Tash sips her wine. 'I think your writing is great. Seriously.'

'But . . . ?'

She hesitates. 'I suppose I was a bit surprised you'd set it in the twenties.'

'Why?'

A light shrug. 'I don't know. I guess because you'd said it was loosely based on Mum and Dad. So maybe I was just expecting it to be a modern-day thing.'

'Well, hence the term "loosely". They're only the inspiration. It's not their biography.'

She sips her wine again. 'Did you get in touch with that guy yet, about joining that writing group?'

I stare at her. 'Oh, you actually hated it.'

Her eyes widen. 'No, that isn't what I meant! I just remembered you were going to try a session with that group, that's all.'

Self-doubt and dismay spread through my chest like a bruise.

There have definitely been times over the years when the world's seemed to be telling me to jack writing in. Like when that pipe leaked above my bedroom at uni and destroyed all my writing notebooks. And when I had that short story accepted for publication in an anthology just before I left, only for the small press to fold before it could ever get printed. The handful of submissions I made to magazines, all returned with form rejections.

I feel humiliated suddenly, exposed. My biggest fear has been that my novel isn't good enough to share, or even exist – and this lukewarm response has proved me right.

Why, why, *did I send it to Caleb?*

'You *encouraged* me to do this, Tash,' I remind her, childishly defensive suddenly.

My sister's eyes get even wider. 'Lucy, it was excellent – honestly.' She elbows Simon next to her. 'Wasn't it?'

He looks up. 'To be fair, I'm not much of a reader, but . . . yeah. It was good.'

Hardly a resounding endorsement.

Tash rolls her eyes. 'Lucy, I swear, I *loved* all the back and forth between Jack and Hattie, and you do tell it so beautifully . . .' She trails off, seeming to sense the need to pick her words carefully. 'I just remembered that writing group and thought, you know . . . it might be useful. Only because you're a beginner. You've never had any formal training.'

I scoop up the glass containing what's left of my fake margarita. If I can't even show my work to my own sister without feeling this way, what chance would I have in front of strangers?

Lifting the iPad close to Simon's face, Dylan starts describing his preferred scooter from a shortlist of three, which thankfully saves us all from having to sit through the world's most awkward silence.

'That came out all wrong, Luce,' Tash says, once Dylan's finished his sales pitch. 'We honestly loved it.'

I meet her eye. 'Really?'

'Really.'

Dylan squeals with delight at something Simon has said and dashes from the room, iPad abandoned. Simon takes the opportunity to top up Tash's glass, then his own. 'So, how's it going with your new bloke?' he asks, clearly sensing a need to change the subject.

Tash looks relieved. 'Yes, come on – what's the gossip?'

I smile. 'No gossip,' I say primly, which is actually sort of true.

'Come on,' Tash says. 'We love gory details.'

I shake my head. 'I've known him – what – two weeks?'

'But you like him, right?'

I can't help smiling. 'Yeah, I do. But . . .' I trail off, unsure as to whether my fears are even real at this stage.

Tash leans forward. 'But what?'

'I'm not sure . . . I mean, he said the reason he and his wife broke up was because they were different people, by the end.'

'Okay . . .'

'And, there's a lot about him I like, but . . . he wants to go travelling, and he's just . . . very different to anyone I've dated before.'

In the past, I've mostly been drawn to guys who were very driven and focused and goal-oriented. That's not to say Caleb isn't any of those things – but it's certainly not what would spring to mind if I were asked to describe him. Still, him not being my usual type actually feels like a good thing.

But I still can't figure out if we're holding back on the physical front because Caleb's not planning to hang around. We've lost hours over the past couple of weeks to getting cosy on his sofa. But we've not taken it beyond that yet, and maybe it's because we both know that this is something that can't last.

'Him being different isn't bad though, is it?' Simon says. 'I mean, those relationships ended, so—'

'Yeah, definitely. No, it's more that . . . I really like him, and I don't want to get too involved if—'

'He's going to up and disappear?' guesses Tash.

I nod.

'You could just ask him,' Simon says, with a shrug.

'It's early days.' I smile. 'I don't want to scare him off.'

'You want to know what I think you should do?' Tash says.

'No, what?'

'Have fun. Just go with it. Who says you have to get serious?'

I swallow, and nod. 'No, I know.' But what I don't say to either of them – because how can I possibly know this yet? – is that I have a feeling, deep down, that I already feel serious about Caleb.

I already know that I don't want to let him go.

The next day, Caleb invites me to his place for supper. I head over to the cottage at six o'clock, my mind gently rippling with anticipation.

I already love Spyglass Cottage and its two hundred years of history, its tiny winding staircase, the bijou bathroom.

Yes, it's shabby – the paint is peeling on the window frames, the electrics are temperamental and some of the floorboards are warping – but it's got character, a personality. There are past lives and memories buried within its walls.

'Something smells good,' I say, after he's let me in and I'm following him through to the kitchen.

He's wearing faded jeans and a lightly crumpled T-shirt, his feet bare and hair fluffed up like it's freshly washed. 'Thanks, but . . . you should definitely reserve your judgement till you've tried it.'

I smile and pass him the dish containing the apple crumble I've knocked up, dessert being my standard dinner party gift in lieu of wine. 'Ditto. So, what's on the menu?' I peer over at the bubbling contents of the Le Creuset on top of the Aga, the pot's orange enamel stained brown from years of use.

'Well, it started out as a veggie curry, but all my spices were out of date, so . . . I think we'd better just call it a stew.' His expression is halfway between a grimace and a smile. 'But all the veg is from the garden, so I'm hoping you'll give me points for that.'

I smile. 'Don't worry. My crumble was going to be a pie until I realised I can't actually make pastry. The apples are from my sister's tree, though.'

'I really don't fancy our chances if the apocalypse comes, Lambert.'

I laugh, flattered by the sudden and affectionate use of my surname.

He throws me a sideways smile. 'Sorry. No idea where that came from.'

'No, I like it.'

He lets out a breath. 'I'm being literally the most awkward host ever. Must be nervous, or something.'

'I don't think you get nervous.'

He smiles and meets my eye. 'Sometimes I do.'

Since it's a warm evening, we eat outside on the back patio, perched on plastic chairs coated in lichen. The garden is long, narrow and wildly overgrown, as though it hasn't been tended to in about a decade – though Caleb has cleared a path to the veg patch through the jungle of brambles and nettles. The burgeoning greenery is daubed with the butter-yellow splash of dandelions, violet clouds of forget-me-nots, the creamy foam of cow parsley. At the far end of the garden, I can just about make out an unruly hawthorn hedge, woven through with honeysuckle and flanked by a line of lime trees, their leaves gently twitching in the breeze. Behind them, the sinking sun is bleeding into a cocktail-coloured sky, the clouds becoming watercolour brushstrokes.

Caleb's been showing me the images from a job he was working on this week – taking photographs for the fish bar and grill on the promenade, which has just received a rave review in one of the broadsheets. The shots are impressive, capturing precisely the grill's rustic, down-to-earth vibe while showcasing bits of fish as if they're works of art.

Once we've finished the stew, which was pretty good, we portion the crumble into bowls, drowning it in custard. 'I take it back, by the way,' Caleb says, examining his spoon after a couple of mouthfuls. 'About the apocalypse. I reckon we'd do all right.'

'My sister should really take the credit for this,' I admit. 'She had to talk me through it. She's a lot more accomplished than me at most things.'

'You're accomplished.'

'Hardly.'

'Don't people always feel that way about their older siblings?'

I lick my spoon thoughtfully. 'Maybe. Do you, about yours?' I ask, meaning his step-siblings.

'Yeah. Which is stupid, really, because I've never been into money and fast cars and . . .' He glances over at me before elaborating. 'My stepbrothers on my dad's side are older, and they both work in property, and making everyone else feel like abject failures is kind of their hobby. Or maybe it's just me. I think they see me as the black sheep of the family. In so far as I *am* family.'

I think back to when I'd just returned from Australia and had withdrawn almost completely from my own family. I don't think even Tash quite knew how to reach me. There was a time when we were only speaking every few weeks. I think, deep down, I felt jealous of how smoothly life seemed to have panned out for her. How easy she appeared to find things. The strength of her relationship with Simon.

But when Dylan was born, everything changed. Suddenly, there was a brand-new little life linking me to my sister. Day by day, Dylan started bringing us closer

– and since we've been living under the same roof, we've more or less recreated the strong bond we had as kids. Improved on it, even.

'So,' Caleb says, meeting my eye with a smile. 'I read your pages.'

Reflexively, I put a hand to my face, still a tiny bit crushed by Tash and Simon's slightly tepid response last night to my writing. 'I'm not sure I want to know.'

He spoons up more dessert. 'Why?'

'Why what?'

'Why don't you want to know?'

I smile, then take a long swig of water, trying to wash my vulnerability away. 'I let my sister and her husband read the same pages I sent to you.'

'And?'

I shrug lightly. 'They were expecting something different, I think. Maybe it just wasn't to their taste.'

As we talk, I can just about hear the faint murmur of waves on the shoreline dancing through the air. It mingles with the whoops and hoots of revellers winding through the town, and the folksy sound of live music drifting over from The Smugglers' beer garden. Shoreley is gearing up now for the tourist season, and though I love how people flock to it like migrating birds in the summer months – it arouses my sense of local pride – I think on balance I prefer it out of season, when the cobblestones are quiet and the beach is a blank canvas and you can always hear the sea.

'Lucy.' His gaze hooks onto mine. 'I *loved* it.'

A warm breeze lifts the hair from my face. I flatten it

back with one hand, then wrinkle my nose self-consciously. 'Really?'

He leans forward. 'Really. God, when you told me about all that Margate-in-the-twenties stuff and we were talking about *The Great Gatsby* and all the hedonism and hope . . . I mean, it sounded *great*. And you completely and utterly nailed it, one hundred per cent. I felt like I was there. I felt . . . transported, just completely absorbed. And the chemistry with Jack and Hattie is something else.'

I feel a blush of flattery rise up my neck. 'Wow. Thank you.'

'I'm serious. Your writing's beautiful. Honestly, Lucy. I'm not sure what I was expecting, but . . . you've got a gift.'

I let his gaze sink into me, pleasure budding in my belly. 'You're not just humouring me?'

'Believe me, I'm a terrible liar.' He smiles slightly help-lessly. 'Look, I get it: I've been putting my work out there for God knows how long. I do understand what it takes to show people your stuff for the first time. So I would never patronise anyone who does. I respect you way more than that, Lucy.'

I realise I'm shaking slightly, and for the first time in years, I find myself craving a long swig of chilled white wine. I take a steadying breath, drawing the scent of honey-suckle into my lungs.

'If I'm honest, I had everything crossed it *would* be good, because I knew I wouldn't be able to fake being impressed. Lucky for me, I didn't have to.'

'Thank you,' I say, finally relaxing enough to be able to

smile. 'That means a lot. Writing . . . It's all I've ever wanted to do.'

'Lucy,' he says, leaning across the table like he really wants me to hear this, 'it's really good. You should keep going.'

I bite my lip. 'Tash got me a flyer for a writing group, in Shoreley.'

'You going to go?'

'I might.'

'Can't hurt.' He meets my eye, like he understands my reticence, even without me spelling it out. 'That's one of the reasons I wish I hadn't dropped out of college, actually. Having that . . . group support goes a long way.'

'Have you ever doubted yourself? With your work, I mean?'

'Only pretty much every day,' he says, a soft smile on his face. 'Look – you do anything creative, you spend your life questioning your choices and doubting your ability. It's part of the deal. But the payback, when it comes . . . That feeling when someone else likes your work, and you manage to pay the rent for another month off the back of something you've dreamed up . . . There's nothing like it, Luce.'

'I'm really glad I met you.' The words leave my mouth entirely without permission. I chase them down with a self-conscious laugh.

But Caleb isn't laughing. He's looking me right in the eyes. 'I'm really glad I met you too.'

From over at The Smugglers drifts an acoustic song I can't quite place but sounds like it might be Jack Johnson.

'I've never . . .' I start, then falter. 'This feels really—'

'Yeah. It does, doesn't it?' And then he leans forward and kisses me, lips sinking against mine, tender pressure that makes me melt inside. His mouth teases mine open, and I have to actively hold back how hungry I am for this, for this amazing man who knows just what it is to be human, whose heart seems to beat exactly in time with mine.

After a couple of minutes, we draw gently apart. Caleb still has one hand at the back of my head. 'Want to go inside?'

I can only make a sort of happy murmur in response, but luckily he understands what it means, so we abandon our bowls and glasses and he leads me back indoors, gripping my hand like a promise. My body is buzzing, almost shivering, with want.

In the living room, he turns to face me, kissing me again. This time, the intensity ratchets quickly up, our movements becoming faster and deeper, greedier. Our mouths are heated and damp, our breath loud and heavy. I grab the hem of his T-shirt and tug it roughly over his head, and as I do, we stumble backwards onto the sofa. I pull him on top of me, he pushes up my dress. A sharp groan flees my throat at the delicious torment of his fingers against my thighs. I sink into his touch, giddy from the weight of him against me, from the feeling of his hand roaming the skin beneath my dress.

We explore every inch of each other's dips and curves and grooves, fingers skating over flesh, the tease of limbs pressing then releasing. I discover that Caleb is not muscular exactly, but toned and lean. He has the physique not of someone who goes to the gym, but someone who's never needed to.

I flick open his belt, delighting in the hot dance of his breath against my neck. And then all I can hear is the rush of my own blood and the throaty sound of him gasping my name as he moves inside me at last and I let go completely, pulsing and shuddering and intoxicated with pleasure.

Go

While Max is away in Leeds, I determine to make the most of my final week of freedom – reassured by the prospect of my forthcoming salary – before my start at Supernova on Monday. I set out to explore London in springtime, as though I'm emerging from the chrysalis of my old life. The trees are twitching with greenery, their branches growing heavy with confetti, as vapour trails carve scars into a blue-skinned sky. Families and tourists and office workers – distinguishable by their varying gaits, curiosity, impatience – are shedding winter clothing like moulting birds. I spend a few days checking out Jools' recommendations for favourite brunch cafés, the best spots for rye brownies, warm croissants, whole-milk flat whites. I browse charity shops, bookshops and markets, pick up artisan doughnuts and freshly baked sausage rolls and armfuls of flowers for the house. And when Jools isn't working nights, we brave the still-chilly water at the lido before filling our bellies on Lebanese mezze at the Common, watching children career haphazardly across the newly mown grass – the tang of it heady as freshly picked mint – delighting in the freedom afforded them by the firming ground, the warmth of the hatching spring.

I go shopping too, update my summer work wardrobe, spend hours on Instagram trying to figure out how the advertising world dresses. I mean, I've worked in advertising before, of course, but only in a hideous brutalist office building abutting a multi-storey car park in Shoreley. Nylon featured heavily. Soho – and Supernova – it was not.

In the evenings Jools and I head out for drinks, sourdough pizza, late-night treats in dessert bars. Sometimes we meet Reuben, and sometimes Sal, who I decide I would definitely want as my midwife if I were ever to fall pregnant.

Originally from South Africa, Sal is one of those people with a story to tell about everywhere she goes, each person she encounters: this pub, where she once had a very long and involved conversation with Jack Dee. That waiter, with his heavy addiction to chemsex and S&M. Those lads over there, who look like football hooligans but are in fact all very high up at a well-known tech giant.

Max and I have FaceTimed a few times since he's been in Leeds. He's walked me to his hotel window, showed me the skyline of the city at night as the promise of Friday burned between us.

That part – the view, and the tour he gave me of his hotel room – actually made me feel a little queasy, brought back unwelcome memories. But I didn't let it show. I just focused on his face, the balm of his voice.

What Might Have Been

I've met some interesting guys in the two weeks I've been here – friends of Jools, acquaintances of Sal or Reuben. But being with Max again has reignited that certainty I felt for so long – a certainty I still feel, deep down – that he and I were meant to be. I've not been able to stop replaying our three incredible nights together – the chemistry, the fun we had, the mind-blowing sex – after which I scroll further back in my mind to how it felt when we were together at uni. To the kinetic pleasure of kissing him, the drug of feeling his hands on me. But that inevitably leads to the sharp thunderclap of our split, a shock close to hitting black ice on a road and waiting to strike a tree.

On Friday afternoon, the day Max is back from Leeds, Jools knocks on my bedroom door as I'm watering the pot plant on my windowsill with a rinsed-out milk carton.

I've spent most of today trying to spruce up this room, because I'm vaguely aware that at some point, I might have no choice but to invite Max back to it. I headed out early this morning to buy fresh white bed linen, a couple of cheap framed abstract prints, three pot plants, a thick grey rug for the floorboards and some throw cushions. I dithered over tea lights too, before deciding they were probably second only to joss sticks in the student bedroom stakes.

'Looks great in here,' Jools says, coming over to the window. She's wearing a pair of tiny denim shorts and a peach-coloured spaghetti-strap top, sunglasses pushed back into her wild hair.

'Not a patch on yours.' Jools spends time and money curating her possessions: she wouldn't need to panic-buy half of Wilko in an attempt to impress a new boyfriend.

'Is this for Max's benefit?'

I nod. 'His flat is the kind of place that should have its own concierge.'

'He wasn't exactly born with a silver spoon in his mouth, Luce.'

'I know,' I say guiltily, because I do. 'I know that.'

She gives my elbow a consolatory squeeze. 'Anyway, just came to say 'bye. Wish me luck.'

Jools is off to Shoreley for a couple of days, to celebrate her dad's sixtieth. Her trips back there are rarely without drama – past visits have involved fist fights, bombshell revelations about affairs and illegitimate kids, and a permanent family-wide barring from one of Shoreley's major hospitality chains.

'As long as no one ends up in A&E, I'll be back on Sunday night,' she says, 'so I'll see you before you go.'

For a moment I can't think what she means, before remembering it's my first day at Supernova on Monday – otherwise known as the opportunity of a lifetime. *Get your priorities straight, Lucy, for God's sake.*

Jools laughs, climbing onto my bed and pulling her legs into a yoga pose. 'Do you actually need me to call you on Monday morning to *remind* you?'

'Ha, no. I'm coming back here on Sunday night.' A pause, then a thought occurs to me. 'Jools. Have I been a crappy friend?'

'What?'

I sit down next to her. 'I mean, I move in here with you and then ... I don't know ... I promptly disappear for days on end with Max.'

Jools places a hand on either side of my face, kisses my forehead. 'I work shifts. We were always going to be ships in the night, a bit. I'm *happy* for you, Luce. You deserve some good karma right now.'

In the aftermath of my break-up with Max, Jools – unlike Tash, and many of my other friends – never disparaged or criticised him, or declared she hadn't liked him all along. She helped me through my heartbreak without once running him down, something I realised afterwards must have taken the self-restraint of an alcoholic at an open bar. I'm not sure I could have done the same, in her position.

We sit quietly together for a couple of moments, our skin scored with shards of afternoon sunlight. Then Jools smiles and says, 'I actually always thought you'd get back together at some point. You were made for each other. Everyone could see it.'

'He might hurt me again.' It's the first time I've voiced it out loud: that Max could just up and leave one day, exactly as he did before. Maybe he's still scared of commitment. For a wild, crazy moment, I wonder if I could get in touch with his ex, ask if any of this sounds familiar.

Jools nods. 'Maybe. So, take it slow.'

'It's a bit late for that.'

A smile. 'I meant, emotionally.'

'So did I.'

★　　★　　★

A few hours later, I meet Max at his flat, this time with a packed bag (he messaged earlier: Stay the weekend?). We're heading to the house party of a friend of his tonight, in Balham.

He's waiting just inside the front door when I arrive. Straight away I drop my bag and we stumble towards the bedroom, our kisses wild and frantic as our clothes come off, no other thought than to be together.

'I have something to confess,' he says through the gap in the en-suite door as I towel off from showering afterwards, the peppery scent of his posh body wash infusing the steam.

'What's that?' I say lightly, though – irrationally – my mind is barking, *Girlfriend? Wife? Kids?*

'The party we're going to. It's at Olly and Joanna's.'

I put my head around the door. Max is in front of the mirror, freshly dressed in dark blue jeans and a black long-sleeved sweater.

'You don't mind, do you?' He apologises with his eyes. 'Thought you might not agree to come if I told you.'

The idea of it does feel slightly awkward: we were at uni with Olly and Joanna, childhood sweethearts from the same town in the Midlands, who were both studying chemistry. They were part of our wider circle, but we all thought they were slightly co-dependent, and already I'm struggling to remember a single thing about who they really were – like what music they were into, or which films they enjoyed, or what drinks they would order at the bar.

'Are you . . . friends, now?'

Max nods. 'Bumped into Olly in Balham one night a couple of years back. He was hammered, so I walked him home. He sent me a crate of wine the next day to say thanks.'

'A crate?' I say, thinking, *What's wrong with a bottle?*

'They're nice, I promise.'

'Is that because they've got more exciting, or you've got more—'

He cuts me off with a laugh. 'I'll let you be the judge of that.'

Olly and Joanna's house is halfway down one of those long, tree-lined streets where every second property is home to a young family, all with identical side-return extensions, bi-fold doors off their kitchen-diners and a particular style of Berber rug in the living room. Max tells me Olly is an analytical chemist now, and that Joanna works as a scientific writer for – get this – the *same* pharmaceutical company.

'They work together now, too? That can't be healthy,' I say, as we climb out of the cab.

'Don't drop that,' Max says, smiling down at the bottle of champagne I am gripping by the neck. 'This isn't a broken-glass kind of street.'

'Do you think they know they're two separate people?'

Max laughs and takes my hand, and we walk up to the front door together and ring the bell like we've been a couple attending house parties for years.

I feel mean, of course, as soon as Joanna answers. She's exactly as I remember – pin-thin in a slightly pinched way, with strawberry-blond hair and unnervingly pale skin, made even paler by the darkness of her navy silk dress. 'Hello, you,' she says to Max, leaning forward to kiss him, before standing back and taking me in, shaking her head proudly like I'm her first-born child on day one of primary school. 'Lucy! Haven't seen you since your famous disappearing act.' And before I can wonder if she's being deliberately snarky, she's pulling me into a kind of long-lost-friends hug, all musky perfume and strands of wayward hair.

Inside, Olly is similarly effusive – *Took you guys long enough!* – and soon we find ourselves with drinks in hand, drifting between groups of Olly and Joanna's neighbours, colleagues and friends, many of whom Max seems to know.

Every flawless room of this house is aglow with lamplight, platters of M&S nibbles on surfaces where we once might have balanced ashtrays and plastic pint glasses. It's all very middle-class and urbane, with most of the conversation seeming to revolve around the much-admired renovation of Olly and Joanna's house, and swapping contact details for builders, plumbers and electricians, as well as the usual debates on the council's approach to policing, schooling, parking. There's a lot of underplayed wealth going on here – the kind nobody admits to but that slips out in offhand references to second homes, nannies, postcodes. I start to feel conscious of my cheap sundress, green-and-white cotton in a bold print – perfect for the weather, I'd thought. I hadn't even worried too much about the creases, thinking, *How posh can a house party be?* But I know a pair of Louboutins and a hundred-quid manicure when I see them.

'Sure you don't want one of these cocktails?' Max asks me, after we've been here an hour or so. 'They're insanely good.'

I smile. 'I don't think drinking in public after ten years dry is a very good idea.'

'Ten *years*?' Max says, but fortunately as he does, he's clapped on the back by a tall, sandy-haired guy with high cheekbones and glinting blue eyes, who turns almost straight away to me.

'Lucy Lambert. Well, well.'

Beneath the chatter of the room, a Mumford & Sons bassline is galloping away. It strikes me that the frantic beat seems to suit this guy's entrance, somehow.

I know those eyes, I think, my mind scrambling to place them. But in the end, it takes me too long. 'Sorry, I—'

'It's Dean,' Max says, at the same time as his friend says, 'Dean Farraday.'

'*Oh*,' I say, my eyes readjusting to the slimmer, sharper, more self-possessed version of Max's friend from his law course. One of the guys he went to live with, after he graduated. I always used to wonder if Dean – or Rob – had persuaded Max to finish with me, in order that they could be three single lawyers in London together. But I eventually concluded that had to be rubbish, because Max was always someone who knew his own mind. 'Sorry – I didn't recognise you.'

'Imagine me several stone heavier.' Dean winks. 'Max finally talked me into the gym.'

I laugh. 'I didn't mean that.' And I didn't, really – my confusion was far more about the poise, the gravitas, that never really existed in the Dean I knew back then.

I ask what he's up to these days. He tells me he's living in Chiswick with his wife and young daughter, that he's a criminal barrister at a chambers in Chancery Lane. 'Unlike your man here – the ultimate sell-out.' He shakes his head, eyes alive with mischief. 'All that potential, wasted behind a desk.'

'Couldn't do what you do, mate,' Max fires back, tongue-in-cheek. 'Too many five a.m. starts and nightmare clients and trains to the arse end of nowhere.'

Smiling, Dean swigs back some champagne, then turns to me again. 'And what are you doing these days, Lucy? Don't tell me,' he cuts in, before I can reply. 'You're a best-selling novelist.'

I smile. 'Not exactly.'

Dean affects mock-shock. '*What?* You mean the rumours weren't true?'

'What rumours?' But I know, of course, because I'd been the one to spread them.

'That you'd quit uni to go and write a novel on a beach in Thailand or somewhere.'

My only option is to style this out. 'Actually, I'm starting a new job on Monday. In advertising.'

'*Ah*,' Dean says knowingly. 'Well then. Welcome to the club.'

'Sorry?'

'Of professions people love to hate. Estate agents, lawyers, ad men. Or women.'

'Ignore him,' Max says. 'He's only trying to justify his non-existent social life.'

But the barrister in Dean starts to dig deeper. 'So, come on, Lucy. What's your story? One minute you're at uni with the rest of us, the next . . .' He makes a motion with his fist which I assume is supposed to represent a puff of smoke.

I smile, even as I feel my body grow warm with discomfort. 'Am I being cross-examined?'

He smiles too, though not unkindly. 'Sorry. Force of habit.'

Back then, I told everyone I was off travelling, that I planned to write a novel. I cringe when I think about it now – how confidently I informed them I'd be writing in hotels, on beaches, from hammocks and in bars.

But the truth was, Max ending it at the start of that final autumn term had floored me – to the point where I hadn't been sleeping, had missed deadlines, seminars and tutorials, had handed in coursework that was sloppy and badly thought through. After a week back in Shoreley trying to pull myself together, I'd attempted to struggle on through to the end of term, avoiding Max completely, who'd moved out of our flat and into a temporary room in town.

But the downturn in my performance had been severe enough that my seminar leader had asked to meet with me just before the Christmas break, whereupon she suggested I might want to consider repeating my final year. Twenty minutes later, on the way out of the faculty building, I'd seen a flyer tacked to a noticeboard, calling for volunteers to work on a community programme in Thailand. And that was it. I'd seen enough signs by now: my mind was made up.

After I dropped out, the texts and calls checking on me persisted for a time. But pretty soon after Boxing Day, when I boarded my flight to Paris – my first stop – they began to dry up, before more or less stopping completely as everyone returned to uni in the new year. I got a new phone, replying from then on only to the odd email, assuring whoever had sent it that everything was fine. That I was revelling in my freedom, travelling and writing, having the time of my life.

Max contacted me too, but my response to him was much less cheery: just a couple of cool sentences – perhaps to punish him – to say I wasn't coming back. My friends ended up filling in the rest, and after that, I didn't hear from him again.

The music switches now to something cheesy, and a smatter of cheers goes up, a few hands lifting skyward.

'I mean, I did go travelling,' I tell Dean.

He nods, thoughtfully. 'Well, good for you. I only seem to make it as far as ski resorts these days. And I absolutely *loathe* skiing.' He exhales, scans the room. 'Right – better mingle. I know every single person here bar two, apparently.'

He and Max shake hands. 'Love to Chrissy,' Max says.

'Don't cock it up this time,' is Dean's parting shot, though I'm not sure which of us it's aimed at.

By now we're at the back of the living room, in a quiet corner next to an oversized standard lamp with a spotless glass shade like an overturned goldfish bowl.

Max turns to me, lifts an eyebrow. 'So. I'm not to cock it up, apparently.'

'I wasn't sure who he meant.'

'I'm going to hazard a guess and say me.' He reaches for my free hand, his thumb skimming the inside of my wrist. 'Sorry about all that.'

'No, he's . . .' I shake my head. 'Dean's nice. I always liked him.'

'So,' Max says, 'what did happen to that novel? You ever write it? Can I read it?'

'Ha! No.'

He smiles. 'Not about me, is it?'

I jab him gently with my elbow. 'Nope.'

'Think you'll ever pick it up again? Writing novels was all you talked about, at uni.'

'Probably wasn't realistic. I mean, at least at Supernova I'll get to write on an actual salary.'

'Well, will you at least show me your travelling photos sometime?' Max says. 'Be nice to see you again . . . as I knew you back then. If you know what I mean.'

'Oh.' I swallow. Now's not the time or place to go into why I don't have a single photo, no evidence at all that I was ever even there. 'Yeah, okay.'

Max smiles, sips his drink. 'Luce, have you had a chance to think yet . . . about what I said?'

Last weekend, I stayed with Max until Monday, when he was up early to catch the train to Leeds. I walked with him through the warm morning, beneath a milky sky, to the tube at Clapham Common.

'I want you back,' he whispered, as we paused on the pavement outside. He smelt lovely, of aftershave and mouthwash. 'I'll do anything to make it work with you again.'

I said nothing, just hugged him back and kissed him, told him I'd see him Friday. And it didn't seem right to discuss it over the phone while he was away. We stuck to lighter topics, like Max's big case in Leeds and my final week of freedom, Jools and the house and Reuben's narrow escape from a psychotic van driver after the pair of them got into a slanging match as he cycled along the Holloway Road.

I look up at Max now, into those storm-grey eyes. And I nod, just once. 'I want to see where this goes. I want to give us a try.'

And in an instant, it is as though I have been momentarily dropped into my old life, because Max is scooping me up and whirling me round, whooping and laughing, just as he would have done in the SU all those years ago. And people are looking over and laughing too, even though they're not in on the joke, and I'm grinning, my face braced against his shoulder, thinking, *Yes. This is our time. It's finally come.*

The next morning, we go for brunch in a café close to Max's flat. He tells me he stops there most days for espresso on his way to work, and sure enough, they greet him by his first name when we walk in. I wonder, fleetingly, how many women he's come here with, the morning after the night before. I'm paranoid the waitress's smile is partly code for, *Your secret's safe with me.*

The café's nearly full, but we get the last table for two by the window, overlooking the road. The space is sunny and high ceilinged, its chalkboard scrawled full of brunch offerings, the scent of coffee beans spiking the air.

It's a warm day, and Max is weekend-casual in shorts and T-shirt, sunglasses propped on top of his head. I keep catching sight of him and thinking, *We're really together. This is finally happening. We actually were meant to be, after all.*

His skin is gleaming, his eyes bright. He snuck out for a run first thing this morning, even after all those cocktails last night and barely a couple of hours' sleep when we got back to the flat.

'I feel guilty, Luce,' he says out of nowhere, as I'm dipping a sourdough shard into the molten middle of my poached egg.

'Guilty about what?'

'That you never got your degree. It was my fault you left uni, wasn't it?'

I pause, leaving the toast speared into the egg like it's been slayed. 'I guess if we hadn't broken up, I wouldn't have quit. But it was my choice. Nobody forced me. I made that decision.'

'Have you ever thought about going back?'

'A degree's just a piece of paper,' I say, though I'm not sure that's true. Being a dropout affects everything – your CV, your self-confidence, your prospects – if you let it, which for a long time I did.

'What did your parents think?' he asks, raising his voice slightly above the pneumatic pulse of a coffee grinder.

'They were sad for us.'

'I meant about you dropping out.'

'Actually . . . they weren't really thinking about that. And neither was I, at the time.' I stop short of saying it was my broken heart that everyone was worried about, to retain some level of dignity if nothing else.

'How are they, your mum and dad?'

Max met them a few times – those occasions when he came to Shoreley, and twice in Norwich, when they visited me at uni. Each time, he was the perfect boyfriend – attentive and polite, but not overly smooth, never trying too hard. I thought back then that maybe Max's particular gift in life was making people fall in love with him.

'They're good. Still working.' Mum's a primary school teacher, and Dad's in middle management at an insurance company – though there's been talk of redundancies lately, which is never great news for someone in their fifties. But I'm not going to bore Max with all that now.

'Still head-over-heels in love?'

'Ah, sickeningly so.' I smile, set down my fork, pick up my coffee. 'And do you remember my sister, Tash?'

He hesitates, probably reluctant to admit he doesn't, not properly.

'I think you only met her a couple of times. But she's doing really well. She works in marketing now. Married, with a son.'

'Crazy,' Max says, like he's struggling – as I have been, over the past few weeks – to get his head around the passage of time, to become reacquainted with everything he'd thought was firmly in the past.

'Tell me about your last girlfriend,' I say, sipping my coffee.

His expression remains open, unfazed. 'All right. What do you want to know?'

'Why did you break up?'

'Our lives were going in opposite directions. I like it in London, but she wanted to give it all up to start a yoga retreat abroad somewhere.'

'Wow.'

'Yeah. We were polar opposites, really, personality-wise.'

'Do you ever think about what might have happened if you'd gone with her?'

Max finishes his espresso and laughs. 'Yeah, I'd have caught the next flight back to Heathrow.'

I smile.

'And you? Why did you and your ex split up?'

'Lack of fire in the belly,' I say, which is a generous way of saying *a bit lazy* and *that amount of online gaming's not healthy for anyone.*

I don't mention, of course, that I thought of Max often while I was with my ex. Sometimes late at night, while he snored beside me. Occasionally out at dinner, as he was asking for a knife and fork to replace his chopsticks. And once – I was ashamed of this – while we were having sex. It was all I could do to stop myself from calling out Max's name.

8

Stay

'I think it's good,' the man with the tomato-coloured face says, doubtfully. 'It's just not to my taste, I suppose.'

He shrugs and looks at me apologetically. As my heart thunders away in my chest, I am about to tell him it's fine, that I completely understand, when Emma – the girl with long blond hair sitting opposite me – says, 'Sorry – good writing's not to your taste?'

'I meant,' says Tomato Face, 'I don't really read *romance*.'

'But this is a writing group,' Emma counters. 'You can't only be prepared to critique dystopian thrillers.'

I'm sensing there might be history between these two.

'I don't *only* like dystopian thrillers,' Tomato Face snaps. 'I like crime, and fantasy.'

His evident irritation rings around the room where we're sitting, which abuts the vestry of a church in Shoreley town centre. It's far too big for the six of us, really, with its high ceilings, enormous stained-glass windows and unnecessary levels of reverb. Though the weather outside is warm, the air in here is cool in the way that churches are, rich with the limey, mineral scent of centuries-old stone. There's a long fabric hanging on the wall opposite where I'm sitting, which says, TRUST IN THE LORD'S PLAN FOR YOUR LIFE. It reminds me of a particular religious studies lesson I had at school, when our teacher had just said something similar, and someone put up their hand and asked why we should try hard at anything, if God already had a plan for us. Our teacher's response was that God knows where you are going, but how you get there is up to you.

For so many years, even after we'd broken up, that's how I felt about me and Max – that we were destined to be together, no matter how circuitous the route we'd take to get there. I'm surprised to realise I don't feel that way any more.

Around the table, a tense silence is simmering. Reluctant to look up and take sides in the stand-off, I stare down hard at my phone, the screen I've been reading from now idle.

'Okay, then,' says Ryan brightly, like a playgroup leader trying to calm down warring toddlers. He glances up at the clock. 'Reckon we've got time for one more exercise before we finish.'

Ryan catches me afterwards as I'm packing up to leave. Dark-haired and sunken-cheeked, he's wearing mostly black, a handful of chains around his neck, like he's off to play guitar in a battle of the bands.

Ryan has had two books published, both dark comedies set in corporate London. Earlier this week I read his first, which was a bestseller on publication nine years ago. It reminded me loosely of Joseph Heller, and I wondered if it was partly autobiographical (except for all the firearms, obviously).

Ryan's enthusiasm for his craft seems at times to border on eccentricity – intermittently throughout our session, he'd plant his hands on the table, leaning his whole body in to make his point, before leaping to his feet and striding the length of the room. I was braced for him to jump up onto the furniture at any moment.

He's calmer now. All that adrenaline came from sharing his passion, I realise, which is very inspiring, in a *Dead Poets Society* kind of way.

'Will you be back next time?' he asks me. 'Hope we haven't scared you off.'

I smile. 'Not at all. I really enjoyed it.'

'Out of interest . . . how long have you been writing?'

'Just a few weeks, really,' I say, shyly.

He seems surprised. 'Seriously? Never before now?'

'Well, I started sketching out the idea years ago, but . . . never went anywhere with it.'

He nods, slowly. 'Life got in the way?'

'Kind of. I feel a bit stupid it's taken me so long to get round to it.'

'Took Margaret Mitchell ten years to write *Gone with the Wind*.'

I smile. 'Ha. There's hope yet, then.'

'Absolutely. You should keep going. Really. You've got talent.'

I almost gave up and went home before the session had even started – I was late, having only just clocked off from a full day at Pebbles & Paper after Ivan's daughter was struck in the neck by a lacrosse ball at school (luckily, she's fine). But when I did finally arrive, I struggled to find a way to the room that didn't involve clattering down the church nave during evening choir practice. Anyway, apart from Ryan and me, four others are regulars: Debs, a grand-mother of four in her sixties who's writing a heavily reli-gious novel set in a hospital; Aidan, a computer engineer and dad of two whose writing reminds me a bit of Jay McInerney; Paul, my tomato-faced challenger from earlier, who's all about the dystopian thriller; and Paul's adversary Emma. Roughly my age, maybe younger, she's writing a novel about a woman who walks out on her own life in order to find herself.

I like Emma: I've only known her for two hours, but she seemed to enjoy my writing, and I appreciated her fierce defence of it against Paul. I met her eye over the table once they'd stopped arguing, and she shot me a little *You're welcome* wink.

I like the idea we might become friends. I've met up with a couple of ex-colleagues from Figaro since I left, but seeing them feels awkward now. The topic of Georgia seems to be off-limits, and we don't really discuss the office, and without that common conversational ground – colleagues, clients, who stole whose biscuits, the slightly scary sandwich man – our chatter quickly ran dry, and so our meetups have become more sporadic. I still have old school friends in Shoreley, but these were never intimate friendships – just surface-level, gossip-based. Good for quick drinks and nattering over coffee, but little more than that. My true friends dispersed across the country after we left school – for university, jobs, relationships – and it soon became clear that Shoreley was fast-becoming a place to be returned to only at Christmas, or for funerals, weddings or holidays.

Caleb's much the same. His friends from school have largely moved away now, and the ones he's made since are mostly London-based. Like me, he has casual acquaintances here, ones he can meet for a pint or game of pool. But his two closest mates are still in North London, and they also happen to be mutual friends of Helen's.

Right at the start of the session tonight, Ryan asked if I'd be comfortable sharing an excerpt from my novel, to give everyone a flavour of my writing style. So, with my pulse buzzing and my cheeks tingling, I read out the first chapter.

I'd been expecting to wilt with regret as soon as I finished – despite Caleb's words of encouragement at the weekend. But then something strange happened. As the group began discussing the work *I'd* written – suggesting improvements, dissecting my characters, debating certain turns of phrase – I could feel my mind start to sing with something resembling pride. The same feeling Caleb was able to stir up in me the other night, for the first time in almost a decade.

'He's probably got unresolved emotional issues,' Caleb says later, when I describe the altercation between Paul and Emma. 'Don't take it personally.'

'No, I mean, the feedback in general was positive. And Ryan was super-encouraging.'

He squeezes my hand happily.

I squeeze him back. 'So, where are we going, again?'

It's late, long after dark. I called Caleb after the session to see if he'd mind me dropping in. He didn't, so I did, but we got pretty distracted as soon as he opened the front door, so it was getting on for ten o'clock by the time he said, 'Fancy doing something a bit crazy?'

'That depends. How crazy is crazy?'

'Well, that also depends,' he said, lifting an eyebrow. 'On your appetite for adventure.'

Of course, I want Caleb to think I'm at the greedy end of the adventure scale, so together we left the cottage and walked hand in hand down to the beach. Now, we're making our way towards the end of the shingle, the section that faces dunes rather than houses.

In front of a row of classic candyfloss-coloured beach huts, Caleb pauses. They've been here as long as I can remember, these sought-after wooden cabins offering high-tide refuge to Shoreley's beachgoers. They're nestled back from the shingle, deep in the dunes as if they've sprung up quite naturally through the marram grass.

'Fancy a swim?'

I let out a sound that's somewhere between a laugh and a shudder. 'What?'

'Come swimming with me.'

'I . . . I mean . . .' *No. No. Not in a million years. If I don't drown, I'll freeze to death, probably, or get arrested for indecent exposure.*

'Sorry, forgot to check – you *can* swim, can't you?'

'I mean . . . I can, but . . .'

'You'll love it, I promise. There's no feeling like it.'

'I don't . . . have a bikini with me.' Even the word is enough to make me shiver.

'Kind of the point,' he whispers, devilishly.

'I think there are laws against that.'

He looks as though he's trying to suppress a smile. 'Well, then, we'll just have to make sure we don't get caught.'

'Also, I don't want to sound like a wimp, but . . . it's *freezing.*'

He rests a palm flat against the beach hut we're standing next to. It's smart and stout, painted in a glossy flamingo-pink. 'Don't worry. We have a good place to warm up afterwards.'

'This is yours?' I say, surprised and impressed. 'These things are like gold dust.'

'Actually, no,' he confesses. 'It belongs to a mate of mine from school. But he moved away years ago and hardly uses it now. So he gave me a key.'

He moves to the front of the hut to unlock it and I follow him inside. Tash had a school friend whose parents owned a beach hut on this row, but it was nowhere near as nice as this one. It's very neat, and smart: all the wood inside is painted cream, there are two banquette benches uphol-stered in deckchair-striped fabric, and a line of brightly coloured bunting is strung across the back wall. It reminds me of a rather grandiose playhouse in a catalogue I once got fixated on as a child. Somewhere magical to escape to, its own little world.

What Might Have Been

Caleb flicks on a garland of fairy lights looping from a shelf before showing me round – as much as you can conduct a tour of a space not much bigger than your average garden shed. 'Okay, so we have towels and blankets, and crucially – a stove, heater and hot chocolate. Shall we go?'

Letting slip a laugh, I realise I'm starting to feel nervous. 'So what – we're just going to go skinny-dipping? Just like that?'

'I'm up for it if you are.'

I release a breath like I've eaten something hot, then laugh again. 'Okay. Okay. All right. Let's do it. Why not? Yes.'

'Ah, you've convinced me,' he jokes.

So we ditch our shoes and outer layers in the beach hut, then Caleb locks up, hiding the key beneath a piece of driftwood before we walk down to the shoreline. The shingle is cold and sharp, biting into my bare feet. I decide as I follow him that Caleb is the only person on earth who could have possibly persuaded me to do this.

We come to a pause at the water's edge. I glance left and right. The only other people I can see are a pair of night fishermen, their little tents glowing like igloos, a quarter of a mile or so along the beach. The air is cool and calm, sublimely still.

'So,' Caleb says.

'So,' I reply.

The only time I've been naked with Caleb before now has been close up, well within touching distance, in the heat of a moment. It's vastly different to the idea of standing still and unclothed in front of him, which I'm worried will feel a bit too much like I'm auditioning for something.

'I'll go first,' he says, gallantly, then starts stripping off.

I sneak a look at him once he's lost the clothes. Tall, toned and lean, with an irresistible, incorrigible smile.

'Your turn.'

So I peel off my dress, then lose my underwear, realising as I'm doing so that I don't feel as self-conscious as I thought I might. In fact, standing here like this with him feels like the most natural thing in the world.

Stars spill like glitter across the velvet folds of cloud and sky above our heads. On the surface of the water, the moon has splintered into a million shivering shards.

Caleb passes me a woollen hat. 'Here. It'll help keep the heat in.'

I pull it on, then grin. 'How do I look?'

He keeps his eyes on the horizon, shakes his head. 'I'm actually trying *very* hard not to look at you right now.'

I laugh. 'Oh, sorry.'

He takes a step closer, grabs my hand. 'Ready?'

'As I'll ever be, I guess.'

Together we step into the sea. It's cryogenically cold, like wading unclothed into snow. As we go deeper, the water reaching first my knees and then my ribs, my chest contracts and I gasp with the shock of it, growing more hesitant with every step.

To my left, Caleb is swiftly becoming submerged. Eventually, his hand slips free from mine. 'Just go for it,' he says, his voice slightly stiff from the shock of immersion. 'It's just like . . . ripping off a plaster.'

My own voice is by now an embarrassing hoot-gasp hybrid. 'It's worse than that!'

But I know he's probably right, so I take a breath, then launch myself inelegantly forward like some sort of hefty sea creature. In an instant the water is up to my chin and my heart is hopping, my breaths rapid and shallow. By my side, Caleb reaches for my hand, then releases a whoop that startles me so much I start laughing. He sounds so buzzed you'd think we were skydiving, or surfing some undiscovered reef in the middle of the Indian Ocean.

It takes me thirty seconds or so to rein in my breathing, my flailing limbs, my galloping heart. But once I do, I start to relax, and I can finally begin to appreciate the tight, chilly pleasure of the sea gripping my body, the sensation of being surrounded by nothing but salt water and stars.

We tread water side by side as it laps gently between us.

'That is . . . an excellent moon,' Caleb whispers.

I look up, taking in the bold, creamy face of it. 'It is. It's beautiful.'

'Are you okay? Cold?' he asks.

I turn my gaze to where he's bobbing up and down next to me, and smile. 'No, I'm fine,' I say, even as my breath is jerking in my chest. 'This is amazing.'

'Isn't it?'

I nod towards the beach. 'Just hope nobody sees us.'

'Ah, isn't that half the fun?'

I laugh, narrowing my eyes. 'You're not about to tell me you're a closet nudist, are you?'

He laughs too, spins round to face me. 'Er, no. Despite all appearances to the contrary, I'm not some kind of needy exhibitionist.' Beneath the water, his hands find my hips, the words leaving his mouth in gasps. 'But the point is, no one can actually *see* us right now, Lambert. Well, only our heads. Hardly indecent.'

'Until the police turn up and order us out with a megaphone.'

'If they do, I'll be demanding a foil blanket.'

'So,' I say, continuing to pedal my feet, my lips starting to swell now with the cold, 'do you do this a lot?'

'Not as much as I'd like. And I have to say, it's really nice to have someone to do it with.' He moves his hands up and down my hips. 'It's supposed to be good for immunity and your skin and have all these crazy health benefits, but . . . I don't know. I just like the feeling of it, being out here, just me and the sea and the sky and the elements.' He delivers a salty kiss to my lips. 'Don't think I'm a nutter, do you?'

I shudder through a smile as my teeth start to chatter. 'Well, if you are, then I guess I must be too.'

Back at the beach hut a few minutes later, once we've towelled off and got dressed, Caleb lights the gas fire then whips up some hot chocolate on the little stove.

'I think this might be the most romantic thing I've ever done,' I say, as we huddle together under blankets on the banquette, sipping our hot chocolate and looking out to sea. Next to our toes, the gas fire roars like a furnace.

Caleb leans over, sets his lips to my neck. 'Really?'

'Really.'

'Fancy making it even more romantic?'

'Yes,' I shiver, turning my head to kiss him. And in the next moment, our still-chilly fingers are seeking out warm skin, eliciting laughter then quiet shocks of pleasure. Outside, the sea twitches and glimmers like a mirror tilted to the moonlight, the blackness above it festooned with a finery of stars.

Go

'Hello,' the photographer says. 'Sorry I'm late. I'm—'

'Oh my God. Hello.'

I'm halfway through my first day at Supernova. So far, I've attended a brainstorming session on a new business pitch for a major cosmetics brand and presented my portfolio – such as it is – to the entire creative team in a breakout area so they could 'get to know me', which also involved random people pausing unnervingly to watch as they passed. I've been shown around the office by Phoebe, my deskmate and fellow creative, who is five years younger than me and was named as the industry's 'one to watch' two years ago by a broadsheet newspaper. She also happens to be a well-known influencer *as a side hustle*. My line manager is Zara, who's super-smart, with a vast and intimidating talent. She's seemingly come up with every famous strapline UK commerce has ever known. I was convinced at my interview that she'd instantly weed out my inferior creativity with the ruthless cool of a neurosurgeon. Her dark hair is cropped close to her head, and she has the kind of face that looks like she's giving you permanent side-eye. She's wearing a black, knee-length dress that appears so effortless and comfortable, I can't stop staring at it. Or her. Zara is just the kind of person who draws you in, makes you desperate to occupy her orbit. A little like Max.

And though it's been hectic, all morning I've been unable to wipe the smile off my face, to the point where I started to worry people might think I'm a bit odd. I just can't quite believe I'm here, at one of the country's biggest ad agencies, and that this time, I'm actually a proper creative, getting paid not for my research and organisational skills, but for my ability to write. The job Georgia kept promising, but never delivering. I'm here. I've made it.

I'm getting these headshots done just before lunch, after which I've got a sit-down with Seb, who's the designer I'll be paired with for the majority of my initial projects. I want to make a good impression: I know how much emphasis they put here on creative chemistry.

But first . . . the strangest thing. The photographer taking my headshots is Caleb – the guy I abandoned in the pub, the night I saw Max in Shoreley. Who slipped a beer mat into my coat pocket with his number on it.

It's clear he's recognised me too, and for a couple of mortifying moments, we stand face to face without saying anything further.

Eventually, I find my voice, feeling my face flare with colour. 'I'm so sorry. You gave me your number, and you—'

'No, please,' he says, laughing, as if he couldn't feel more awkward. 'That was the cheesiest move I've ever made. It didn't deserve a response.'

'It wasn't anything . . . against you, I promise. It's just that that guy I saw out of the window . . . It was my ex, Max, and . . .'

He smiles. 'You absolutely don't owe me an explanation of any kind, Lucy. It was always going to be a long shot.'

I release a breath to try to soothe my embarrassment, as I attempt to work out whether he remembers my name from that night or if he's been told it in advance of today. 'Still. I should have messaged you, to explain.'

'Hey, not at all. We talked for a sum total of what – two minutes?'

I smile, thinking a change of subject might help. 'So . . . what are you doing here?'

'Supernova's one of my corporate clients. I'm based in Shoreley, though. Hence my tardiness, sorry. Trains were a nightmare.'

It turns out we went to different schools, on opposite sides of town. As he's setting up, we chat about our lives in Shoreley – he describes a childhood mostly spent on the beach, then gaining a place at art college despite flunking his exams, before promptly dropping out of his course.

We must have talked for nearly twenty minutes before he checks the time with a grimace. 'Sorry. Better get cracking. I've only been given half an hour.'

'They are pretty hot on timing here,' I say with a smile, recalling the lecture I was given by Zara earlier about billable hours.

'Let's try over here first,' Caleb says, motioning behind me to a hot-pink wall. 'They want a pop of colour in the picture.'

'Do you want me to look serious, or . . . ?'

Caleb leans down to shunt a table out of shot, flush against the nearest wall. As he does, his T-shirt falls forward to reveal his toned stomach.

'Just completely relax,' he says, as he straightens up. I can feel myself trying not to blush about his patch of taut skin catching my eye.

In the next moment, the flash goes off, startling me. 'Sorry. Think I blinked.'

He smiles. 'No worries. Would it help if I counted down?'

Oh, he's so nice. I try to keep my eyes off his body, remembering afresh how attractive I thought he was in The Smugglers that night. 'Maybe. Although then I might overthink it.'

'I'll count to three,' he says. 'Blink on two.'

We try it, and of course I blink on two *and* three. *It's a sodding photo, Lucy, it can't be that hard.* And now I am starting to feel self-conscious and stiffening up, but Caleb quickly distracts me with a story about the time he shot nearly an entire wedding reception before realising he'd been taking photo after photo of the groom's identical twin brother. And it's only as I'm laughing – properly laughing – that I realise Caleb's been snapping away the whole time.

'See what you did there,' I say, tipping my index finger towards him.

'Well, I do have all the tricks.' He smiles at me and winks, one of the few men I've met who can do so without seeming creepy. 'So, anyway, what brought you to Supernova? The night I met you, you'd just quit your job, and now . . .'

'I know. Actually, that was also part of the reason I didn't call you. My friend had a room going free in London, so I thought . . . why not move here, make a fresh start?'

He meets my eye, and for a moment I think he's about to ask me about Max. But he just smiles and nods. 'Why not indeed. Well, it was great to meet you again. Good luck with everything.'

'They didn't scare you off, then? You're going back tomorrow?'

Max and I are sitting against opposite arms of his expansive mustard-yellow sofa, our legs and feet intertwined, awaiting a delivery of sushi – an order, I noticed in horror, that cost as much as my weekly food bill.

Sushi, I've recently discovered, is Max's all-time favourite food. Getting to know him again has been such a strange hybrid of the old and the new, a combination of the familiar (his sense of humour, that ever-present thoughtfulness, his kisses) and the new (his tastes having evolved from instant noodles, Britpop and beer to sushi, electronica and top-quality wine).

Though my head is still hazy with first-day fog, I smile and nod. 'I'm going to work there till I retire. Or die. Seriously. They'll have to prise that job out of my cold, dead hands.'

Max laughs. 'Wow. I could use someone like you in my team.'

'Honestly. I can't believe I'm actually being paid to write.'

'Why not? You've always been a great writer. Why shouldn't it be you?'

'Writing's different to the law, though. I mean, you have a vocation. You train for five years—'

'Six.'

'Sorry, six. And then you're qualified. I mean, don't get me wrong,' I add, with a prickle of guilt, because I know how hard Max worked to get to where he is, especially at a prestigious firm like HWW. 'Obviously you had to put the graft in. But with writing . . . there's no clear path. It's not like you do a course, then, bam – you're a qualified writer. There's no such thing.'

'Doesn't matter. You're doing it now.'

'Took me long enough.'

'Well, don't they say the best things in life come to those who wait?'

'They do, yeah.' Our eyes meet, and I smile. 'Hey, the strangest thing happened this morning.'

'Yeah?' He pushes a little bowl of wasabi peas towards me.

I wrinkle my nose, shake my head. 'I'm more of a . . . Scampi Fries kind of girl.'

He laughs. 'God, haven't had those for years. Do they still make them?'

'Not sure. We should go to a proper pub and hunt some down.'

'Is it weird that I think I'd prefer wasabi peas now anyway?'

'Yes. That's the weirdest thing I've ever heard.'

He grins and throws a couple into his mouth. 'Sorry. You were saying.'

'Yeah – the photographer taking my pictures, for my headshot . . . It was the guy I got chatting to in the pub in Shoreley, that night I saw you in the street, remember?'

'In The Smugglers?'

'Yep.'

'Didn't you say he gave you his number?'

'Yeah, he did.' I laugh a little stiffly.

'That must have been awkward.'

'It was a bit, at first.'

'Didn't it feel weird, him taking your picture?'

'No, he was super-professional.'

I'm not really sure why I'm telling Max this. I'm not trying to make him jealous. He's never been a jealous kind of person. Maybe it's just because bumping into Caleb was an odd little coincidence, and that's the kind of thing I want to share with Max.

I tell him more about my day – the morning's meetings and my afternoon with Seb, who showed me some of his recent work: an animation for a high street bank, a social media campaign for a recipe box delivery service and a series of billboard posters for a big-brand lingerie company.

The whole time Seb was talking, I kept trying not to stare too hard at him, because I was so fixated on this moment – that *this* was my new creative partner, that I was now a writer at *this* agency with talented people like *this*. Given my lack of writing experience, I wouldn't have blamed Seb for being wary, or for worrying that he might have to carry me creatively. I know it's down to me now to prove I deserve to be there.

Still, self-doubt didn't entirely stop me enjoying the moment. In fact, the longer Seb and I talked, the harder it became to resist jumping to my feet and performing a kind of victory lap around the breakout area, weaving in and out of beanbags and high-fiving passing creatives.

'I'm kind of proudest of this one,' Seb told me, passing me the lingerie scamps to flip through. 'The client wanted to go for this sleazy campaign straight out of the eighties, and eventually what we talked them into was—'

'Classy,' I said, seriously impressed by the elegance of the design concept and copy. 'Really classy.'

Seb nodded, uncrossed his legs. He's very thin and tall, and his trousers today were so short they rode halfway up his calves when he sat down, revealing a particularly jazzy pair of socks. 'And they had this one really overbearing guy on their marketing team, so to talk *him* round felt like a real win.'

'There's always one,' I said, thinking back to my planning days at Figaro, to how many meetings I'd had with that *exact* same guy.

'Isn't there?'

I smiled. I could tell I was going to like Seb already.

'So why'd you leave your last place?' he asked.

'I wanted to move to London, have a fresh start,' I replied, which although not entirely true, didn't feel like too much of a leap.

Seb laughed, his Adam's apple bobbing. 'Most people want to move *out* of London to do that.'

What Might Have Been

When I describe for Max the Supernova offices, right down to the custom-printed toilet paper – designed, apparently, by an ex-intern who's now very high up at Supernova in New York – he says, 'God, a bar at work. Think I could sell that to my VP?'

'Definitely. Is there any reason why lawyers should be more serious than anyone else?'

'Yeah. The lawsuits when we get stuff wrong.'

'Isn't it quite difficult to sue a lawyer?'

He laughs. 'Nope. That's why we have insurance.'

I sip my ginger beer. 'Now I'm picturing you all being very businesslike, taking everything super-seriously.'

'Well, not all the time.' He describes his colleagues: some he's worked with for years and is very close to, others are mere acquaintances, others get seriously under his skin.

'I can't imagine you getting wound up about anything. You've got to be one of the most patient people I've ever met.'

A particular memory stands out for me – Max receiving a call, in our second year, to say his mum was seriously ill. I went with him to Norwich station, where we learnt from another passenger that all trains were cancelled due to leaves on the line. No staff were seemingly anywhere to help, and meanwhile the minutes ticked by, and with them the surreally terrifying possibility that Max's mum might die before he reached her. Eventually, he found a member of staff and, given the disdain with which she spoke to him – a scruffy student whose wild-eyed worry she'd clearly interpreted as drug-induced – Max was calm, polite and immeasurably courteous, when he had every excuse not to be. I never forgot that.

I ask Max now how Brooke is. He always called her that
– never Mum. When I first got to know him, I thought this
was pretty cool. It's only all these years later that I realise
it's actually quite sad.

'Nothing much ever changes in the world of Brooke
Gardner,' Max says. His voice carries zero affection, as
though he's narrating a slightly unkind documentary about
her life.

Max never knew his father. Brooke had always been a
drinker and used to claim, in her crueller moments, that
she had no memory at all of having even slept with him.
She worked a variety of jobs, often several at a time, and
when she wasn't doing those, she was 'unwinding with her
friends', as she liked to put it. She left Max alone at an age
when it was illegal and shocking to do so, until someone
pointed this out to her: after that, she would land him on
various neighbours, friends-of-friends. He told me once
he thought that was when he first learnt to make conversation with anyone, even people who were very different to
him.

'Is that why you want to be a lawyer?' I asked him, the
night he first confided all this to me, a couple of weeks
after we'd met. I guessed his childhood must have led him
to develop strong feelings about justice, about right and
wrong. We weren't together then, but I already knew there
was no one else I preferred spending time with.

He nodded. 'Partly. A social worker told me once that
kids like me go one of two ways: either well off the rails, or
sticking to the straight and narrow like glue. Guess I'm the
latter.'

'Have you ... lost patience with her?' I ask Max now, because back then, he would still visit, call, text and email Brooke, make an effort.

I see a tiny muscle flicker in his jaw, but as he starts to speak, the sushi arrives.

'So,' I prompt, once we're sitting at the table in Max's kitchen-diner, the sushi boxes open between us. Max has flicked on a chillout playlist, dipped the lights.

He picks up a piece of yellowtail nigiri expertly with his chopsticks, takes a bite and continues the story. 'Well, I made the mistake of taking a girlfriend back to Cambridge for the weekend. I thought I'd introduce her to Brooke, who swore she'd be sober and pleasant and make an effort.'

'Who was your girlfriend?' I ask, hoping my voice sounds light and mildly curious, as opposed to frenziedly desperate for details.

'Allegra. We met at work. This was about ... seven years ago.'

I nod, mentally chastising myself for wanting to whip out my phone and yell, *Hey Siri, show me Allegra!*

'Brooke had been trying to get sober at the time, and she'd dumped her leech of a boyfriend, so I was hopeful. We arranged to meet at this restaurant – nothing fancy, just a chain place, thank God – and when Brooke got there her eyes were glazed and rolling. Like, she was *out* of it. I could tell the second she walked through the door.' He shakes his head. 'I just felt this ... uncontrollable anger inside me. But I managed to keep a lid on it, we sat down, and then ... literally the first thing that came out of her mouth was to ask me for money. She hadn't even looked at Allegra, or said hello.'

I frown, set down my crab roll. 'That's awful.'

'Yeah, and I just . . . lost it. Started yelling at her. Allegra literally had to drag me out of there. And afterwards I thought, God, if I'd started throwing stuff and something had . . . I don't know, bounced off a surface and hit some-one . . . I could have been arrested and charged with God-knows-what and my whole career might have been over. All that work . . .' He shakes his head. 'Just one stupid move could have changed my entire life, that day.'

I realise I've been holding my breath as he's been talking. 'Do you still see her?'

'Brooke? Or . . . ?'

I hesitate. 'You still see Allegra?'

His gaze finds mine, steady and sincere. 'She's at a different firm now. But we occasionally bump into each other at events, and networking stuff.'

'Why'd you break up?'

'She was cheating on me. With a barrister we used to use all the time.' His laugh is brittle. 'Don't use him any more. Which is a shame, actually. He's really good.'

I wipe my mouth with a paper towel. My lips are sticky, sweet-tasting from the sushi. 'Are they still together?'

'Yep. Married, expecting a baby.'

I don't know why I feel so sad for him, when he says this. Because if they hadn't split up, Max and I wouldn't be here now. Or maybe we would. Who knows? I think vaguely back to something my religious studies teacher said at school, about God knowing your destination but you deciding how to get there. If Max and I are fated to be together, then Allegra and the barrister and everything else were just distractions en route to the main event. Weren't they?

I lift my hand to the back of his neck, run my fingers along his hairline, a small gesture to let him know I feel for him.

'Anyway,' he says, tipping back his head like a cat enjoying a scratch, 'I don't see much of Brooke any more. She's got a new man, other stuff going on. I think she always saw motherhood as a kind of obligation. Something that got in the way of what she really wanted to do. And when I stopped making the effort, I think she felt . . . relieved of her duties. If that makes sense.'

I don't want to say it does, because it shouldn't. Nothing like that should ever make sense.

It always used to surprise me that Max was such an optimist, given his rough start in life. So perpetually hopeful. I realise now that that was a coping mechanism. If he looked hard enough at the horizon, he wouldn't have to contemplate the shifting ground of his present, or the rocky terrain of his past.

'So, Luce,' he says, turning his head to look at me, 'mind if I ask you something?'

'Go for it.'

'Why did you stop drinking?'

I wonder suddenly if he thinks it's because I had a problem, like Brooke. If, in the back of his mind, he's wondering if perhaps Brooke and I aren't so different. Which is a fairly horrific thought.

'Nothing dark,' I say, though of course that isn't really true. 'I just . . . decided I was happier without it.'

I try to remember how it used to feel, to recall the sensations that ended up scaring me the most: losing control, waking up with no memories of the night before. Being made to feel weak.

Luckily, I struggle to summon them.

'Happier how?' Max asks, setting a hand against my leg.

'Well, I just want to remember everything,' I say. 'All the best moments in life. I don't want to forget any of them.'

He doesn't reply, just leans over to kiss me instead, moving his hand up my thigh as he does so. And I kiss him back, slightly sad to be relieved that we're not talking any more.

A few hours later, I blink awake. At first, I'm not sure why – it's dark and quiet as a cellar in Max's bedroom.

Or maybe that's exactly why.

Don't panic. You're with Max, in his flat. Breathe. Breathe.

I grope in the direction of the nightstand on my side of the bed, lighting up my phone to check the time.

A message preview is waiting for me, from Tash. I scan it, then scan it again, completely confused.

> Max. This is Tash. You need to do the right thing. I don't know why you've started something up with Lucy again, of all people, but you need to –

Frantically, I tap into the message and read the rest.

What Might Have Been

My heart begins to behave strangely, at first speeding up, then migrating from my chest to my throat. I reread the message in confusion again, and then again.

By the time I realise Tash must have sent it to me in error, my phone has started to ring, over and over and over, a shrill jangle that slices through me, like hearing a scream in the dead of night.

Max sits up in bed, snaps on a light. 'Luce, you okay?'

'I . . . I'm not sure.'

What would I not be able to take? What does Tash not want me to find out?

I get up, groping for the skirt and T-shirt that ended up on the floor a few hours ago. I pull them roughly on, then stand where I am, unsure what to do next and feeling slightly foolish.

'You going to get that?' Max says with a wince, as from the nightstand, my phone continues to ring.

'No, I . . .' *I need to think.*

'Luce, what's going on?'

'I don't know.' Thoughts are starting to bounce around my brain like tennis balls. *If I found out what? Why does Tash want Max to end it with me? If I found out what? If I found out what?*

'Luce?' Max reaches for my hand but misses. His voice is more urgent now, perhaps out of frustration. He rolls over to my nightstand, picks up my phone and glances down at the screen, where I've left the message open. As he

149

looks at it, his face becomes clay, like his blood has stopped pumping completely.

My phone begins to ring again.

'Max, what . . . What does Tash not want me to find out?'

Max looks up at me, but he doesn't say anything. His eyes look almost empty. If he wasn't sitting upright, I might think he'd passed out.

'Max?' I've never seen him lost for words before, and it's this sudden inability to speak that lets me know this is bad. Really bad. He has done something bad, something so awful he can't even bring himself to open his mouth.

But how does this involve my sister? Tash can't stand him, she flinches whenever I so much as mention his name, she . . . *Oh no.*

I feel the floor fall away from me as we look at each other, and something unspeakable passes between us.

Not that. Please, anything but that.

'Max . . . what did you do?' I manage to whisper, though my mouth feels dry and unwieldy, like I've been chewing on flour.

He just shakes his head in response, and I know that if he can't even say it out loud, it's the worst possible thing I can imagine.

So I start gathering up my stuff, because I know the only move I can make right now is to run – as far away as I possibly can, don't stop, keep running, running, running.

'We shouldn't jump to conclusions.'

I'm back at home, in Jools' room, sitting with her on the bed. She's switched on the light and made us both a cup of camomile tea, and I've changed into joggers, washed my face, brushed my hair. I feel a little calmer now that I'm here, and have had a chance to think.

'I mean, yes – it's a weird message. But it could mean anything.' Jools hesitates, presses her lips together, tactful as ever.

'Go on. I've literally thought of every scenario.'

She clears a tumble of hair from one side of her face, flipping it over with a tilted hand. 'Well, isn't the most likely explanation that Max just did something a bit shady and Tash found out? I can't imagine in a million years it involved Tash and Max . . . doing anything *together*. For a start, when would they even have had the opportunity?'

The screen starts to flash on my phone. I turned it off as soon as I fled Max's flat and caught the night bus home, and I've only just switched it back on.

It's Max, my tenth missed call from him. Tash, meanwhile, has racked up fifteen.

Jools nods at me. Reluctantly, I return the call.

'I'm outside.' His voice sounds shaky, keyed up. 'Please let me in.'

I head downstairs, but I don't let him in. Instead I move onto the front step, pull the door to behind me. The night air is warm and still, the sky above our heads spattered with stars. I hear the rumble of vehicles on the main road and feel a quick pulse of panic in my chest, the familiar urge to flee.

Usually so smart and composed, Max looks crumpled, undone. He's thrown on a T-shirt and joggers, and on the road, a 4x4 – presumably his – is parked at a ludicrous angle from the kerb, the way detectives park in TV crime dramas when they're chasing a hot lead.

I didn't even know Max had a car.

'If I found out what?' is all I say, because right now, that's the only question I want him to answer.

And now his expression turns almost feral with – what is it? Fear? – and my knees begin to fold as I hear him confirming the worst, and then I feel Jools' arms around me, apparently alerted by some kind of noise I've made. A swarm of angry voices rises and falls above my head, and I can hear Reuben threatening to call the police, but the whole time there is only one word in my mind I can grip onto: *No, no, no, no, no.*

9

Stay

Caleb has said I can use the beach hut to write in, so every afternoon, after my morning shift at Pebbles & Paper, I walk down to the beach, stopping at the deli en route for a takeaway coffee and crabmeat sandwich. Then I make my way to the dunes, passing pleasantries with walkers and day trippers and fishermen as I go.

There's something about the vista from the hut – the mercurial landscape of the water, the braying of gliding seagulls, the push-and-pull of the tide like a creature drawing breath – that fires my imagination. Through the front door, I watch the weather twist and shift: sheets of summer rain that slice into the sea and drill down on the roof, intercut by splashes of bright, brilliant sunshine. I watch the sky in its catalogue of colours – from the rarest of silvers to a flawless afternoon blue – as clouds tumble through it like cashmere on a breeze. The view from where I sit is an ever-changing artist's canvas, my daily spur of creativity.

Thanks to Caleb's encouragement, and the inspiration I'm getting from the writing group, I'm beginning to grow in confidence. The words are flying from my fingers. I feel them like a second heartbeat inside me. I write for hours at a time, stopping only when I realise I'm thirsty or hungry. Each day my mind spins with new worlds, my blood rushing with possibilities.

Maybe whoever said the best things in life are free had it right after all.

'Luce, I love him,' whispers Tash.

I've invited Caleb to Tash and Simon's for Sunday lunch. We're in the living room, and Caleb's sitting with Dylan on the carpet near the fireplace, helping him out with the component parts of an airport-themed Lego set. He must have said something funny, because Dylan is laughing loudly in that throaty way small children do, and just at the point he's begun to calm down, Caleb says something else, detonating another full round of hysterics, resulting in Dylan tipping his head to the carpet then falling onto his side, completely unable to contain himself.

'Are you absolutely sure he doesn't have children?' Tash says.

'Positive,' I whisper.

'So are you two . . . you know, officially together now?'

'I mean, I guess so. We haven't really said it in so many words . . . but it kind of feels like we don't have to. You know?'

She nods, thoughtfully. 'I see what you mean about him being different to anyone else you've dated.'

I turn to look at her. 'Go on.'

'Well, he's very . . . self-assured, isn't he?' she whispers. 'But not in an arrogant way. He just seems like someone who's comfortable in his own skin. Like he wouldn't be into playing games.'

'Yeah,' I say, as I watch Caleb help Dylan stick the wings onto his plane. 'I feel like I know where I stand with him.'

'You know what he is, don't you?'

'No, what?'

'He's a proper grown-up.'

'Ugh, that makes him sound boring.'

'No, not boring, just . . . what you see is what you get. That's good, isn't it?'

'Yeah,' I say, smiling as I lean back into the sofa, sipping my sparkling apple juice, today's version of an aperitif. 'It's very good.'

And really, the past couple of months have been just that. Caleb and I have spent the onset of summer drinking in the joys of Shoreley before the main tourist season hits. We've meandered hand in hand through the cobblestoned streets, pointing out all our old childhood haunts to each other – the bandstand on the green where my friends and I used to congregate after school, the little courtyard behind the old-fashioned sweet shop where Caleb had his first kiss, the hill sloping towards the north end of the beach where I sat with my friends on the last-ever day of school and watched the sun setting between bouts of dramatic sobbing as we swigged from a bottle of cava, heartbroken at our forthcoming separation. We've waded in wellies through the creeks behind the harbour as seagulls swooped low above our heads, the sails of moored boats ringing against their masts like percussion in the breeze. We've walked barefoot across the salt flats, both of us laughing till we cried when Caleb slipped into the mud and then couldn't get up, pulling me on top of him as I tried to help. We've plucked fresh samphire from the ground then taken it back to Caleb's cottage, blanching it on the Aga and drenching it in butter and black pepper before devouring it with our fingers. We've eaten way too much salted caramel gelato from the ice-cream parlour on the promenade. We've been crabbing and skinny-dipping, we've watched raspberry-ripple sunsets drizzle into the sea from the harbour wall, we've kissed under lamp posts on moonlit streets. It's been the best, most romantic time, and it's cast my hometown in an entirely new light. I've rediscovered its romance, its charm and appeal, worthy of all those postcards and jigsaw puzzles and fridge magnets. It's reminded me why people come here now. Shoreley sells them a dream, and this year, I have fallen for it, hard.

'Are you going to introduce him to Mum and Dad?' Tash asks.

It's always an intimidating idea, introducing a boyfriend to our mum and dad: lifelong soulmates, the lighthouse keepers of their own epic love story.

'Thought I'd ease him in with the older sibling. Anyway, it's only been two months. Feels a bit soon.'

Tash grins as Simon bellows, 'Lunch!' from the kitchen. Dylan jumps up and leads his new best friend out of the living room, following the scent of Sunday roast. Caleb glances over his shoulder at us, shrugging happily as he's led away.

Tash shakes her head, watching them go, then nudges me. 'Remember when you first met him, you thought you knew him from somewhere? Like you'd met before?'

I nod. 'Yeah. But I never did work out why.'

Tash presses her lips together like she's trying to hold in some excitement. 'Well, apparently, that's a sign you've met your soulmate.'

I snort softly. 'I thought you didn't believe in soulmates.'

She shrugs. 'This girl at work was talking about it on Friday. She'd read a whole magazine article about it. It all sounded quite convincing, actually.'

I smile. 'Well, Caleb doesn't believe in soulmates either, so don't be sharing that over the Yorkshire puddings, will you?'

'But you do.' She sneaks me a hopeful smile.

'Maybe,' I say, coyly. 'I'm just seeing how it goes.'

I don't want to admit that what she's just said has made sense to me in a way that's weird and perfect all at once.

It's quite sweet how much effort Tash and Simon have made with lunch today. The table is groaning under Met-Gala quantities of decorations – three enormous, peony-stuffed vases, an excess of gold cutlery, pink glass-ware, printed linen and co-ordinating crockery. Tash, Simon and Caleb are drinking the posh wine, brought up from the basement, and Simon's put on some classical music.

I hope they don't think we're ungrateful for the effort, given Caleb's just in his usual faded jeans and T-shirt, and I threw on a green-and-white cotton sundress without bothering to press it first.

'So, Lucy was telling us about your beach hut, Caleb,' Tash says, topping up his wine as we're eating our roast beef.

'Was she?' Caleb says with a smile, and I kick him gently in the shin, because I get the feeling he's probably thinking about all the sex we've been having in there lately.

'What's a bee shut?' Dylan asks Tash.

'A beach hut. It's like a little house on the beach,' I explain to Dylan, 'where you keep your buckets and spades and shelter if it rains.'

'We don't go to the beach often enough, do we?' Tash says to Simon. 'We definitely don't make the most of living so close to the coast.'

'I know what you mean,' Caleb says. 'I missed it, when I lived in London. Don't get me wrong, I loved a lot about the city, but ultimately—'

'You're not a city person?' Tash guesses.

He shrugs. 'I suppose I just knew I wouldn't want to live there for ever.'

'I actually feel the opposite,' Simon says.

Caleb sips his wine. 'Yeah?'

I frown and turn to Simon. 'What? You don't want to live in London.'

He shrugs. 'Sometimes I crave a bit more life than we have here. You know – culture on tap, a better choice of takeaway than a single sub-par Chinese . . .'

What Might Have Been

Tash sighs impatiently, suggesting this isn't the first time this has come up. 'There's plenty of culture in Shoreley, Simon. You just have to make a bit more effort to find it. And there's nothing actually wrong with that Chinese. You just had dodgy king prawn balls there one time.'

'Mum, what's culture?' Dylan asks, pushing the vegetables around his plate.

She looks down at him distractedly. 'Eat your carrots, please, darling. Um, culture means things like plays and music.'

'Like what we're listening to now,' Simon says to him, as on the speaker, the orchestra crescendos to a single, trembling note.

'Caleb and I went to see *Romeo and Juliet* a few weeks ago,' I point out. 'What's that if it's not culture?'

'I'd hardly call the Shoreley Players the height of culture,' Simon deadpans, though I suspect that deep down, he's joking.

I laugh, hoping Caleb isn't offended. 'Don't be such a snob!'

'Sorry. I just crave something other than Shoreley from time to time, that's all.'

'Isn't that what holidays are for?' says Tash. She keeps her tone light, but I can still see her jaw clench. It can't be easy, I suppose, listening to her husband making throw-away criticisms about the life they've built together.

Grinning, Dylan starts repeating the word *snob* between vigorous snorts of laughter.

This makes Caleb laugh too, which then starts me off as well. The joy that Dylan can derive from a single, supremely unfunny word is adorable.

'So, you don't miss London at all?' Simon asks Caleb, as Dylan's face starts turning pink and unruliness threatens to descend.

'Well, there's some stuff I miss,' Caleb says, and I wonder if he's starting to feel a bit uncomfortable, given London is where his life with Helen was, 'but on balance, no. There's nowhere else I'd rather be.'

Later that evening, we make the most of the long daylight by heading down to the beach hut, where we fling open the door and settle down together to drink in the view. It's that grainy half-hour now before dusk turns into darkness. The moon in the sky is dulled by cloud, like a lamp in mist.

'Thanks for today,' I say, rocking into Caleb with my shoulder. 'Tash and Simon really loved you.'

He smiles. 'They're great. I liked them too. You're very lucky.'

I draw the scent of sea-soaked sand to my chest. Tiny lights speckle the horizon – ships, maybe? Oil rigs? The air tonight is warm and calm, still balmy from a day of un-broken sunshine.

'How often do you see your family?'

He wrinkles his nose. 'Not often. It's always a bit like walking on eggshells. Everyone trying not to offend each other. Surface-level chat. The kind of get-together you need a drink to recover from.' He hesitates. 'Sorry.'

I shake my head, to let him know it's okay. 'Well, Dylan adored you, too. You've got a friend for life, there.'

He smiles. 'He's such a little dude.'

'He is.' I sip my tea. 'Did you ever think . . . you might have kids with Helen?'

I know it's an intensely personal question, but it doesn't feel like personal's off-limits between us. Plus, Caleb is the sort of guy who'll be straight-up if he doesn't want to talk about something.

'Yeah,' he says, then clears his throat. 'We actually tried, for ages.'

'You did?' I say, pulling away slightly from where I've been tucked up against him, my head on his shoulder. I don't know why I'm so surprised – I suppose I just imagined they broke up before they got serious about starting a family. I mean, you wouldn't try to have kids with someone if you thought they wanted completely different things to you, would you?

Caleb glances down at me without quite meeting my eye. 'Yeah.' But he doesn't elaborate.

'Didn't you . . . break up because you'd grown apart?'

'Eventually, yes. But we were in denial for a long while before then, I guess. Or maybe I was. I think I convinced myself I could be happy staying in London, if we had a family.'

I wait, sensing he has more to say.

'We went through six rounds of IVF.' His voice is heavy with admission. 'Unsuccessful, obviously.'

Six rounds of IVF?

'Helen's five years older than me. She was worried about . . . you know. Leaving it too late.'

I struggle for a moment to find the words. So . . . surely it was those six unsuccessful rounds of IVF that broke them – not disagreeing on whether to hike the Inca Trail or keep their own chickens?

'Caleb, I thought . . .' But then I don't know what to say.

I take a moment to collect my thoughts, absorbing as I do the peace of the windless night, the sound of sea meeting shingle in soft, briny bursts.

'What?' he says, gently.

'Do you think you'd still be together? If the IVF had worked.'

He exhales. 'That's . . . impossible to answer.'

Hardly the reassurance I was hoping for. 'I thought you broke up because you wanted different things.'

'We did. I guess it just took all the stress of the IVF to fully realise it.'

'Wow.' I mouth it more than say it, which I suppose comes across as slightly snarky.

He frowns. I feel his hand grip my shoulder. 'Lucy, me and Helen . . . we weren't right for each other.'

I nod, but I don't really know how to respond. I'd been thinking their marriage had just come to a natural end, and now I find out that in fact they went through this huge, life-altering thing. That they wanted to start a family. What if they *had* become pregnant – would they still be together in London right now, proud parents to a toddler, their very own miracle baby?

I shake my head, an attempt to dislodge the image from my mind. 'So . . . who broke up with who?'

He waits a long time before answering. 'It was mutual. We realised that without the prospect of a family, we didn't really have . . . anything left.'

I frown, pulling my hands up inside the sleeves of the sweater I'm wearing, which is a little too long for my arms.

I feel Caleb shift his weight against me. He dips his lips to mine, kisses me softly. I catch the woody remnants of the aftershave he wore to lunch, almost faded now, and find myself wondering if Helen picked it out for him. If it was a birthday present, a Valentine's surprise.

'It doesn't really matter *why* we broke up,' he says. 'I mean, the point is, we did.'

I'm not sure I fully agree with that, so I remain quiet.

'And just so you know, there was nothing "wrong",' he says. 'Medically, I mean. It just . . . wasn't happening.'

'Don't, Caleb. You don't have to tell me stuff like that.'

Another long pause. 'Is it . . . something you ever think about?'

I turn my head to look at him, let out a tight half-laugh of surprise. 'Come on.'

His eyes remain wide, his expression unruffled. 'What?'

'It's weird, asking me that. When you've just told me . . . You only broke up with Helen eight months ago. It's too soon to—'

'Okay,' he says, seeming to accept this. 'But I just want you to know . . . I still see all that stuff as part of my future. If it's not too much to say that.'

I swallow. 'Can we please change the subject?'

'Sure. Okay.'

But for a couple of minutes, we don't say anything else.

'Want to go swimming?' he asks eventually.

'Yeah,' I say, surprised to realise I do. There's something appealing right now about the thought of jumping into the sea, plunging my head beneath cold water, washing away the strange tension that's settled unexpectedly between us.

Caleb gets to his feet, offers me his hand. As I stand up, he pulls me close to him. 'I'm sorry,' he whispers, 'if I wasn't completely straight with you, about why me and Helen broke up. I was probably trying to downplay it because . . . well, I really like you, Lucy. I mean, a lot.'

'Let's not talk about it any more,' I whisper into his chest. 'Let's just go and find the sea.'

Go

Tash has been trying to reach me for a whole month when, finally, early on a Sunday in mid-June, she catches me as I'm popping to the shops.

She ambushes me in the street as I step outside the house, which makes me think she's been waiting there since dawn.

I wonder if Dylan and Simon have come to London with her. I wonder what Simon knows.

It's the first time we've been face to face since I found out, since that unthinkable night in May when my whole world collapsed.

'Lucy,' she says, like I might not have seen her standing right in front of me. She's lost a lot of weight – so much that I'd find it shocking, if I wasn't already in receipt of a string of infuriating WhatsApps from my mum informing me Tash has barely been eating.

'Go away, Tash,' I mutter. She watched me spiral out after the break-up, questioning everything. And she's had ten years since to come clean.

'This is crazy,' Tash says. Already she sounds like she might break down. 'Please, Lucy. I just want to talk to you.'

For a sliver of a second, I hesitate, then shake my head and start walking away.

'Where are you going?'

'Shop. Go home, Tash.' I start striding towards the end of the street, where I turn right and onto the main road. It's just beginning to rumble with life, with traffic and joggers and people with prams. The strip of sky between the building tops is drab and crammed with grubby clouds, but the air this morning is warm.

I glance over my shoulder to check she's not following me, then cross the road to the newsagents. It's only once I'm inside that I realise I'm shaking, and that I've completely forgotten what I came out to buy. I end up grabbing milk, bread, coffee and biscuits, before heading back home, praying she'll have gone by the time I return.

She hasn't, of course. She's waiting on the doorstep, like a cold caller who won't take no for an answer.

'Lucy, *please*. Just let me give you my side. And if . . . you never want to see me again, you don't have to. But will you at least just hear me out?'

I say nothing for a few moments. I realise I haven't yet met her eye, afraid that if I do, I'll be confronted with a vision of her and Max that I won't be able to un-see.

Behind her on the street, a group of women pass by, all in NHS lanyards, presumably having just clocked off from a night shift at the hospital. I stare at them, trying desperately to conjure Jools so I'd have an excuse to turn Tash away.

'Lucy?'

The women walk on. 'Fine,' I say, eventually, my voice clipped and cold. 'You can come in, say what you've got to say, then leave. I've got work to do.'

She follows me inside. Thankfully, I'm the only one home right now – Sal's on nights at the moment too, and Reuben stayed over at his girlfriend's again yesterday.

I wasn't lying about work. Though Supernova is everything I'd hoped for and more, the days are long and intense, especially when there's a big pitch coming up. I regularly get home at eight or nine o'clock, and have worked until midnight at least once a week in the month since I started, plus a couple of weekends.

My most recent project has been creating a new brand identity for a well-known healthy living company, run by a semi-famous celebrity. The feedback Seb and I received on Friday about our latest presentation was brutal in a way I hadn't been expecting from someone with a sideline in meditation clothing – so much so, it left me hyperventilating in the ladies' for forty minutes. When I eventually emerged, Seb was waiting outside to assure me that Zara wouldn't sack me off the back of one C-lister's opinion. Still, until my six months of probation at Supernova are up, I can't relax.

I wasn't lying, either, when I told Max they'd have to prise this job out of my cold, dead hands. Already, it's impossible to imagine working anywhere else. I feel as though I've finally found my calling, the career I was always meant to pursue.

Still, most weekends I feel mentally wrung-out – which is why, this morning, I have about as much enthusiasm for listening to Tash's phony professions of remorse as I do for sitting down to read the complete works of Shakespeare, or learning ancient Greek. Seb and I have agreed to put our heads together first thing Monday morning to come up with some new ideas for the healthy living company, and despite working most of yesterday, I still haven't hit on anything I can realistically pitch to him. Which means I need to focus on work today, and nothing else. I'm certainly not about to let Tash – or Max, for that matter – distract me from the best job I've ever had.

I kick off my shoes, then head upstairs without offering Tash anything, shutting my bedroom door behind us. It's been a warm night and the space is already stuffy, so I push open the window, letting in the gentle hum of the city waking up, and the balmy, urban air.

I sit on the chair beside my boarded-up fireplace, and wait.

Tash removes her denim jacket and perches on the edge of my bed. Her green top has a plunging neckline, revealing the bones newly outlined beneath her clavicle.

'Lucy,' she says, her voice shaking. 'You should know. What happened with me and Max meant nothing.'

I feel my tear ducts firing up, but I fight it. 'Come on. It's been a month. No, actually, it's been *ten years*. Surely you've had enough time to come up with something more original than that?'

She doesn't reply, and I wonder for a moment if that's all she's got, the sum total of her crappy apology.

'Well, at least it all makes sense now,' I say, coldly. 'I could never fully understand why he finished it, and he could never properly explain it, either. I blamed myself for a long time. Thought I'd asked too much of him, scared him off. But you already know all that.'

She wipes a tear away. 'All I can say is that I'm *so sorry*, Lucy—'

'God, all those times I thought you hated him because he'd hurt me, when actually it was because he reminded you what a terrible person you are.'

She rummages in her handbag for a pack of tissues, takes one out and wipes her eyes.

'I literally have no idea why you're crying.'

'*Please*, Lucy. Please don't be so cold—'

'Cold? Are you joking right now?'

'Have . . . Have you spoken to Max?'

'Nope.' We haven't spoken since that night on my front doorstep last month, when he confessed to having sex with my sister. He's tried – turning up at the house and my office, messaging, voice notes, calling, even writing me a letter. But whenever I think of him, my imagination pairs him up with Tash all over again. *My sister*. The person who's supposed to love me most in the world. I've tortured myself wondering whether the sex was good, memorable, mind-blowing; I've tried to work out how many times I've slept with him since he did the same with her; I've gone over and over the impact the whole thing has had on my life over the past ten years, without me even knowing it.

Anyway, he's backed off this past week, since Reuben threatened to report him for harassment.

It ended like this.

I'd bumped into Max's friend Rob in the little campus supermarket on that warm September Friday. He dropped into our brief conversation – casual as you like – that Max wanted to live with him and Dean the following summer, when they all moved to London for the LPC. I felt the shock of this claim like a slap – only the previous night, Max and I had been checking out flats of our own, making plans for our big move to the city in nine months' time.

I confronted Max that afternoon, under a vast cedar tree outside the law school. He was already edgy and tense, thanks to a ton of coursework he'd just been given on intellectual property law, and the logistics of arranging another internship at HWW for the Christmas break. He refused to ring Rob – as I wanted him to, right then – to tell him unequivocally he'd be moving in with me next summer.

Convinced he was being untruthful, I walked away, told him over my shoulder I was cancelling Tash, who'd been due to come and visit us in Norwich that evening. She was planning to drive up after work, and we were going to spend the weekend together.

I messaged her not to come, then stayed out late with friends, not wanting to return to the flat I shared with Max. The future I'd been so certain of seemed suddenly to be under threat – but was it my fault? Had I overreacted, behaved unreasonably? Was Rob simply getting ahead of himself, misunderstanding the conversations he'd had with Max?

By the time I got back to the flat in the early hours, I'd convinced myself I was in the wrong. Max was just too popular – hardly his fault. Of course his friends would want him to move in with them next year. That didn't mean he would. I planned to crawl into our bed, cover him with kisses, whisper my apologies and make it up to him the best way I knew how.

But it seemed the damage was already irreversible. Max pushed me away that night, turned his back, wouldn't speak to me. And for the whole of the next week or so, he was distant, closed off. He refused to discuss our fight, wouldn't mention the future, flinched from the subject like it burnt. And then, on the following Friday, he ended it. I don't remember much about that conversation, I felt so dazed with disbelief. But I do recall hearing him say perhaps he would move in with Dean and Rob next summer after all.

It was like handing him my heart, then watching him snap it in two.

'I never got your message that night,' Tash says pleadingly now, her blue eyes wide, like a baby's. Her voice is thick and clammy. 'I drove up to Norwich like we'd arranged, and turned up at your flat, but you were out. Max said you'd had a fight.'

I shake my head. Despite the full month I've had to process all this, I'm still not sure I can bear to hear the details of what happened next, between my sister and the love of my life.

'We got drunk,' she says. 'Like, crazy-drunk. He had a bottle of gin.'

'You don't even like gin,' I say, stupidly.

Briefly, she shuts her eyes. 'No, because that night put me off it for life.'

A memory drifts back to me – seeing an empty gin bottle in the bin the next morning, partially hidden beneath a pile of egg shells. It struck me as odd – firstly because Max had bought it only a few days earlier. But also because sinking so much gin seemed strange when I knew he'd had a long run planned for that morning, ten miles with a friend.

Tash is gabbling now. 'I'd been having a horrible few weeks at work, and . . . I guess Max wasn't having a great time, either. You'd had this fight, and he was worried about his exams, and his friends—'

'This isn't seriously going to be your defence – that you were both *stressed*?' My voice feels hollow and flimsy, like I'm seconds from being sick.

Through the open window drifts the urgent scream of brakes on the street outside, followed by the sharp blast of a horn, doors slamming, swearing.

Tash's forehead crimps into a frown. 'I want you to know, Lucy, it was hardly even . . . The whole thing lasted less than five minutes.'

Unbearable images begin to ricochet through my head. Kissing. Clothes coming off. Hands, body parts, noises, breathlessness. 'Who came on to who?'

'He was reaching over to take my glass, and . . . I thought he was going to kiss me.'

'*Why* would you think that?'

'Like I said. We were drunk.'

As I look at her, it suddenly strikes me, the worst part about all this. It's not – hard as it might be to believe – the physical act of them being together, although that, of course, is horrible. The worst part is finding out that my sister is a complete stranger. That the person I thought she was – honest, kind, principled – doesn't actually exist. That she never did. That every single interaction I've had with her since that day has been a lie. Yes – there was a period after I returned from Australia when I pushed everyone away, including her. But in the years since Dylan was born, we'd been closer than ever, and I can honestly say rebuilding our relationship was one of the things that made me most proud.

'I quit uni because Max finished with me, and I was too much of a mess to carry on. I went travelling and . . .' I catch my breath, push away the spectre of Nate. 'And then I went for the first job I could get because I didn't have a degree. I could never understand why Max had finished it. It just . . . didn't make sense. He was the best thing in my life, and we missed out on . . . *so much*, after we broke up. And you watched all that happening, when the whole time, it was your fault. You let me *live with you* . . .' Hot tears are tumbling down my face now, wetting my lips as I speak. 'You've had nearly ten years to tell me the truth. You've watched me grieving what we had, everything I lost . . .'

She's crying again too, now. 'I know. I'm so sorry. I should have told you straight away, but the longer I left it . . .'

I find myself distracted for a moment by her earrings, a pair of ostentatious drop pearls that Simon gave her for their third wedding anniversary. Posh to the point of pompous, hardly befitting a woman who's shagged her sister's boyfriend. 'Does Simon know?'

She shakes her head, wipes away more tears. I get a petty twist of satisfaction from watching her smudge mascara and eyeliner all over her face. 'Not yet.'

Simon and Tash met after all this happened, so technically it's irrelevant – but I guess she's kept it quiet because she wants him to think she's principled and virtuous, morally flawless.

Well, maybe I'll tell him, I think savagely. *Just so he can be aware of the type of person he married.*

'You know, it's funny,' I say. 'When I came back from travelling, you said I was a different person. Like I'd changed, forgotten how to have fun, or take risks' – she nods but says nothing, clearly too ashamed to speak now – 'and when Max came into my life again, I remembered what you'd said. And I thought, *I'm going to take a risk, and go for it with Max.*' I shake my head. 'What an idiot. I should *never* have risked my heart with him again.'

She exhales and goes to speak, but no words leave her mouth. So we just sit in silence for a few moments, like two completely broken people.

'You need to leave now,' I say.

'Please, Lucy. We can't—'

'Get out,' I say, not looking at her. 'I don't ever want to see you again.'

Jools must have wondered why I'm not up when she gets home a couple of hours later, because she taps my door, opens it and sticks her head through the gap. 'Morning.'

I'm back in bed, where I've been flicking through the notebook from my travels, my sole souvenir from that time, containing the sketchy first seeds of the novel I'd wanted to write. I'm recalling afresh how every page was coloured with self-recrimination about Max, with heartache and regret over my lost soulmate. And now those words have taken on a completely different meaning, like the language I wrote them in is obsolete. Because all my confusion about the way Max and I ended seems foolish suddenly, childish and naive.

I shut the notebook, shuffle into a sitting position, draw my knees into my chest. I rest my chin on top of them. 'Tash was here earlier.'

'Oh God.' Jools sits down on the edge of my bed. 'Did you talk to her?'

I nod. 'She said it meant nothing, her and Max. That it lasted less than five minutes. Like that makes it okay.'

I stopped crying an hour ago and my head just feels blank and woolly now, like I've swallowed a sedative. My brain's way of shutting down, I guess, when I've been thinking for too long and too fast.

'Oh, Luce,' Jools says, taking my hand. She looks exhausted from her night shift, and I feel instantly guilty.

She needs to eat and sleep, not listen to me complain about my ridiculous life.

'Sorry,' I whisper. 'How was your shift? Shall I make you some toast?'

'Shut up and come here.' She pulls me into a hug. 'Make me nothing, and tell me everything.'

So I relate the conversation to her and afterwards we sit quietly together, like we're surveying the broken glass of my relationship, trying to figure out how best to clean it up.

'So, what's worse,' I say, eventually. 'A meaningless, drunken shag, or a passionate affair?'

'Neither. End result's the same, isn't it?'

I'm so glad Jools is here. As well as my closest friend, she's also a long-time expert in familial drama. Literally nothing can shock her.

'You know, since I got back from Australia, Tash has always made such an effort with me. You know – like she's been so desperate for us to be close. I thought she was just worried about me . . . and sometimes I even felt guilty for not telling her what happened with Nate. But now I realise she did all that because *she* felt guilty, for what she'd done.' I brush away a fierce tear, trying not to picture Max's face. Max, who I thought – until a month ago – was my soul-mate, fated to come back into my life. Who I would look at in bed, thinking, *This is exactly how it's meant to be.* The man I was falling in love with all over again, unable to quite believe he was mine for a second time around.

'Jools, can I ask you something?'

'Always.'

'Am I overreacting?'

Her eyes narrow. 'About your sister and your boyfriend . . . sleeping together?'

'It was nearly ten years ago. Max and I were twenty-one. Don't we all do stupid things when we're young?'

'I mean . . . a stupid thing is nicking a lip balm from Boots. Or drink-dialling someone shady. Or eating a kebab from that dodgy chicken shop. What Tash and Max did . . . It was cruel.'

It feels unusual, to hear Jools speak out against Max. She's always been so good at treading a neutral line.

From out of nowhere, an image of Dylan floats into my mind, and I feel heat rise behind my eyes. What the hell do I do now? Because I can't just cut my nephew out of my life. And I don't want to. But I can't face talking to his mother again, either.

'Time,' Jools says, like she's reading my thoughts. 'That's the only thing that's going to fix this.'

'I'm not sure it is fixable.'

'You just need space. Won't happen overnight, trust me.'

I feel exhausted suddenly, like I haven't slept in a week. 'I know. You're right.'

'What about Max?' Jools says. 'How do you feel about talking to him, now you've spoken to Tash?'

The only thing I know is that even hearing his name is enough to make me cry, and right now, I'm too weak to fight it. So I just stay where I am in bed and sob while Jools holds me.

Once I've pulled myself together and Jools has gone to shower and get some sleep, I open my laptop and do some healthy living brainstorming for the morning, eventually deciding there might be something in the strapline, *Do it for you*. (Don't get healthy to impress your friends, or your colleagues, or your cheating ex, or your lying sister. Do it for you.) I triple underline it so I don't end up pitching the wrong idea to Seb tomorrow, then start to work up some potential creative routes.

I must have fallen asleep after that, because the next thing I know, the room is an avalanche of bright light and my Monday morning alarm is drilling through every cell in my body, and there's no time to think any more.

10

Stay

'I'll stay in Nigel's room. You guys have mine,' Jools says, almost as soon as we've walked through the front door of her house in Tooting.

Jools and Nigel, the financial auditor who brought muffins along to his viewing, have been seeing each other for a couple of months now. It's going well, because Nigel, apparently, is as normal and sensible as they come – in other words, Jools' ideal man. He works in financial services, has no dirty secrets involving rehab, revenge porn or dubious opinions he's aired on social media, and – like Jools – has staunch views on people who claim to love immersive theatre (not shorthand for having a personality), courgetti (an insult to pasta) and road bikers in Lycra who think they're the next Bradley Wiggins (they literally never are).

'My sister thinks he's boring,' Jools told me last week. 'But if boring means he's sweet, and mature, and doesn't say arsehole things just to spice up a conversation, then I'll take it.'

★　　★　　★

What Might Have Been

I wasn't sure about inviting Caleb to London, when Jools first suggested it. The IVF revelation had a strange effect on me for a few days, to the point where I even started wondering if I was emotionally ready to have a relationship with a man who'd been in as deep as it can get with someone else – bar actually having the kids to show for it. During the month since that conversation, we've seen each other a few nights a week, and in every other respect, spending time with him has been as intoxicating and pleasurable as ever. And yet ... the Helen thing has been itching incessantly in the back of my mind. Sometimes I find myself mulling over the worst kind of questions: *Does he wish the IVF had been successful? Does he still love her? Does he actually have any plans to get divorced?* And worst of all, *Am I the consolation prize?*

But I don't really feel comfortable asking him any of this, partly because I don't want to risk stirring up emotions he might not yet have confronted. Eventually I had to conclude that no matter what, I'd rather have Caleb, and if that means some questions going unanswered, then that's how it'll have to be.

Inviting him to London for the weekend did feel a bit strange, given that less than a year ago, it had been his home with Helen – the place where they thought they might have a future and family together. But as Jools pointed out, he goes back there for work occasionally anyway, and it's not as though we're staying next door to his old house in Islington. There's a whole river and several boroughs between us.

After drinks at the house, where we're joined by Sal and Reuben, and Reuben's girlfriend Beth, we head out to

Jools' favourite Lebanese place, a few minutes' walk down the road.

Outside, the air is swollen with July heat. The street is humming with traffic, a flurry of moving faces and bikes zipping past. Even if Shoreley was on amphetamines, I'm still not convinced it would ever come close to London, with its constant whirl of stimulation, the city like a tide that takes you by the feet.

'Do you miss this?' I ask Caleb tentatively as we walk, sensing him observing everything almost as though he's seeing the city for the first time. We're walking hand in hand a few steps behind Jools and Nigel, who are loping along the street with their arms wrapped around each other, occasionally pausing to kiss and giggle and nuzzle in a way that all looks amusingly post-coital.

'Actually,' Caleb says, voice low like he's worried Jools and Nigel will hear him, 'I was just thinking about how relieved I am to be living in my tumbledown little cottage on a back street in Shoreley.'

I feel my heart lift slightly, like a kite breaking free in a breeze.

'There's a reason I left London,' he says softly, squeezing my hand.

We sidestep a sullen group of people who look as though they've just been forced at gunpoint to attend the world's worst work night out.

'How about you?' Caleb says.

'Me?'

'Well, you said you almost moved here with Jools. Ever have regrets?'

What Might Have Been

It feels strange even to think of it now – that I might have moved to London, and not ever contacted Caleb again. 'No,' I say. 'And just think, if I had taken that room, Jools would never have met Nigel.'

Caleb laughs. 'Okay. I was hoping there might be something else you'd regret more than that.'

I laugh too, and glance across at him. 'Sorry! Of course. Thought I already said that.'

He's smiling, but I detect the faintest shade of bemusement in his eyes. 'No . . . you definitely didn't.'

'*Of course* I'm pleased I stayed in Shoreley. That I get to be with you,' I say, squeezing his hand.

'Moment's gone, Lambert,' he teases, whispering now because we're joining the queue for the restaurant. The thought that I might have hurt his feelings is suddenly so alarming it's all I can do not to pull him into the nearest alleyway so I can smother him with kisses, and tell him over and over again just how happy I am that I made the choice I did, on that day three months ago.

The restaurant is small and unfussy, with hard seats and tiny tables, so popular we had to queue for our own reservation. It's just two small rooms connected by a narrow corridor passing the serving area, and the space is packed, so we have to raise our voices to be heard.

Our table is crammed with plates and dishes – grilled fish and charcoaled chicken, flaky pastries and yellow rice, bowls of creamy hummus and the fluffiest of flatbreads, all adorned with fresh herbs and golden splashes of oil, plump pomegranate seeds, shards of lemon.

Jools is asking Caleb how long he's been a swimmer.

'Definitely wouldn't call myself a swimmer,' Caleb says with a laugh. He looks so lovely tonight – perfectly dishevelled in his checked shirt, jeans and trainers. 'I just bob about, really. Only because I read cold water's supposed to be good for your circulation and immune system and mental clarity and all that stuff.'

Jools nods thoughtfully. 'We swim in the lido sometimes. Not quite the sea, but close enough.'

'It's as *cold* as the sea,' Nigel chips in. He's holding Jools' hand between refilling her wine glass and intermittently offering the different dishes to her, and I'm struggling to remember a time when I've seen her so happy.

They ask Caleb about his photography, and he's too modest, so I have to keep interjecting with examples of his talent – the awards and grants he's won, the numerous accolades and endorsements to his name, that time he got to shoot a famous influencer's thirtieth birthday party after someone recommended him on Instagram. 'I almost didn't take the job,' he says, laughing, 'because it was so ridiculous. I mean, she was nice enough, but she'd hired *zebras* because they fitted in with the colour theme.'

Nigel smiles. 'A photographer's dream, no?'

'I mean, kind of. But she wanted everything to look very staged and dramatic. Which was easy, obviously, with all the animals and the fire-eaters and the dry ice. But I just prefer taking pictures of stuff that's real, you know?'

'Bet the fee was out of this world,' says Jools, with a smile.

'Oh, yeah, don't get me wrong – that party paid my bills for a whole year. But the big-ticket stuff really isn't my bag. Her PR people wouldn't let me out of their sight. Every single shot was signed off. Post-production was ridiculous, bordering on unethical. I prefer low-key gigs. Jobs where I can actually see the impact of my work.'

I ask Nigel how he got into financial auditing. I sense he's the kind of person whose appearance rarely alters between the office, the pub and his living room. He's delicately featured and exceedingly well groomed in a collared shirt and chinos, his dark hair neatly side-parted and weighted-down with product.

He turns to Jools, poker-faced. 'You were supposed to tell them I'm a stuntman.'

I laugh. My taste buds are dancing from the warm spices and mint, the soft cheese, pickled vegetables. 'She wouldn't date you if you were a stuntman.'

'No? How come?'

'Risk-averse,' Jools says, winking at me.

Nigel looks pleased. 'Then we're *definitely* the perfect match.'

Caleb leans forward. 'What is it you audit, exactly? Sorry to be dense.'

I love this about Caleb – how interested he is in other people, how attentive. How little time he'd actually spend talking about himself, if it were left up to him.

'Well, essentially, I review company accounts. Check everything's in order, and above board.'

Nodding earnestly, Caleb starts asking more, even though I know Nigel's job is about as far as it can be from the stuff Caleb finds inspiring.

Eventually, Nigel smiles, meeting Caleb's eye. I can only hope a bromance is brewing. 'At the end of the day, it's not my *passion*, but . . . I couldn't turn my passion into a long-term thing, so this is my backup plan.' He shrugs, takes a sip of wine. 'I mean, it's not bad. I like the company I work for, the people I work with.'

Caleb tears off a piece of flatbread and dabs it in hummus, the elbow of his shirt dangling dangerously close to a bowl of yoghurt dip. 'So, what *is* your passion?'

'Nigel was going to be a professional pianist,' Jools says, as though she can't hold back any longer.

'Wow, seriously?'

Nigel nods. 'Yeah. I had an agent, was doing well on the session circuit, had a couple of hotel residencies lined up, and then . . . bam.'

Caleb and I wait, breath held, to find out what the bam was.

'Arthritis. My fingers swelled up like sausages. I could barely use them for a year or so.'

'Oh God,' I say. 'What . . . What caused it? I mean, you're so young.' He's just a year older than Jools.

Nigel shrugs. 'No idea. But it was severe.'

'And now?' Caleb asks.

'Not bad.' He wiggles his fingers, which look perfectly slender and firm to me. 'I'm on some pretty hardcore drugs. But I've no idea how long they'll work for, or if funding could be withdrawn for them tomorrow, so . . . thought I'd better find something else to do.'

I nod. 'Hence the auditing?'

Nigel laughs. 'Yep. Being meticulous was literally the only other thing I was good at.'

'Do you still play?'

I notice his eyes going slightly glassy as he nods. 'Just for fun. Could never . . . step into that world again. Too . . . you know. Heartbreaking.'

'I'm sorry,' I whisper.

The faraway look in his eye recedes then, and all his features seem to contract suddenly, as if he's just woken abruptly from a dream. 'Hey no, hate to kill the mood. It's all good.'

Jools smiles. 'He's being modest, but he literally plays piano like a *demon*.'

'Let's find one,' Caleb says, sitting up a little straighter and wiping his mouth. 'Let's go to a bar and find a piano. There must be one around here somewhere.'

Nigel shakes his head. 'Ah, I couldn't. Way too rusty to play in public. I'll give you a tune back at the house later, if you like. I've got a keyboard.'

'What did I say?' Jools says, looking at us. 'Too modest. Come on, Caleb. It is our duty to find this man a *real* piano.'

Eventually, we do – a battered-looking upright at the back of a bar that occasionally hosts live music nights. It's a cramped, badly lit place where the colour theme is basic dungeon, and which could do with all the windows being left open for about a week. Still, Caleb strides up to the bar, and after a little back and forth with a surly barman, he returns, triumphant, brandishing a bottle. 'Piano's yours,' he says to Nigel. 'For the price of a bottle of cava.' He slings an arm around me, kisses my cheek. 'Got you a Virgin Mary. That okay?'

I smile and kiss him back, because he knows it is, that a plain old Virgin Mary will for ever remind me of the night we met.

We find a booth with a small table near the back, and after virtually draining his glass, Nigel strolls up to the piano, like the idea's just popped into his mind to sit down and have a go. As he rolls up his sleeves, takes a seat and starts to play, it's clear that he's much less buttoned-up than you might think on first appearance, that he has music running through his veins.

I'd been expecting – I'm not sure why – something jazzy, the kind of thing you might hear in a Park Lane hotel lobby, or a piano lounge in Manhattan. But he surprises me by kicking off with Coldplay, then Lady Gaga's 'Shallow', then 'God Only Knows' by The Beach Boys. After a while, I realise a small crowd has gathered, though I'm not sure where from, since the place was virtually deserted when we walked in.

I settle back in the booth and into Caleb's arms. His fingers tap out the melodies on my forearms.

'Loving this dress, by the way,' he whispers to me at one point, brushing the hair from my neck, his voice grazing my ear as Nigel plays a tune by Stereophonics. He drops a hand to my thigh, fingering the hem of my dress in a way that I know to be far less absent-minded than it looks. I feel a current begin to race through me, and for half a moment I consider grabbing his hand and pulling him into a dark corner, or to the bathroom, or onto the street outside.

And then I start to worry, regretting again my fleeting doubts of the past few weeks, those stupid fears about Helen that are really nothing more than my own insecurity. So Caleb has been serious about building a life with someone else, in his past – hasn't everyone? Haven't I?

I lean over to him, squeeze his hand. 'You and me,' I say, the words barely distinguishable above the piano and the crowd and the sound of Jools whooping. 'If I'd moved to London – not being with you would have been the worst thing.'

'What?' he shouts, leaning right into me.

'You and me,' I shout back. 'That was the best thing that happened, when I decided to stay in Shoreley.'

Nigel finishes his song with a flourish, and the crowd erupts.

'Sorry, Luce,' Caleb mouths, shaking his head. 'Didn't catch any of that.'

I determine to say it all again as soon as we're out of the bar, but by then of course we're all riding high on Nigel's musical triumph – which culminated in the barman perking up and inviting him to pop in next week to discuss a regular gig – and by the time Caleb and I are on our own again, in Jools' bedroom back at the house, it feels as though the moment has passed.

★   ★   ★

And then. Like a really bad joke from some higher power, it comes.

I'm downstairs in Jools' kitchen, fetching water to take to bed while Jools is talking Caleb through how to use the shower, and showing him the best way to jiggle the bathroom door so the lock actually works, when my phone buzzes.

A message.

From Max.

Max Gardner.

Hey, Luce. It's been too long. It was so great to see you in Shoreley back in April.

Kind of wish I hadn't dashed off that night.

I'd love to catch up.

Let me know if you fancy it. I still think about you. M x

I stare at the phone for so long that when I next look up, I wonder if hours might have passed and the whole house has fallen asleep. But then I realise Jools has snuck into the kitchen, and is leaning against the sink with an odd expression on her face.

'Everything okay?'

'I don't know. I just got this . . . from Max.' I pass her the phone. Above our heads, the kitchen strip light flickers ominously.

Jools scans the message, then looks at me. 'Is this the first time—'

'Yep. Haven't heard from him since that night.'

'The night you met Caleb,' she says, meaningfully.

'Also the night my horoscope said I'd cross paths with my soulmate,' I say – I'm not sure why. It sounds stupid the moment it's left my mouth.

Jools tilts her head, meets my eye. 'Come on, Luce.'

I put a hand to my face. 'I know, I know.'

She passes the phone back to me. 'You haven't done anything wrong. But you should delete it.'

I say nothing. Suddenly, the grimy malfunction of the kitchen – the leaky tap, the fizzing light, the mound of dirty dishes in the sink, the cupboards with their badly angled doors – seems to echo the abrupt dip in mood.

Jools peers at me. 'You're not seriously considering getting in touch?'

'No, I—'

'Oh God, you *are*.' She sighs, shakes her head.

'No, but . . . I don't know. All this stuff with Helen . . .'

'All this stuff with Helen is in your head. They split up six months before you met.'

'And went through some fairly life-defining stuff together.'

'So what? So Caleb has some baggage – who doesn't?'

'Max, probably,' I say, as a sort of joke. 'He was always pretty good at processing things.'

'Clearly not, if he's still messaging you after all this time.'

'Caleb and Helen . . . they're still married. They're not divorced.'

'So, what are you saying?' says Jools, her voice softening. 'You think he's still in love with her?'

I sigh, and frown. 'No, of course not. I just . . . it's so weird Max has sent me this when . . . I always used to think he and I were meant to be, you know?'

'Max is in your past, Luce. Caleb is very much in the here and now, and to be brutally honest, I think you'd be an idiot to answer that message.'

I'm about to reply when I see a shadow momentarily darken the slice of light at the edge of the kitchen door, which is slightly ajar. Then comes the sound of footsteps making their way upstairs.

Horrified, I stare at Jools. 'Was that Caleb?'

She bites her lip. 'No idea. Could have been Nigel, or Sal, or—'

I shut my eyes. *Or Caleb.*

She puts a hand on my arm. 'Go upstairs, be with Caleb. Forget about Max. You've moved on now. Max Gardner is your past, nothing more. Caleb is your future.'

Go

'I'm just asking you to think about it. Please. You've been so desperately unhappy since all this happened.'

I sigh, shift the weight to my other leg. Mum's right, of course – I have been miserable since finding out about Tash and Max. But her view on how easy it could be to fix is optimistic to say the least.

I'm standing in the street outside the Supernova offices, waiting for our pizza delivery to arrive. Seb and I are working late again, on one of the first campaigns I was assigned when I started at Supernova. It's a series of animations for

190

a global wildlife charity, reimagining well-known children's stories in the light of climate change.

'Dylan's birthday isn't the time or the place,' I tell Mum. 'I can't bring all that . . . anger and tension to his party. It wouldn't be fair.'

'But Lucy – that's my point,' Mum says. 'I think you'd only have to look at his little face to feel better about everything.'

'You reckon I'd feel better . . . about the fact that Tash slept with Max?' I say, to check I'm understanding her correctly.

'Well, it *was* a long time ago. I'm not condoning what she did,' Mum clarifies, before I can interrupt, 'but nearly a decade has passed now. Are you going to let one drunken mistake destroy your relationship with your sister?'

It wasn't just a drunken mistake, I want to say. *It was the very worst kind of betrayal.*

I tip my head back, stare up at the indigo sky of the evening and the ungainly clatter of pigeons flapping between the rooftops, the only nature visible from this particular patch of Soho pavement. It's a hot Friday night, almost steamy, and for a moment I imagine I'm somewhere in the southern hemisphere, as far as I can be from reality.

To think, the whole time I was travelling through climates like that all those years ago, I was pining for Max and questioning myself . . . when all along, he'd done the most unthinkable thing.

'You need to find a way to move forward,' Mum's saying. Then, generously conceding my sister *may* also have a part to play in all this: 'Both of you.'

I try to think of a way to explain it to her that might topple her from whatever maternal fence she's claiming neutrality from the top of. 'How would *you* feel, Mum? If Dad had slept with . . . Auntie Kath?'

There's a short silence, during which I can't tell if Mum's trying not to laugh, or seriously attempting to picture it. Could be both, I suppose: whether Auntie Kath – Leicester's fiercest head teacher – has ever so much as kissed a man is a mystery my mother is no closer to solving now than she was thirty years ago.

'Well, I think the big difference is that you and Max weren't married with children when all this happened, darling.'

No, I think, bitterly. *But we might have been, one day. And that's what Tash stole from me: a future, possibility, a shot at true happiness. What if I never meet another Max in my lifetime?*

'Tash has apologised, hasn't she? Can't you at least try to meet her halfway?'

Mum knows she has. Flowers to my office and home, a voucher for a two-night stay at a health spa in Berkshire so 'we can talk', which I promptly sent back. Five long emails, two letters, multiple messages, voice notes and missed calls.

But I'm not ignoring her to make a point. I'm ignoring her because I honestly don't know what to say, how to even take one step towards forgiveness. Do I even *want* to forgive her?

On the street in front of me, a guy about my age passes by. He's an office worker with swagger: sunglasses on, tie loosened, confident gait. He glances at me, and for a moment I feel self-conscious standing here in my flimsy chiffon dress. I catch the edge of his smile, but it doesn't make me feel good. It just makes me ache for Max.

I switch my gaze to my feet, scuff at a protruding paving slab with the toe of my sandal. 'Mum, you've always said you and Dad are ... soulmates, haven't you? That you were meant to be.'

Down the phone, there's a scuffling noise, as though Mum's covering the speaker with her hand. But I can still hear her snapping at Dad – 'Yes, all *right*, Gus!' – which kind of weakens the point I'm trying to make, if I'm honest.

It's weird. I've never heard Mum bark at Dad like that before. This Tash and Max stuff must be getting to us all more than I realised.

'Did you ever think,' Mum says, her voice softening, like I'm six years old again and this is her umpteenth attempt to talk me through a particular times table, 'that maybe Max sleeping with your sister means he isn't the person you're supposed to be with after all?'

And suddenly, I feel stupid, because of course, this *is* elementary-level stuff. Max slept with my sister. *Of course* he's not the man I'm meant to spend my life with.

Soulmates don't cheat. They just don't.

At least, that's how everybody else – quite logically – sees it. And yet ... I still can't shake my feelings for him. Even after everything that's happened.

'Please come to Dylan's party,' Mum says again. 'You haven't seen him for two months. The time flies by so fast when they're that age.'

But now a moped's speeding up to the kerb, which means I'm either about to be mugged or collect a pizza.

Either way, I'm relieved to have an excuse to end the call. 'I've got to go, Mum.'

The rider flips his visor and climbs off, balances the moped on its stand and opens the box on the back.

'Just think about it,' Mum's saying. 'Please?'

'Okay, I will,' I reply, which is the most I can assure her of right now.

Seb tosses a pizza crust back into the box. 'Okay, so we're saying the twist is, the Ugly Duckling *is* actually ugly. Because of the oil slick.'

Seb and I are sitting on beanbags in one of Supernova's breakout spaces, our enormous pizza half-eaten between us. It's almost ten o'clock, but the time has melted away, and we're finally making progress on the core components of our campaign.

'*Yes*,' I say, scribbling away on my sketch pad. 'And all the other birds stop migrating because . . . the winters are no longer cold, because of—'

'Climate change,' he says, lowering his index finger towards me before grabbing another slice of pizza.

I frown. 'It's pretty bleak, but . . .'

'But that's what they said they wanted.' He flips through a pile of papers, then reads from the relevant page of the amends brief. '"We need this to be more hard-hitting."' He takes a bite from his slice and chortles. 'Hey, bet you never thought working at Supernova would be this depressing. Last year was literally all high fashion and fast cars.'

What Might Have Been

I smile and shake my head. 'Believe it or not, this is the opposite of depressing to me.'

I feel him observe me as he chews. 'You really should have done this years ago, you know. You're a great writer.'

Touched, I look up at him. 'Thank you. Writing's all I ever wanted to do, so . . . that means a lot.' And it does, especially coming from someone as talented as Seb, and when I've had so much to prove here. But now, for possibly the first time since I started at Supernova, I realise my fears about my lack of writing experience are starting to ebb away. I have earned my spot in this team – I contribute at least as much as Seb to our joint assignments, and whenever the entire creative team put their heads together on a brief, I'm never short of ideas, some of which get taken forward and worked on for major pitches and campaigns.

Seb shrugs, like he was only speaking his mind, which makes what he said even more meaningful, somehow. 'So, what else have we got for this?'

I flip back through my sketch pad. 'Jack and the Beanstalk – the beanstalk doesn't grow because, global warming. And in Little Red Riding Hood—'

'The forest's being cut down by Big Agriculture.'

An idea begins to nudge the edge of my consciousness, some wordplay that's been staring me in the face that, somehow, I've been missing. I tap pencil against paper. 'Oh, hang on.' I look up at Seb and smile. 'There must be something we can do with *Grimms' Fairy Tales*.' I scribble it down, triple-underlining GRIMM.

We do a little fist-bump. 'Right. On that note, shall we call it a night?' He stretches his arms above his head and yawns.

'You can take the rest of the pizza.'

'Nah,' he says. 'We'll be back in tomorrow, won't we? Let's just leave it here for lunch.'

Seb lives in Battersea, so we expense a cab together. He gets straight on the phone to his girlfriend to discuss some plumbing emergency at home, which leaves me time to think about something other than work for the first time in hours, or maybe even days. As the cab heads across the river, the lights of the city sliding like rain over the rear window, my thoughts turn to Max.

Working all these crazy hours has had an almost tran-quillising effect on me: filling my brain with Supernova, fighting to prove myself, has stemmed the constant flow of doubt and questions and longing. It's stopped me from dwelling very long on how I feel, or wondering what Max is doing right now – whether he's also working himself into the ground, because stopping to think for even a second just hurts too much.

I manage to achieve a lie-in the next day, before letting Jools drag me to the market, where we slide into our favourite café for a brunch of coffee and toasted sand-wiches. The air balloons with the scents and sounds of the market late morning on a Saturday – flowers and fish and fruit, the clamour of voices and crates and roller doors shuttering.

'Sorry if we made a bit of noise last night,' Jools says as we sit down, a mischievous glint in her eye.

For a moment, I can't think what she means, before I remember she had a date after work yesterday. Another nurse, who's recently moved to London from Edinburgh. I must have already been asleep by the time they got in.

She tells me they went to see a Tom Stoppard play, followed by cocktails at one of those bars that used to be a public toilet. 'The urinals were built into the tables. Which was a bit weird, considering we both spend all day at work obsessing about hygiene.' She brightens. 'But other than that, it was great. He's funny, quite old-school chivalrous. Holds doors open, that kind of thing.'

Max holds doors open, I think automatically, before the alarming thought occurs to me that perhaps now he's started holding them open for other people. It has been two months since I broke it off, after all, and Max never did go short of female attention.

'Do you think you're going to see him again?' I ask Jools, through a mouthful of mushroom and Emmental.

'Maybe. Yeah. I think I will.'

I lean forward, trying to dislodge Max from my mind. 'Sorry, what did you say his name was again? Victor?'

Jools laughs and sips her coffee. 'Vince.' She peers at me. 'Are you okay, Luce? Sure you're not working too hard? If you don't mind me saying, you look a bit . . . you know. Under the weather.'

It's a fair observation: I seem to spend most of my life looking and feeling under the weather, these days. To try to take my mind off Max and my sister, my days have melted together in a series of skipped breakfasts and lunches, dinners snatched from boxes, too much coffee, late nights, zero sleep . . .

I check the time on my phone. 'Actually, I'd better not be too long. I'm meeting Seb at one.'

'Can I say something?' Jools says.

''Course,' I mumble into my coffee, the steam dampening my lips.

'I know what happened with Max was awful and horrible . . . but you can choose how you deal with it. You know?'

'I am dealing with it.'

Finishing her sandwich, Jools brushes crumbs from her fingertips. 'No, you're denying it. Massive difference.'

'I'm just focusing on work. And it's going really well,' I say, remembering the high of our creative session last night, and the compliments Seb paid me.

A couple of teenagers push past our table, almost sending our coffees flying. We snatch up our cups with the dart-fast reflexes of the caffeine-dependent, then smile at each other.

'And that's brilliant,' Jools says, 'but you haven't resolved things with your sister, and working like a maniac won't do that. You're going to have to face up to what happened sooner or later.'

I nod slowly, because I know she's right: Tash has been drifting into my head more and more lately, and the harder I try to push her away, the more persistent she becomes.

'My mum wants me to go to Dylan's birthday party next month,' I say.

'Well, that could be a start.'

'Yeah, maybe,' I say, nibbling my bottom lip.

'I'll come with you, if you need the moral support. I'm an expert in family crises, remember?'

'Thanks, but I wouldn't subject you to mine on top of yours.'

I finish my sandwich, then we order two more flat whites to take out.

'Have you heard anything else from Max?' Jools asks, as we head back out into the market, dodging a group of men carrying babies in slings. For some reason, the sight of them makes my blood pulse with sadness.

I shake my head. 'Just that last message a couple of weeks ago. Think he's given up.'

She nods. 'Is that . . . a good thing?'

I swallow and take a sip of coffee, instantly skinning the roof of my mouth. 'Yeah, it's got to be. I couldn't go back now. Not even if I wanted to.'

Because I'd be ashamed to admit that, in my darkest moments, I *do* want to. I find myself imagining that maybe I'll just go and knock on Max's front door, and we won't talk, or say anything at all, because speaking's too painful. Instead we'll just let chemistry do its thing, which is easy, because that – to my mortification – has never really gone away, for me. And I won't worry about whether he's my soulmate, or just a guy I can't forget. I won't allow my brain to get involved at all – I'll just leave it up to my heart. And maybe we'll do that once a week after work, and sometimes at the weekends, and conversation – the thing that feels so impossible – will never actually factor into it.

I indulge in this fantasy so often that sometimes, I actually find myself reaching for my keys, my wallet, my bag, and tapping through to the Uber app on my phone, before remembering that's all it can possibly be now, a fantasy, one that can't ever be realised.

On the tube en route to Supernova, I re-read Max's last run of messages to me.

I won't contact you any more after this. I promise. I just need to say . . . that I know how good things could be between us. And yes, I messed up what we had in the worst way possible. But I'll do whatever it takes to put it right.

If there's even a chance I can save this, just tell me how.

Okay. Won't message you any more, I swear.

Just please know that this has been the best few weeks of my life, and I'd give anything to have you back in it. M xx

11

Stay

On the morning of Dylan's birthday, I wake to find he has climbed onto my bed and started tapping my face gently with a magic wand. 'Auntie Lucy,' he whispers, 'I'm six.'

'Happy birthday, darling,' I whisper back, reaching up to ruffle his hair. 'Fancy being six.'

'I'm going to turn you into a rabbit,' he whispers with a grin, waving the wand around my face.

After I've obliged by making bunny ears with my fingers and chewing an imaginary carrot, I pull him into a hug. He curls up in the crook of my arm and rests against my shoulder. I put my nose to the crown of his head and draw in the comforting scent of him, of vanilla and sleep and innocence.

'Is Uncle Caleb coming today?'

It's the first time he's called him that. I wonder if I should gently point out that, technically, Caleb isn't his uncle, before remembering that (a) it's his birthday; (b) he's six; and (c) who the hell cares? It just means Dylan enjoys spending time with him, and surely that's all that matters.

'Of course,' I say, kissing the top of his head. 'He can't wait to see you.'

Dylan shuffles his little body even more tightly to mine. And I cross both my fingers, pray I haven't just told him a lie, given I've hardly seen my boyfriend at all since our weekend in London with Jools.

Dylan's YouTube obsession has recently graduated from young toy recipients to teenage magicians, so after he'd gone to bed last night, we festooned the whole house with magic-themed decorations in black and red and silver: top hats, wands, and huge alphabet balloons spelling *ABRACADABRA*, courtesy of the Pebbles & Paper stockroom. There's a vast pile of gifts from Tash and Simon waiting on the coffee table downstairs, and she's ordered a cake with more constituent parts than you would for your average wedding.

I messaged Caleb last night to remind him of the party's theme, but when I woke up this morning, he still hadn't replied.

He finds me in the kitchen later, where I'm taking refuge from all the parental politics and school-gates gossip by mixing up more colour-changing cocktails for the kids.

'Hello,' Caleb says, from the doorway. It's hard to tell how long he's been standing there. I try to read his expression, but it remains coolly neutral, detached in a way that instantly unsettles me.

'Hi.' I feel shy suddenly, like I'm trying to impress a long-time crush at a house party. 'You made it.'

'You look nice.'

'Oh, thanks.' I adjust my party hat faux-flirtatiously. On Tash's request, I'm wearing silver to complement the magic theme, though the only thing I could find was a revealing strappy top more suited to a nightclub than a kids' party. 'So do you.'

His T-shirt bears a single white star on the front. It's years old, I think, an ancient band T-shirt, and it's hard to know if he's sticking to the theme or just fancied wearing it.

'Sorry,' he says, slightly gruffly, 'that I've been a bit AWOL these last few weeks.'

I swallow. 'That's okay.' I have a horrible feeling it's because he overheard the conversation between Jools and me in the kitchen when we were in London. I didn't want to bring it up that night, for fear of us falling out while we were staying with Jools. But ever since, he claims to have been busy, either out with friends or swamped with work, splitting his time between corporate jobs in London, a wedding in Whitstable, and a mid-week job for one of his stepbrothers in Devon.

'Have you seen Dylan yet?'

'Er, no.' He holds up a gift-wrapped parcel. 'Where should this go?'

'Oh, you didn't have to—'

'Got him the Harry Potter Lego in the end,' he says brusquely, almost cutting me off, and then we both just stand looking at each other for a moment or two. I feel something resembling dismay creep through me, and almost have to blink back tears.

'Caleb, are we—'

'I'll just go and find Dylan,' he says. 'Catch up with you in a bit.'

Catch up with you in a bit. Like we're office nemeses bumping into each other at a networking do, and he'd been secretly hoping to avoid me.

Twenty minutes or so later I manage to track him down, once I've handed round more drinks and helped to herd the kids into the dining room, where their communal hyperactivity is currently being contained by a man with a beard pulling stuff out of hats.

I watch Caleb for a few minutes before I approach him. He seems familiar with a fair amount of the people here. I know he's taken pictures for Dylan's school before, and I guess he's done work for quite a lot of the parents too. He moves smoothly between groups, chatting easily, cracking jokes, laughing at all the right moments. Perhaps it would be a cliché to say he lights up the room, but I can't deny it seems a whole lot brighter for having him in it.

Eventually I see him extricate himself from a particularly involved conversation with two of the mums, one of whom kept touching him on the arm and laughing uproariously whenever he opened his mouth. It was at this point that his eyes found mine, the smile he shot me seeming to say, *Could do with some help here.*

'Do you need rescuing?' I whisper, my hand finding his next to the 'Pin the Scar on Harry Potter' poster, willing him to say yes.

A flurry of delighted screams erupts from the dining room, and he smiles. 'Well, if I didn't before, I do now. Shall we go somewhere quiet?'

'Yes please,' I say, immediately, but as we're turning to go, a woman I half-recognise but can't quite place taps me on the shoulder. 'Lucy! God it's been *years*.'

She obviously decided to ignore the memo about the touch-of-magic dress code, being perfectly groomed in the manner of Gwyneth Paltrow – tall and slim with long sandy hair, in skinny white jeans and a teal-coloured silk T-shirt, her skin beach-holiday brown.

'Briony,' she prompts me quickly, saving me the embarrassment of having to confess I can't remember her name. 'I was at school with Tash.'

'Of course.' I give her a hug, trying not to cough as I breathe in a powerful punch of perfume.

'Listen, hate to pry, but is your sister okay?'

I frown. 'Yes, she . . . Yes, I think so. Why?'

'I saw her *crying* just now,' Briony says, in an exaggerated whisper, tipping her head towards the hallway.

'Sure it was Tash?' Maybe they were happy tears, like the ones she shed this morning at Dylan's present-opening session.

'Yes – blond bob, silver playsuit?'

Feeling my smile fade, I decide to try to find her and check, but then Briony turns to Caleb. 'Max, is it?'

'No,' I say quickly, heat rushing to my face. 'This is Caleb.'

'Oh, sorry. I thought . . . I thought your boyfriend was called Max, for some reason.' She lets out a shrill sliver of laughter. 'God, sorry! I must be thinking of someone else.'

'No, Max lives in London,' I say, completely without thinking, before instantly wishing the man with the beard would come and magic me – or preferably Briony – away from Caleb and this excruciating conversation.

We chat for a couple more painful minutes about Briony's children, and Caleb's photography – her curiosity piqued by the camera hanging around his neck – and then she asks what I do.

'Oh, I'm . . . writing a novel.'

'You're a novelist?'

'Well, no,' I say hastily, feeling instantly fraudulent. 'Not yet. I'm just writing a first draft, really. Actually, I work part-time at Pebbles & Paper too. You know, the—'

'What's your novel about?' she asks, eyes glimmering almost intrusively.

'Oh, you know. Girl meets boy. That kind of thing.'

'A love story?'

'I guess so.'

'Is it about you?' she asks Caleb, winking at him and smiling conspiratorially at me.

Looking uncharacteristically uncomfortable, Caleb clears his throat. 'Not as far as I know.'

Just as I'm opening my mouth to say something – anything – that isn't to do with Max or love stories not featuring Caleb, the dining-room doors fling open, and the kids start streaming through it in magicians' hats, babbling about magic and whacking each other over the head with little plastic wands.

'Nice to talk to you both,' Briony says, patting me on the arm, and then she is gone.

'Let's go outside,' Caleb says, his voice terse, and I sense a curl of dread in my stomach, something I've never felt with him before.

We head into the garden. The air is lemony with sunshine, rich with the scent of damp grass from the sprinklers ticking over the vast lawn in an attempt to offset August's record temperatures. It's newly cut, mown weekly into English country stripes by a gardener who's also cultivated the multi-coloured mass of dahlias, roses, chrysanthemums and geraniums bursting from every border.

The sky is a vast blue lake, its surface unbroken except for the occasional dart of a song thrush or blue tit. At the garden's furthest point, I can just make out Tash's recently created outdoor office, nestling beneath the long tendrils of a silver birch, the facing wall made almost entirely of one-way glass.

It feels good to be out here, away from the cartoonish playlist Tash has on loop in every room, the clamour of over-excited children, the heated undercurrent of parents gossiping.

'I'm sorry,' I say, the words tumbling from my mouth as we pause by the side of the house, out of sight of everyone inside.

Caleb shakes his head as we face each other, and I can't quite read his expression – sadness? Anger? Embarrassment?

'I overheard you that night,' he says. 'In Jools' kitchen.'

I shut my eyes for a moment, the recollection of what I said trickling through me liked iced water. 'I'm so sorry.'

'It was a bit weird,' he says. 'I thought everything was going pretty well between us, but then you suddenly start acting distant, and then I overhear you saying you think I've got baggage and that you feel weird about me and Helen still being married . . . and to top it all off, you tell your best mate you always thought you and Max were meant to be, that he might be your soulmate . . .'

The tears brim in my eyes. I reach out to touch him, but he's stuffed both his hands in the pockets of his jeans. '*No,*' I say, fiercely. 'I was just . . . Max sent me a message out of the blue, and I was momentarily confused about—'

'Good to know.'

'Not like that. I'd been feeling a bit strange about Helen, and . . .' But I trail off, clueless as to how I might explain away emotions I no longer fully feel.

'Lucy, you're going to have to fill me in here, because I have no idea where Helen comes into all this.'

I say nothing for a couple of moments. My right hand finds the wooden bracelet around my opposite wrist and spins it anxiously. 'I suppose . . . the IVF thing freaked me out slightly. And you *are* still married.'

'Yeah – on paper,' he says, stiffly. 'As far as we're both concerned, the next step is divorce.'

I swallow, feeling relief ripple through me, despite everything. 'Okay.'

'So, what are you saying, Lucy? Do you think you've made the wrong choice, between me and your ex?'

'*No.* I never asked Max to send me that message.'

'But you still thought about replying.'

'I didn't. I wouldn't. You've got it all wrong.'

'Actually, I got it from the horse's mouth,' he says, his eyes horribly cool against me. He tips his head back towards the house. 'And then that woman in there says she thought you were with Max.'

I swallow and shake my head. 'No. Honestly. I don't have any feelings for Max. I'm not in touch with him. I don't *want* to be in touch with him.'

I feel a hot sweep of shame whenever I reflect on that night in Jools' kitchen. Time apart from Caleb over the past few weeks has made me realise just how much I want to be with him, and how stupid it was to feel thrown-off by the idea of him trying to have a family with Helen. Perhaps he shouldn't have downplayed its role in his split with her, but as Jools pointed out last week, if it's not a deal-breaker, it's crazy to waste any more time worrying about it. I hate being apart from Caleb. I think about him all the time. The idea of splitting up makes me feel cold with misery.

I've realised – perhaps too late – just how strongly I feel. How convinced I am that Caleb – not Max – is the one for me, the person I'm *meant* to be with.

'So is this what these past few weeks have been about? You've been punishing me?' I say quietly.

Caleb shakes his head. 'Actually, I've been trying to figure out what I'd do if you told me you were getting back with . . . him. Because the truth is, Lucy, I love you. I've fallen in love with you.'

I stare at him, my breath suspended in my throat.

The smile appears first in his eyes, then at the corners of his mouth. 'Seriously, I love you. You're the best person I've ever known, hands-down. I've even started to believe—' He breaks off, then looks down at his feet.

I reach out and touch his arm. 'Believe what?'

He swallows. 'I've never bought into the idea of soul-mates, Lucy. All that stuff about it being written in the stars. Not even when I was married. You know that.'

I nod, hoping very hard that the next word I'll hear will be *but*.

'But I've finally been starting to wonder if maybe all this time I've had it wrong. That actually, I was meant to meet you that night at The Smugglers. That you and me . . . we're meant to be together.'

My heart begins to pelt with happiness.

'And the idea that you might not feel the same way . . . it's just been killing me. I'm sorry.'

'I do,' I breathe. 'I *do* feel the same way. I love you too. I'm so sorry for nearly messing everything up. I don't want to break up with you. Ever.'

His smile broadens. 'Serious?'

'Serious,' I repeat.

He takes a step towards me, close enough now that we're almost touching. My back is pressed against the sun-warmed brickwork. Then he lifts his hand, places it on the wall above my head, his eyes steady on my face. His expression is so fiercely charged I get goosebumps. And then he leans forward, kissing me with an intensity I feel right down to my toes. He presses himself against me, and all at once I am burning for him. 'I've missed you, Lambert,' he breathes.

'I've missed you too.' I'm so desperate to suggest we sneak off upstairs to my bedroom, or even down the lawn to Tash's garden office, but my conscience just about reins me in. This is my nephew's sixth birthday, after all, not a university house party.

'Later,' Caleb murmurs, the word landing square in my solar plexus. 'We'll make it worth the wait.'

I kiss him again, my stomach stormy with wanting, then lean back against the wall to collect my stolen breath. Over on the lawn, a squirrel hops across the grass before scaling the silver birch, making its leaves shimmer like water with the disturbance.

'I think,' I say, after a few moments, 'I used to believe Max was my soulmate because I never really got closure.'

He nods. 'Maybe if you'd stayed together, you would have realised eventually that you weren't actually . . . meant to be.'

I smile. 'You know, the night I first met you, at The Smugglers, my horoscope told me I was going to bump into my soulmate.'

He cocks an eyebrow. 'Oh, really?'

'Yep.'

'How come you're only just telling me this now?'

I reach out and prod him gently in the ribs with a single finger. 'Because you never believed in soulmates, remember?'

Exhaling, he smiles. 'All right. I've been giving you a hard time about this, but . . . I have something to confess.'

I wait.

'I wanted to tell you this when we first got together, but I thought you might think it was a bit weird.'

I smile. 'Should I be nervous?'

He scratches the back of his neck, then releases a breath. 'That day I met you in The Smugglers, when you ran outside to talk to Max, you both looked so . . . I don't know. Giddy, or something. To be seeing each other. Anyway, I walked out the front door to leave, and I was going to say goodbye to you, but you were so absorbed in each other that . . . Anyway, I had my camera with me, so I took a quick shot. It just struck me, how you were looking at each other. I was going to email it to you, if you got in touch. I thought maybe it could be an ice-breaker, or something . . . until I realised that'd be slightly shooting myself in the foot.'

'Do you still have it? The photo?'

He shakes his head. 'Deleted it. Felt a bit weird about keeping it once we'd got together.'

I frown. 'Why are you telling me this?'

He shrugs. 'I could see that night how much Max meant to you, and I guess . . . it goes some way to explaining why I feel a bit . . . sensitive about him. Aside from him being some sort of over-achieving Adonis, obviously.'

'He's not,' I say quickly. 'But thank you. I appreciate you being honest.'

He dips his face to mine. 'Any chance you could kiss me or something, so I don't feel like quite such an idiot?'

I laugh, lean forward, and oblige.

We're just about to head back inside when, from the back of the house, a door slams, making us both jump.

I peer around the brickwork to see Tash and Simon on the patio. Tash is crying, her face covered in blotches.

I glance at Caleb, eyes wide. He shakes his head, raises a finger to his lips.

'Tash,' Simon is saying. 'You're overreacting.'

'*Overreacting?* You went for a drink with *her*, of all people, and you think—'

'For the hundredth time, it wasn't a drink, it was a sodding work thing! There were about a hundred other people there!'

'I *said* to you that if you saw her again, that would be *it*—'

'I haven't been *seeing* her, I bumped into her. What did you want me to—'

'Natasha?' My mum is stepping out onto the patio, her timing impeccably ham-fisted as only a mother's can be.

My dad's bedridden at home today with a migraine, apparently, which is odd – I can't remember the last time he was ill, and I didn't know he suffered from migraines, either. Not to mention the fact he adores his only grand-child. Maybe all the redundancy stuff has flared up again: I know how much that stresses him out. And Mum's looked pretty miserable today, though she's been trying to put a brave face on it. I guess she's just used to always having Dad by her side.

'Dylan wants to know if we can cut the cake,' Mum's saying. There follows a pause as she clocks Tash's face. 'Are you . . . okay, darling?'

'I'm fine,' Tash snaps, her voice so caustic it chills me. 'I'll be in in a minute.'

There's another pause before Mum retreats, pulling the door shut behind her.

I feel my pulse invade my throat. I've seen my sister get angry before, but I've never seen her lose control like this.

'Tash,' Simon says, his voice strung-out like it's being physically tugged from his chest. Ridiculously, he's still wearing his top hat, hired – I hope – to align with today's theme. 'Andrea was a mistake. I don't know how many times I need to tell you that.'

'If you can't stay away from her, then I don't even know what we're doing, Simon.'

Across the lawn behind them, a blackbird whooshes past in a flurry, as if startled by all the commotion.

'Tash. It's Dylan's birthday.' Simon is pleading now.

And then she simply nods, turns and walks back inside. Simon follows her, closing the door behind him, and the garden goes quiet.

I turn to Caleb. 'Who the hell is Andrea?'

It's probably the first time I've ever confronted someone about an argument I've witnessed by eavesdropping, which must be why I get it so wrong.

I catch Tash as we're clearing up in the kitchen. Dylan's enduring a painful comedown from his sugar high in the living room with Mum, sobbing about some boy who kept snatching his deck of cards, while Caleb's helping Simon dismantle the decorations.

'Tash,' I say, clumsily, glancing over my shoulder to check nobody's hovering behind us, 'who's Andrea?'

The stack of paper bowls in her hand goes limp as she stares at me. 'Have you been talking to Sarah Meadows?'

'No, I—'

'Where did you hear that name, then?' she says. Her eyes have gone weak and watery. In this moment, she looks utterly broken – and it breaks me to see it. My instinct is to put my arms around her, but I have a sense she'd shake me off. Her sadness has a particularly angry edge to it.

I'm unsure how to answer without revealing our presence in the garden earlier. For some reason, I can't bring myself to confess we heard the whole thing. Probably because right now, she doesn't seem as though she'd take it too well.

Luckily, her question seems to be rhetorical. 'I don't want to talk about it, Lucy.'

'I just want to know if you're okay—'

'I'm okay. We're okay. But please don't say her name again. I mean it.'

Go

Tash and I agreed beforehand, over a series of scantly worded messages, that we wouldn't sit down to talk until after Dylan's birthday party was over. Fortunately, the abundance of people makes it fairly easy to avoid her until Dylan's safely in bed being read to by Simon, and Tash is leading me to the new garden office she's had built beneath the silver birch at the end of her garden. It's so far from the house I have to squint to see it at first.

215

Surprisingly large inside, the space is simply furnished, with a desk, printer, pot plant and bookshelf, and a sofa with two matching chairs arranged around a dormant wood burner. The air is thick with the lingering scent of damp grass and the freshly cut timber of the roof and walls. There are several monochrome canvases of Tash, Simon and Dylan on display, grinning between various poses, the best shots from a photography session Mum got Tash for Christmas last year.

I'm not sure if Tash sees me smiling sourly at the sight of them, but she passes me a throw (cashmere, of course – 'In case you get chilly'), then gestures for me to sit. I take the sofa next to the glass wall facing the garden, so she perches on a chair, tucking her feet up beneath her like a child. She's wrapped herself up in a vast black cardigan that comes down to her knees, completely covering the minuscule silver playsuit she's been wearing all day. I'm relieved, since this means I no longer have to look at her bare skin and picture Max stroking it, or take in the sight of her trim legs and imagine them wrapped around him.

Still, Mum was right. She has lost weight, an alarming amount. Her clothes are so big on her now she looks like a child playing dress-up.

'Thank you for coming,' she ventures, our eyes locking properly for the first time since she door-stepped me two months ago. 'I know how hard it must have been for you.'

'Well, I'm glad I did.'

Her expression lifts. 'That's good.'

'Dylan's . . . None of this is his fault.'

She swallows. 'No. He wasn't even born when all this happened.'

I nod agreement.

'And . . . thanks for his present,' she says. 'You really didn't have to spend that much.'

I bought Dylan a pricey box of Lego in my lunch hour on Thursday, barely even looking at what was in it, just wanting to get him the best set I could to make up for not having seen him for so long.

'Do you want me to explain more about that night?' Tash says. 'Or—'

I shake my head.

'Would it help if I told you . . . I know how you feel?'

I frown at her, confused. 'Well, unless I've somehow slept with Simon without realising, I don't think you do, actually.'

'Simon had a one-night stand,' she says, quietly. 'Just before Christmas, the year we got married. A woman called Andrea. She worked with him.'

I stare at her. Simon, Dylan's father? The most passive, harmless man I know? 'But you'd only been married—'

'Five months.' She nods. 'Yep.'

I want to say I'm sorry, but the words won't come. So instead, I just say, 'Oh. Right.'

'Simon changed jobs not long afterwards. And somehow, we got through it. We went to therapy. We're still going, actually. Although . . .' She trails off, looks down. 'People still gossip. I overheard someone saying her name earlier, and it was all I could do not to . . .' She shakes her head. 'But I didn't want to cause a scene, do anything to make you think coming here today was a mistake.'

I lift the cashmere throw from my knees. It's humid in here, the air still hot from the mini-heatwave of the last few days. Or maybe it's just the years of unspoken betrayal simmering between us. 'Why . . . Why are you telling me this? It's hardly the same.'

'No, but I guess I wanted to say . . . that good people can do awful things, sometimes, Lucy.'

'I'm confused. Who's the good person here? You? Andrea?'

She flinches slightly as I say her name. 'I just mean people can make mistakes, sometimes. That's all.'

'But you're my *sister*, Tash,' I say, surprised that I'm managing to stay relatively composed. 'Do you know what it *means* that you did that to me?'

'Believe me, I do, and I'll never stop questioning why I did what I did.' Her eyes fill with tears, her voice cracking and wobbling. 'But I want you to know . . . I'm not going anywhere. You can be as angry as you need to be, and I'll *never* stop trying to make it up to you.'

'If it wasn't for Dylan—'

'If Dylan ends up being the only reason we stay in each other's lives, then . . . well, he's even more of an angel than I thought.'

I think about Nate, about how I'd probably never have met him if Tash and Max hadn't got together that night. I consider telling Tash about him now – describing my experience in full and chilling detail, to make her feel even worse. She doesn't know. I've never told her. Only Jools knows the truth.

But I won't. I can't. Somehow, I can sense that blurting it all out in bitterness wouldn't bring me satisfaction.

'I've not been able to stop picturing it,' I say instead, pulling my arms tight to my body. 'You and him.'

'I know,' she whispers, wiping her eyes. 'I was the same, with Andrea.'

'Please don't compare that with this. It's different.'

She breaks my gaze, then releases a breath, rubs at an invisible mark on her ankle. 'I know. Sorry.'

A silence descends, so uncomfortable it makes me feel queasy.

'Have you spoken to Max?' she asks, eventually.

'No point. I have to pick between you and him, don't I?'

She seems to consider this for a moment. 'I don't see why.'

'Because I can't have both of you back in my life. How exactly would that work?'

'Well—'

'Family gatherings? Exchanging presents at Christmas? Making small talk over Sunday lunch? Getting rounds in on birthdays? Come on. Be real.'

Tash leans in, the lick of her blond bob bouncing in the lamplight. 'I never thought I'd be able to so much as kiss Simon again, let alone let him touch me. But over time . . . you *can* get past stuff you thought was impossible, Luce.'

'Really? Or are you just trying to appease your own conscience?'

She swallows, hard. 'Actually, nothing would appease my conscience about this. Apart from maybe the ability to turn back time.'

I find myself staring dazedly down at her perfectly pedi-cured feet as a breeze skirts the windows and roof, slides between the leaves of the trees.

There's a long silence before she speaks again. Her scarlet lipstick is now little more than a raspberry-coloured smear, like she's overdone it on the jam sand-wiches. She looks sorry, and slight, and full of regret. 'You still love him, don't you?' she says. 'Max. You still adore him.'

Now, I do start to cry. 'I shouldn't. What kind of person does that make me?' *Weak,* sneers a voice in my head. *Pathetic. Foolish.*

'Max is the one for you,' Tash whispers. 'Anyone can see it. And you'll never know how much it kills me, Lucy, that I have might have destroyed that for ever.'

I realise now there's nothing more to say. That it all comes down to a simple choice: move forward with my life, or stay still and let this crush me.

The following morning, I conclude my long drive home from Shoreley by pulling up outside Max's flat, my heart thrashing, barely able to believe what I'm about to do.

I get out of the car and walk unsteadily up the front path and into his storm porch, where I press the buzzer firmly before I can change my mind.

There's an agonising wait before it clicks. 'Hello?' He barely enunciates, mumbling the word like he's only just got out of bed.

'Max,' I say. 'It's—'

What Might Have Been

My words are buried in a buzz before I can finish, and in the next moment he's standing in front of me, grey eyes wide and his body quite still, like he's trying to remember how to breathe.

'I'm literally amazed you're here,' he says, once we're sitting in his living room. He's barefoot in shorts and a T-shirt, hair careless and eyes a little bloodshot. His skin looks rough and his cheeks are pinched, like he's spent the past three months subsisting on little more than coffee and a punishing workload, much like me.

One end of the sofa is strewn with documents and open files – piles of Land Registry reports and oversized papers that look like title deeds. His laptop's open next to them, and there are a couple of large Starbucks cups on the coffee table.

The room is warm from the morning sun, light striping our skin through the angled shutters.

'Me too, actually.'

He laughs, even though what I've said isn't remotely funny, and puts up a hand to rub his chin. His usually clean-shaven jawline is grainy with stubble. He looks slightly more muscular, too, than the last time I saw him – not much, but enough for me to notice, like he's been putting in extra hours at the gym. 'So . . . how come you are?'

The truth is that missing him has just become too hard, but I won't tell him that. 'I spoke to Tash,' I say.

A cautious nod. 'How'd it go?'

'We're going to try to . . . work things out. For Dylan's sake.'

'That's really great, Luce.' His voice is full, sincere.

'So . . . how've you been?' I ask, sipping the tea he's made me.

He rubs his jaw again. 'Not great.'

'How's work?'

'Busy. You?'

'Same. I haven't stopped, these past few months.'

'Helps, doesn't it?'

I try out a smile. 'Yep. Thank God we didn't work together.'

He smiles back, but in a way that doesn't quite reach his eyes. 'Actually . . . I don't really want to talk about work.'

I nod, because neither do I.

'I miss you, Luce. I meant what I said in my message. I'd do anything to have you back in my life.'

A small storm of tears starts to gather behind my eyes, but I make an effort to hold it back. 'Tash told me . . . Simon cheated on her, a few years ago. They . . . went to therapy, sorted everything out.'

'Do you want to go to therapy?' he says quickly.

I shake my head. 'I can't think of anything worse.'

Max leans forward, forehead crumpled in earnest, the deep grey of his irises seeming somehow to intensify. 'So . . . ?'

'It just made me think that maybe we have to . . . make a choice. A conscious decision to live with what happened, and try to move past it. If that's what you want.'

He closes his eyes momentarily, as though, in a twist of irony, a jury's declared him not guilty of some terrible crime. 'That's *all* I want. It's the only thing I've been able to think about.'

The relief when he says this feels like hitting air after being underwater.

Max comes over to the sofa, sits down next to me and takes my hand. 'I realise I don't deserve this. Or you.'

I look down at his fingers wrapping mine. I can feel a pulse passing between them like a current. 'I know you're sorry. And I know how bad Tash feels, too.'

'The only thing I care about,' he whispers, putting his face to the base of my neck, his breath dancing over my skin, 'is that you feel able to trust me again.'

'We have to take it slow.'

'As slow as you want.' His voice wavers like he's going to beat me to the tears. 'I'm just so happy you're here.'

We've talked all day, not even pausing to eat, and it must be late now because it's dark outside. My mouth is dry and tacky, a headache taking root inside my skull.

Max has closed the shutters. The living room is lit only by a single floor lamp, and I'm struggling to fully make out his features or the expression on his face, since he's sitting back in the armchair near the fireplace, a couple of metres between us. But I can decipher the inflexions of his sentences, the pauses he leaves between words, sentiments all of their own.

'Do you want to talk about Tash?' he asks at one point, because we still haven't.

'No,' I reply, honestly. 'You?'

He shakes his head. 'No.'

From outside the bay window drifts the rattle of a taxi idling, then a door slamming, followed by a snatch of laughter that I want to grab onto, try to absorb some-how. I'm not actually sure if I've laughed properly since May.

'You were right earlier,' Max says, swilling tea that must be cold by now around the bottom of his cup. 'About making a choice. A conscious decision.'

I nod. 'I used to think you were . . . The One, you know? My soulmate. That we were destined to be together, or something.'

'And now?'

'I'm not sure I believe in that any more. Maybe . . . we're a good match, but it's still down to us what we do with that. Not fate, or destiny, or some higher power. Maybe what actually happens is, you meet someone, you fall in love, and you do everything you can to make it work.'

I think about what Tash said to me last night, about Simon and Andrea. *Good people can do awful things. You* can *get past stuff you thought was impossible, Luce.*

Max seems to reflect on this for a moment or two, and I can't tell if he's offended, confused, or a little of both. 'Can I be brutally honest?'

'From now on, let's only be that.'

'Okay. Well, there've actually been three people in my life who I've had that . . . meant-to-be feeling with.'

I nod, ignoring the brief blaze of jealousy I feel.

'But there's only ever been one person who I don't want to live without.' He clears his throat. 'What I mean is, I agree. I want to work this out, Luce. And I do mean work. Whatever it takes. I love you too much to let this go.'

I glance at him, half-wondering if he might get to his feet, cross the room and kiss me, but he doesn't. He simply looks soberly into the space between us, like we're way out at sea, fighting to keep our heads above water. And in this moment, all I can do is hope with everything I have that we make it back to shore.

12

Stay

I'm in the pub with Emma – the girl from my writing group – and our tutor, Ryan. Over the past few weeks, the three of us have become friends, settling into a routine of post-session drinks to talk writing and books and our passions and life.

'I'm serious,' Emma's saying, driving her index finger down onto the table, as if she's arguing with it and not me.

I laugh. 'I can see that.'

Emma's not laughing. 'But . . . ?'

'I'm not ready,' I say, shrugging.

'Look.' She leans forward, blond hair dangling perilously close to her glass, the threat of a red-wine balayage alarming me momentarily. Our table's next to an open fire-cum-furnace, so the sleeves of her sweater are pushed right up to her elbows, affording her a particularly no-nonsense demeanour. 'If you won't listen to me, at least listen to Ryan. An expert in his field, and all that.'

I glance towards the bar, where Ryan is chatting to two young guys. I guess they're into writing, because they seem to be hanging off his every word, like they've bumped into

Stephen King and not publishing's greatest has-been (Ryan's words, not mine). One of them has a notebook in his hand, and the other is clutching a copy of . . . Oh God. It's *Ulysses*.

Summer has surrendered to autumn's advances now, the greenery turning gold, the air thickening with damp. I always think of Shoreley as a place better suited to cold weather, despite it being somewhere people flock to in summer. To me, the town improves the further you walk from the beach, when you reach the cobblestones and winding back streets, and the medieval houses all lean against one another like they overdid it on the mead, and everywhere is lit up by those old-fashioned street lamps that look like they're straight out of a Dickens adaptation. I think the town's history is at its most beautiful draped in lights and kissed with frost, when all the windows are glowing amber, and everyone's walking around in hats and gloves, clutching hot drinks and taking selfies beneath the stars. I've even surprised myself by getting excited about planning festive displays at Pebbles & Paper, pitching stock ideas to Ivan – seashell wreaths, starfish tree toppers, beach sand baubles – and suggesting we put on a Christmas shopping event, with complimentary mulled wine to tempt in the punters.

'If you edit that chapter any more,' Emma says to me, 'you'll kill it. You'll squeeze all the life out of it. You know I'm right. Tell her, Ryan.'

'Tell who what?' Ryan says, returning to our table with another round of drinks on a tray.

Ryan and Emma have been nagging me to enter my novel into a first chapter competition being run by a major literary prize. The winner gets their chapter published in a glossy magazine, plus a meeting with a senior editor at a big-name publishing house, and a top agent. The deadline's in a week.

Briefly distracted, Emma nods at the drinks, her cheeks pink from the heat of the fire. 'You're such a rock star, Ryan. Did you get those on the house?'

He sits down and distributes our glasses before sipping from his pint. 'Ha. I wish.'

'Did those lads recognise you? Were they angling for a selfie?'

'The guy behind the bar told them I was a bestselling novelist.' He rolls his eyes and shakes his head. 'Christ knows how he knew.'

'Maybe you got a bit braggy one night after too many red wines,' Emma teases, to which Ryan elbows her.

'Must be nice,' I say, nodding over at the lads again. For some reason, I'm desperate for Ryan to have his moment. 'To get recognised for something you've achieved. They looked pretty starstruck.'

He grimaces. 'Yeah, for about two minutes, until I told them I haven't actually been published for seven years. Which to them, of course, is like half a lifetime ago.'

Ryan's told me a few times that he keeps wondering if he dreamed ever having had a book deal – that these days, the closest he gets to feeling like an author is handing out copies of his second and final novel, *The Away Day,* to new members of our writing group, at which point he always has to endure a spell of gentle heckling from Emma.

Ryan looks at Emma now. 'Talked any sense into this one yet?' He means me.

'Nope. She's more stubborn than my nan when we tried to make her wear compression stockings.'

'Lucy,' Ryan says, like he has a million times before, 'it's ready.'

'I just don't feel like it is.'

'But why?'

I think about it. I've been writing my novel for nearly six months now, and although I've almost finished the first draft, I feel as though it's taken me until now to really find my feet with it. I've been writing feverishly and greedily in the beach hut every afternoon, the hours passing by unnoticed, sometimes without looking up until it's dark. I've been lost in a frenzy of compulsion and inspiration, fuelled by coffee and Haribo and not a lot else. It's made me feel more alive creatively than anything else I've ever done – sometimes it even takes me half an hour before I've cleared my head sufficiently to be able to hold a simple conversation with Caleb, the thoughts still hurtling around my mind like the spacecraft in that video game Dylan's so fond of. But I have an almost-finished novel to show for it, and for the first time in my life, I am starting to feel like a writer. I have created something, and stuck with it, even though at times it's felt like an impossible hill to scale. After all this time, I have become reacquainted with my old means of self-expression, the way I used to make sense of the world and my own feelings. Writing this novel has been as cathartic as keeping a journal: I feel lighter after every writing session, as though

I've unburdened myself, upended my mind onto the page. I guess, if I were to be really cheesy about it, I'd say writing was my therapy.

But I still don't feel confident enough to show anyone beyond Caleb and the group yet.

'You need exposure,' Ryan insists.

I sip my lemonade. 'Maybe I'm not ready to be exposed.'

'I'm telling you, you are.'

Emma looks as though she's about to say something smutty, before thinking better of it.

Ryan's not giving up. 'You need to take a risk on this. I promise it'll pay off. This could be one of those conversations you look back on when you're a bestselling novelist. You know: "I almost didn't enter the competition, but my incredibly talented writing tutor, Ryan Carwell—"'

'"And my friend Emma Deacon, herself a literary star in the making . . ."' Emma chips in.

I shake my head. 'Why don't you two enter, then?'

'You can't be previously published,' says Ryan, with a shrug I'd interpret as smug if I didn't already know he doesn't have a smug bone in his body.

'Or be really, really bad at first chapters,' Emma says, wrinkling her nose. 'Whereas you, on the other hand . . .'

Ryan turns to me. 'Do me a favour and become a literary sensation. And I do mean favour: I could really do with the career boost.'

'Very funny,' I say with a smile, shaking my head.

★   ★   ★

Caleb's working late tonight, so after finishing my drink and promising the others I'll think seriously about the competition, I head over to his studio.

It's a chilly October night, feathered with the scent of wood burners and the promise of winter. My breath becomes wisps in the air as I walk, salt clinging to my skin from the onshore breeze. The cobblestones carry a cool sheen, the air around the street lamps opaque with the finest of mists.

As I approach Caleb's studio, I slow my pace. He's standing outside, embracing a tall, dark-haired woman I'd recognise anywhere.

As they're pulling away from their hug, he spots me. Following his gaze, Helen turns. I can't tell from here if she's smiling – I'm rooted to the spot about a hundred metres away – but if I had to guess, I'd say her expression remains steady, unyielding and entirely unflustered.

Caleb calls my name, but I've already turned and started walking away.

'Lucy.' I hear his footsteps behind me. 'Lucy.' He grabs my arm, pulls me to a halt.

I turn to face him, but say nothing. He urges me a few steps further along the street, presumably to escape earshot of his wife.

'Lucy . . . it's not how it looks,' he says, his breath like hot smoke in the air between us.

The cliché is so bad, I have to resist the urge to wince.

Caleb sighs, glances down at his feet. 'As in, she just showed up.'

'Right.'

'I had no idea she was coming.'

I nod again, more tightly this time. 'What does she want?'

'Just to talk.'

I'm not too sure why that had to involve bodily contact – especially considering he's always claimed things weren't amicable between them – but I say nothing further. It's up to him to explain, not me to ask.

'Listen.' I can tell he wants to take my hand, but is sensing I might snatch it away. 'Would it bother you . . . if Helen and I went and got a bite to eat?'

I swallow, feeling my stomach tip and pitch. *Yes, it would bother me. Why is she really here? What is her game, showing up out of the blue like this?*

I glance over Caleb's shoulder back towards her. She's not even looking at us, is staring down at her phone instead, her face made ghoulish from the blue light of the screen. Her lack of interest fits perfectly with the mental image I have of her – high-flying, someone utterly unaccustomed to hearing the word *no*. You don't rise to the top of magazine publishing hierarchy without having a shard of ice somewhere inside you. I picture her at work in the West End – a corner office, floor-to-ceiling glass – with assistants running around after her as she stalks between appointments and meetings, yelling at people to *just get it done*.

Does her indifference mean she has no interest in Caleb, or that she sees me as entirely inconsequential?

'I thought you said things weren't amicable between you,' I say, folding my arms, already resenting him for turning me into someone with suspicions, a role I have no interest in playing. I think slightly bitterly back to what my sister said about him the first time they met, back in June: *He just seems like someone who ... wouldn't be into playing games.*

'They're not, particularly. But ... we've got stuff to discuss, and I've not eaten, so ...' He puts a hand to the back of his neck. 'Can we meet at the cottage, later?'

I wrinkle my nose. What could be more pathetic than waiting at my boyfriend's house for him to get home from dinner with his wife? 'No, I'll stay at Tash's tonight. Call me tomorrow.'

'Luce.' And now he does grab my hand, before I can walk away. 'I swear, this is just ... business.'

Business? Stuff to discuss? Is he being deliberately evasive, or is he trying to protect my feelings? Does business mean divorce? And isn't that what solicitors are for?

Maybe it's just a clumsy choice of words, but calling it *business* seems slightly disingenuous. Because since when was having dinner with your wife to discuss your divorce devoid of all emotion, something towards which you have no significant feelings at all?

I'm half-expecting him to try to kiss me, but he doesn't. He just squeezes my hand, then lets it gently drop before walking back along the cobblestones towards her.

Go

Max has joined me and a group of people from Supernova for after-work drinks. It's not often he finishes early enough, so I felt my pulse quicken with excitement when I saw him walking into the bar earlier. I still feel that way every time I catch sight of him, even after all these years.

The bar is a favourite of Zara's (she's related in some way to the owner, I think) and is popular with the advertising and media crowd. It's one of those underground places with a secret door, so dark inside you can barely see. As a rule, I hate spaces without windows and an obvious escape route, but if Zara suggests somewhere, you don't chip in with an alternative.

I've been here once or twice before. Because the room is so small, it always feels rammed, thus perpetuating its exclusive, popular vibe. You end up feeling almost lucky to be here, which is ridiculous. It's just a bar.

'Lucy tells me you're in property litigation,' Zara says to Max, once I've introduced him to everyone. He's just bought a round, which has made all eleven people in this corner of the room fall a little bit in love with him.

'I am, for my sins,' he says, with a friendly wink.

'You might be able to help me, then.'

'I can certainly try.'

'My neighbours. Nightmare couple. They're building an *annexe*,' Zara says, in the same way most people would say *sex dungeon*. 'I've seen the plans. Completely unnecessary, and a hideous eyesore. It's going to take all the light from my kitchen.'

Max clears his throat politely. 'Okay. Sometimes that's more of a planning issue, but it depends on—'

'Tell me about it.' Zara leans forward, martini in hand. Her chunky gold bracelet keeps banging against our table, and she's wearing a navy-blue jumpsuit that on anyone else would look prison-issue, but on her resembles something at the top of a magazine trendometer. 'Who *are* these jokers at the council? I objected, but they granted it anyway.' She shakes her head. 'They're building it for their teenage devil children, who are only going to use the thing to snort drugs and play loud music. Nothing you can do? Send them a threatening letter, or something?'

People do this a lot to Max – imagine they can engage him over a swift half down the pub. I smile into my Virgin Mary. It's the drink I order more often than not these days, because it reminds me so much of seeing Max that night in The Smugglers, when he appeared outside the window and back in my life.

He asks Zara some questions, starts talking about the enforceability of restrictive covenants. Zara, eager, gets out her phone. I appreciate the effort Max is making: he could so easily have dismissed her, spelt out in no uncertain terms that her complaint is legally baseless – but he knows how important Supernova is to me, and how eager I am to earn brownie points with the toughest woman in the world to impress.

Phoebe, my deskmate, leans over. She's wearing a headband and crop-top – the weather never seems to be a factor when she's choosing what to wear – and I envy her easy confidence. She called a member of senior management *dude* in a meeting last week and he blushed more than she did. 'Anyone in for karaoke later?'

As Zara gives Phoebe a look I can only describe as withering, I smile. 'Unless Max is keen, I think we'll—'

'Actually,' he says, 'I wouldn't mind blowing off some steam.'

I stare at him. Back in the day, we always used to laugh at karaoke, maybe even feel a little smug that we didn't have to get up on stage to prove we lacked inhibition. 'Really?'

'What's your song?' Kris asks him.

'"Wonderwall",' Max says, without missing a beat.

Kris looks surprised. 'Huh. I'd have had you down as more of a "My Way" kind of guy.'

I meet Max's eye and smile. He used to sing 'Wonderwall' to me at uni, whenever it came on in a bar or at a gig, and every time he did, my whole body hummed with happiness.

It's been just over a month since I agreed to try again with Max, to put the past behind us. We didn't even kiss before I left his flat that night, but forty-eight hours later, I called him, suggested a supper club Jools had recommended. The idea of eating around a table with strangers appealed to me – I thought it might be a simple way to ease back into each other's lives without the pressure of a one-to-one meal, or the temptation of jumping into bed together if we spent our first night hanging out at home.

In the end, though, I realised I hadn't fully thought it through – we had to answer lots of awkward questions about where we'd met and how long we'd been together. Still, it served as an ice-breaker, and we did meet some interesting people, including a weather presenter whom

Max and I both half-recognised, and a former X-Factor contestant, whom we definitely didn't.

The idea of being physically intimate with Max again felt a bit like approaching the top of a rollercoaster. My biggest fear was that Tash would rear up in my mind like a jack-in-the-box whenever he tried to touch me. But in the end, it didn't work out that way. After supper, Max and I went back to mine, our nerves slightly quelled by the preceding hours of conversation. And that first kiss, which I initiated, on the doorstep, felt entirely natural, like something I'd been craving after many weeks of abstinence. In fact, I was surprised by how hungry I felt for him, by how much I wanted to go straight upstairs and start where we'd left off three months earlier.

Once we were in my bed, Max let me lead, and for the first few minutes I imagined we were back at university, on that very first night before we went home for Christmas. I pretended we were starting all over again, that the past had been erased. And then my body took over, the pleasurable twitch of muscle memory, and everything felt better than even I had thought possible. Afterwards, we lay naked on the bed together, breathing hard, the curtains still open, listening to the sound of kids passing by on the street below, swearing and shouting and laughing through the single glazing. And I felt strangely at ease, like I'd just found the missing last piece to a jigsaw that had been driving me crazy.

Since then, we've been a little stop-start. I know Max wants me to set the pace, to say how often I want to see him, to suggest the things I fancy doing. Which is thoughtful of him, and in some ways helpful. But sometimes I just want to pretend the whole Tash thing never happened – I definitely don't want to discuss it any more than we already have – and I think Max is aiming for some kind of middle ground that doesn't really exist.

The worst part has been wondering what everyone else thinks. Only Jools and my immediate family know the true reason behind our temporary split, and when we're out with friends or colleagues, I occasionally catch a sideways glance, an uncertain smile. Like they're thinking, *Who cheated on whom? Is he bad in bed? Is she actually really boring? Is he an unbearable snob?*

I try not to think too hard about what they'd say if they knew the truth.

On the pavement outside the karaoke club, I dither for a moment. For some reason, I feel nervous about going inside. Maybe it's the prospect of another dark space with no windows, being crammed into one of those hot, airless booths together. I don't want to take the risk.

'You okay?' Max asks, as I hesitate, watching the others go in ahead of us.

We could just go home, I think. Zara's gone back to Highgate. Everyone's drunk already. I wouldn't be letting anyone down.

'Come on. Let me be all cheesy and bellow "Wonderwall" at you.'

I smile and squeeze his hand, because to be honest, that's an offer that's hard to resist. So I take a breath and follow him inside.

As we're waiting to be shown to our booth, my gaze is drawn to a tall, dark-haired figure in front of us. He's with another group, and I can only see him from the side, but he looks horrifyingly familiar. Same slim build and pale shirt. A demeanour rippling with confidence, a self-possession that chills me. He's only a couple of metres away. He could turn, and . . .

I feel for a moment as though someone's clamped their hand across my mouth. My body goes stiff and rigid, skin prickling all over like I've been pushed into nettles. If a fire broke out now, I wouldn't be able to flee. My pulse becomes an urgent, fluid rush between my ears.

Nate.

No. It can't be.

Nate. He's here. He's found you.

Finally, I force my body to move, and in the next moment I'm back out on the street. Heaving cold air like I've just run the race of my life, I bend over in an effort not to pass out, but my heart is beating so fast, it's touch and go.

Feeling a hand on my back, I jump, before realising it's Max.

'Luce? You okay?'

'Sorry,' I gasp. I'm ridiculously relieved to see him, like I've just woken up from a nightmare.

'God, what's wrong? You've gone grey.'

It takes me a couple of moments to find the words. 'I just saw someone in there who . . .'

He waits, but I can't say it.

'Someone you know?' he prompts.

I shake my head. 'Someone who . . .' *Maybe it's time to finally tell him.*

I must look quite ill, because Max doesn't ask any more questions. He just removes his coat and wraps it around me – it's only now I realise my teeth are chattering – and orders us a cab.

13

Stay

'What – so you actually saw them hugging?'
I frown, nod. 'Yep.'

I'm with Tash in her kitchen, the morning after seeing Helen and Caleb embracing outside his studio. I've been reading through the latest hard copy of my manuscript since dawn, scribbling all over it with red pen. I've realised recently that whenever anything's troubling me – no matter how serious, or trivial – delving into my writing has become my way to deal with it. Or not deal with it, depending on how you look at things. Anyway, it helps, being able to lose myself in something. Whatever's playing on my mind, I always end up finding some version of it somewhere on the page.

The kitchen is bright with chilly light and filled with those homely start-of-the-day scents – browned toast and brewed coffee and freshly laundered clothes. Simon and Dylan have already left the house, and now it's just me and Tash, grabbing half an hour together before she's due in at the office and I open up at Pebbles & Paper.

'Did Caleb call you, afterwards?'

I smile, grimly. 'Yeah, at one a.m.' I didn't pick up, and he's not sent me a message since. So as to how his dinner went with Helen, I'm still firmly in the dark.

Tash winces. 'Ouch.'

I shake my head. 'I don't know – maybe it was too much to expect, that she'd be out of his life so soon after they split up.'

'What, you think . . . he still has feelings for her?'

The idea of Caleb rediscovering his love for Helen at dinner last night – laughing at her jokes, flirting through dessert, not wanting to leave the restaurant – makes my chest contract and my heart spin. 'I didn't think so, but . . . he messaged me at one o'clock. So they must have gone out for drinks, and . . .' I sigh. 'Who knows? Maybe.'

This is what comes, I think grimly, *of risking your heart with someone who seems too good to be true.*

'You could check his phone.'

I laugh, glumly. 'Come on.'

She shrugs. 'Why not?'

'If you reach that point, you're better off not being together at all, aren't you?'

Tash swallows, then looks down at her hands, spins her wedding ring a couple of times. 'I don't know. Sometimes . . . if you just need that reassurance . . .'

For some reason, the expression on her face takes me back to the argument she and Simon had in the garden at Dylan's birthday party.

'Tash,' I say, softly, though my heart is thundering. 'Did Simon cheat on you?'

What Might Have Been

She waits for what seems like minutes before answering, her forehead creasing like a mask beginning to crack. 'Yes. Once. With this woman called Andrea, a few months after we got married. She worked with him.'

I swear under my breath, grab her hands across the top of the kitchen island. 'God, Tash . . . why didn't you tell me?'

'I was ashamed,' she admits, her voice suddenly reed-thin. Her hands are quivering slightly. 'It was embarrassing. We were newlyweds. I felt humiliated. I just wanted to pretend it had never happened.'

I think of what she just said, about checking Caleb's phone. 'You don't think Simon's still—'

'No.' She shakes her head. 'We worked it out. We got through it. And I actually think it was the right thing at the time, not telling you, or Mum, or anyone, because . . . Simon's the most amazing dad to Dylan, and he's a really brilliant husband, and . . . we chose to make it work, Luce. And every day, I'm glad we did.'

I'm pleased to hear her say that, obviously, but I'm not sure what she thinks that means for me. 'So, what – if something's happened between Caleb and Helen you think I should just . . . be cool with it?'

'Of course not. But you can be in charge of how you deal with it.' Her frown deepens a little. 'You know, this is why I never really bought into that whole soulmates idea, Luce. I think love is a choice, not a feeling. I think it's something you have to work really hard at.'

I smile faintly. 'Didn't you say a girl at your work read a magazine article about soulmates that sounded terrifically convincing?'

She shrugs softly, like everything I've just told her has put paid to that brief dalliance with sentimentality. 'Must have just got caught up in the moment.'

I might not align with my sister's pragmatic approach to love, but I have to admit, it does all sound impressively mature. I squeeze her hands. 'It's amazing. That you could forgive Simon, move past it.' It would be hard to argue that this wasn't a good thing – because if she hadn't, Dylan wouldn't exist.

'Don't get me wrong,' she says quickly, not quite meeting my eye. 'If he'd had a long-term affair, that would have been different. But I'm hardly perfect myself. I've done my fair share of . . . crappy things in the past. I guess I just tried to remember that . . . people make mistakes, you know? Good people can do bad things sometimes. Life isn't black and white. It's a million shades of grey, except nobody seems to accept that these days.'

'So what you're saying is, don't be too hard on Caleb?'

'Well, hear what he's got to say at least, then go from there.' She looks up at me, eyes suddenly shining with sentiment. 'I love you, Luce. I'm so lucky to have you.'

To my surprise, she starts to cry. It must be the emotion of talking about Simon and Andrea, so I go over and wrap my arms around her, kiss her hair and tell her I love her too.

Shortly before lunch, the door to Pebbles & Paper jangles, and Caleb walks in.

It's been a slow morning – so far, I've sold only some deckchair-shaped candles and a handful of greetings cards

– and I'd just got to the point of starting to scribble notes for my novel onto the back of the complimentary gift wrap.

'Hey.'

I swallow as I try to work out if he looks as though he's spent the night having sex with his estranged wife. He certainly seems tired and wrung-out, like he needs some coffee and a plate of food.

'You're barred, you know,' I remind him, as a sort of joke. (It's true – he actually is. On my first day, Ivan handed me a sheet of paper bearing the names of six people no longer welcome in the shop, one of whom was Caleb – though quite how he expects me to ascertain the full names of the offenders on sight, I have no idea.)

'I literally could not care less.' Caleb stands where he is in the middle of the shop, next to the sheepskin soft furnishings, hands stuffed into the pockets of his charcoal wool coat. His hair looks damp, and I realise with a thud that he must have had a late start. 'How are you?'

I nod, slowly. 'Okay. You?'

He nods back, his expression sombre. 'Can we talk?'

'I get off at one.'

'Meet me at the beach hut?'

'All right,' I say, realising as I do that he could be about to break my heart. That he might tell me he slept with Helen last night, that they're getting back together, that splitting up with her and being with me has all been a horrible mistake – a mere bump in the road on his journey through married life.

* * *

When I get to the hut after my shift, Caleb's lit the stove and boiled a kettle. I sit wordlessly down on the seat opposite him, and he passes me a coffee.

'You had a good night, then,' I say, my voice heavy with resignation.

'What makes you say that?'

I shrug. I know I risk sounding petty, but I can't help myself. 'One o'clock's pretty good going.'

He just nods, like he's conceding some sort of point, and sips his coffee. 'It was . . . a weird night.'

I don't say anything, just watch him and wait. I'm not going to help him out here – he has to start talking, to be straight-up with me about whatever went down between them.

He pauses for a long time before elaborating. 'Helen . . . wants me to move back in with her, in London.'

My stomach becomes a fist. 'Oh.'

I feel his gaze barrel into me. 'Lucy, you need to know, I told her straight away that I was in love with you. That that's *never* going to happen.'

Relief radiates through me like some sort of narcotic. Still, I can't help thinking there must be more to the story than that. 'That sounds like a pretty quick conversation, though. What took you till one o'clock?'

'She was upset. We went back to the cottage.'

I picture them there together, in the tiny wonky living room I've grown to love. Did Helen crack open a bottle of wine, put his favourite music on to tempt him to reminisce? Maybe under that coat she was wearing a dress he always liked. Or worse . . .

'But you're separated,' I say, exasperation flickering

inside me like a failing light bulb. 'You moved out, you live two hours from London now. Have you been . . . ?'

'Have I been what?'

I frown, clamp my hands a little tighter around my coffee cup. 'I don't know – giving her a different impression, or something? I didn't think you were in touch.'

'We weren't. I promise, this came totally out of the blue.'

'She just . . . changed her mind about being separated? Just like that?'

'She says she's been seeing a therapist about . . . the kids issue. She thinks she's ready to face the idea of a future without them, now.'

I feel my heart climb up my throat and into my mouth. 'Caleb.'

'What?'

'Were you two . . . on a break?'

'*No.*' His eyes widen in alarm. 'We'd split up. The next step, as far as I was concerned, was divorce.'

I shake my head. 'So now what?'

'I told her nothing's changed. That I love *you.*'

Despite his reassurance, I feel guilt pressing irrationally against my chest – as though perhaps I've come between them, got in the way of something good. Maybe it's actually Helen and Caleb who are meant to be – not us. I find myself wondering if the right thing to do would in fact be to tell Caleb to go back to her, to give his marriage another try. Isn't that what marriage means, after all? For better or worse. The rough with the smooth. Wouldn't *that* be the right thing to do?

The words pop and fizz on my tongue. But then

something far more pressing comes out instead. 'She stayed over, didn't she?'

He waits a long time before answering. 'Yes. But ... I slept on the sofa.'

I shake my head. 'Wow.'

From the roof of the beach hut, we hear the thud of a seagull alighting, triggering an abrasive chorus from other birds nearby. They sound furious, somehow. Or maybe I'm just projecting.

'I *swear* to you, nothing happened.' Anguish is etched across Caleb's face. 'It was just ... at one in the morning, there wasn't really any other option.'

I stare at him, my mind in limbo. I so desperately want to believe him, but ... am I just being gullible, idiotically naive? 'I saw you hugging her, at the studio.'

He works his jaw for a moment or two. 'I know. She'd been crying, and she asked me for a hug. It would have felt ... I don't know. Cold-hearted to say no.'

I sip my coffee. 'Did you ask her where she was staying, before you took her out drinking?'

'She said she had a room at a B&B. And I didn't "take her out drinking".'

'An imaginary B&B?'

He nods, softly. 'I guess she thought the evening would go differently to how it did.'

'Did she try to kiss you?' Helen's unquestionably beautiful, and apparently desperate to have him back. I can hardly bear to ask, but I can't believe she wouldn't have tried her luck, even once.

He swears softly, runs a hand through his hair. 'Yes.'

I feel my stomach clench. 'So when you said nothing happened, what you meant was, something happened.'

'No,' he counters. His eyes are urgent, filmy with distress. 'She tried to kiss me and I pushed her away. We *didn't kiss*, Lucy.'

'God, how would you feel? If this was me and Max?'

He looks down at his hands, shakes his head. 'Well, I'd want to punch him, obviously.'

'Constructive.'

He looks up. 'What do you want me to say? Obviously, I could – *should* – have played things better last night. I should have told her to go home as soon as she turned up. But . . . I never once gave her mixed signals, or any reason to think I was even slightly interested in getting back together. I'm sorry this all had to happen, but maybe . . . Maybe she's got closure now. I probably should have done this a long time ago, if I'm honest.'

'How have you left it?' I say, trying to ignore the gnawing sensation in my stomach as I picture Helen making one last lunge for him on the doorstep this morning before speeding back off to London in her Porsche.

'I've told her I want a divorce. Me and Helen . . . we're over. It's you I want, Lucy. No one else.'

I don't say anything. On the one hand, I want yesterday not to have happened at all – but at the same time, perhaps he's right. Maybe she'll have closure now.

I think about my sister again. If she can get over Simon having had a one-night stand, then shouldn't I be able to surmount Caleb having given his wife the brush-off – however clumsily?

Caleb sets down his coffee, then crosses the hut and gets to his knees in front of me. 'My life with you, here, is *ten times* what it was with Helen.' He dips his head to kiss the knot of my hands, clasped together in my lap. 'This is how love is *meant* to feel, Lucy. What we have. You and me.'

I know he's right, when he says that: that this is how love is meant to feel. I've known it the whole time we've been together – that being with Caleb feels like walking into a lit room after too long spent stumbling around in the dark.

But I still can't help feeling a ripple of unease pass through me, like the lights might blow at any moment, and I'll be left in the dark once again.

Go

Max and I don't speak at all between leaving the karaoke bar and arriving back in Tooting. He just holds my hand in the cab, and I turn my head away from him, letting a few tears fall, smearing the window with my breath.

How can I still feel this terrified, so many years later?

Back at the house, we head upstairs, where I take off my shoes and Max's coat and climb onto my bed, pulling my feet up beneath me. The heating's on and the room is warm – which I'm grateful for, because I still feel cold from the shock of having encountered Nate's doppelganger.

There are people downstairs in the living room. I can hear Reuben talking over everyone, and that honking seal-laugh Sal does when she's stoned, or drunk. They're play-ing music, and the bass snakes up through the ceiling and into the space between us, along with a ripe twist of weed. Their presence down there is comforting, reassuring.

Jools is out tonight, seeing Vince. She might break it off. After a promising start involving late-night conversations, flowers to the house and all the hallmarks of him having good manners, it's not been going well. He keeps telling her he wants to take things to the next level – whatever that means – then failing to reply to her messages, sometimes for days at a time.

Max sits in the chair next to the fireplace. 'What happened back there?'

I realise I'm still leaking tears. I reach over to my night-stand for a tissue, and wipe them away with a shaking hand. Max is watching me, his face distorted with concern.

Jools is the only person I've ever told. A part of me wishes she was here right now, holding my hand.

'It's something . . . and it's nothing. I mean it's bad, but my mind plays tricks on me. Sometimes I wonder if I'm overreacting. I mean, I'm alive—'

'Alive?' Max looks alarmed. 'You need to tell me what's going on, Luce. Right now.'

So I swallow, then start to talk.

It was nearly ten years ago. Since Boxing Day, I'd been travelling through Europe, Morocco, Thailand and Malaysia after leaving university in Norwich, with Australia my final stop. In March I landed in Sydney, with plans to stay in Australia for a while, then move on to New Zealand and after that, North America.

It was my first night in Australia. What an idiot.

There are some people in this world whose charm is undoubtedly pathological. Max has charm and charisma in abundance, but he also has a good heart. The best heart.

But Nate's charm, when I look back now, was nothing more than a chilling, brilliant performance.

He must have followed me, I realised later. I couldn't have made a more perfect target, walking alone from the backpackers' hostel to the Opera Bar, where I planned to take some selfies. I was checking my phone for directions the whole way.

Tash had set dinner up for me with a friend and her husband for the following evening, but that first night was mine to enjoy.

It had been an overcast, humid day. The bar was crowded, thick with bodies. I ordered a drink and after managing to bag one of the last available seats right next to the water, started flipping through a guidebook. Yes, I literally did that. I must have looked the picture of innocence. It could only have been more obvious if I'd had *MUG* scrawled across my forehead in lipstick.

'Erin, is it?'

For a moment I didn't react, but when the shadow by my seat failed to move, I looked up. He was handsome as a movie star – green eyes, dark hair, features so perfect he almost looked unreal, like he'd been CGId into the space next to me.

The worst thing was, I was instantly on my guard. I knew from the start. I *knew*.

And yet, I let him in.

I smiled politely, shook my head. 'Nope.'

'Oh! I'm sorry. You looked like . . .' He shook his head, raised a hand in apology. 'Never mind.'

And right there was his in: he looked so embarrassed, I felt sorry for him. I think he was even blushing slightly – God knows how he pulled that off.

'Meeting someone?' I said, regretting my suspicion.

He looked smart, date-ready, in a light denim shirt, a conspicuous watch peeking out from beneath one cuff. It was the biggest, chunkiest timepiece I'd ever seen, the kind of thing most people would need a small mortgage to afford. He grimaced, lifted his wrist. 'Well, I was. An hour ago. You were my last hope.'

I winced an apology. 'Sorry.'

'No, *I'm* sorry. For disturbing you. Have a great night.'

I watched him head over to the bar, shaking his head, putting one hand to the back of his neck, making a call on his phone. Looking back – because this part remains so clear in my mind to this day – he played the role of the hapless, handsome stranger to perfection.

After twenty minutes or so he passed by my seat again, presumably on his way home. He looked up, snuck me a sheepish expression, paused.

'British?'

I nodded, feeling slightly shy.

He smiled, then hesitated, matching perfectly my timidity. 'My aunt lives in Bath.' (Another genius move: who doesn't love Bath?)

'Oh, really? Bath's lovely.'

'It is.' He hesitated again, as if he was entirely unused to chatting up girls in bars. How the hell did I fall for it? 'Can I . . . get you a drink?'

I have replayed that moment over and over in my mind in the years since it happened. *Say no. Wish him a good night. Get up, walk away and don't look back.* But I didn't, of course. I just felt flattered that this sharply dressed Australian with the killer tan and magnet eyes and kindly auntie in Bath wanted to buy me a drink.

When I asked what he did, he even rummaged in his wallet for a business card, which purported to show he was senior management at a well-known bank. It turned out afterwards, of course, that they'd never heard of a Nathan Drall.

'Call me Nate,' he said.

And not long after that, my memories cut out completely, like he'd knocked me to the ground with a single punch.

I woke the next morning – at least, I assumed it was morning – with a stiff neck and a headache that felt like my skull was being dismantled. I felt disoriented, unable to place where I was.

The room was dark, but it wasn't the hostel. I knew that instinctively. It was too quiet, too still. Too air-conditioned.

Something was wrong. I felt panic scramble up my throat.

And then: the blast of a bell sounding over and over, a discordant jangle so sudden and urgent it sent my heart catapulting from my chest. It took me ten seconds or so to realise a phone was ringing.

'Good morning,' said a smooth voice, when I finally picked up. 'This is a courtesy call to advise you that check-out is eleven a.m.'

Check-out?

I mumbled something, then blinked and hung up, struggled into a sitting position. The pain in my head was getting worse.

A hotel. I was in an enormous bed, the curtains tightly drawn. The room had the hushed, unventilated feel of an airline cabin. I was still fully dressed, in the same clothes I'd been wearing last night.

A chill passed through me.

Nate.

Where was he? Was he still here? Why was *I* here?

I switched on a lamp, scanned the room. It was large and disconcertingly messy – there were empty bottles and glasses on a coffee table, two room service trays. I had no recollection of any of it. I wrinkled my nose and inhaled, maybe for the first time since I'd woken. The air smelt of fried food, and something else. I tried to find my phone, but couldn't see it anywhere.

I climbed out of bed and made my way unsteadily to the bathroom, but the stench made me recoil. The sink was full of vomit.

My panic intensifying now, I ripped the duvet from the bed, upturned cushions, flung open doors and drawers, wrenched the curtains apart. I felt almost dizzy when I looked out of the window – dazzled by the sunshine, confused by the sight of the Opera House sitting calmly across the harbour like nothing had happened.

I stepped back from the view – which ordinarily would have been breathtaking – as though it burnt. My bag – which, the last time I checked, had contained my phone, money, wallet, passport, everything – was gone.

Stupidly, I scanned the room for a note – *There's been a misunderstanding, he's taken my bag by accident, he's just popped out for breakfast and he'll come back soon with croissants and coffee like they do in the films* – before the dark thump of reality struck. Nate was gone, and so was everything else.

I felt so shocked and dazed that I started to wonder if I had somehow acquired a head injury. I chugged a bottle of water, attempted to clean up the bathroom – whose vomit was this? – then headed down to the lobby to check out, vaguely aware that if I just walked out, it might constitute theft of some kind.

I was too embarrassed to say anything, at reception. I just took the bill for the early morning room service and shedload of alcohol I'd apparently ordered, and got out of there.

At first, I thought I'd got so drunk that Nate had checked me in himself then left me there, embarrassed on my behalf. The business card he'd given me was nowhere to be seen, so I couldn't even call him to apologise.

Things got worse when I returned to the hostel. Whoever had stolen my bag had used my room key to steal the stuff I had there, too. The only thing they'd left behind was the notebook under my pillow.

Every cell in my body was screaming to leave the country,

go home, feel safe. So I called Jools. I must have sounded another level of frightened, because we'd barely exchanged more than a couple of sentences before she insisted on booking me a flight home, talked me through getting emergency travel documentation, and said she'd take care of cancelling my cards.

I flinched from the thought of going to the police, the idea of it like pressing bare skin against something hot. Because what, actually, was my story? I had no proof Nate had stolen my things. How could I accuse someone of that, with no memory of it? Maybe I'd just left my bag in the bar. Maybe he'd checked me into that hotel so I'd be safe. I'd clearly been wasted to the point of blacking out. What crime would I even report?

Later, though, I concluded it must have been him. Because my bank account was empty and my credit cards maxed out, and he was the only one who could have discovered my PIN. He must have asked for it while I was hammered – or perhaps he'd watched me use it, at some point during the course of the night.

Anyway, he got lucky, because I used the same number for all three of the cards in my wallet.

It was only a week later, once I was back home in Shoreley, my travels cut short by two months, that Jools asked if I thought Nate had drugged me.

I'd told her all I could remember about him. Which honestly wasn't much. I felt so embarrassed, so naive, so unsure of what had taken place.

But in an instant, what had been baffling and unsettling me for so many days snapped sharply into focus, like wiping dirt from a lens.

'I mean,' Jools said gently, 'you never black out when you drink.'

And she was right. Now that I thought about it, that night with Nate had been the first time I'd ever experienced all my memories cutting off at a certain point. It was so weird, so unlike me.

And right then, in my heart, I knew. Nate had slipped something into my drink.

To this day, I still don't know if we had sex in that room.

I mustered up the strength to visit a clinic, where I got checked out and took a pregnancy test, but everything came back clear. And I never told them the truth.

But once I'd done that, of course, I realised I had to tell the police, because Nate was most likely a monster on the loose. Although at that point, nearly a month had passed, I was out of the country, and the chances of catching him were virtually non-existent. Still, I contacted the police in Sydney and told them everything I knew. Or thought I knew.

In the weeks that followed, I spent entire days fixating on what had happened, straining to remember until my brain hurt. I knew I was fully dressed when I woke on that awful morning, but had I *felt* anything, physically?

I searched obsessively for him online too, but turned up nothing, of course. Because Nathan Drall, as I well knew by now, wasn't real.

I was tormented by the whole thing, sleeping only in brief, fevered snatches. And when I did manage to drop off, I would wake a couple of hours later like a bolt had ripped through me, convinced Nate was standing at the foot of my bed.

I didn't have sex for almost two years afterwards, and I haven't touched a drop of alcohol since that day. For a long time, my ability to concentrate was shot to pieces, as was my sense of humour. I became snappy and irritable, the worst kind of company.

I told my family I'd come back early because I'd run out of money, had been mugged for my camera, was sick of travelling. That for me, jet-setting obviously just wasn't meant to be. Tash remarked more than once that I'd returned from Australia a completely different person: that I'd forgotten how to have fun, be spontaneous, take pleasure from life. And I could tell from the way that she said it – sadly, so gentle – that, somehow, she knew I'd lost more than my stuff out there.

After I reported Nate, I longed so desperately for a call to say they'd caught him – so I'd know that through my shock and failure to act during those first weeks, I hadn't unwittingly endangered someone else.

But the call never came.

Max stares at me, his eyes budding with tears. 'God, Lucy. I'm so sorry.'

'It's why I've found it . . . quite hard to trust.'

I can tell the irony isn't lost on him. His face pales, and he looks away from me. 'I just . . . I can't believe this. Why didn't you tell me before?'

I hesitate, draw shapes against the cushion I've pulled onto my lap for comfort, like a child. 'I mean, I still don't even know what really happened.'

'I think you do,' he says, softly.

Yes, I do. But as Max is so fond of saying, instinct isn't evidence. 'I know he stole my stuff. But I don't know . . . the rest. Not for sure.'

The sound of a speeding motorbike shoots through the room from the road. It sounds like it's going so fast, I wait for the ensuing sirens, but for once they don't come.

'That's why you don't have any pictures,' he says, slowly. 'You keep making excuses not to show me, but you don't have any. He took your camera.'

I nod, feeling my forehead knit together. 'The worst thing is having no way to find out the full story. It makes me feel sick, if I think about it too much. It's why I don't drink any more. The thought of ever losing control like that again . . .'

Listening to every beat of regret between us now is one of the saddest sensations I've ever known.

'Did they investigate?'

I nod. 'As far as they could. He was on CCTV, so they know it was him that stole my things. But they don't know the rest. And they never caught him.'

'Have you ever talked to anyone about this?' Max is fiddling with a pine cone, turning it over and over in his hand. It must have fallen from the little pile I've balanced in the grate of my redundant fireplace.

'Only Jools knows.'

'Not your family?'

I shake my head.

'Not a professional?'

'Nope.'

'I think you should. It's really serious, what happened to you.'

'I don't want to go over it all again. I actually just want to forget it.'

A few more seconds tick by. 'God, Lucy, I'm just . . . so sorry.'

He doesn't say what we're both thinking: that if he'd not slept with Tash, we might never have split up, I might never have gone travelling, I might never have met Nate . . .

If . . . if . . . if . . .

But the truth is, I don't want Max to feel guilty. Not about Nate. There are plenty of other things I could blame him for. But not that.

From downstairs, a cheer erupts, like they're about to start a conga, or someone's just lost at strip poker. It makes me smile, despite myself.

'I take it . . . it wasn't really him you saw tonight?' Max asks me, gently.

I shake my head. 'He'd be ten years older by now. He'd look different. It was just my mind playing tricks on me. It's happened a couple of times before.'

Once in a restaurant, with my parents and my ex-boyfriend. And once at Figaro, when I walked into a meeting room to encounter a new client, who just so happened to be Nate's double. On both occasions I fled, locking myself in a toilet to throw up, thereby convincing most of the people involved I was pregnant.

Max comes over to the bed and takes my hand, and then we just lie down next to each other, breathing in sync and not speaking. And when I next look around it is morning, and for a horrifying moment I think I'm back in that hotel room. But then I turn my head, and it is Max by my side and I am wrapped in his arms, both of us still fully clothed. And in this moment, to know I'm safe is the most precious feeling on earth.

14

Stay

I'm swimming with Caleb, a Saturday morning in November. Well, I say swimming: I'm actually just float-ing, face-up to the sky as I scull with my fingers, staring into the vastness of another mottled dawn. The cold clings to my skin like frost to the earth, and every now and then I feel the deep, electric strike of it afresh as the water shifts around me. The water is pearl-grey, the sky dappled with brightness and cloud, like a marble lifted to the light. Occasionally, birds make a dash for clear sky above our heads – snow buntings and knot, bar-tailed godwits and sanderlings. On the beach, other waders dabble tentatively at the shoreline, as if the water's too bitter today even for them.

But the cold's doing a pretty good job of invigorating me. I need waking up – we were out late last night with my sister, Simon and my parents, celebrating Simon's recent promotion.

I couldn't help sneaking the occasional sideways glance at Simon last night – finding myself wondering, as he poured the wine and joked with my mum about golfing his way to that promotion, whether it's really true that once a cheat, always a cheat.

I noticed, as my mum was laughing at something Caleb had said to her, that she wasn't wearing her wedding ring. 'Where's your ring, Mum?'

'Oh,' she said. 'I've lost it.'

'*Lost* it?'

'Ssh, ssh. It'll turn up.'

'But Mum . . . it's your *wedding* ring.' I glanced over at Dad – I knew he'd be devastated.

'I know. Ssh. I'm sure it's in the house somewhere.'

Unexpectedly, I felt my eyes cluster with tears. 'Mum, you can't lose your wedding ring. After all these years—'

'I told you, Lucy. It's in the house, somewhere.' And then she turned back to Caleb. 'Actually, no, I've never been to Newcastle. What's it like?'

Beneath the table, Caleb rested a hand on my leg, just high-up enough to make concentrating on my goat's cheese starter a near-impossible task.

My parents adore Caleb. The first time they met, he spent a full two hours talking to them about their jobs and politics – their two favourite subjects in the world (and I hadn't even briefed him beforehand). It was nearly time for us to go home before they eventually looked up and seemed to notice I was there.

Last month, Caleb and I headed to Devon, so I could meet his dad, stepmum, two older stepbrothers and their wives and kids for the first time. We stayed in a B&B just outside Exeter, meeting his family at an Italian restaurant on our first night. The whole thing was very polite and civilised, with lots of passing the bread and friendly questions about Shoreley and my novel and my own family. But I could see what Caleb meant about feeling like something of an outsider: he was so different to everyone else around the table, with their cars and second homes and investment portfolios and opinions on the best places to play golf in Europe.

'Not that there's anything wrong with all that,' Caleb said afterwards, 'but it's just hard to feel like I have anything to add to conversations about skiing and show jumping, you know?'

As the weather's got colder, we've tried to keep up our habit of swimming a couple of times a week, albeit in wetsuits now to deflect the worst of the cold. Still, the first minute or so is pretty hard – that initial, masochistic act of plunging a duvet-warm body into glacial water. But once I've adapted, and my breathing's found its rhythm, I can stay in for around fifteen minutes, the ultimate effect of which is pretty similar to downing a couple of strong espressos. We see seals in the water some days, and if we swim after dark, one of my favourite things is looking back towards Shoreley from the water, at the town's lights glimmering, like a cruise ship docked at night. Afterwards, we cross the shingle back to the beach hut, where we shiver together under a blanket and share mugs of hot tea.

Beside me in the water now, Caleb touches my arm. 'Think I'm done.'

I bob back into an upright position. 'Okay.'

'I need to talk to you about something.'

I smile cautiously. 'Sounds serious.'

He finds my hand beneath the water and squeezes it. 'See you back at the hut?'

I nod. 'Okay. Five minutes.'

We go back to the cottage for breakfast, because it's so cold today that the lure of the wood burner is just too strong. Caleb chops the wood, while I make tea and a plateful of buttered toast with the loaf we picked up from the bakery yesterday.

After he's lit the fire, I set down the toast and two mugs of steaming tea, and we sit on the sofa together, watching the flames gyrate hypnotically through the glass.

'So, what's up?' I ask him, sipping my tea. He's not said much since we got home, his demeanour seemingly a jumble of preoccupation.

'Helen messaged me yesterday. She's agreeing to the divorce.'

Though my heart does a little somersault, I know this is hardly the moment for a fist-pump or high-five. So I just keep my face straight, and nod. 'How do you feel?'

He slings his head briefly back against the sofa cushions and exhales. 'Yeah. I feel . . . well, *good*'s probably not the right word. Positive.'

I put a hand on his leg. 'Sorry. I don't know whether to . . . congratulate you, or . . .'

He looks across at me and smiles. 'You can if you like. It's not as if I'm . . . you know, mourning the death of my marriage, or anything. But anyway. It got me thinking. About what to do next.'

I feel a pendulum of fear swing through me. Here it is – the conversation I've been dreading since he first brought it up, seven months ago now.

'I'm loving being back in Shoreley, and work's going well, and you . . .' His smile shoots straight to my toes. 'You are amazing.'

'But?' I say, forcing myself to smile back, even though my body's telling me to do the opposite.

He holds my gaze. His cheeks are tinged slightly crimson from the heat of the fire. 'I got chatting to someone on a job this week. He's just got back from a round-the-world trip. And it got me thinking. I was wondering . . . if you'd fancy taking off somewhere.'

I swallow. 'Where were you thinking?'

He hesitates, takes a bite of toast. 'Haven't exactly thrashed out all the details yet. I guess I just wanted to know if in principle you'd fancy going travelling for a bit.'

'A round-the-world trip?'

'Not necessarily.'

I feel my forehead pinch together. 'So . . . do you mean a holiday?'

He shakes his head. 'I was thinking more like . . . six months or so.'

A silence settles between us.

'Okay,' Caleb says eventually, laughing lightly. 'I'm not sensing *overwhelming* enthusiasm here . . .'

I resist the urge to clamp my eyes shut and deep-breathe for a few moments. 'I'm not sure.'

Another pause, the seconds ticking ominously.

'Well,' he says, 'how about if we picked up where your trip left off all those years ago? We could go to all the places you never got to see.'

The rest of Australia. New Zealand. North America.

Caleb doesn't know the real reason I cut my trip short – only that I ran out of money. Which, technically, was true. Every time he's asked to see my travelling photos, I've made an excuse, gabbled something about the memory cards being in Tash's loft.

I hesitate, trying to work out what I should say. There are plausible reasons for me not to go: I'd be reluctant to abandon my novel – being a writer is what makes sense to me, right now. Coming home each day exhausted and creatively spent, but kind of high on it, feels almost spiritual some days, like … I've found myself. Some people, like Caleb, might want to travel halfway round the world to do that, but I've done it right here in my hometown. And what if I got long-listed for that first chapter competition (I eventually entered at the last minute, following unrelenting pressure from Ryan and Emma)?

But realistically, I know I can write from anywhere. Isn't that supposed to be the beauty of it? And even if I couldn't, taking six months off wouldn't be the end of the world, would it? If I really wanted to go away with Caleb, none of these would actually be reasons, and he's smart enough to know that.

'I think,' I say carefully, 'if you want to travel, you should definitely do it.'

What Might Have Been

'Okay,' Caleb says, searching my eyes for something more. 'But I'm asking if *you* want to do it.'

Unable to articulate everything that's going through my mind, I shake my head. 'I don't think so.'

He nods, but slowly, like he's trying to understand and can't. Unsurprising, considering I've not offered up a single reason so far for turning him down.

'I'm not saying I'd want to break up,' I say, because I'm desperate to make that clear. 'We could make it work, long-distance for six months. It just depends on how you'd feel about that.'

He laughs lightly, rubs a hand along his jaw. 'Er, I think I'd feel pretty crap about that. Wouldn't you?'

I try to picture it – Caleb calling me late at night from some bar on the other side of the world, WhatsApping me from a mountain peak, sending emails from a hostel in the middle of nowhere. And it feels all wrong. The idea of being parted for six months sits like a brick in my stomach. But it's been his lifelong dream to see the world, and I'm certainly not about to be the one who holds him back. I know too much about unfulfilled ambitions to do that.

'Of course,' I say, quietly, sipping my tea. 'But I'd wait for you. We'd make it work.' And I know we would, because the alternative . . . well, as far as I'm concerned, there isn't one. Caleb is my person. There's no one else in this world I'm meant to be with.

He gets up, then paces a quick circuit of the tiny room before returning to the sofa. 'Honestly, forget about it – it was only an idea.'

I sit up a little straighter. 'No, it's your *dream—*'

'Yes, one of them, but I've met you and you're more important to me than indulging a bit of wanderlust.' He takes my hands. 'What we have is too special to jeopardise.'

I shake my head. 'Caleb, this is one of the reasons you and Helen split up – having different ideas about what you wanted from life. You can't sacrifice your dreams for me. Six months apart would be hard, but that shouldn't be a reason for you not to go.'

He nods, like he's thinking about it. 'I guess I'm just wondering why you dismissed it so quickly. I mean, it's not like you haven't travelled before. Won't you at least even think about—'

'Believe me, *nothing* could persuade me to step on a plane right now.'

And it must be something about the way I say it – the edge to my voice, the chill in my tone – that makes him pause. I feel his eyes on me, taking in the stiffness of my shoulders, my shifting gaze.

'Please, talk to me, Luce.'

I glance at him, then make a slow exhale. Why am I fighting so hard to hide a part of myself, my past, from the man I love? And perhaps it's because the fire is roaring, and the tea has soothed me, and I feel utterly loved and secure, that I feel able to take a breath, and finally start to talk.

When I'm finished, Caleb doesn't speak for a really long time. We just sit and listen to the sound of the fire spitting and crackling in the wood burner until eventually, I can't take it any more. 'Say something.'

He rubs a hand through his hair. 'I . . . I'm trying to find the words.'

'It doesn't have to be anything profound or meaningful. Honestly. I mean, I've dealt with it.'

He drums his fingers rapid-fire against the arm of the sofa, like what he'd really like to be doing is tearing Nate to pieces with his bare hands. 'I'm . . . I'm so sorry, Luce. This is . . . why you don't drink?'

I nod. 'Yes.'

He looks across at me, his expression stricken. 'Why didn't you tell me?'

'Because . . . I hate talking about it. And I don't want what happened to rule my life. I've dealt with it, and—'

Almost absent-mindedly, he moves one of his hands to gently grip my knee, a gesture that feels reassuring and protective. 'You know he's still stealing from you.'

I recoil slightly, a hot flicker of defensiveness in my throat. 'No, he's not.'

'Well, you don't want to ever set foot on a plane again . . . what is that if it's not stealing experiences from you?' His voice is gentle, but the point he's making hits me right in the gut.

'I'm working through it in my own way.' I set down my now-empty mug on the coffee table.

'I get that, and I wouldn't ever presume to tell you how to handle it. But it makes me furious, to be honest, to think that bastard's grounded you here for the rest of your life.'

'Plenty of people don't travel. It's ridiculous to assume you can't have a fulfilling life without going abroad.'

'You know that's not what I'm saying. I wouldn't care if we stayed in Shoreley for ever, but I'd hate to see you make that decision out of fear. Are you . . . afraid that it'll happen again?'

'No, of course not—'

'Because you know I would *never* let anything happen to you.'

'Caleb, it isn't that I need you to protect me. It's more . . . subconscious than that. I get nervous just thinking about it, the experience wouldn't be worth the stress—'

Caleb suddenly takes my hand. 'I know it doesn't seem like it now, but there'll be a way to take something positive from this.'

'Something positive like what?'

'Well, at the very least,' he says, 'not letting that arsehole win.'

Go

'So, come on – is this your weirdest birthday ever?' I ask Max with a smile.

'Christ, no. When I was a kid Brooke dropped me off with this random family down the road and I spent the day watching back-to-back episodes of *Bottom*.'

I stare at him, regretting my flippancy. 'Oh. That's . . . awful.'

He laughs. 'Ah, it's all right. They let me eat my body weight in crisps.' He glances around the ballroom. 'And things are looking up now, right?'

What Might Have Been

It would be hard to argue with that. Max and I are at the bar in the ballroom of a swanky Hyde Park hotel, attending the *London Rising Star Awards – 40 Under 40*. The awards, run by a national newspaper, name forty peer-nominated under-forties living and working in London, and flying high in their particular industry. Mortifyingly (certain business journalists have gone wild for this story, which makes me think they need to get out more), Max and I are both on the list.

Max's award recognises his fast-growing reputation as one of London's fiercest property litigators, due to his recent work on a number of high-profile cases. Well, I say high profile: unless you subscribe to *The Lawyer* and have a niche interest in property disputes, you're unlikely to be up on them. My award was for my contribution to *A Whole New World*, the climate-change fairy-tales campaign I worked on with Seb, for the wildlife charity. (He's here somewhere too, with his girlfriend.) The reward of a promotion at Supernova has so far eluded me, but then again, I have been there only six months. It seems a little early to be demanding a pay rise. Though Zara's pleased with the positive publicity, and the uptick in client enquiries off the back of the work, I'm pretty sure she'd say I'll need to do a lot more than create one decent campaign before she'll consider me for promotion.

'So,' Max says, pulling me close. 'I think we should take a moment to appreciate the fact that only six months after starting at Supernova, you're already winning awards for your writing.'

'Stop,' I say, mock-bashfully.

'No, I'm serious,' he whispers. 'You're smashing it, Luce. I'm so proud of you.'

'Well, it's better than being a starving novelist, I guess.'

He smiles. 'Yeah, I reckon.'

I think about my long-abandoned notebook, how tough it would have been to ever make that idea pay. I smile back up at Max. 'Yeah, I'm pretty happy with how things have worked out.' In the middle of the crowded bar, I pull him into his millionth happy birthday kiss of the day, prompting someone nearby to mutter, 'Oh, get a *room*,' in an upper-class accent.

Max laughs. 'Now *that* is an excellent idea.'

'That wasn't me,' I say, out of the side of my mouth.

'No – I actually *am* going to get a room,' Max says, grey eyes sparking with mischief. 'Back in a sec.'

I grab his hand. 'Wait, what? The rooms here probably cost—'

'I'm sorry,' he says matter-of-factly, cutting me off, 'but that dress is *way* too incredible for a twenty-minute cab ride home.'

In the end, the dress only stays put in the lift up to our room because I keep swatting Max's hand away and laughing. 'Don't! Someone might come in.'

He leans his head back against the lift wall and groans. 'Why. Is. It. Stopping. On. Every. Floor?'

'See? A cab would actually have been quicker.'

Max exhales dramatically, though the way he catches

my eye in the mirror as he does so makes my stomach tug with lust. He's in black tie tonight, and though I've always admired how he looks in a suit, I have to say the extra level of suave is really doing it for me.

The hotel's been decked out for Christmas – all baubles and garlands and oversized foil bows – even though it's still only November. There was a Christmas tree the size of a national monument in the ballroom, and they're playing carol instrumentals in the lift.

'Imagine if we got trapped in here,' Max says, 'and the last music we ever heard was the panpipes cover of "Frosty the Snowman".'

'Oh, don't.'

'I can just picture the headline: *Britain's Smuggest Couple Perish in Festive Lift Tragedy.*'

I know he's joking really, but I find myself wondering if he might actually be right – if we are in danger of becoming just a little bit smug. Dressed in our finery, clutching our awards, dropping hundreds of pounds on a hotel room for the night, just because we can. *Is this the life I'm supposed to be living?* I think to myself, as I stare at the sight of us in the lift mirror. The thought arrives unbidden, out of nowhere. Suddenly, we seem to look like strangers – a couple I don't recognise at all.

The lift pings for our floor. 'Finally,' Max murmurs, feeling for my hand, our keycard between his teeth. I shake off the sensation of unease, allowing the heat of anticipation to spread through my stomach instead.

What was that all about? I think, as we make our way along the corridor.

Our room is a level of plush the students in us still pause to draw breath at. Floor-to-ceiling views of Hyde Park, art deco decor – all blush pinks and mint greens – with furniture edged in rose-gold, and a bathroom clad in marble. The carpet is so soft and thick, it almost swallows my feet.

I notice a box of chocolates and a vase of dusky roses on a table near the window. 'Max. Did you—'

'They threw them in when I told them it was your birthday,' he says, slipping his arms around my waist from behind and kissing the top of my collarbone.

I laugh. 'But it's your birthday.'

'Oh. My mistake,' he whispers, and in the next second my dress is a glittering black puddle on the floor, his dinner jacket and bow tie going with it, and we're falling into bed together for the second time today.

'Did you hear from Brooke?'

We've ordered mocktails to the room, which are pleasingly creative and pretty tasty. I'm relieved by the brief distraction they've provided, because something about this room – its opulence, maybe, or the freshly cleaned scent – reminds me of another room, long ago, in Sydney.

'Nope,' Max says. Though it's pretty warm in here, we're both wearing our complimentary towelling robes. We put them on as a joke at first, because I said I thought parading about in matching white dressing gowns was all a bit Swiss Toni. But now I have to admit Max looks quite hot in his, though I shouldn't be surprised, really – he looks hot in pretty much anything. 'We don't really speak much.'

I perch on the miniature couch next to the window, tucking my legs up beneath me. The room is dark now, the only light from a standard lamp in the corner. 'I know, but . . . not even on your birthday?'

From the bed, Max shakes his head. 'She doesn't really go in for stuff like that. Doubt she even remembers when it is. But . . . maybe it's better that way. I send her flowers on her birthday every year – some stupid overpriced bouquet she probably dumps straight in the bin so she doesn't have to put them in a vase. But it's cursory, just a gesture. She probably wouldn't notice if I never sent them again.'

I consider briefly how crazy it is that Max could have had such a dysfunctional childhood and yet . . . here we are, tonight, seemingly with everything we could ever want.

I sip from my mocktail. It buzzes on my tongue, the sugar and sparkle of it spinning through my stomach.

'Was there ever . . . ?' I begin, and then trail off, unsure how to continue.

He waits. I feel the warmth of his gaze as he watches me.

'Was there ever a moment when you were a kid, when you were tempted to go the other way? You know – blank everything out, or make yourself feel better somehow by—'

'Going off the rails?' Max says, lawyerly effective as ever in summarising my meandering train of thought. I've heard him do this on the phone sometimes, smoothly cutting clients off when they start to ramble, which is good of him, considering his hourly rate.

I nod. 'Yeah.'

From beyond the window, we hear the muted wail of an ambulance siren.

Max nods too. 'I guess so. I did get in with the wrong crowd one year.' He laughs lightly. 'I think about that quite often, actually. Brooke wasn't around, we didn't have any money, and I started to think that maybe . . . this was how my life was meant to be, you know? Just a bit . . . crap. And when I went back to school after Easter, I started being a bit mouthy, I think, and my PE teacher, Mr Janson . . . he pulled me to one side one day, and asked me to join the athletics team.'

'Oh,' I say, surprised. I'd been expecting him to say he'd been given a good talking-to, threatened with expulsion, or something.

Max gets off the bed and crosses the room to the desk beneath the mirror where the Bluetooth speaker is, pairing it with his phone. Music fills the room and with it, my heart: it's an old Tom Baxter album, one we'd listen to on repeat at uni.

'I can see now that it was actually a stroke of genius,' he says, walking over to the bed again and sitting down with his back against the headboard. 'Because I was pretty good at running, and there were . . . girls there who I wanted to impress, and other boys who I wanted to beat, and . . . I swear he saw what was happening to me and came up with a way to step in. I started training after school instead of tagging buildings and smoking and drinking. So, it turns out Mr Janson sort of saved me.'

'Good old Mr Janson. Wonder what he's doing now.'

'Still teaching,' Max says, with a smile. 'I emailed him last year to say thank you. I'm going to take him for a pint when I'm next in Cambridge.'

'Do you know what happened to the crowd you were hanging out with?'

A solemn nod. 'One's dead, actually. And another lad's inside.'

I feel a twist of anger in my stomach towards Brooke, for neglecting Max so badly. *What a stroke of luck,* I think, to have been saved by a single teacher's brainwave that summer.

'You're so lucky,' Max says, putting a hand behind his head. 'Having parents like yours.'

I nod – I agree, of course I do, though it's with a touch of regret. Because in a parallel life, my mum should be taking on Brooke's role now – mothering Max, lavishing him with love, treating him like the son she never had. But that won't happen – at least, not in the way it might have done, since Tash.

The last time my parents saw Max was a whole decade ago – they'd been to visit me at uni in Norwich, not long into my final term. When Max and I got back together this April, it had felt too early to reintroduce them, and soon after that came the revelation about Tash. I've been half-pondering the idea of inviting him back to Shoreley with me this Christmas, but that kind of chutzpah needs military-grade preparation, and I haven't yet had the headspace to think it through.

It makes me sad to know that what happened will always taint us, a stain created by carelessness that will never quite scrub clean. On the face of it, my family have accepted Max and me, but I worry that – over time – a natural distance will open up between us all, if I sail off into the sunset with Max, the man who did a thing none of us can actually bear to talk about.

My phone buzzes. I glance down at it: Jools. She's ranting about Vince again, who, after she broke it off with him last month, has been struck with the revelation – which had previously eluded him – that Jools is the love of his life, that he wants them to be exclusive (what a guy), that he wants them to *move in together*.

I mean, says Jools' message, the absolute RAGING CHEEK of him.

'What will you do?' Max says.

'Hmm?' I look up from my phone, then feel bad, setting it down on the little gold table next to me. It is his birthday, after all.

'If Jools moves in with . . . What's his name again?'

'Vince. Vincent.'

'Yeah. I mean . . . would you stay in the house?'

'Oh, she won't move in with him. He's just crying because she dumped him. He virtually confessed to having been seeing other people right up until she ended it.'

Max smiles, and for a moment, I can't quite interpret his expression. 'Humour me.'

A beat. 'About what?'

'Well, say Jools *did* move out . . . would you consider moving in with me, for example?'

I stare at him. Is he saying what I think he's saying? I admit it has crossed my mind, the fantasy of living with Max – reaching out to touch him every day when I wake, sneaking into the shower together before work, hearing the turn of his key in the lock after a long day. Doing those twee coupley things that feel stupidly exciting the first time around – cooking supper together (fancy pasta, always fancy pasta), clearing space in the wardrobe for my things, play-fighting over the remote, buying trinkets we both love for the home we'll make together.

All the stuff we'd been planning to do a decade ago, before everything went wrong.

'I've been trying to hold off asking,' Max says, smiling down at his glass like he's making a speech at a wedding. 'But ... I'd really love it, Luce, if you'd move in with me.'

'God,' I breathe, trying to tread the line between excitement and restraint. 'I'd have to see how Jools feels. They'd need to find someone else for the room, and—'

'Is that a maybe?' Max says, his grey eyes gleaming.

'Yes,' I say, breaking into a smile. 'It's definitely a maybe.'

He gets to his feet, crossing the space between us and tipping his glass to mine. In this moment, we could be back in Norwich, in the SU bar clinking plastic pint glasses together, madly in love and planning our future, our whole lives ahead of us. I shut my eyes and fantasise – just for a second – that I'm back there, before anything went wrong, when the world seemed to be full only of possibility, an abundance of good things.

'Well,' Max is saying, 'that's a reason to celebrate, don't you think?'

Pulling myself back to the present, I laugh. 'How much more celebrating can two people do?'

He gently takes the glass from my hand before leaning down, putting his lips against mine and tugging on the cord to my dressing gown. 'Oh, you'd be surprised.'

A couple of hours later, I wake with a jump, my skin slippery with sweat. I blink into the blackness, trying to remember where I am. For a moment I think I am back in Sydney, in a strange hotel room, and that Nate is by the bed, leaning over me.

I try to call out, to shout for help, but my breath is a knot in my throat.

I fumble for a light, half-falling out of bed, then make my way over to the window, where I rip the curtains open. Part of me is expecting the room to flood with daylight, that I'll see the ominous sight of the Sydney Opera House looming in front of me.

But outside, it is dark, except for the diffuse amber glow of Hyde Park Corner at night, backlit by a colourful jumble of Christmas lights. I swear and shut my eyes, try to calm the leaping sensation in my chest.

I feel a hand on my shoulder, and I spin around. But it's only Max, of course. I draw another deep breath. 'Sorry. I'm just . . . I thought I saw . . .'

He pulls me into a hug, and we are quiet for a couple of moments. I try not to fixate on how still and soundless this room is, about how much I want to flick the TV on, or play some music. I'm suddenly feeling almost unbearably hot, too. But these windows don't open. I have no way to escape.

'I didn't think,' Max whispers eventually, softly.

'What do you mean?'

'About staying somewhere like this. That it might . . . bring back memories.'

I shake my head, my mind beetling with frustration. 'Oh no. God, it's okay. I should be able to sleep in a sodding hotel room, shouldn't I?'

There is a long pause as we stand in front of the window together. It should be the most romantic view in the world, yet here I am wondering if I'll ever feel safe in a place like this again.

'You know, my company . . .' Max begins, then trails off.

'HWW?'

I feel the graze of his stubble as he nods, his chin dipped into the crook of my neck. 'I have private medical insurance, and partners are covered. Partners as in girlfriends, boyfriends . . .'

'Okay,' I say, unsure where this is going.

'I've been thinking . . . you could use it to see a psychologist, if you want. I think it would cover a few sessions. If you feel like that might help.'

I peel away from him, go and sit on the edge of the bed. Any romantic vibes have evaporated from the room now completely. 'Jesus, Max. Do you really think I'm—'

'Yeah,' he says, softly, staying where he is by the window. 'I do. I think what happened to you was really serious. And I don't think you've fully . . . accepted that.'

'I don't *know* what happened to me,' I remind him.

'Well, exactly. God, Luce, isn't that fact alone enough to mess with anyone's head?'

The question flickers between us for a minute or so, while I try to think of a way to save tonight. I don't want to spend our time here discussing the state of my head, or Nate, or whether I should use HWW's health insurance for psychiatric assistance.

'It was just a bad dream,' I say, eventually.

'Yeah, one that you're still having ten years later,' he says gently. 'Just . . . promise me you'll think about it.'

I look over at him, this incredible man whom I've loved for almost half my life, who wants us to live together, who cares for me so deeply. 'Okay,' I say. 'Okay. I'll think about it.'

15

Stay

Caleb and I are having dinner in the little courtyard garden of the French bistro in Shoreley – a little optimistically, admittedly, for late evening in May – when he leans forward and sets his glass against mine. It's a romantic space out here, with antique brick-weave paving so uneven it makes all the tables wobble, and twinkling lights spanning the rear wall. The air is fragranced by tiny vases of sweet peas, the breeze rich with the rumble of a restless sea.

'So . . . it came through.'

I hold my breath. I know what he's referring to, because we were expecting it today – his decree absolute, the final document confirming he and Helen are no longer married – but I need to hear him say it.

'We're officially divorced. It's over.'

I exhale, unsure whether to smile or stay solemn. It's a strange thing, watching the person you love untangle themselves from someone else – who just so happens to be the person *they* once loved most in the world. The process has been remarkably frictionless – aside from some minor quibbling over a car and some savings – but I still feel relief spill through me like a breaking wave.

'Is that why you suggested dinner?' I say, venturing a smile. Caleb called me this afternoon, asked if I fancied eating out tonight, and I sensed from his voice he had something to tell me.

'Kind of,' he says, not quite meeting my eye.

Suddenly, he looks so uncomfortable that my relief evaporates, and is replaced by that snow-cold feeling you get in your gut when someone decides to explore a darkened cellar in a film.

But then he seems to shake it off. 'Anyway, tell me about your news,' he says, abruptly changing the subject.

I park my trepidation. 'Hardly news,' I say resignedly, with a grim smile.

After failing to make the longlist for the first chapter competition that Ryan and Emma were so adamant I should enter last year, I finally mustered up the courage recently to enter a different competition, one I'd spotted in a writing magazine.

The email came through today, and again – the same result. Not even longlisted.

'Maybe this is a sign,' I say glumly. 'You know – a nudge from the universe to stop me pouring all my energy into writing.'

'Come on.'

'I'm serious.'

Caleb hesitates for a moment or two, frowning into his wine glass. 'So, what you're saying is, people should only have to try once at a thing before they're successful?' He looks up and meets my eye. 'I think even you know that's complete bollocks, Lucy.'

And there's something so matter-of-fact and pragmatic about the way he says this that I have to laugh. 'All right. Maybe that sounded a bit self-indulgent.'

He leans towards me, holding my gaze. His eyes are sweet and dark as treacle. 'Look – as I see it, if you want to be a writer, you only have one option right now.'

'And what's that?'

'Get up, dust yourself off and keep going.'

I've recently finished the whole first draft of my book. Writing the last few chapters was pretty tough – Ryan and Emma had to practically tug them out of me – but now, finally, the words are all there on the page. There's lots of polishing still to do, but at least I finally have a full story to work with.

And Caleb's right. Of course he is. I didn't come this far only to jack it all in now.

'So,' I say, keen to stop pressing on the bruise of my rejection, 'was there another reason you wanted to have dinner tonight?'

That look again. Discomfort and unease. Something on his mind. I pull my cardigan more tightly around me, and wait.

Is it to do with Helen? Us? His happiness – or lack of it?

He takes a couple of moments to reply, swilling what's left of his wine around the bottom of his glass. 'All right. So, after I got the email about the divorce, I had a dentist's appointment, and in the waiting room . . . there was this magazine.'

'Okay . . .' I say slowly, not yet able to imagine where this is going.

'It was one of those *National Geographic* type of things, and there was this advert in the back.'

He passes me his phone, open on a photo.

The advert is for a not-for-profit cultural heritage organ-isation that's seeking a photographer-in-residence to docu-ment overseas cultural sites across South-East Asia, in return for a modest salary and all expenses paid. The application deadline's in a month, and the trip would last for six.

'Oh,' is all I can think of to say.

I don't often wish I drank, but a nice neat shot of some-thing would come in very handy just about now.

Caleb waits. I know he won't launch into a sales pitch, and I'm glad. He shouldn't have to sell it to me. Instinctively, I understand this is something he has to do.

So – though I already feel selfishly sick with self-pity – I reach across the table for his hand. 'You *have* to go for it.'

All his features seem to soften, his expression now daubed with guilt and uncertainty. 'Lucy, I—'

'I'm serious. You have to do this.'

He's quiet for a couple of moments. His hand is grip-ping mine fiercely. 'It just . . . feels pretty weird to be suggesting this when you're literally the best thing that's ever happened to me.'

I feel my forehead crumple slightly, succumbing to the weight of my emotions. 'Look, I know they say love is about compromise, but I don't think that should ever mean giving up on your dreams.'

He lets his head drop forward, releasing a long breath as he does so, and I realise he'd been nervous about telling me. 'I guess the timing just seems off, somehow.'

'No – the timing's *perfect*.' I squeeze his hand. 'Caleb, seeing this advert on the same day as your divorce being finalised . . . That can't have been coincidence. It's meant to be. You *have* to do this.'

He raises his head now, swigs back some wine. As our gazes meet again, I try not to think about how much I'm going to miss him.

'It's still all theoretical at this stage, anyway,' he says. 'I'll have to apply, and there'll be loads of competition, and—'

'You'll get it,' I say, already absolutely confident that this is true.

His smile is bashful. 'Well, we should talk. About what it would mean, and you know . . . if you'd want to fly out to join me – at any point along the way?' He phrases this last part like a question.

We've discussed Nate a lot over the past six months, ever since I disclosed to Caleb what happened in Australia. At first, it felt weird to be talking about something I'd kept inside for so long – but at the same time, unexpectedly cathartic. Caleb never avoids the subject, shuts it down or flinches from it because it's hard to put into words. He wades right into the middle of it, repeatedly encouraging me to share my feelings, and even – after many weeks of conversation – asking me whether I could ever conceive of taking a trip abroad together. It's actually started feeling strangely soothing to discuss it lately, to share my dread and sadness with someone whose only goal is to help me overcome it.

Still. My head is responding to his question with a firm no. And yet . . . I sense my heart flexing with the unfamiliar sensation of temptation.

'Sorry,' he says, when I don't reply straight away. 'Getting ahead of myself.'

'When would you have to leave?'

'Early December. So even if I got it, we'd have half a year before . . .'

'It would make me . . . *really* happy. To see you go out there and do all that.' Despite my premature sadness, I feel my whole body smile at the thought of it. 'I'd be chuffed to bits for you, honestly.'

'But I'd miss you so much,' he whispers. His eyes are glimmering with reflected candlelight.

I brave a smile. 'Yeah, but just imagine the reunion.'

He laughs and rubs a hand through his hair. 'God, yeah. Imagine that.'

'So, would you actually consider going out there?' Jools whispers to me, the next morning. She and Nigel have made a rare last-minute trip back to Shoreley for the week-end, and I'm walking with her along the promenade, a few steps behind Caleb and Nigel. It's just before midday, and after a late start we're heading to the crab shack for lunch.

'No,' I say. 'That would be a bit too long-haul for me. Plus, I feel like it's something he needs to do by himself. It's a work thing, you know?'

'But . . . ?' Jools guesses with a smile.

'But maybe . . . Maybe I'd be up for a short break to Europe sometime. A long weekend. Something like that.'

She slips her arm through mine. 'I'm so pleased you told him, Luce. About what happened in Australia.'

I nod as above our heads, seagulls orbit steadily, seeking unsuspecting tourists' chips to snatch. The tide is high now. Weekenders have filled the promenade and the remaining slice of biscuit-coloured shingle, ambling four or six abreast, making an early start on oversized cones of artisan ice cream.

'He's just so . . . calm and logical about it all, you know?' I say. 'Like, he gets all my pain and heartache, but he also really wants to help me move forward.' I gaze at Caleb's back as we walk. He's laughing at something Nigel's said, gesticulating like he's doing an impression of someone or something.

'Nigel's exactly the same,' Jools says. 'He's making it his mission to help me build bridges with the . . . let's say, more dysfunctional members of my family.'

'Imagine if I'd moved in with you, Jools, last year. I mean, no offence – but you would never have met Nigel, and I'd probably never have called Caleb back.'

She smiles. 'Actually, I think we'd have all found our way to each other eventually.'

I smile back at her. I love that idea. 'You reckon?'

'I *know*.' And then she hesitates, like she's hanging on to the sentiment, not quite wanting to let it go. 'Oh, I can't wait any longer.'

I frown. 'Wait for what?'

'Nigel!' Jools calls. He and Caleb turn, and now she's waving them frantically back towards us with one hand.

'You can't wait for what?' I say, touching her arm.

Jools ignores me. 'Can we tell them now?' she says to Nigel as he and Caleb reach us.

Nigel smiles, like he's amused by her sudden flustering. 'Sure, if you want to.'

'Tell us what?'

Jools turns to face me, taking both my hands in hers. She looks beautiful as always, with her pebble-smooth skin and her mermaid's hair catching and lifting in the sea breeze. She glances at Nigel again. 'I'm sorry, I know we said we'd do it over lunch, but . . . I can't hold it in any more.'

'Jools!' I exclaim, laughing with frustration and anticipation.

She releases my hands, then moves over to Nigel. She slings an arm around his waist, takes a breath and looks up at him. Above our heads, the sun brightens suddenly as it evades a cloud, as if to gild her announcement. 'We're getting married.'

I gasp. My knees threaten to fold with surprise and delight. By my side, I feel Caleb grab my hand.

'We know it's quick,' Nigel says, looking down at his wife-to-be. It was their one-year anniversary this week, just a couple of weeks after our own. 'But—'

'When you know, you know,' Jools says, beaming.

I throw my arms around her so I can squeeze her as tightly as humanly possible, then I do the same with Nigel. He and Caleb man-hug, then we all come together as a foursome, our arms around each other. I feel as though my heart's just been torpedoed, but in the best way ever.

Jools is totally right. When you know, you know.

Go

'Your poor flat,' I say to Max, standing back to survey the mound of boxes we've just finished lugging in from the van – a mismatched jumble of supermarket cardboard that once held crisps, nappies, cereals, orange juice. There are a couple of vast IKEA bags too, plus several stuffed black bin bags. I look as though I'm en route to a car boot sale, not moving into the world's most beautiful flat.

'It's all right,' Max says, deadpan, rubbing his chin. 'I mean, I presume you'll be unpacking at some point?'

I laugh. 'The stuff inside them isn't much better, believe me.'

He sneaks up behind me, slipping both arms around my waist. 'Is this why you put off moving in for so long? You thought I'd stuff-shame you?'

Yes and no, I think, even though I know he's only joking. It's May now – six months since Max first suggested I move in. At first, I mainly felt bad for Jools – after all, we'd only been living together for seven months, and I was already considering shacking up with my new boyfriend. It felt weirdly unsisterly, though of course Jools never made me feel that way. And so I sat down and had a word with myself, tried to dig down into why I was *really* feeling hesitant – and I realised that in the back of my mind, perhaps it still just felt too soon. Max was the man I loved most in the world – but he was also the person who'd betrayed me in the worst possible way.

Since getting back together, things between us have been good – no, better than good. We spend most evenings eating out, or at the theatre, or going to gigs, or having supper with friends. I've met Max's colleagues from HWW. We've become close with Dean and his wife Chrissy. From the outside looking in, our relationship couldn't be better.

And yet. As I considered moving in, a tiny note of doubt still occasionally sounded in the back of my mind, telling me to give it a bit more time. Subconsciously, I was probably half-waiting for a tidal wave of secondary emotions to hit at some point, and I wanted that to happen before I moved in, not after.

But actually, it never has. So, last month, I told Max I was ready.

'Fill this flat with whatever you like,' Max whispers into my ear now. 'I couldn't care less. The only thing I care about is that you're here.'

I can't resist. 'But what will your interior designer say?'

He laughs. 'I should think he'd be thrilled for me, if I'm honest. I could tell he thought the whole bachelor pad thing was a bit tragic.'

I smile. 'Have you made space in the wardrobe?'

'Of course. A full half is now yours.'

'Wow. I'm impressed.'

Max takes my hand and pulls me down onto the sofa next to him. His expression is soft and keen, his marl-grey eyes seeming to search my face for something. 'Luce, in all seriousness, I want you to know . . . this place is yours as much as it is mine. I don't want you to ever feel like you're . . . staying with me.'

I press my lips together and nod. Momentarily, I am transported back to our student years, when we'd sit together on various decrepit sofas and talk for hours about our feelings and the future, the life we had ahead of us. 'God, I used to dream of this day when we were at uni.'

He nods too. 'Yeah.'

'Not so much our first move to London . . . but more what we're doing now. With proper careers, and good friends, and an idea of where we're headed in life, you know?'

Max hesitates for a second or two, then lifts one hand to brush the hair from my face. 'Can I ask you something?'

'Of course.'

'It might freak you out.'

I smile. 'Why?'

'Just a hunch.'

'Try me.'

'Okay. Well, we always used to talk about . . . getting married, and having kids, and . . . I know we haven't done that lately, and obviously I get why. But I guess I'm just curious . . . if you still see that stuff in our future. I mean, I don't know what you see when you think of us in five years' time . . . ten . . .'

I swallow hard, an attempt to prevent my heart cleaving and my eyes filling up. But I know, actually, that I couldn't play this cool if my life depended on it. When Max and I got back together, we agreed we'd be one hundred per cent straight with each other, always. So that's what I'm going to do. Screw it – the worst has already happened. 'Of course. Every day. Getting married and having a family with you . . . I still want all that stuff, Max.'

He swears softly, then lowers his head, resting it in his hands. I put a palm flat against his back. He is breathing hard. 'I thought you might not,' he says. 'I thought I might have blown the chance of that ever happening.'

'The heart wants what the heart wants,' I whisper, with a soft shrug and a smile.

He looks across at me, his disquiet turning to curiosity. 'How many kids?'

I let a beat go by. 'Three. No, four.'

'Big white wedding, or . . . scarper off to a beach somewhere?'

'Both?'

'City or suburbia?'

'City. For now. Or then. You know what I mean. None of this is happening yet.'

He leans over to kiss me. 'I love you so much.' Picking up his phone, he angles it for a selfie. 'One for posterity?'

I kiss him on the cheek for the shot, then we put Coldplay on and start unpacking the boxes. And every time I catch his eye, or our elbows bump, I feel happiness billow inside me as I think, *Right here. Here is the guy I am going to grow old with.*

Later, Jools rings me. Max is out of the room, having had to take a call from his poor working-at-the-weekend-to-prove-himself assistant. We've spent the last couple of hours on the living-room floor flipping through photos from our university days, laughing at the red-eye, the grainy quality, the bad composition. Heads cut off, people looking in the wrong direction. Nothing was posed, back then. Selfies were still new. We didn't really care about our clothes. We were never curated – we were captured at our imperfect, carefree best.

'Don't take this the wrong way,' Jools says. 'But *thank you* for moving out.'

Sipping from my tea, I smile. 'I mean, you're welcome, but I'm going to need some context.'

'That girl who was moving in has changed her mind.'

'What?' It was all lined up for today – a friend of Sal's, who works in production at the actual atelier of a major fashion designer. Jools had been so excited about her moving in, insisting whenever I ribbed her about it that it was nothing whatsoever to do with the prospect of tapping the girl up for free clothes.

'Yeah, something about a last-minute move to Milan.'

'Like you do.'

'Yes, but then Reuben called that guy – the one who came to view it last year, remember, with the muffins?' Jools' voice becomes slightly hectic and high-pitched. 'You know – he turned up to view the room after you did and we had to send him away. *Anyway*, he's just been round to see it again, and he's—'

'Did he bring muffins?'

'Screw the muffins,' she says, 'he is *dreamy*. His name's Nigel. He's going to move in next weekend. Apparently he used to be a professional pianist.'

I dunk a custard cream into my tea, hold it down for the regulation three seconds. 'So, what does he do for a living? I mean, if he's an ex-pianist.'

'He's a financial auditor.'

'That sounds promising,' I say, thinking, *Sensible. Reliable.*

'Yeah, and he's one of those people who makes proper eye contact, and actually listens when you speak.'

I realise it's been a long time since I heard Jools really enthuse about a guy.

'So anyway,' Jools continues, 'what I'm saying is, much as I loved living with you, Luce, Nigel definitely has more long-term potential, romantically speaking.'

I laugh. 'God, Jools! You never get all mushy about guys.'

'I know! What's wrong with me?'

'Are you drunk?'

'Sober as a judge.'

'Well, then I guess it must be love at first sight.'

'I guess it must.'

16

Stay

Sunday night, and Caleb and I are sitting in the little courtyard of my parents' cottage in Shoreley. They've spent the weekend in Sussex, and as Tash and Simon have been in Bristol visiting Simon's brother, we agreed to house-sit, because Mum's paranoid about burglars and Dad worries about their cat, Macavity, starving to death. We'll lock up tomorrow morning before they get back, post the key through the letter box.

They've seemed under strain over the past few months. Not quite themselves. Dad's migraines have been persisting, and talk of redundancies at his company has started up again. So I was pleased when they announced they were getting away for a couple of days.

Caleb and I are wrapped up in our big coats, scarves and gloves. The metal of the seat I'm on feels icy through my jeans. We've just finished eating, a feast of local scallops and bacon fried in butter. It's a clear night, the sky spangled with a million stars, so Caleb suggested making hot chocolates and lighting Mum and Dad's little firepit, so we could sit out here in the darkness and wonder at the array of hot-white constellations above our heads.

We've been discussing my novel, which he's just finished reading the full draft of. There are a few minor tweaks and edits left to make, but I wanted Caleb to read the whole thing before he goes, in case he's got any salient feedback.

He got the South-East Asia job, of course. And I'm so excited for him. He's a genius behind the camera, and he more than deserves this opportunity. He flies to Bangkok in a fortnight for orientation, and will be away six months.

I'm going to miss him hard. Really, really hard.

'Honestly, I think it's epic,' Caleb's saying. 'Seriously. You are such a talent, Lucy.'

'I don't know about that.'

'Well, I do. The ambiguity of that ending . . . It's genius.'

I bite my lip. I mean, if I were to be really honest, the ending was actually Ryan's idea, dreamed up over post-session drinks in The Smugglers. 'You think?'

'No, I know.' He leans over and kisses me. His lips are warm and sweet from the hot chocolate, and the kiss is long and deep and slow, like we're marking the moment.

'Thank you. Shame it's taken me so long.'

He draws back from me, tilts his head. 'Didn't it take Margaret Mitchell ten years to write—'

'*Gone with the Wind.*' I smile. 'So they say.'

And I suppose, in a way, I've been writing my novel for ten years, too. Maybe not on the page – but it's been in my head ever since I boarded that flight at Heathrow on Boxing Day eleven years ago.

I burrow deeper into my coat, shuffling a little closer to the firepit in an effort to ward off the icebound November air. An occasional fit of wind is laced with the briny scent of the sea as it stirs.

Caleb leans back in his chair, gazing up at the stars. 'I'd go as far as to say the world *needs* to read your book, Lambert.'

I snort. 'No. The world does not *need* to read my book. The world needs . . . equality, and human rights, and an end to corruption and famine, and—'

'All true. But as long as books exist, yours should too.'

'Ah, you're biased.'

'Nope. When are you going to let Ryan show it to his agent?'

I smile. The four of us – Ryan, Emma, Caleb and I – have become pretty close over the past eighteen months. We cook dinner for one another, meet for drinks and Sunday roasts at The Smugglers, go out to see films and plays and poetry readings.

Ryan's been badgering me for weeks to let his agent in London have a sneak-peek at my draft. But I'm not quite ready yet.

'Soon,' I say, obliquely.

Caleb reaches for my hand, his fingers twining with mine. 'Promise me something.'

'Anything.'

'Don't go and get published while I'm away. All right? You *have* to wait till I'm home. I want to be here for your big moment. It would kill me to hear about it over Skype.'

I smile at his faith in me before slinging my head back, readjusting my eyes to the glinting galaxy in the sky. 'Okay. I'll try my very best not to achieve the impossible while you're away.'

By my side, he exhales. 'Six months.' His breath ices the air between us. I feel him looking at me, but I don't want to look back, because I know it might make me cry.

So instead I just nod, and wash away the sadness with the last of my hot chocolate. 'It's going to be the best six months of your life.'

I'll be staying in Caleb's cottage until he gets back. I'm so pleased he's not giving it up. I mean, yes – it has leaks and loose tiles and bits always falling off it. But it's cosy and ramshackle, decrepitly romantic. I picture myself sitting in it alone while Caleb's gone, listening to the sea, the gentle rumble of the waves reassuring as a heartbeat.

As we're getting ready for bed, my phone buzzes. It's Jools, about next weekend, when Caleb's agreed to do an engagement shoot for her and Nigel in London. We're travelling to Tooting on Friday, then I've organised a surprise going-away party for Caleb on Saturday night. I can't imagine a better way of spending his last weekend before he goes.

Jools and Nigel are getting married in Shoreley next summer, and Caleb will be taking the pictures. Before meeting Nigel, Jools never showed much interest in marriage, largely because her parents couldn't even take their own on-off engagement seriously. But since saying yes, she's become the white-wedding enthusiast none of us saw coming. We've been dress shopping and venue hunting, we've sampled catering and cakes, we've spent hours gazing at honeymoon destinations and fantasising over gift lists. One of her colleagues even jokingly called her *bridezilla* last week, and she beamed as she told me, as if she'd just been promoted, or Reuben had finally paid her back all that money she's subbed him for rent.

In the middle of the night, I wake to a tarry, acrid smell. It burns the back of my throat like smoke, turning it raw. I lie there for a few moments, confused, trying to remember if we ate anything last night that tasted smoky.

Then I realise. It *is* smoke.

Next to me, Caleb is sitting up. 'Lucy,' he says, very calmly. 'I think the house might be on fire.'

'Er, Mum,' Tash says. 'Do you need a brandy, or something? You look really pale.'

Tash rushed round as soon as she heard, and I've taken the morning off work. I told Ivan I'd escaped from a house fire, which was a bit of a white lie, given only part of the living room was actually destroyed in the end. A socket behind the TV was overloaded and ignited in the night, but the fire service was able to put it out before too much damage occurred. We were permitted to re-enter the cottage just minutes before Mum and Dad arrived home from Sussex. Luckily, Macavity was perfectly fine.

The five of us are crammed around the breakfast bar in Mum and Dad's tiny kitchen, shivering because all the doors and windows are wedged open. I've always loved this room, with its handmade wooden cabinets and uneven ceiling and cherry-red Aga. It has character. Soul.

The stencilled words on the wall above the corkboard catch my eye. *What's meant for you won't pass you by.* I've been known to rib my parents about the triteness of that saying, but today it seems painfully poignant.

Caleb's made a pot of tea, is passing round cups. I meet his gaze as he hands me mine, and feel comfort sink through me like an anchor gently dropping.

What am I going to do without him?

Mum shakes her head to the offer of brandy. 'No, thanks, darling. I always hated that picture, anyway.'

Tash shoots me a funny look. Mum must be talking about the oil painting of poppies above the TV. It's not the only thing that was burnt: many other items went up in flames, including – ironically enough – the copy of *Jane Eyre* I was reading last night, but I guess she's focusing on that painting because she's in shock, or something. I'm pretty sure Dad bought it for her, once upon a time.

'It's just so *lucky* you and Caleb were here,' Mum says to me, shaking her head. 'Imagine if you hadn't been. The whole house would have gone up, and Macavity would have . . .' She breaks off, clamping a hand over her mouth, unable to continue.

Caleb reaches over and squeezes her hand. 'Don't think about that, Ruby. We *were* here. That's what counts.'

What Might Have Been

She looks up at him, her eyes shimmery with tears. 'Thank you, Caleb.' I know she's grateful for him right now – I think we all are. If I've learned anything from the eighteen months we've been together, it's that Caleb is someone you want around in a crisis. He's so cool-headed, pragmatic and dependable. Even just to look at him makes me feel calmer, somehow. A few months ago, we were on a train to Newcastle – my first time meeting his mum and younger step-siblings – when an elderly passenger across the aisle slumped suddenly over in his seat, his skin completely grey. Caleb was the model of composure – clearing the man's airway, directing the other passengers to call for help, talking a nearby woman down from her frenzied panic. The man regained consciousness by the next stop, where medical help was waiting, and we found out later that he'd fully recovered. But it made me think Caleb had missed his vocation as a member of the emergency services. It's quite a skill to be unflappable in any crisis, I think.

By my side, Tash is uncharacteristically quiet. She diverted here on her way to the office, which is why she's looking so businesslike in her camel-coloured coat and dove-grey suit. She seems horrified by what's happened: at first I thought she might blame me, for leaving the TV plugged in when we went to bed, but she hugged me when I asked and said of course not, that she was just in shock.

I know she's been struggling with the idea of me moving out of their place and into Caleb's cottage when he goes away, having taken so much pleasure from watching me and Dylan bond over the three-and-a-half years I've been living with them. But there comes a time to move on, and I think we both know that time is now. Maybe I'll use the money I've saved up to buy a place with Caleb when he gets home. Or maybe I'll use it for something a little more adventurous. Anyway, it's lovely to have options, and I feel a thrill in my stomach whenever I think about my future with this man I love so much.

'Listen, kids,' Mum's saying now, clearing her throat, 'we've got something we'd like to talk to you about.'

Next to me, Caleb shifts slightly. 'Did you want me to—'

'No, Caleb,' Mum says. 'You should hear this too.'

God, she sounds very serious.

I glance at Dad. He's looking down at the cup in his hands, and he's sitting quite far apart from Mum. They've been doing that a fair bit recently, and it still looks weird to me. My whole life, they've always sat so close together, could never stop touching each other. I've lost count of how many comedy vomit faces Tash and I have made behind their backs, over the years.

Mum looks meaningfully at Dad. And then the bottom falls out of my world.

'We were at a marriage retreat,' he says. 'That's where we were, this weekend.'

'A marriage retreat? What's that?' I say dumbly, assuming he's going to say it's somewhere you go to . . . what? Enjoy being married? Isn't that what most of us call a dirty weekend?

'I don't follow,' says Tash.

'We went to . . . try to save our marriage,' Mum says, slowly. 'Our friends recommended it.'

'Our friends John and Roz,' Dad says, pointlessly. 'You know – with the barge?'

I can tell you that John and Roz could wander in here with their barge right now and I wouldn't even blink. I feel as though I've just had a knock to the head, that all the words I used to understand are no longer making sense. Maybe I inhaled more smoke than I realised last night. I glance at Tash, desperate for clues.

'What do you mean, *save your marriage*?' Tash says, like she's trying really hard to be tactful but would actually quite like to upturn the teapot over both their heads.

Neither Mum nor Dad replies for a very long time, like they're waiting for us to read between the lines. But it feels like we're on completely different planets, never mind conversational planes.

Eventually, Mum takes a deep, dramatic breath. She's fiddling with the silver locket around her neck, the one containing the photo of my grandparents. She's had her hair cropped recently, shorter than I've ever seen it, and she's wearing a pale pink lipstick with a frosted finish, which for her is a bold move. She usually complains lipstick makes her look old. 'We're getting a divorce.'

I gape at her, then at Dad. He's sitting very still, staring down at his knees like a drug smuggler at a press conference. He's got a new hairstyle too – but his is long and unkempt, almost like an act of defiance, a statement of something. I look back at Mum.

'What are you *talking* about?' Tash's voice is skipping octaves now.

'The idea of the retreat was to try to find a way forward. It was a wonderful, very enriching experience, and the facilitators were *incredible* . . .'

For God's sake. Mum sounds like she's talking about the sugar crafting course at her night school.

'. . . but we've decided that the best thing for us is to go our separate ways.'

I stop just short of letting rip with every expletive she's ever told me off for, plus a few new ones. 'Why would you want to do that? You belong together. You're . . . You're meant to be.'

Next to me, Caleb squeezes my hand, a silent show of support.

Mum looks at Dad, and there is real sadness in their eyes. And for the first time ever, I'm forced to wonder if what I've been seeing all these years hasn't, in fact, been a reflection of reality. If their fairy-tale love story is just that: an illusion. Something they've told us to make us feel better, or restore our faith in love, or worse – entertain us.

I look at Dad, the lingering smell of smoke catching the back of my throat. 'I know you've been having migraines lately, and you've got all that redundancy stuff hanging over you, but surely this is—'

He shakes his head. 'The migraines . . . we lied.'

Mum winces. 'Sorry, darling. We needed to tell you *something* when . . . we'd fallen out.' She says *fallen out* like I used to say *women's troubles* to my boss when I was pulling sickies at my first-ever temp job.

'But . . . what have *you* got to fall out about?' says Tash helplessly, as though she thinks people simply cease having feelings or any brain function at all once they hit a certain age.

'We want different things,' Dad says. 'And our love life—'

'*No!*' Tash and I squawk in unison, putting up our hands to cut him off. And after that we all just sit in our little circle around the breakfast bar, staring down at it in silence like the world's most dysfunctional group therapy session.

I'm struggling to remember a time when I've ever felt quite so blindsided by sadness. I tug at a loose thread on my cardigan, wonder if I could unravel the whole thing right here, if I just pulled hard enough. I feel Caleb glance across at me, and I wish we could be transported away suddenly, to a place where he could be wrapping me in his arms, telling me he loves me, whispering reassurance into my hair.

Tash is first to speak again. 'You've been married for *thirty-five years.* You can't chuck all that away because ... you're going through a rough patch.'

I think about Simon and Andrea, and about Caleb and Helen. And then I look at my mum and dad sitting in front of me, self-professed soulmates who we all thought were destined to be together.

They've been my role models my whole life. They made me believe in the kind of love that's fated to last a lifetime. How can this be happening?

'Is there ... anyone else?' I look between them, searching for tell-tale hints of sheepishness. The thought appals me, but I have to ask.

'No,' Mum says, sipping her tea. 'But of course we've discussed the idea that ... there might be, one day.'

It's so ageist and unkind, I know, but the thought of my fifty-something parents joining Shoreley's dating pool makes me recoil far more than any of the PDAs they've subjected me to in the past.

'You always used to tell us you were destined to be together,' Tash says, like she thinks they might need reminding. 'Was that a lie, then?'

'Of course not,' Dad says, glancing at Mum again. He's hardly touched his tea. 'I believe we were destined to meet, because wonderful things have come out of that: you, and Lucy, and building a life together. But now it's time for a new chapter.'

Mum nods. 'We don't see it as the end, more as a fresh beginning. We're choosing to look forward – not back. The retreat helped enormously with that.'

'Some marriage retreat,' Tash says, 'where you come away planning to divorce. I assume you've asked them for a refund?'

And then, despite ourselves, we all smile, and soon we are laughing, and before very long we are wiping away tears of both mirth and sadness as we hug each other. I'm pretty sure we're all already wondering exactly what our future will look like as a family now, since everything we thought we knew has gone up in smoke.

Go

I'm jolted into consciousness in the small hours of Monday morning. Max and I have only just gone to bed. A brunch in Battersea yesterday afternoon turned into an evening bar crawl that ended up in Belgravia via Chelsea. Olly was there, and Dean Farraday, and a couple of people from Max's work. And Jools brought Nigel. They've been seeing each other for nearly six months now – almost since the day I moved out of the house – and they're the kind of besotted where they'll break off mid-sentence to kiss, and forget the rest of us are standing there, wondering how long we should wait before edging away. It's been pretty special, watching Nigel fall in love with Jools. And the best thing is, he knows how lucky he is. I was able to stop worrying within days of her meeting him that he'd ever be the kind of guy to take her for granted.

Sal and Reuben tagged along too last night, and some Supernova folk. At one point, one of our group – Nicola, I think her name was, a senior associate at HWW – congratulated me on 'bagging the most eligible bachelor in London'. Jools was standing next to me at the time, and we both just about kept our faces straight before turning to each other with bulging cheeks as she started chatting to someone else, pulling that face people do when they're trying not to throw up in public. But – much as she'd phrased it *horribly*, and I could never actually admit it out loud – I privately agreed with Nicola. Max *is* a catch: I've always felt that way, ever since we were students in Norwich and people flocked around him in bars like he was famous. He's always just had that . . . aura about him.

Living with Max, just the two of us, has been everything I hoped it would be. Six months on, we're still making each other late for work several times a week, unable to bear leaving the bedroom. We take showers together and pin love notes to the fridge and message each other to rush home. We eat our bodyweight in takeaway sushi and I've taught him to cook my famous paella crowd-pleaser. At first, I even joined him on the odd morning run, though my enthusiasm has slightly dropped off now. We've done so many of the tiny, trivial things we said we would over a decade previously, and every one of them has been worth the wait.

Perhaps it's even better now than it would have been back then. Because maybe now is our time. Our careers are on an upwards trajectory, we know who we are and what we want. This is the life we've chosen, not one we arrived at by accident.

And yet, somehow, I occasionally catch myself not quite recognising the life we're living – the show-home flat and our flashy jobs and increasingly expensive tastes. Maybe it's because we broke up as students, and a part of me still thinks of us that way. Or maybe it's ever since finding out about Tash, because nothing after that has turned out quite as I always thought it would.

But even if Tash hadn't happened, and we'd stayed together all those years ago, I know we still might not have made it. Perhaps we'd have moved to London together, hearts full of hope, and parted ways six months later. Because life is complicated. Best intentions get buried beneath work, money, social lives. Love falls victim to circumstance.

'That yours or mine?' Max murmurs now. He's spread-eagled on his front, face wedged between the pillows like he's been dropped there from a height.

What Might Have Been

The sound of my phone is about as welcome as a pneumatic drill. I pick it up, praying it's not Zara calling me to the office early for an emergency pitch meeting. I worked until midnight three days last week. I *need* a reasonable start time this morning.

'Hello?' I croak, alarmed to realise I sound as though I chain-smoked my way into bed.

'Lucy?'

I sit up. My hair is all over my face. I push it back. I need water and an open window, to breathe in some fresh dawn air. 'Mum?'

'Oh, darling, thank *God* you're okay.'

Dread spreads slowly through me like treacle. 'What . . . What do you mean?'

'There's been a fire.' Her voice cracks on the last word.

Max drives us to Shoreley, breaking every rule of the road, plus a few extra ones. The whole way, I can barely think, the guilt like a swarm of bees in my brain.

'It'll be okay,' he keeps saying. He's had his hand on my leg since we left London, only moving it to change gear or navigate a roundabout. Zara, and Max's boss Tim, both gave us today off when we explained about the fire. But a small, selfish part of me is so scared of what we're about to discover that I almost wish they'd said no.

Mum had asked me to house-sit for the weekend. She and Dad were going away – three nights in Sussex – and they're always so paranoid about burglars, and their cat, Macavity, starving to death. Tash and Simon were in

313

Bristol with Dylan, visiting Simon's brother, so I said we would, but on Friday night it was impossible to get out of London. The A2 was gridlocked – a seven-car pile-up, apparently – so we turned the car around. Both Mum's and Dad's phones were switched off (I tried not to think too hard about why) so eventually I rang their neighbour, Paula. She'd been away all week herself, which I guess is why Mum didn't ask her.

Straight away, Paula suggested we stay in London, save ourselves the trip altogether. Everything would be perfectly safe until Monday, she said, and she'd be sure to pop in on Macavity. She promised to contact Mum and Dad to let them know.

I had her on speaker at the time, and Max was kissing my neck, his fingers slipping in between the buttons on my shirt. 'Say yes,' he mouthed, and I very nearly groaned out loud on the phone.

We'd both been working long hours all week and were exhausted. What we really needed to do was spend the weekend between the bed and the shower and the sofa, eating proper food. Not that it worked out that way in the end, but our intentions were good, if slightly lust-fuelled.

So I said yes to Paula, made a note in my iCal to send her some thank-you flowers, then promptly forgot about the whole thing.

And now, it seems, that split-second decision has cost my parents everything.

★   ★   ★

What Might Have Been

I shouldn't have let Max come. It's always so awkward now when he's with my family: he and Tash studiously avoid eye contact, and my parents deal with the discomfort by pretending he's not there. All of which only draws attention to the one thing we'd all rather forget.

We're wrapped up in our coats, standing on the pavement across the road from the cottage, like mourners watching a funeral cortège. Above our heads, seagulls are sailing briskly on the breeze, like it's an ordinary winter's day. But it's not, of course, because the fire service is still working on the slowly smoking wreckage of the cottage. The air smells noxious. Only the lower floor is still intact, and what's left is ragged and charred, like blackened tree trunks in the aftermath of a wildfire. The ugly remains of it alter how the whole street looks, and passers-by are stopping to stare. For a moment it feels as though this can't be real – like we're on the set of a film about our life, gaping at the plot twist they've seen fit to throw in.

'I'm so sorry,' I say again, my stomach grinding with guilt. I feel horrible not only about the fire, but about the fact this is the first time I've visited Shoreley in three months. I've been so busy and loved-up, but that's no excuse. Aside from anything else, I haven't seen my nephew since his birthday.

Next to me, Max squeezes my hand. I know he's desperate to reassure me, tell me none of this is my fault, but he probably feels he can't – not out loud, anyway.

On my other side, I feel Tash glance at me, and for a moment I think she's going to lecture me about how selfish I am, how I need to sort my life out, that I'm a terrible person and look what I've done. But she doesn't. She just slips an arm around me, hugging me so close I can smell her shampoo.

By the time we've talked to Paula and the authorities and the insurance people, it's mid-afternoon, so Max and I head back to Tash's with Simon while Tash goes to pick Dylan up from school. Bizarrely, Mum and Dad took an unscheduled diversion to a coffee shop at lunchtime, and have been there ever since. Simon said we should leave them to it, as they're obviously in shock. We figure they'll join us back at the house when they're ready, along with Macavity, who's thankfully safe and currently gorging on copious quantities of tinned tuna at Paula's.

'You can go if you want to,' I tell Max in the car, en route to Tash's. 'I can get the train home later.' We're following Simon, who drives surprisingly slowly, like he's about five decades older than he actually is. Either that, or he's got six points on his licence. He keeps stopping at roundabouts like they're T-junctions, and I can tell Max is starting to find it quite funny.

'Go where?'

'Back to London.'

'Are you saying that because you think this is going to be awkward?'

I run my tongue over my teeth. I feel strung-out and a little wired, like I've drunk too much coffee, even though I've only had a single cup today. I shake my head. 'Just thought you might want to get off.'

'I'm not going anywhere.'

Ahead of us, Simon dithers at a slip road. 'You could be right about that,' I say, and Max laughs.

Simon inches into fourth gear on the dual carriageway, and finally we leave Shoreley in our wake. Everything I can see is the colour of charcoal – the road, the sky, the fume-stained bark of the leafless trees.

I turn my head towards Max, taking in the sight of his hands on the steering wheel, the quick flick of his eyes between lanes and signs and slip roads and traffic, his freshly shaved jaw, the dark neckline of his jumper against his collarbone.

I switch my gaze to the road again. 'I have no idea how I'm going to come back from this, you know. I'm not sure they'll ever be able to forgive me.'

'Nobody in their right minds would blame you for this, Luce. It was an overloaded socket. Even if we'd been there, there was nothing we could have done.'

I frown, look down at my hands. I got a manicure yesterday afternoon, in a colour called *siren red*, which not only seems now like the height of self-absorption, but also cruelly ironic.

Max puts a hand on my leg, making me good-shiver, despite the sombre mood. 'Don't you think it's lucky we weren't there? The fire service said your parents' smoke alarm wasn't working. What if we'd been asleep and not realised?'

'I still let them down.'

'No,' Max insists, his voice firmer now. He taps the brakes as, up ahead, Simon does the same for no reason. 'I think saying yes to Paula on Friday might have been the best thing you ever did.'

I smile, faintly. 'I'm not going to win this one, am I?'

'Afraid not. I won't let you punish yourself for what's happened.' He flicks on his indicator, moves into the outside lane. The car surges forward. 'Right, are you holding on? I'm about to top forty.'

As it turns out, trying to buy children's affection with expensive birthday gifts doesn't work, because when Dylan gets home with Tash, he frowns when he sees us.

I smile. 'Hi, Dylan. Remember my friend Max?' I stop short of saying, *Uncle Max*.

He might not, I suppose. Max has only met him once.

Dylan is so sweet in his oversized St Edmund's blazer, his blond hair neatly combed into a side parting. He reminds me of Prince George that time he met Obama in his dressing gown.

But Dylan's frown deepens now, and he looks up at Max. 'My mum doesn't like you.'

Simon's still not home, which is what doing thirty on the bypass does for you, but Tash has been hovering in the hall with their coats and Dylan's book bag. She pretends she hasn't heard, but she must have done, because Tash never misses a thing. 'Right, Dylan!' she trills from the doorway, clapping her hands. 'Homework time.'

'Sorry,' I mouth to Max, as Tash ushers Dylan upstairs. I hear her whispering to him as she goes.

Max shakes his head. 'No, I'm a fan of straight-talkers. He'll go far.'

'He doesn't mean it.'

'I think he probably does.'

My stomach swings with apprehension. The situation's impossible, really: yes, Max did a terrible thing, but he and I have made a choice to move on. Still, I guess you can't assume everyone else will come with you. That's not fair, either.

'This is no more than I deserve, Luce,' Max says, calmly.

'You don't need to self-flagellate.'

'I know. I'm not.'

'You can honestly head off if—'

'Luce, if I feel a bit awkward for a few hours, it's fine. I can handle it. I promise.'

Mum and Dad arrive an hour or so later, as it's getting dark, with Macavity in a pet carrier. They're moving in here with Tash and Simon until the cottage is sorted out.

As Tash makes sure everyone's warm enough – I notice she's tactfully avoided lighting the fire – Simon passes round brandies. He misses out me, and Max because he's driving, making us both a latte from the posh machine instead.

I don't know why, but as soon as we're all sitting down, I start to cry – the great, hiccupping, ugly tears I've been holding in all day.

Max reaches out to rub my back, Mum and Dad make soothing noises, and Tash pleads with me not to blame myself. I know how this looks: that I've turned on the waterworks so no one gives me a hard time. But I feel genuinely awful about messing up.

'It's just *stuff*, darling,' Dad says, from the opposite sofa. 'The important thing is that you're safe. God knows what would have happened if you'd been there. We're glad you weren't.'

'I keep telling her the same thing, Gus,' says Max.

At the sound of Max's voice, there's a pause so uncomfortable it makes my scalp prickle. It's like they've all been pretending so hard he's not here, they're genuinely shocked to realise he actually is. Like a mannequin moving in a shop window. I'm unused to feeling this way around Max: he's personable and warm, quick-witted, the kind of person everyone wants to sit with at the pub. Painful silences usually don't get a look-in.

'So, tell us about your lovely weekend in Sussex,' Tash says to Mum, sipping her brandy. 'Something to cheer us all up.'

Mum glances at Dad, then clears her throat. 'Well, we weren't sure whether to mention anything . . .'

Tash and I share a look. A film-reel of mortifications spools through my mind. *Oh God. What are they going to say? They're not nudists, are they? Was it a sex party? Please don't let it have been a sex party.*

Mum and Dad are sitting very close together on the sofa, holding hands. It strikes me that I haven't seen them do that in a while. The last eighteen months have been tough for them – I know Dad's suffered from some bad migraines lately, and talk of redundancies at his company has started up again.

'This weekend . . . we were at a marriage retreat,' Mum says. The words come out in a whoosh.

Mum's had a funky new haircut recently, and I realise as she speaks that she's wearing lipstick, which she never normally does. Dad's got a new hairstyle too, but his is a bit more cabin-in-the-woods.

'What's . . . a marriage retreat?' (Tash is clearly also thinking *sex party*.)

Mum glances at Dad. 'It's where you go . . . to work on your marriage.'

'Why do you need to work on it?' Tash says, with about as much tact as Dylan when he asked where babies come from.

Next to me on the sofa, Max shifts. 'Do you want me to—'

'No, stay,' I whisper, squeezing his hand.

'We've been having some . . . *problems*, and we decided . . . this was our last shot.'

'John and Roz recommended it,' Dad chips in, like we're talking about a box set, or the best place to buy lawnmower parts. 'You know, with—'

'Yes, yes, John-and-Roz-with-the-barge,' Tash says, irritably.

Mum turns to me. 'We actually want to thank you, Lucy.'

'Me?'

'Yes. What happened last night . . . It's put everything into perspective for us.'

'I don't follow.'

Mum's face brightens suddenly, like her favourite band have just walked on to an invisible stage. 'We're going to do something *wild*. Aren't we, Gus?'

Dad beams at Mum. I haven't seen him look so happy in . . . well, a really long time. 'Yep. We're going to take advantage of being nomads. Give married life another go.'

'What do you mean, another go?' Tash says, her voice becoming more and more agitated. 'You're already married. And I don't understand what all this has to do with Lucy, or nomads, or—'

'Losing everything in the fire . . . it's made us re-evaluate,' Mum says. 'And we realised . . . we don't want to lose each other.'

'I'm going to take voluntary redundancy,' Dad says. 'And we'll bank the money from that, and the insurance, then do something crazy with it.'

I notice Simon meet Max's eye with the shadow of a smile. I'm pretty sure they'd get on, if they officially had permission to – Simon knows now about what Max and Tash did one night before he'd even met her, and to his credit, seems entirely unfazed by the whole thing. There is a level of understanding there, perhaps, reminding me – not for the first time – of Andrea. Maybe, because Simon did something stupid once too, he refuses to judge Max for having done something similar.

'Crazy's about right.' Tash is leaning forward now, her blond bob dancing in front of her face. 'Listen. I think you're both in shock—'

Mum doesn't blink. 'Actually, this is something we've been thinking about for a very long time.'

'Thirty-five years, in fact,' Dad says.

I feel Tash glance at me, perhaps for support, but I can't take my eyes off Mum and Dad. They're gleaming like two kids in love, flushed with excitement. I haven't seen them like that in so long.

'You don't know this, but when we met on holiday in Menorca, when we were twenty,' Mum says, 'we actually spent the fortnight talking about wanting to sail around the world.'

'You can't sail,' Tash points out.

'Tash, *please*,' says Simon, uncharacteristically sharp, like she's talking over all the good bits in a film.

'And when that holiday was over and we came home,' Dad says, 'me to Shoreley and your mum to Somerset, we started making plans.'

'You didn't realise you were pregnant,' I say, the picture slowly slotting into place.

'Oh,' says Tash, the culprit.

Mum shakes her head like we're misunderstanding. The beads on her earrings rattle. 'Having you girls was the most *wonderful* gift we could ever have hoped for, but now . . . it's as though this fire was a sign.'

'Take the money and run,' Dad chortles. 'Or buy a boat, anyway.'

'But Mum, what about your jobs? Your pensions? I mean, you're not millionaires – you're a teacher, and Dad works in an office.'

Mum tilts her head. 'So, only millionaires can have dreams?'

Tash shuts her eyes. 'No, of course not. I just don't think . . . I mean, how can you go from your marriage collapsing to going off round the world in the space of twenty-four hours?'

'Sometimes, if you don't know what to do next, you just have to look for a sign,' Dad says, reaching over to take Mum's hand.

I smile faintly, realising it's been a long time since I looked to a sign from the universe for guidance. Probably not since I found out about Max and my sister. I kind of miss it.

'And can you really learn to sail at your age?' Tash says. 'Don't you think that's just a tiny bit irresponsible?'

'At our age?' Dad echoes, then laughs.

'Lucy?' Mum says, and everyone looks at me. 'You're being very quiet.'

I swallow. My mouth feels tacky and unsupple, as though I haven't spoken out loud in about a hundred years. 'In principle . . . it's a brilliant idea. But yeah – I think you should take some time to think about it. Tash is right: you're in shock.'

'Very often in life,' Dad says, 'you don't know you needed a shock until you get one.'

'I can still remember that first day I met you at uni,' Max says, as we're driving along the M2 back to London, the orange motorway lights flying over the car roof like tiny UFOs. It's dark now, late, getting on for midnight. 'And you were telling me the story of how your parents met, and I thought it was this . . . crazy, unattainable fairy tale. It was so different to what I'd known with Brooke.'

I smile, lean my head against the headrest. I know exactly what he means: I'd wanted to write a whole goddamn *novel* based on that fairy tale. 'And what do you think now?'

He makes a hopeful shrug. 'Well, I don't really believe in fairy tales. But it is pretty romantic – I mean, they want to go and do the thing they first talked about thirty-five years ago. They're *literally* sailing off into the sunset together.'

'Things must have been pretty bad, though. For them to go on a marriage retreat.'

'Well, isn't the point that they went on it in the first place? They obviously wanted to save it.'

I turn to look at him. 'Max?'

'Luce.'

'Would you ever want to quit your job to buy a boat and travel the world?'

'Nah.' He looks back at me briefly. 'Farraday's right – I'm too much of a corporate sell-out.'

I smile. 'Someone's got to be.'

He smiles too. 'Yeah. And to be honest, I like it that way. Life's good, and with you, it's pretty much perfect. So long as we're together, that's all I care about. I'm just glad we made it.'

I feel him glance at me again, but he doesn't have to ask: he knows my travelling days are done. And I'm fine with that. London is my home now. I belong there, with Max. We're building a life together, a life that I love.

For a moment I shut my eyes and enjoy the warmth of the car, the engine's comforting rumble, the feeling of knowing Max will always be by my side.

'Wasn't it funny,' I say, laughing, 'when Tash started saying they couldn't sail a boat, like Mum and Dad are going on ninety? They're in their fifties.'

Max rarely lets slip any kind of opinion on Tash. So he just keeps his mouth steady and says, 'Yeah.'

We drive the rest of the way back to London without talking much, listening to Snow Patrol. The music takes me straight back to Norwich and to loving Max with my whole heart, from the first moment I met him.

17

Stay

'God, I'm sorry, Luce. I really thought he'd love it.'

I'm facing Ryan by the door in the now-empty church room. He asked if he could have a word after the session, and I could tell by the look on his face that it wasn't good news.

It's March now. Caleb's been gone for three long months. The tail end of winter by the sea – though vividly scenic, and lavish with frost-filled panoramas – has started to feel incessant. I am yearning for warmer weather.

A few weeks after Caleb left, I said Ryan could pass several chapters of my novel to his agent. And for the first time maybe ever, I felt quietly confident. It was ready, this sentimental story about love, and about longing and hope, that I'd poured my whole heart into. It tackles a few tough themes – including some similar stuff to what I went through in Sydney, with Nate – and I'm privately proud of the result. In that respect, I feel as though I've partly rewritten my past, regained control over some of the trickier parts of my own history.

We thought a response – either yes or no – might come

quickly. But the weeks slid unremarkably by, even though Ryan nudged him a couple of times.

Today, finally, the email came. One of the few professionals, aside from Ryan, who's read my work, and the response was a hard no.

Ryan looks as remorseful now as if I've caught him graffitiing appendages on the church wall. 'I honestly would never have sent it to him if I thought he'd turn it down.'

I nod. 'I know.'

'But, listen, Lucy – it's true what he said. This is no reflection on your writing, it's just that he represents more . . .' He trails off.

'High-brow stuff?' I supply, with a half-smile. 'It's okay, you can say it.'

He looks at me for a couple of moments. His dark eyes are dewy, the expression on his face intense. 'This isn't going to make things weird between us, is it? You know I'm your biggest fan.'

I smile. We've known each other almost two years now. Ryan's a friend, and a good one. I lean forward and hug him, so he can be in no doubt. His frame feels fragile and wiry in my arms, so different to the sturdiness of hugging Caleb. 'Not at all. If I ever do get published, your name's getting top billing in the acknowledgements.'

'Not *if*,' he says, sternly, pulling back from me. His words echo against the high ceiling, the stone walls. '*When.*'

I think we're about to leave, but though he's set his hand on the doorknob, he doesn't turn it. 'How's Caleb?'

I can see the teacher in Ryan is trying to end on a positive, which is sweet but also unfortunate, because talking about Caleb's pretty tough for me right now. 'He's really well, thanks,' I say, trying to keep my voice light, my tone upbeat.

'Where is he at the moment?'

'Myanmar.' To stop myself becoming too emotional, I get out my phone, tapping through to the most recent pictures Caleb's sent me, of the rust-coloured temples and hazy sunrises, the elaborate pagodas and formidable stone Buddhas.

Ryan swipes through them, seeming impressed. 'Remind me why you didn't go with him?' he says when he's done, handing back my phone with a gratified smile, like he's just been flipping through a holiday brochure.

'I wasn't really . . . in a place in my life where I wanted to go away. Maybe I will, some day.' I realise with surprise as I'm saying this that for the first time in more than a decade, it might possibly be true.

'Big deal, isn't it? Saying goodbye to the person you love for six months. Not sure I could do that.'

Ryan never talks much about his love life, other than occasionally making reference to having been on a (usually disastrous) date. Emma says he broke up with the love of his life in his mid-twenties and never fully got over it. Which kind of makes sense, when I think about it. His writing makes a lot of references to regret. Chances missed, opportunities squandered.

I nod. 'Yeah, it's a big deal. Bigger than I first thought, maybe. But . . . it'll work out.'

On the morning Caleb flew to Bangkok, I dropped him off at Heathrow. We parked up in the drop-off zone, then sat together for a while without saying much. The sky was a rich, pre-dawn purple, and together we watched it gradually brighten then dissolve into daybreak. We listened to the roar of ascending planes, their lights skimming above us like shooting stars.

'This feels all wrong,' he whispered, when it was nearly time to go.

Despite every synapse in my body throbbing in agreement, I shook my head firmly. 'It'll feel right as soon as you get there.'

We'd had this conversation so many times – late at night in bed, first thing in the morning through the shower curtain, across currents in the sea, over candles flickering in restaurants. And every time, I told him the same thing – if it was right for him, then it was right for us.

'God, why does this feel so impossible?' He laughed then as he welled up. 'If this is what leaving you is like, I'm never going to do it again.'

And then we hugged, hard, heads tucked against each other's shoulders, breathing through our noses. We hugged like you do when someone's died. It *was* a kind of grief, I think: I suddenly couldn't bear to say goodbye. I tried to draw in for the last time the exact sensations of being close to him – the broad solace of his shoulders, the press of his arms around my ribcage, the sweet scent of his skin.

'Six months,' he whispered as we eventually drew apart, his eyes damp, the words wavering.

'Six months.' It had seemed so straightforward when we first talked about it, like an exam we simply had to prep for and sit. But now the prospect felt overwhelmingly daunt-ing. I was dreading having to miss him, go to sleep alone, love him from a distance of thousands of miles.

After we said goodbye, I drove straight from Heathrow to Jools and Nigel's new flat in Tooting. Jools let me in, and I crawled into their spare room and stayed there. I'd taken a rare week off from Pebbles & Paper, earmarking it purely for eating pizza and ice cream and watching box sets and wallowing. That had always been my plan – seven days of self-pity, before getting straight back into my writing, and making something exciting happen for myself.

I can't lie – there've been moments when I've wondered if I should have been braver, taken a risk and agreed to join Caleb for part of his trip. But then I remind myself this is Caleb's adventure, not mine. We'll have plenty of time for making memories of our own when he gets back.

'Fancy coming for a drink?' I ask Ryan now.

'No, I . . .' He jerks his head, like there's somewhere he needs to be. 'Got plans.'

I nod, then hesitate. 'You know . . . even if this book never sees the light of day, I'll always be so grateful for how much you've all supported me. You and Emma, and the group.'

Ryan bats the sentiment away with his eyes. 'We can't take any of the credit here. You're a writer, Luce. It's in your blood.'

I smile bravely, remind myself not to assume the rejec-tion from Ryan's agent is terminal. *It's just a bump in the road*, I think. *What's meant for you won't pass you by.*

★   ★   ★

Emma's messaged to say she's already in the pub, getting in our usual post-session drinks. She left me and Ryan alone earlier, sensing he had bad news to impart. I said I'd catch her up.

But I can't see her anywhere when I arrive, even though the place is half-empty. The bar smells of beer and bodies and hot chips. As I'm opening WhatsApp to find out where she is, I feel a tap on my shoulder.

'Lucy?'

Turning around, I come face to face with Georgia, my old boss from Figaro.

It's almost two years since I walked out, and though I haven't thought about Figaro much over the past twelve months or so, in the immediate aftermath it was *all* I could think about. Whether I'd overreacted. Whether I'd done the right thing. Whether Georgia would find another planner to take my place, and whether the business would be okay.

Georgia draws a breath, breaks the awkward pause. 'Lucy, I just wanted to say ... I'm sorry. For everything that happened when you left. I treated you really badly. I know how much I took you for granted.'

She seems almost as surprised to be admitting this as I am to hear it, but her green eyes are wide and sincere. She looks slightly less groomed than she used to, casual in jeans and a grey cable-knit sweater, and trainers instead of the vertiginous heels she always wore to the office. She's pulled her dark hair into a messy ponytail, her whole demeanour far more chilled than I remember. 'I still feel *terrible* about it,' she continues. 'I should have messaged you afterwards, or emailed, but . . . I convinced myself I'd bump into you at some point, so I could say it to your face, and now . . . here we are.'

I shake my head. 'No, it's . . . I shouldn't have just walked out the way I did. It was selfish, leaving you in the lurch like that.'

'I *deserved* to be left in the lurch. I treated you horribly. No wonder you felt like I'd betrayed our friendship – because I had.'

We pause for a few moments, eyeing each other reflectively.

'So . . . how's everything going?' I ask, cautiously.

'Well, that's sort of what I wanted to say, as well. I sold the business about nine months ago, and honestly . . . it was the best thing I've ever done. I'm actually retraining to be a teacher.'

Without even really intending to, I step forward and hug her. 'Georgia, that's amazing. Congratulations.'

'And I met my boyfriend Adam on the course too, so . . .' Her eyes are bright – brighter than I ever remember them being while she was mired in the day-to-day stresses of running her own business. 'What I'm saying is, none of this would have happened if you hadn't walked out that day, Lucy. I'm convinced of it. After you left, I couldn't stop going over everything you'd said, and it really got me thinking about making a change. I needed a shock to wake me up. I *needed* someone to call me a selfish cow.'

I feel myself colour slightly. 'Yeah, sorry about that.'

'No!' She grasps both my hands between hers. 'Do not apologise. You had every right to do that. I had it coming to me. Really.'

I let my face soften into a smile. 'So, what will you teach, when you qualify?'

'Hopefully A-level business studies.'

'That's really brilliant, Georgia.'

'And what are you up to, these days?' She's looking at me hopefully, like I'm a lover she once dumped and she's praying I'll say I'm married with two kids, never been happier.

'Well, I work mornings at Pebbles & Paper. You know, the gift shop in town?'

'Oh yes? Adam gave me one of their salt lamps for my birthday.'

I smile without telling her those damn salt lamps are the bane of my life. Ever since Ivan made the questionable decision to stock them, customers have been queueing up to tell me they've broken, or haven't cured their insomnia, or have failed to resolve their many allergies.

'And . . . I've been writing a novel,' I say quickly, to move on from the sodding salt lamps. 'Which I probably wouldn't ever have done if I was still at Figaro. All I ever wanted was to be a writer, so—'

'Wow, that's . . . Are you published?'

'Not yet.' I think of Ryan's agent, the disappointment still churning in my chest.

Behind us, someone wins on the fruit machine, the coins paying out with a clatter that resembles applause.

'Have you finished it? What's it about?'

I nod. 'I have. And, I guess . . . love, at its heart.'

'Well, look,' Georgia says, 'since you've written a novel, maybe I can do something to finally make amends for having been such a crappy boss.'

I frown. 'How do you—'

'Adam's sister is a literary agent. If you're up for it, I'd love to send it to her. Her name's Naomi Banks. Email me the manuscript – I'll happily forward it on and ask her to take a look.'

Naomi Banks? Naomi is my Secret Dream Agent. She represents several authors I love, and – according to her website – is on the hunt for exactly the kind of book I've written.

Georgia gives me her email address. 'But,' I falter, as I'm tapping it into my phone, 'you haven't even read it yet.'

She smiles at me. 'Happy to take a chance on that. I know how good your writing is. I should have recognised that while you were working for me. You *deserved* someone to recognise it.'

I smile, then reach forward again, pull her into a hug. She smells impeccable, of perfume and fabric conditioner. 'Thank you.'

'You're welcome. I'm so happy I've seen you again, after all this time.'

After she's left, I stand where I am for a few moments, trying to remember what I've come here to do. Finally, I check my phone, which is still on silent after the writing session, and see a string of messages and missed calls from Emma.

I ring her. 'Where are you?'

'The White Hart. Waiting for you, two glasses of wine later. Why – where are you?'

'Ah. The White Horse.'
'You're in the wrong pub.'
'I'm in the wrong pub.'

When I get back to the cottage a couple of hours later, I email my manuscript to Georgia before nerves can get the better of me. Then I slip on my coat and hat and head down to the beach.

The end of winter is tantalisingly close. The days are getting longer and warmer. Greenery is bursting from the trees and hedges, pushing up through the pavement cracks. I'm still swimming occasionally, and every time I do, the sea feels slightly less like taking a dip at the South Pole. That tingle of risk has started to ebb away.

In the early hours, I video call Caleb from the beach hut, warming my hands around a cup of sugary tea. We try to talk a few times a week, but it can be hard to co-ordinate, because of the time difference, the patchy Wi-Fi, and our conflicting schedules.

Though it's just after breakfast in Myanmar, Caleb's still in bed, propped up bare-chested against the headboard. He gave me a little virtual tour when they first arrived a few weeks ago – his room is wood-panelled, with a view of the hotel swimming pool, the tips of the temple spires just visible over the treetops beyond. I like to imagine him there sometimes, as I'm falling asleep – going over his photographs, updating his blog, sending messages to friends and loved ones.

'Hey,' I say. 'I miss you.'

'Hello, you.' He seems to get more handsome every time we speak. His eyes are sparkling with the thrill of adventure. Even his teeth look brighter than I remember, whitened by the depth of his new tan. I want to reach into my phone, touch his skin, kiss his face. 'Miss you too. What's the weather like there?'

I smile. 'Still pretty cold. You?'

He laughs. 'Roasting.' His hotel is basic, no air conditioning, so he relies on a ceiling fan which he tells me has a highly lackadaisical approach to whirring.

He asks how my parents are doing. After they lobbed their break-up bombshell at us, Mum moved in with Tash and Simon while she and Dad decided what to do with their money and the cottage and their thirty-plus years' worth of stuff. It's so weird now, to think of them as two separate people. They were always Mum and Dad. Now they're Mum, and Dad.

What I haven't told anyone – not even Caleb – is that I'm harbouring a private belief that they can get over this. That this isn't the end of their story – merely a detour along the way.

'Dad had a date,' I tell Caleb.

His eyes go wide. 'Wow.'

'I know.'

'Who with?'

'Didn't ask.'

'Did it . . . go well?'

I shake my head. 'Apparently she was only looking to make a friend.'

Caleb winces sympathy. 'Your dad okay?'

I smile. 'He'll survive. He said she wasn't his type anyway.'

'God, dating at their age must be brutal.'

I nod, not quite ready to share my secret theory that none of my dad's dates – or my mum's, come to that – will result in anything meaningful, because their love story isn't actually over yet. I'm well aware how ridiculously naive this sounds, and yet . . . I just can't shake the sense that they'll get through this somehow.

Caleb slings a hand behind his head. His chest is as tanned as his face. I miss that chest, its taut contours. I miss lying on it, kissing it, running a finger along it. I miss listening to the drum of his heartbeat.

We chat for a bit longer. He tells me he's heading out with the team in an hour or so to photograph a local monastery. I try to conjure up the heat-laden air, the lushness of the vegetation, the gilded temples. They're just approaching the wet season, and temperatures have been in the high thirties. They're a long way inland, and – believe it or not – Caleb says he's missing swimming in the Channel.

So I carry our call outside, into the inky night and onto the shingle. The air is blunt with cold. I feel the salt hit my skin and coat my lips, mingling with the sugar from my tea.

I walk him down to the shoreline so he can see the water, passing a clutch of night fishermen in pop-up tents as I go. I hold up the phone and let him listen to the sea as it shifts and heaves, its surface spangled with moonlight. I wonder if we see the same patch of sky when we look up, from our distant time zones on faraway spots of the earth.

Caleb groans thirstily. 'What I'd give to jump into that.' His pupils look larger, greedy for cold water. 'Swimming in a pool out here doesn't even come close. I never feel properly refreshed.'

'Well, I wouldn't mind a bit of sultry weather right now,' I admit. 'Winter's felt long without you. Mind you, there's something to be said for living in a place with all four seasons. I like knowing change is always somewhere on the horizon.' I sit down on the shingle and finger some chilly pebbles, wishing his hand was holding mine.

On the screen, our eyes meet, and I am riveted with the desire to feel his skin next to my own, to be kissing him, undressing him. I breathe in, secretly hoping to catch the scent of sun cream and Caleb and frangipani flowers. But all I get is the faint pungency of fish and seaweed.

'Twelve weeks tomorrow,' I whisper.

'Twelve weeks,' he whispers back. 'Can't wait.'

'What's the first thing we'll do together?'

'Go back to the beach hut and I'll tell you.'

So I do. Holding Caleb in my hand, I go back to the beach hut and close the doors and switch off the lights, and let him talk me through *exactly* what we'll do together, the first night he's home. And afterwards, as we whisper about laughing and kissing and loving each other, I know there's no other person I'd rather be thinking of as winter segues into spring. No one else I'd want to love over the longest of distances, as I dream of a future I can't wait to begin.

Go

'How's the conference?' Jools asks.

I'm sitting on the bed in my hotel room with Jools on speaker, wrapped in a dressing gown with a staggeringly expensive seaweed mask tacked to my face, a vain attempt to minimise my pores before tomorrow.

'It's very … conferencey. I mean, everyone's trying to pretend it's not a conference, because we're "creatives", but it is. There's lukewarm coffee and custard creams and PowerPoint and breakout spaces. It's definitely a conference.'

It's my second night at this four-star golfing resort in Surrey, where I'm attending the Association of UK Creatives' annual conference, on behalf of Supernova. Today has been a mad dash between masterclasses, work-shops and roundtables, where I've listened to industry experts speak about everything from behavioural data to junk food advertising to the agency-client symbiosis. The programme finished about an hour ago, and I've got another forty minutes or so spare before networking drinks and then dinner.

I've been invited to deliver a presentation tomorrow on my contribution to *A Whole New World*, the now-acclaimed campaign I created with Seb over a year ago, which, un-believably, is still getting traction. It seems that pretty much anyone who's anyone in the advertising world is a delegate at this conference – including Zara, plus a couple of other senior Supernova executives. The room I'll be presenting in holds up to two hundred people; Zara's also been hint-ing over the past couple of months that a promotion might be on the cards for me. If I mess this up, the repercussions won't be good.

The hotel's pretty nice. I even managed to sleep peacefully last night. Since the new year, courtesy of Max's medical insurance with HWW, I've been seeing a psychologist, Pippa, once a week. She's been helping me explore what happened with Nate, and I've started taking some risks in baby steps, to overcome my tendency to panic in unfamiliar spaces. I hadn't known how much I needed to talk to someone about it until I finally did.

I don't talk too much about it with Max. Though he's been nothing but supportive, I can tell he thinks psychological intervention is best left to the professionals. And maybe he's right. I've said things to Pippa I would never say to Max. Your boyfriend can't fulfil every relationship role in your life. Sometimes it's healthier to offload onto someone else.

'What time's your presentation?' Jools asks.

'Ten.'

'Feel ready?'

I've been prepping for two months now, working on the thing non-stop at evenings and weekends. It's fair to say it's the most pressure I've ever been under, professionally speaking. But it's a good kind of stress. Like walking up the aisle, or buying a house. Seb's been helping me out, animating parts of my presentation so there's no risk of death-by-PowerPoint. I can recite my speech in my sleep, I've repeated it to myself over and over – in the shower, on the tube, in the loos on girls' nights out – and I've even recorded it on my phone, so I can listen to it whenever I get a free moment. I've asked Max to film me speaking; I've invited friends and family to the flat and forced them to listen to me practise. This needs to be twenty minutes of gold. I *have* to nail this.

'Yes,' I tell Jools firmly, because at this point, exuding confidence is almost as important as the words I'll be saying. 'Yes, I'm ready.'

I ask how Nigel is, and Jools sighs dreamily. They've been together nearly ten months now. I suspect they're going to be one of those couples for whom the honeymoon period never ends.

'We had this little impromptu gig at the house last night,' she says. 'All these people turned up. I didn't know most of them. But Nigel played for everyone, and they *loved* it. Everyone was dancing around the living room.'

I prod at the stiffened face mask with my fingertips, wiggle my mouth a bit. I really want to smile, but whoever made this mask clearly modelled it on cement.

'The finale was "God Only Knows" by The Beach Boys,' Jools continues. She loves that song. 'It was so beautiful, Luce. He's so talented.'

'You're welcome, again,' I say.

'For what?'

'Me moving out.'

She laughs. 'How long am I going to be in debt to you for that?'

'As long as you and Nigel are together. So . . . for ever?'

I hear her bite into an apple. 'Come on then. Thrill me – what's on the conference agenda for tonight?'

'Oh, the usual. Drinks, networking, dinner. Then a quiz, I think. All very dull.'

'But you love your job.'

'Exactly. I love my *job*. I don't love pretending to get excited about the history of advertising so I can win a hamper full of jam.'

'What's Max up to tonight?'

'Oh, working. He's got loads on at the moment. Macavity's helping out.'

We adopted Macavity after Tash and Simon discovered Dylan was allergic to pet hair. Mum and Dad are holding firm on their sailing-around-the-world plan, so Max and I said we'd take Macavity. He's twelve now, so he's pretty low maintenance, and he's always been an indoor cat, which means we don't have to freak out about passing cars or decapitated mice.

Max wasn't sure about having a cat at first, but the pair of them are best buddies now. I love sneaking up on them late at night, finding Max dozing on the sofa with Macavity purring contentedly on his chest.

'Well, good luck for tomorrow,' says Jools. 'I'll be thinking of you. You'll boss it.'

'Thank you. I hope so.'

'I know so.'

Our dinner is classic conference, whereby they seat delegates from the same company at different tables as a sort of icebreaker, although to be honest, the free wine mostly takes care of that anyway. I've found myself next to Jon, a graphic designer. He works for a rival agency in Shoreditch that I happen to know Zara absolutely loathes. After a couple of glasses of wine, he tells me he's just found out his wife of eight years cheated on him with his best friend, a matter of months after they got together.

He's blond and a bit manic, talks very fast. He might be high. His eyes are bloodshot and his clothes are slightly crumpled, like being asked to look smart is an affront to his creative genius.

I've tried to go classy tonight in a midnight-blue knee-length lace dress, with capped sleeves and a high neck, plus the Jimmy Choos I wore for my date with Max, that night he got back from the Seychelles. I felt fancy earlier, when I stood dressed-up in front of the mirror in my room, so I sent Max a selfie, which he replied to with a string of complimentary messages.

'I mean, what I can't figure out is, does it actually *matter*?' Jon's asking me. He's swaying a little as he speaks, like he might be about to faceplant into his panna cotta.

'Only you can answer that.'

'She keeps saying, "Eight years versus three months, Jon."' He mimics his wife's voice at a bitter, unflattering pitch. 'But that doesn't mean I don't picture them together every time I shut my eyes.'

I sip my orange juice, blink away an image of my sister with Max. 'Mmm-hmm.'

'You married, Lottie?'

'It's Lucy, actually.'

He frowns. 'Your place card says Lottie.'

I pick it up, waggle it at him. 'Nope . . . it definitely says Lucy.'

'Okay, *Lucy*,' he says, like I'm being particularly obtuse. 'You married?'

I shake my head.

'Boyfriend?'

'Yes.'

'So then you know.'

'Not . . . exactly.'

'Well, put yourself in my position. We're creatives, aren't we? Let's use a *little imagination*, for God's sake.'

'All right,' I say curtly, because he's talking to me as if this is all my fault.

'What would you do, if you were me?'

I glance at him, and it's then that I notice there are tears clinging to his eyes, just waiting for him to blink so they can fall. I feel bad for him suddenly, recalling the anger I felt myself, when I first found out what my sister and Max had done.

I wait for a couple of moments. 'If I were you . . . I'd go upstairs, drink a pint of water and sleep it off. And whatever you do, don't drink-dial your wife. Or your friend.'

He nods, and it's hard to tell if he's mulling this over, or if his mind has just popped off on a detour. 'She loves that I have this job, you know.'

I guess it's the latter. 'Does she?' I say, weakly.

'Yeah. The money. The kudos. She *brags* about it.'

'What does she do?'

He speaks over me. 'You know what would really annoy her?'

'No, what?'

'If I just . . . quit. Without telling her. Just got up one morning and said . . . *I don't have a job any more, you figure it out.*' He's slurring his words now, his face growing flushed and damp, a combination of red wine and outrage.

'Sounds like the only person that would hurt would be you.'

'I've got a whole novel in a drawer, you know.' He swigs back more wine. His lips are stained purple from it, his teeth gradually greying. 'Sci-fi, like . . . Asimov, but better.'

I suppress a smile. 'Really.'

'Yeah. But whenever I talk about it, she tells me to grow up and stop dreaming, like she doesn't think I could do it.'

'I'm sure she doesn't think that.'

'In fact, you know what? Screw it.' He jabs an index finger a little too close to my face for no apparent reason, then gets to his feet. 'I'm going to tell them to stuff their job, right now.'

'No, Jon . . .' I get up too, grab his sleeve. 'Don't be silly. You're drunk, you'll regret it . . .'

He shakes my hand away. He's so out of it, his eyeballs are beginning to roll as he talks. 'Nah, I've always hated this job anyway. And my boss is a grade-A tosser. Time for some *home truths.*' And before I can stop him, he's weaving his way over to another table.

'Is he okay, do you think?' asks the girl on my other side, about twenty minutes too late.

I shake my head. 'I think we're about to find out.'

Jon has stopped by another table, and is now doing his little finger-jab at an older man, who's sitting down. I'm guessing it's his boss. Other people start getting to their feet. One of them grabs Jon's arm, which doesn't go down too well. He starts shouting, then grabs a full glass of white wine and slings its contents at the man, who by now is on his feet too. There is a collective gasp from the room, before it falls completely silent. I'm too far away to see the exact expression on the man's face, but I'm guessing if Jon's not already out of a job, he will be by the morning. He'll probably open his email tomorrow, head throbbing, to see that immortal subject line: *Meeting with HR*.

I can't watch any more, so I grab my handbag, stumble out of the dining room and head for the lifts. It'll leave my table mates two down for the quiz, but it's not like we're playing for a five-star holiday. I mean, the top prize is a hamper full of condiments.

'I should have done more.'

'Luce. He didn't jump off a bridge. He got a bit lairy at a work do. Who hasn't done that in their time?'

It's about nine o'clock now. I'm lying on the bed in my room, sipping my complimentary water and nibbling a shortbread biscuit. It's a much nicer room than I'd imagined before we arrived: I'd been expecting a travelling salesman vibe, with flat-pack furniture and warning stickers on all the appliances. But it's actually very swish and country house, with sturdy furniture and a plush carpet, heavy curtains and designer toiletries.

Max is in his car – apparently he's had to pop into the office for a couple of files. His voice keeps patching in and out.

'I bet *you* haven't,' I say, in reply to his question.

'Well, no, but only because I like my job. Sounds like this guy's got a backup plan anyway. He'll be all right.'

'What – to be "Asimov, but better"?'

A pause. 'That doesn't actually mean anything to me. The last book I read was *Gale on Easements*.'

I smile. 'Let's just say, I should have tried harder to talk him out of it.'

'It wasn't your job to. You don't even know him. And hey – when you see his book in the window at Waterstones next year, you'll be glad you didn't.'

There was a time, many moons ago, when I dreamed of the same thing for myself.

'You're a hopeless optimist, Max Gardner – do you know that?'

'Well, wasn't quitting Figaro the best thing you ever did? You'd never have moved to London. You wouldn't be working at Supernova. We'd probably never have gone on that date . . .'

'Yeah. I think everything worked out pretty well in the end.' I smile dreamily. 'So, are you pulling an all-nighter? It's late to be picking up files, isn't it?'

Max clears his throat. 'Actually . . . you know how I said I was in the car because I'd just popped to the office?'

'Yes . . .'

'Well, what I really meant by that was . . . I'm coming to see you.'

My heart does a little back-flip. 'What?'

'Yeah. I was thinking . . . you could sneak me into your hotel room. We'll have some fun.'

I laugh. 'You can't. Aren't you working tomorrow?'

'No meetings till the afternoon. Anyway, the hotel's got Wi-Fi, hasn't it?'

'Max, I—'

'Sound like a plan?'

I don't say anything for a couple of moments. From the corridor I can hear shrieks and muffled laughter, probably other like-minded delegates ducking out of the quiz.

'No,' I tell Max. 'I'm sorry. I need to get an early night. This presentation tomorrow is a big deal.' I don't go as far as to say *career-defining*, but I really do think it could be.

Anyway, I shouldn't feel bad. Max knows this already. He's made a romantic gesture, but he'll wake up tomorrow and realise this was the right call. I need to run through my notes again, charge my laptop, press my clothes, get eight solid hours of high-quality sleep.

'Swear I'll behave myself,' he says, but the mischief in his voice tells me otherwise.

I suppress a shiver. 'No, Max. You know you won't. You know *we* won't. I can't handle any distractions. Not tonight.'

He laughs. 'I promise I won't distract you. I'll just . . . raid the minibar and eat all your Pringles and test you on your slides.'

'No!' I smile. The thought of it is so sweet, but I know it'll be even sweeter tomorrow, once all this is over. 'Turn the car around. I'll see you tomorrow night. I'll take you out for dinner. Somewhere nice. I love you.'

So we say goodnight, and he turns the car around.

I wake to the sound of my phone ringing. I have to tug my eyes open, unsnag the sleep from my brain. There's an ocean-floor depth to the darkness that tells me it's the middle of the night.

I can't hear any music or laughter. The world is still, waiting for what comes next. The silence is so loud it almost buzzes.

Switching on a lamp, I grab my phone, blinking at the screen. I tap to answer it, even though I don't recognise the number.

'Am I speaking to Lucy Lambert?'

My heartbeat becomes liquid. I can hear it rushing between my ears. A question like that at this time of night can only ever be bad news.

I have never felt more desperate to hear someone promising me a special price on new guttering, or offering to fix my computer. But the female voice on the other end of the line is clear and steady, pin-sharp. I know from just those six words that she is no cold caller.

An image of my parents lurches into my mind. *Who is it? What's happened?*

'Yes,' I manage to say, eventually.

On the carpet next to the bed, one of my blue Jimmy Choos has fallen on its side, like it's fainted.

'Lucy, this is Kirsten Lewis from Surrey Police.'

Surrey? Why Surrey?

'Are you the partner of Max Gardner?'

And just like that, my whole world goes black.

18

Stay

'I've just been almost killed,' I gasp into my phone.

Jools is laughing – I guess because escaping death is better than succumbing to it. 'What?'

'Mopeds.' I turn to survey them, buzzing like bees along the road I've just jumped out of. 'They're everywhere.'

I've been in Bali for less than an hour. According to the map (and Caleb's super-helpful colleague from the cultural heritage team, Gabi), the beach hotel I need to head for is just a short distance from the airport. But the reality is much more confusing than Google Maps. I can only see streets and trees and tall buildings and dense clumps of people, all of whom look like locals, not tourists. Every road seems to loop onto the next, and none of them appear to lead anywhere that isn't the airport periphery. And I can't see the beach – nor are there any signs suggesting where it might be. It feels a bit like I've wandered out of Heathrow Airport and attempted to walk to Covent Garden.

Anyway, I was so intent on trying to navigate that I forgot to check both ways before crossing the road, which was when I almost got knocked down by a speeding moped, whose rider didn't flinch, swerve or even brake.

I hitch my rucksack higher up my shoulders. I'm already sweating. The air when I first left the terminal felt like stepping inside a preheated oven. Why did I think it would be a good idea to walk? For some reason, I'd imagined Bali to be blue sky and sea breezes. But so far, it's just sticky and muggy and noisy, the sky the colour of a dirty puddle.

'Luce,' Jools says calmly, like the nurse she is. It's morning in London, and her day off. I picture her sitting in the cool shade of her back garden in Tooting, sipping a coffee. 'Please just go back to the airport and get a taxi.'

I rotate slowly on the spot, searching for anything that could hint to where the terminal might have gone – an ascending plane, for example, or a person with a suitcase. Maybe I should FaceTime my dad and his sixth sense for direction – he'd probably be able to tell which way I should walk just from checking out the clouds above my head.

'That's a good idea in theory,' I say. 'If the airport hadn't vanished into thin air.'

It's now May. I haven't seen Caleb for five months, and somewhere around the four-month mark, the missing him began to get too much. The drawn-out goodbyes at the end of our phone calls, the pangs of regret when I saw a couple holding hands in the street, the shameful rushes of envy whenever Jools WhatsApped me with another update on her wedding plans. The wanting to touch him and kiss him and feel the warmth of his form lying next to me in bed.

'You could do that,' Jools said casually, one day in early April. I was in Tooting for the weekend and we were having a lazy start after a late night out with Nigel and his extended family, lounging on her sofa, watching *Friends* for the umpteenth time as we mainlined buttered crumpets.

'Do what?'

Jools nodded at the screen. Emily had just turned up in New York, having flown in from London to surprise Ross. 'Fly out there. Surprise him.'

I snorted. 'What?'

Jools shrugged, like the suggestion was no big deal. 'You've been missing him like crazy. You could do something to show him . . . just how much you love him. It would be *so* romantic, Luce – flying out there, turning up at his hotel. I mean, why not?'

'Because,' I said, a little too sharply, before I could help it, 'you know why.'

Jools smiled conspiratorially, like this objection was so weak it wasn't even worth acknowledging. 'Imagine how much he'd love it, though.'

We didn't talk about it again that weekend, but she had planted a seed. I'd thought until then that my no-long-haul-travel stance would never soften, but over the next few days, I did begin to imagine how much Caleb would love it if I joined him. I started mulling the idea over, rolling it around in my mind ever so gently, like a ball of clay that I knew had the potential to be something exciting, though I wasn't sure quite what. I let it linger in the recesses of my mind, daring

– while I was showering, or walking to work, or cooking – to picture myself getting on a plane. I even wrote it down on my laptop: a short story about two unnamed characters being reunited after a long time apart, though in the end I had to stop because things got a little too steamy.

After a few days, I realised that the lurch in my stomach whenever I thought about actually doing it didn't resemble fear as much I'd thought. It felt more like excitement. Butterflies rather than wasps. A tiny thrill at the prospect of possibility – the realisation that if I wanted to, maybe I *could* change the way I saw the world. I *could* do things I'd previously thought were beyond my reach. Maybe it had just taken missing Caleb this much for me to realise it.

I was still afraid, but – perhaps for the first time ever – I was starting to wonder if being afraid wasn't, in fact, a reason not to do something. Maybe it was even more of a reason to try.

The taxi reaches its destination and I pass the driver a handful of rupiah. He retrieves my rucksack from the boot, and I thank him, then stand back and look at the hotel. It's a modest place, one road back from the beach, its entrance shaded beneath a pagoda roof and crowded by palm trees.

This is it. Five months apart, and Caleb is now just metres away from me. I stay where I am on the pavement for a moment, staring up at the building like I'm standing at the steps of a castle in a fairy tale.

I venture inside, nod politely to the man behind the desk and walk through the lobby. Gabi's told me Caleb's in room 12, so I follow the signs and make my way along the corridor, flip-flops slapping the floor tiles as I go. I'm paranoid I'll bump into him heading out somewhere, headphones in and camera around his neck, which would be disastrous. Because here in this corridor is not where I want to do this. Our reunion has been on loop in my mind ever since I booked my ticket: he'll open the door, I'll throw myself at him, he'll respond, and we'll barely be able to breathe or speak until much, much later.

Room 12. Here it is: an innocuous brown door, with a fair bit of its varnish rubbed off. I take a breath, rest my palm against the peephole just in case, then knock.

There's a long pause. For a moment I'm afraid he's gone out, or that he's on the phone, or in the shower. I've been dreaming about this moment for so long, I don't think I could bear it if it didn't go exactly to plan, after so many hundreds of pounds, thousands of miles and countless skipped heartbeats.

And then, a muffled, 'Hang on.'

The door opens.

He blinks at me for several moments. And then, 'Oh my God.'

'Hey,' I say, my whole heart bursting open with joy.

'Lucy . . . Oh my *God*.' He steps forward. He is deeply tanned, his dark hair slightly lighter, and he seems taller somehow – though that's impossible, of course. He looks tired, but a good kind of tired. The kind of tired that says he's ready to stop missing me.

'Thought I'd surprise you,' I whisper, even as the tears are beginning to swell behind my eyes. 'Being apart was getting too hard.'

'Please tell me I'm not dreaming,' he whispers back. Then, without waiting for me to reply, he takes my face between his palms and sets his lips against mine, like he absolutely has to check I am, in fact, real. And now his hands are in my hair, and mine in his, and we are kissing the way they do in films – what Jools would call apocalypse-kissing – fierce and frenzied, a kiss on fast-forward because it's just been too long.

We stumble together into his room, which I can already feel is hot, under air-conditioned. But it doesn't matter. A groan falls from Caleb's mouth into mine as we find our way down onto his bed, grabbing at limbs and pulling at clothes. We become quickly slick with sweat, burning and hungry. The mattress squeaks comically with every small movement, but neither of us cares. And soon after that he is pushing up my dress and I am tugging down his shorts, and all I can think about is drinking in every second of this moment I've been craving since the day he left.

Afterwards, we lie unclothed on the mattress together, the ceiling fan spinning hypnotically above our heads as we collect our scattered senses. From outside drifts the soundtrack of a foreign country, horns sounding and traffic shunting, woven through with the reeling of mopeds.

Next to me, Caleb shakes his head. 'I still can't believe you're here.'

I smile, shuffling round on the pillow to face him. 'Are you surprised?'

356

What Might Have Been

He turns his head to mine so we're nose-to-nose. His eyes are shining. 'Surprised doesn't even come close.'

'I couldn't wait another month.'

'You have no idea how happy that makes me.'

'Knowing I'm impatient?' I tease.

'Well, if this is what impatience gets us,' he says, 'please never, ever change.'

I roll onto my front and prop myself up on an elbow, drawing shapes against his chest with one finger. 'Look at that tan. I feel so pale next to you.'

He smiles. 'Pale and beautiful.'

'God, I've missed you. This is . . . *so* much better than I even imagined it.'

He reaches out and tucks my hair behind my ear, his eyes flitting over me, seeming to drink in the sight of me. 'You look amazing. I love your hair like that.'

I've been wearing it loose a lot more recently. Rapunzel hair, my mum calls it. It's spilling out across my shoulders, albeit temporarily roughed up from Caleb grasping it. 'Thank you,' I whisper.

'Just . . . tell me you're not in transit or something. That you didn't win some sort of . . . twenty-four hours in Bali competition.'

'Nope,' I say, happily. 'Ten whole days.'

He shakes his head again, like he's still half-thinking I'm some sort of mirage. 'Perfect.'

'Although . . . I totally get that you're working. You don't have to be a tour guide, or anything. Just so long as we can do this every day.'

He arches an eyebrow. 'I'm not going to take much persuading to do this every day.'

I smile, let my gaze roam over the room. 'This is really nice.' Though basic, the space seems bright and in good order – if slightly messy, with Caleb's clothes and photography kit strewn across every available surface. There are books too, and maps, ticket stubs and travel documents. I can only think housekeeping don't attempt a daily clean.

'Sorry about the state of it. I'd have tidied up, if I'd known you were coming.'

I smile. 'Believe me, I could not care less.'

He runs a hand down one side of my face, like he's finding it hard to stop touching me. 'So . . . what changed your mind? About travelling. I mean, you've literally come halfway across the world, Luce.'

I shrug gently. 'After you left . . . I started thinking a lot about what you said. About Nate stealing experiences from me, and not letting him win. And I was missing you so much, and I started to get . . . I don't know. Sort of angry. I couldn't stop thinking about you, and then me and Jools watched that episode of *Friends* where Emily flies to New York to see Ross—'

He nods sagely. 'Classic.'

I smile. 'And I know we *can* be apart, but I just . . . didn't want to be any more. I wanted to see you, and if getting on a plane was what it took to do that, then I wasn't going to let Nate be the reason I chickened out.'

He's stroking my shoulders now. 'So, was the journey okay? Did you feel all right?'

I nod. 'Yeah, actually. It was pretty good. I brought my laptop. Spent most of it writing.'

Just forty-eight hours after Georgia sent her my manuscript two months ago, Naomi Banks got in touch to ask if we could meet at her offices in Bloomsbury. We discussed the book – why I wrote it and her vision for it – and chatted through her comprehensive list of edits. I'm working on those right now, after which we'll submit the finished version to publishers. It's a long game, with absolutely no guarantees, so I'm still working at Pebbles & Paper, which to be honest I do really enjoy, despite Ivan being something of a control freak who's added two more customers to his barred list over the last five months alone.

I do know, though – however the novel works out – that Naomi and I are the perfect match. We work together so well, and are so aligned in many of our thoughts and ideas. She *gets* my book, and me. I'm now convinced Ryan's agent turning it down was so Naomi and I could be brought together, even though at the time it felt like such a kick in the teeth.

Caleb sketches the outline of my collarbone with one finger. 'This is going to be the most amazing ten days, Luce. I'm so happy you're here.'

'Me too,' I whisper, and then for a moment we are just looking into each other's eyes without speaking, our happiness hopscotching through the space between us.

'So, what do you fancy doing now?' he says, eventually. 'Do you want to go out? This is a hot surf spot, apparently. Loads going on.'

I shake my head and lean forward, pressing my lips to his. He responds instantly, his hand moving to my back and trailing down between my shoulder blades, a tease traced out across my skin. 'Maybe later,' I murmur. 'I'd say we've got some more reuniting to do yet.'

We spend every spare moment of the next ten days together. Caleb shows me the work he's been doing and introduces me to his colleagues, and I get to go with them on trips to Hindu temples and museums, and to restaurants after-hours when they've clocked off, plus a Balinese dance show, a couple of nightclubs. When Caleb's not working, we explore together, venturing out to the palaces of East Bali, hiking Mount Batur at sunrise, visiting the rice paddies, sinking our feet into the sand of countless beaches. We eat breakfast in cafés and lunch at stalls, drink in what feels like a thousand sunrises, enjoy massages at a local spa. And we end our days with what we've been missing most – to touch and undress and soar sky-high with pleasure before lying bare-skinned together in the throbbing heat, almost numb with bliss, talking into the night and making plans for our future, as outside, the sky pops with a million stars.

On my last night, Caleb tells me he's made a booking at a fancy restaurant overlooking the beach. So I wear my nicest maxi-dress and leather sandals, twist my hair up and add a flick to my eyeliner, and put in the silver earrings he bought me on our trip to Seminyak a couple of days ago.

What Might Have Been

As we stroll hand in hand towards the beach, I think about what I'd be doing if I was back in Shoreley right now, if I'd never come out here. Probably FaceTiming Caleb as I walked to Pebbles & Paper on an overcast morning, feeling that deep gnaw of longing in my stomach, oblivious to the magic of being here with him. I think about how glad I am that I pushed myself to do this, that I didn't let fear overtake me and Nate steal this experience from both of us.

The restaurant is on a vast decked area right on the sand, candlelit and fringed with palm trees, raspberry-pink frangipani flowers adorning the tables. The setting sun makes the sky look ablaze, a tropical bonfire.

Once our drinks have arrived, freshly squeezed watermelon and pineapple, Caleb reaches out across the table and takes my hand. A warm breeze is trickling through the air, waltzing across my bare arms and shoulders.

'This . . . has been the most amazing ten days,' he says, eyes glimmering with emotion.

I nod and grip his hand. 'I'll remember it for ever.'

'Really wish I was coming back with you tomorrow.'

'Just a month,' I remind him. 'Four weeks. That's it.'

'It'll feel longer now.'

I smile. 'That wasn't the idea, but . . . I know what you mean. I feel the same.'

Caleb clears his throat. 'You know, if you being here has made me realise anything, it's that . . . I don't want to be apart from you ever again, Lucy.'

'Me neither,' I say, a warm tingle of relief spreading through me. 'From now on, let's just agree to be a couple of co-dependent limpets, okay?'

He laughs, then trails off. I feel a leap of love for him and, momentarily, I can almost see it suspended between us, like hot breath on a chilly day.

Caleb sets down his glass, and before I can fully register what's happening, he's getting off his chair and dropping to one knee in front of me. The restaurant is full, and straight away I can sense heads turning. Somebody whoops. My pulse begins pumping hard, my heart breaking free from my body.

In the next moment, Caleb has slipped a hand inside the pocket of his jeans and retrieved a ring. I catch my breath. It's the one I lingered over in Seminyak the other day, momentarily entranced by the dazzle of its stone. I didn't say anything to Caleb – I hadn't even known he'd been watching me examine it – but he must have gone back to get it. It's slender and silver, studded at its centre with a bright blue sapphire. He holds it out to me now between finger and thumb, his hand shaking slightly.

'Lucy, I love you so much. My whole life . . . I never believed in soulmates. But then I met you, and you proved me so wrong. I don't ever want to be without you again. Will you marry me?'

There's not a single breath of hesitation inside my body. 'Yes. Oh my God. A million times, yes.'

And now we are kissing, and crying, and laughing, and the other people in the restaurant are whooping and applauding, and Caleb's slipping the ring onto my finger, the man I am meant to spend the rest of my life with, the man whose heartbeat feels like home.

Go

I'm just going through the motions when I find it. Drifting from room to room with Macavity at my ankles, picking things up then putting them back down, pretending to clean the flat but in reality doing little more than moving stuff around. Max's vitamins. That slightly intimidating book he was reading on the power of habits. The aftershave I don't dare smell. Dumbbells, cufflinks, breath mints. His work scarf, soft as satin. His running shoes, one pair of many. The box of belongings from his desk at HWW that his boss, Tim, dropped solemnly off last week. Two copies of the *FT*, from the days preceding the accident, which have now, inconceivably, become precious artefacts.

The flat just feels ludicrous without Max in it.

It's now a mess of crusty crockery and strewn items of clothing and half-drunk cups of tea and sauce-stained takeaway cartons. I know I need to do something about this, if only out of respect for Max, because he always took such good care of his things. And it's as I'm putting some of his T-shirts away – I've been wearing them at night, but I can't bear to wash them – that I see it, nestled deep inside the drawer. A small box, in leather the colour of cream.

I prise it open, and my world caves in all over again.

I try calling Jools, but she's at work and her phone just rings out. So, in desperation, I call Tash.

For the first couple of weeks after the accident, I couldn't even look at my sister. There's nothing quite like losing a loved one to bring past resentments springing vividly back to life. I just couldn't square the idea of her being sad on my behalf, because she had, albeit years ago, tainted me and Max in a way that would be there for ever. Like a chip in a precious object, not constantly on show, but unmissable if you tilt it just the right way, or hold it to the light. An imperfection, a flaw that can't be fixed.

But then I rang her one night, when Jools couldn't pick up, a little like I'm doing now. And I realised after we'd spoken for a few minutes that I was clinging to the sound of her voice, to the knowledge that my sister was probably more invested in being there for me than anyone else I knew. The time had come for her to really and truly prove herself, and I knew she would rise to the occasion.

Two months ago today, shortly after I told him to turn the car around, Max's SUV was crushed against the central reservation of the M25 by an articulated lorry. The driver escaped without injury, but Max died at the scene. The police investigation is ongoing.

His funeral was a month later, my only chance to say goodbye, as I opted not to see him at the mortuary due to the nature of his injuries. Nearly one hundred people gathered at Lambeth Crematorium to pay their respects, after which we scattered his ashes at the garden of remembrance. It was never in question that he would stay in London. His heart was always here, not in Cambridge.

I found it bizarrely hard to cry that day, even when we played 'Wonderwall' at the end of the service. I was still in shock, I think, struggling to feel anything but numb. My memory of those first few weeks is so foggy. They say love is a drug – but so, I've learned, is grief. I was having a hard time believing Max was actually dead: I kept checking my phone for messages from him, staying up into the small hours in case he walked through the door. I would think I'd spotted him at the shop, or crossing the street in front of the flat.

Only his mother, Brooke, was conspicuous by her absence at the funeral. I'd asked Tash to track her down with the details, as I couldn't face speaking to her myself, so soon after the accident. And Tash did manage to find her, but Brooke didn't show up. And I hated her for that. Because even after Max had died, she couldn't bring herself to be there for him.

I wondered afterwards if she was angry, because it turned out that Max had recently written a will, in which he'd appointed his friend, Dean Farraday, as executor. Dean told me Max had left his flat, money, everything – aside from a few items for Dean and his family – to me. Brooke got nothing. Dean said Max had made the arrangements shortly after the fire at my parents', but decided not to tell me because he was worried I'd argue it should be Brooke's name on that document, and not mine.

Max knew me so well. Because at the time, yes – I probably would have said that. Now? I'm not so sure.

It wasn't until after the funeral that I think I finally understood – the realisation as brutal as swallowing dynamite – that I would never see Max again. That the only man I'd ever truly loved was gone for ever, because I'd told him to turn the car around.

Since then, I've been surviving from hour to hour, moving through the days but not experiencing them. The grief has seeped into my bones, invaded my body like a disease. People think you're sad when you're grieving, but it's so much more primal than that. That's why grief has its own word. It becomes a part of you, alters you without permission.

Every time death takes a life, it steals a few more too, just for kicks.

'You okay?' Tash asks when she picks up.

I start stammering into the phone. 'I found . . . I found . . .'

'Lucy? What did you find?'

I've been off work since Max died. Zara's been amazing – far more compassionate than I might have guessed she would be. She even gave me that promotion *in absentia*, in recognition of the nearly two years of hard work I'd put in at the time of the conference. When she told me, I burst into tears. It should have been such a proud moment, not the bittersweet wrench it was.

I have no idea what Tash is doing right now, or even what day it is: it could be the weekend, or perhaps she's just stepped out of a meeting at work. But you'd never know: she talks to me as though she's my own personal helpline, like she's got nothing better to do right now than listen to me gabble.

'A ring. A ring in a box. *A ring in a box.*'

'Oh, sweetheart.' I can hear precisely the moment my sister's heart breaks with mine.

I tell her I'll call her back, then run to the toilet and throw up. I can't keep anything down at the moment. Last week was my first session back with Pippa, the psychologist I'd been seeing before Max died (yes, *died*: if one more person says *passed*, I won't be responsible for my actions). Pippa explained that nausea is a common physical manifestation of grief, as is my lack of energy and complete loss of appetite, as well as the constant metallic taste in my mouth, which only serves to further put me off my food.

I look awful, I know it. Like a ghost of myself. And the only thing that would bring me back to life would be if Max were to walk through that door again right now.

'How you holding up?' Dean kisses me on both cheeks. He smells of spicy aftershave, and I am suddenly conscious of my state of unwash. He passes me a coffee and a paper bag from Gail's. 'Thought you could use some sustenance.'

'Thank you,' I say. Gail's is my favourite, but I'm not sure I can stomach cake at the moment. We head into the living room, where I sit down in an armchair, drawing my cardigan around me. It's May now, warm, and London is at its gleaming best, exultant with early summer skies and sun-dappled parks and drinking at dusk. But my mood is more suited to January: grey, cold, never-ending.

Like always, Macavity springs silently onto my lap. He's been clingy ever since Max died, and I'm convinced he's pining for his lost companion. I take so much strength from the warmth of his little body against mine, from the rhythmical, comforting percussion of his purring. *He has loved Max too*, I often think. *He understands.* Max's hands have stroked the same patch of coat I am stroking now.

Macavity is like my little lifebelt, tethered by time to the man I love.

It's Saturday, I've realised – early afternoon, and another warm day. Sunlight is glancing off the furniture, my reward for having cleaned up. This time last year, Max and I might have been walking hand in hand through South Bank, the Thames shifting and heaving beside us like a serpent. We might have lunched in Borough Market, picked up some things for dinner, then meandered back to the flat eating our favourite gelatos, our hearts and bellies full.

I motion for Dean to sit, which he does, on the sofa. He's wearing Ray-Bans pushed up onto his head and a T-shirt, his face faintly bronzed from the last couple of weeks' sun. I suppose he's been out somewhere with Chrissy and his daughter, enjoying some much-needed family time. Because it's Saturday, and life goes on. Or at least, it does for Dean and Chrissy, and they'd be crazy not to make the most of every single second.

I've got to know them well over the past year or so. Chrissy works in television, is high up at a production company specialising in factual entertainment. We'd become quite a tight little foursome, hanging out at our flat or at their house in Chiswick, picnicking on the Common, enjoying long, lazy weekend lunches, walking the Thames Path on Sundays with their daughter Sasha on her little bike. It's hard to know how our friendship will change, now that Max is gone. I suppose, inevitably, it will. I'm fairly sure there'll only be so many times they'll let me play gooseberry: that's not how socialising's supposed to work.

I messaged Dean after finding the ring. I had to know the story, and I was pretty sure Dean would have it. He and Max had become super close in the years since leaving uni – perhaps because as everyone's friendships evolved, broke up or moved on, they discovered they had even more in common as adults than they did as students.

'Can I see it?' he asks now.

I pass him the box. He lifts the lid, then smiles, like it brings back a warm memory. 'That's the one. I helped him choose it. Hatton Garden. It's five carats, emerald cut—'

'When?' I whisper.

Dean is never lost for words, but he takes a really long time to answer. 'The week before he died,' he says, eventually, his voice gentle as an echo.

'Did he say . . . how he was going to . . . ?'

Dean smiles faintly, then shakes his head. His blue eyes look watery. He's lost weight too, since Max died. Chrissy told me recently he's been working non-stop. 'He mentioned some ideas. Like doing it at the Observatory, or the Eye, or the Shard. But to be honest, I think he probably would have just dropped down on one knee right here in this flat, Lucy. He didn't need to perform some grand gesture to prove how much he loved you.'

I shut my eyes, let his words swim through me. I would trade anything – *anything* – for Max to walk into this room right now, if only for a few moments, so I could give him my answer. *Yes. Oh, I love you so much. A million times, yes.*

'I'm sorry I didn't tell you before,' Dean says. 'I didn't know what was best. Chrissy's been saying I should, but . . . I thought it might make everything worse.'

'No,' I say softly, shaking my head. 'It's the opposite. It's like ... me and Max have just had another conversation, and I never thought I'd get that chance.'

We don't say anything else for a few moments, just sip from our cups, contemplating. I get that strange metallic taste on my tongue again, try to wash it away with the coffee.

On my lap, Macavity shifts, stretching and flexing a paw before tucking it neatly back where it came from.

'In case you ever doubted how much you meant to Max,' Dean says, eventually, 'you should know, Lucy, that you were his whole world. He'd been so happy since you guys got back together.'

My eyes fill with tears, and though I can't speak, I nod my thank-you.

Dean wipes away a couple of his own tears now, leaning forward to grab some tissues from the box ever present on the coffee table. He passes me one. 'God, I miss him.'

I blow my nose, then decide that since Dean is here, I will ask the question that plagues me constantly. The one always flickering in my line of sight, like an insect I can't dispatch. 'Dean, do you blame me?'

Until the family liaison officer confirmed that Max had died twenty minutes after we'd finished speaking that night, I'd been tormented by the thought that our conversation on the phone had had a part to play in his death. To know the two events were unconnected didn't make losing him any more bearable, but at least it put that particular fear to rest.

Still. Max had been on his way to see me, and I'd told him to turn around. If I'd said yes, got excited, seen it for the romantic idea it was, he would still be alive.

What Might Have Been

Dean already knows what I said to Max that night – in the immediate aftermath of the accident, I seemed to be on a mission to tell as many people as possible, maybe because I was seeking the punishment I felt sure I deserved. But he's never displayed even the tiniest glimmer of resentment towards me for it. Still, the nature of grief is so fluid, so fickle. Perhaps now he's had time to think about it, he's realised I am partly culpable.

'Nobody blames you,' he tells me firmly, leaning forward so I'm obliged to meet his eye. 'Nobody would, not ever. You couldn't possibly have known, Lucy.'

I nod, then look away from him and down at my hands, which are dry and neglected, much like the rest of me. 'But I just keep thinking . . . if only I'd said yes.'

Pippa's been encouraging me to stop this – questioning everything, agonising over every tiny decision I've ever made. Because, she says, even if I had all the answers I'm looking for, the reality of losing Max would be exactly the same.

Dean nods as though he truly understands. 'That was Max all over, wasn't it? Just wanting to help.'

I pause. When you're grieving, people say a lot of odd things to you – sometimes because they feel they just need to say *something* – and occasionally you have to stop and work out what they mean.

'Help?' I repeat.

'You know, with your . . .' Dean clocks my expression, trails off.

I feel a coldness wash over me. But not cold like a breeze – cold like a deep, deep chill. 'With my what?'

He waits for a couple of moments. 'Ah, sorry. I've put my foot in it.'

'Please tell me what you mean.'

He hesitates. 'I had lunch with Max that day. He said you had this . . . thing about being on your own in hotel rooms, so he was going to drive to Surrey that night and surprise you. So you wouldn't be by yourself.'

And now it's like the armchair has slid sideways, because my face has somehow landed in a cushion, and Macavity has fled my lap. And I am sobbing hot, messy tears for the sweetness of Max's gesture, feeling like I've lost him all over again.

Dean stays with me until it gets dark, only leaving once I've assured him he's not made everything a hundred times worse. I'm not sure if he has or hasn't, really – my head is swarming with new questions and self-recriminations, but at least my brain is busy. It makes me feel less alone, somehow.

I curl up on the sofa with Macavity after Dean goes, thinking – as I do most days – about what would have happened if I'd told Max to come to the hotel that night. If I'd never met the man who gave me my phobia of strange places. If Max had never slept with Tash. If we'd never split up.

But eventually, as the darkness drains into a pink-stippled dawn, I realise Pippa is right. No amount of rumination or soul-searching will change the fact that Max is gone, and he isn't coming back. What Dean told me last night doesn't change anything, not really. It only confirms what I already knew – that Max loved me to the tips of my toes. He'd made mistakes, sure. But he had more than made up for them in the nineteen months since we'd got back together.

It's Sunday now, so beyond the living-room window, the world is quiet, though I do hear the occasional sprinkle of conversation, the slapping of trainers running past on the pavement. Then I realise I'm nauseous again.

It occurs to me as I rush to the toilet that I haven't eaten in twenty-four hours. The cake Dean brought me lies untouched on the coffee table. A waste of quality patisserie, but I can't stomach anything sweet. So at eight a.m., I make canned macaroni cheese. I don't have the energy to create anything more nutritious, which is just as well, because I throw it up about twenty minutes later, at the same time as Jools' number starts flashing on my phone.

'Again?' she says, once I'm back in the kitchen and have returned her call, told her why I couldn't pick up.

'It's fine,' I say, thinking about what Pippa said. 'It's normal, apparently.'

'But you threw up yesterday. And the day before. And the day before that.'

'I know,' I say vaguely, sensing she might be trying to make a bigger point, though I can't quite grasp what that is. It's not up to me how my body responds to losing Max, is it?

'Lucy,' Jools whispers. I hear her voice wobbling slightly down the phone. 'Is there any chance ... you might be pregnant?'

For a few moments I don't reply. I just stare straight ahead of me at the letter magnets on the fridge, which Max arranged to spell *MAX LOVES LUCY 4 EVER XO*. I'm so paranoid about someone messing them up I must have taken about fifty photos of them on my phone.

Working saliva onto my tongue, I dare to taste the magic of Jools' words, just for a moment. And then – for the first time since Max died – I detect the faintest wisp of something unfurling, spiralling to the ceiling like a smoke signal. It is strange, and at first, I can't quite tell what it is.

And then I realise. It is hope.

So, thirty minutes later, I head into the bathroom with a pregnancy test in one hand and my heart in the other. Jools offered to come round and sit with me, but I need to do this alone.

Almost robotically, I take the test, then perch on the edge of the bath to wait. My hand is shaking.

I wish you were here, Max. I wish you were sitting next to me, squeezing my hand. I wish we were praying together for that little blue cross to appear. I never actually believed in the afterlife until you died. But now, I do. Because I know you're here. I know that somewhere, your heartbeat is hammering just as hard as mine.

A mewl slides through the gap beneath the bathroom door before it nudges open to reveal Macavity, like he's as impatient to know the outcome as I am.

I take a breath and turn the test over. And there it is: my hopelessness diminished, my despair drifting away. Because against all the odds, Max is still here. His baby boy or girl is two months old and nestled inside me, gifting me with a joy I thought I'd never feel again.

What Might Have Been

I think back to the day I moved in here with him. To him asking me, playfully, how I saw our future panning out.

How many kids?

Three. No, four.

I steady my racing heart, stare down at my stomach.

Just the one, as it turned out. But you're the most precious gift I've ever been given.

In a few more months' time, I will look into the eyes of my baby and whisper, *Oh, hi. It's you. I've missed you so much. I'm so glad you're home.*

Epilogue

One year later

Stay

I n the café next to the birth centre at Queen Charlotte's
and Chelsea Hospital, I look up as I'm waiting for my
Americano, and catch my breath.

Max Gardner. The man who haunted my dreams for so
many years is standing just inches away, ahead of me in the
queue. He looks older, of course – not a boy any more – but
the extra years flatter him. I can see straight away that all
his best qualities remain: that he is confident and charming
as ever, a magnet of a man with a wholehearted laugh and
reel-you-in eyes.

The hospital's pretty warm, and I've lost layers since
three a.m. this morning, when we came in. I'm now down
to just a cotton dress and some cheap rubber flip-flops,
which compared to Max – in his designer shirt and smart
jeans – suddenly feels unsophisticated, almost childlike. It
strikes me that we probably would never have been as good
a match as grown-ups as we were as students.

He doesn't look tired like I do – in fact, at first glance he
appears pretty wired. Must be the adrenaline rush of

impending fatherhood. Or maybe this is his fifth coffee since he got here.

His smile when he sees me suggests this is the happiest coincidence ever. '*Lucy*. Hello.' Laughter lines spring to the corners of his eyes.

We stand to one side as we wait for our drinks.

'Are you—'

'Yep.' Max half-turns, tips his head back towards the birth centre. 'My wife, Camille. Our first.'

I glance down, notice the dark matte ring around his finger. *How strange,* I think, *that I used to dream about seeing a ring on his hand because* we'd *got married.*

I might once have made a mental note to google Camille as soon as I'm alone. But I'm relieved to realise I have no feelings deeper than mild curiosity about the woman Max has married. Which is, of course, exactly as it should be. 'Congratulations. Do you know what you're—'

'A little girl,' he says, eyes burning with pride. I see him take in my flat(ish) stomach (maternity units, I guess, are the only place in the world where it's half-acceptable to do that). 'But you're not . . . ?'

Hopefully soon, I want to say, but instead I shake my head. 'I'm here with Jools. Remember Jools? She's two weeks early. Her husband's up north for work. Racing down the M1 as we speak.'

Jools and Nigel got married last August, and they'll happily tell anyone who'll listen that they conceived on their wedding night. (I'm not too sure about the accuracy of that, but who am I to argue with such a romantic thought?)

Max smiles, then turns his gaze meaningfully to the rings on my finger. 'So, you're married?'

I nod. 'Caleb. He's a photographer. We actually got married just last month.' Even saying his name brings a flush of warmth to my belly.

'Newlyweds,' Max says, with a smile I can't quite interpret – reminiscence? Envy? 'Congratulations, Luce.'

Four weeks ago today, to be exact. It was at Shoreley Hall, an outdoor wedding in the walled garden where we watched *Romeo and Juliet* that night three years ago. The whole day was luminous and heartfelt, filled with colour and joy. We decorated the fruit trees with bunting and pom-poms, strung lines of bulbs between the branches to glow when darkness fell. Caleb had a raft of friends taking care of the catering, pictures and music. Two of his nieces were my bridesmaids, along with Jools, and Dylan was a page boy. Our guests squeezed together on long trestle benches for the ceremony, umbrellas at the ready in case it rained. My parents even spent the day by each other's side, despite still being separated. There was dancing, and a few tipsy speeches, and a vast Mediterranean feast. And laughter, so much laughter.

Towards the end of the night, Caleb and I stole a quiet couple of moments together, perched hand in hand on top of a hay bale. I rested my head on his shoulder as we watched the happy, swollen throng of our friends and family in front of us, jiving and joking and throwing arms around each other. I was barefoot at that point, exhausted from all the dancing, and Caleb asked if I was happy.

'The happiest,' I whispered. And it was true. I couldn't imagine ever being happier than I was in that moment.

'Funny,' Max says now, an expression on his face that falls somewhere between nostalgia and regret, 'how life works out. I sometimes think how great it would have been to have had a crystal ball at eighteen.'

'Would you have done anything differently, if you had?'

He waits for the briefest of seconds as our gazes latch together. 'A few things.'

I look down. There's some stuff I might have done differently too. But I know I wasn't meant to end up anywhere other than where I am right now.

'You know what else is funny?' Max says. 'I actually have you to thank for meeting Camille.'

I frown with bemusement. 'Me?'

'You probably won't remember this, but . . . a few years back, I sent you a WhatsApp.'

'Oh, right.' Of course I remember: standing in Jools' kitchen in Tooting nearly three years ago, trying to decide if I should respond. Panicking when I realised Caleb might have overheard. I never did reply. 'Sorry I didn't—'

'No, I mean, it worked out for the best, right? I have to admit, when I sent you that message, I was kind of hoping we might . . . I don't know. Hook up again.' He laughs. 'I was a bit crazy about it. I kept checking my phone, but you didn't reply, and I was feeling a bit glum. So I went out for a few beers to cheer myself up and . . . that was actually the night I met Camille.'

I smile. 'And now you're about to become a dad.'

He looks at me for a couple of moments. 'I know. Mad, isn't it?' And with that, any lingering fragments of wistfulness evaporate from his eyes.

Max's name is called then, and he collects his coffee. We hug goodbye. It's a strange feeling, holding him in my arms again after so many years. His body feels broader and firmer – more adult, I guess. Like he's found his place in life.

As I watch him walk away, I realise there was a time when I might have called after him, when I might have thought meeting him here was a sign of some sort. And maybe it is – but only as a friendly reminder from fate that I made the right choice, not moving to London three years ago. Perhaps, finally, it's the closure I was looking for all those years before, when he broke my heart.

As he's about to round the corner and disappear from sight, Max turns. Our eyes meet, and just for a moment, a universe of possibilities and what-ifs unravels and waltzes through the space between us. And it makes me smile.

He raises a hand, and I do the same. And then he is gone.

Much later, back in Shoreley, I slip into bed next to Caleb. It's the early hours of the morning now, and I've just driven home from the hospital, where I've left Jools and Nigel falling in love with their new daughter, Florence.

The bedroom window is open, the sound of the slumbering sea drifting through it like a symphony. The bedroom feels almost unnervingly cool and peaceful after the heat and racket of the postnatal ward – though Jools, of course, high on oxytocin, seemed oblivious to the surround-sound wailing and sobbing. Instead, she looked completely serene, as though the midwives had wheeled her straight from the labour ward into a five-star health spa.

Caleb stirs as I slip my arms around him. He smells of soap and toothpaste, his skin warmed and softened by sleep.

'Hey,' he mumbles, turning over to face me.

'Hey.'

We kiss and he strokes the hair from my face. 'How's Jools? How's the baby?'

'Both completely perfect. Jools is a total warrior.' I was with her right up until the final moments, when Nigel suddenly appeared, stricken with panic that he might have missed his baby being born. I'd always known Jools was tough, but until I saw her in labour, I had no idea what that actually meant. But within minutes of her contractions kicking in, she became so primally driven, so fiercely focused, that I knew Florence would never have to worry about a thing.

'So, how did it feel,' Caleb says, 'being surrounded by all those newborns?'

I smile. 'Amazing, obviously. I was fawning over all of them. Probably a good job I left when I did.'

He grins. 'You're ready for some hardcore godmothering then.'

'No other godmother's going to come close.'

'Lucky Florence.'

'No, lucky me.'

He moves forward to kiss me again, releasing a slow breath that becomes a question against my skin. 'So, does this mean we might be ready to . . . ?'

We've talked about our future, and the family we both want, a lot since we got married. But we've not actually started trying yet, because I've been so caught up with Jools and writing lately, and Caleb's had a hectic few weeks at work.

A few months ago, Naomi and I decided, after much back and forth, that my book wasn't quite ready for submission to publishers. We agreed something was still missing; that what it needed was a present-day element, so I'm undertaking a hefty rewrite to incorporate a second timeline of a young couple striving to uncover the secrets of a love affair begun in Margate before the war. I've been working on it between shifts at Pebbles & Paper, where the people who drift through the door every morning have provided a surprisingly rich source of inspiration for my characters.

But now, at last, I'm over the hump with the rewrite: the end seems to be within touching distance, finally. And Caleb's workload is easing off slightly too. The timing feels as though it might actually be right.

'Yes,' I whisper, with a shiver of excitement. 'I want to make a baby with you.' I press my mouth to his, feeling elation spread through me as we start to embark upon the next chapter of our lives. And all I can think about is how happy I am to be creating a future with this spectacular, brilliant man; that the choice I made on a warm spring day three years ago brought me together with my soulmate.

And if I hadn't made that choice? Well, I still feel sure Caleb and I would have found our way into each other's lives eventually. But as it is, I'm spilling over with gratitude that I don't have to wait another second to love this man with every last particle of my heart.

Go

I am with Hope by the pond at the Common, close to the café. It's May now, and the air is sparkling with the brightness of early summer. The sky is an aquatic blue, the trees newly weighted with blossom and greenery. I have shed my jacket, and Hope is content in her little dungarees and striped T-shirt. On the opposite side of the pond, model boats are sailing serenely in circles, steered by children watched over by eager fathers.

I suppress the familiar lurch in my stomach, and focus on my daughter.

Hope, as ever, is delighted by the ducks. She is smiling and gabbling, mashing pieces of the bread we've brought for feeding into paste with her squidgy fists. God, I love her so much.

It's a year since I discovered I was pregnant. During the seven months that followed, I barely dared to move, for fear of doing anything that might sever my last – miraculous – connection to Max. I assumed I'd feel less nervous once Hope was born, once she was actually living and breathing in front of me – but of course, the living and breathing just sent my protective instincts into overdrive. It's only thanks to the support of my therapist Pippa, and of course my family and friends like Jools, that I've developed enough confidence to ever leave the flat with her.

Our baby daughter is now five months old, and I miss her father every day. Each morning I search her tiny face for more clues to him, my little treasure map of Max. And I'm convinced I find them daily, though perhaps I'm only imagining it. The mildness in her grey eyes. The lightness in her laugh. Her apparent enthusiasm for life.

Jools comes striding back towards us with two coffees, sunglasses on. 'God bless this sunshine.' She passes me a cup. 'How are the ducks today?'

Hope and I are, it has to be said, prolific duck-feeders. She absolutely adores them, and I like to think that's because she's inherited her father's good heart, his compassion.

Jools and I sit down together on a nearby bench. Above our heads, pigeons tack back and forth across a spotless blue sky. The air is rich with the music of chiff-chaffs, blackbirds, song thrushes.

I jiggle Hope on my lap with one hand, sip my coffee with the other. 'It's days like this that I miss him the most,' I say, after a few moments.

She nods. 'I know. He'd love this, wouldn't he?'

That's my overriding feeling about Max being gone, these days. That it's just not fair. He's missing out on so much. I never let myself dwell on *just* how much he'll miss out on – the rest of my life, the whole of Hope's, and most of the lives of *her* children too – because that thought is too gut-wrenching to comprehend. But he's in my thoughts constantly – on the tube and at the café, the streets around our home, in every room at the flat. And even in Shoreley, whenever we're back there seeing Mum and Dad, because every time we are, I deliberately take a detour to walk past The Smugglers.

I'd give anything for just one more day. Or even a few precious hours, so Max could hold his baby daughter, and I could lay my head on his shoulder and tell him one last time just how much I love him.

I started back at Supernova last week, which felt very strange, like I'd wandered into an alternate reality. Because some things were the same – most things, in fact: my colleagues, my clients, my desk, my lunch routine. But other things – the big things – were astonishingly and irreversibly altered. Max being gone. And Hope having become the new centre of my world. It's been tough, readjusting to the noise and pace, the buzzing industry of the office, after spending so long in my Hope-shaped bubble. But I wanted it. I *needed* it – I knew I had to come back before I got too comfortable and our lives became defined by my grief. I kept imagining Hope as a teenager, shrugging her shoulders and saying, 'My dad died before I was born, so that's why my mum's a bit . . . you know.'

I don't want to be a-bit-you-know. I want to make my daughter – and Max – proud.

Along the pavement in front of us, a young couple are walking with their son. He's small – a year old, maybe – and looks adorably wobbly on his chubby legs. Jools smiles and says hello to them as they pass, but I have to look away.

I do get jealous. I can't help it. I got jealous while I was pregnant – at NCT classes when the other dads showed up, in the waiting room at my antenatal appointments, at the hospital when I gave birth. And I get jealous here, and in coffee shops, and at my mother-and-baby group when everyone's griping about their husbands or partners. Sometimes when they start, I just walk off, grabbing Hope and abandoning my coffee or whatever it is I'm doing. My new friends know why, and they don't give me a hard time about it, but that doesn't stop them complaining about their other halves, either.

I had to watch the grey-faced driver in court last week admit to causing death by careless driving. Sentencing is next month, but it won't bring me any kind of satisfaction. It was an accident, Max is gone, and nothing can change that. I've been surprised to realise I don't harbour any bitterness towards the driver: haven't we all changed lanes without looking properly before, had a split-second near-miss, sworn to pay more attention in future? It could have been me as much as it was him.

'Oh, I nearly forgot,' Jools says, probably sensing I'm getting stuck in a thought-bog. 'They had these on the counter in the café.' She pulls a piece of paper from her pocket, unfolds it and hands it to me.

I look down at it. It's a flyer advertising a local creative writing group.

'What's this?' I say, bemused.

She shrugs. 'Just thought you might be interested. Didn't Pippa say writing might help?'

'Yeah, but . . . I write for a living.'

'For work, yes. This would be for you, though.'

I look down at the flyer again, nibble my lip. It would be easy to say I don't have the time, or the inclination right now . . . but I definitely don't hate the idea of it. In fact, I'd go as far as to say it appeals. And I can't exactly explain why. Maybe it just taps into a version of me I'd thought was long gone, and that feels surprisingly comforting.

'Hey, you said you knew a good photographer in Shoreley, didn't you?' Jools is asking, as she sips from her coffee.

I bend over to kiss the top of Hope's head. She wriggles a bit, but otherwise she's still captivated by the panorama of the pond and the mallards. 'Er, yeah. He did my head-shots at Supernova. Caleb. He was nice.' I let out a half-laugh. 'The guy who wrote his number on a beer mat.'

'Reckon he does weddings?'

Jools and Nigel have been together for two years now. And six months ago, Nigel got down on one knee, having hidden the ring inside a muffin that Jools very nearly choked on. Before Max died, Jools had never really been that big on marriage. But I think she and Nigel have decided now that life is too short. That if you find the right person, you'd be crazy to procrastinate, even for a second.

'Not sure. But I could email him, if you like.'

'Would you mind?' Jools sips her coffee. 'We met with a couple of people last week, but we didn't get a very ... chilled-out vibe from them. You know?'

I nod. From what I remember of Caleb, he seemed like someone who'd put you at ease straight away.

Later that night, Hope is dozing on my chest, weighty and warm as a hot-water bottle. I press my nose against her head, inhale the sweet, milky smell of her.

I've just polished off a giant takeaway tray of sushi. I rejected food for so long after Max died – feeling, somehow, that I didn't deserve nourishment – but now I shovel it down, knowing it's fuelling life with my baby girl. The world seems less daunting when my belly is full. And right now, I need all the strength I can get.

The flat is calm and still, neat and orderly, just as it would have been when Max was alive. I have lit a candle someone gave me after he died, a Jo Malone with a scent faintly similar to his favourite aftershave. It comforts me, somehow, helps me to imagine he's still here, watching over us.

I've employed a cleaner recently, and have a nanny to care for Hope while I'm at Supernova. The life insurance payout of four times Max's salary ensures Hope and I will always be able to muddle through. It means I can afford childcare so I can go to work, pay the mortgage, continue to live rather than just survive. I know how fortunate I am to have that. I can be a mum to Hope, and pursue my career, and do all the things that make me feel fulfilled. Stuff that propels me forward, so I don't end up stagnating and full of regrets.

Mum and Dad were in the latter stages of planning their sailing trip when we got the news about Max. And then, of course, came the miracle of my pregnancy. They've put the journey off for a few months, and there's a part of me that's selfishly relieved. If Max can die driving at sixty-eight miles per hour in the middle lane of the M25, I'm not too thrilled about my parents casting off in Portsmouth and heading for Antigua via Gran Canaria in a twelve-year-old yacht. They're still determined to go, having spent thousands on preparing the boat, upgrading the sails and rigging, putting together a comprehensive inventory of spares and qualifying as skippers. But I'll think about that when the time comes.

What Might Have Been

In the fourteen months since Max died, I've rarely been without company. Tash, Simon and Dylan are coming to visit this weekend, and Jools usually stays over a couple of nights a week. And the upside of receiving so many bouquets of flowers in the early days is that I've got to know my neighbours much better, too – Jed, Toby and Magda, and Nadia. We pause to chat in the hall, pop in and out of each other's flats, go for the occasional drink. All of which means I feel much less stressed when Hope decides to exercise her lungs in the middle of the night.

I'm doing a spot of work on my phone now, replying one-handed to emails and messages, giving the thumbs-up on artwork, and I'm just swiping between apps when my gaze lands on the old horoscope app I used to look at almost daily. I haven't used it for more than three years. In fact, the last time I did was that night in The Smugglers, when it informed me I would bump into my soulmate.

I smile faintly. *Soulmate.* It's a while since I believed in those. I think back to how I'd wavered at the time between thinking it was referring to Max or Caleb.

My email pings.

I switch apps and look down. Surprise traps my breath momentarily in my chest.

It's from Caleb.

> Hi Lucy. Nice to hear from you. I'm so sorry about your partner. I really hope you're holding up okay. Yes, I do the occasional wedding – send me your friend's number and I'll be in touch.

I don't know why I felt the need to tell him about Max, in my rambling email enquiry that should really have only been two lines long. I'm not usually in the habit of burdening people with the story of me and Max, but it seemed oddly fitting, somehow, to fill Caleb in.

I suddenly realise he's attached something to his email, and I scroll down.

> I remember you saying when I did your headshot that the guy you went to talk to outside The Smugglers that night was called Max. (Don't ask me how – maybe I googled him.) Anyway, that night, you both looked kind of . . . giddy. I was heading off, and I was going to say goodbye, but you were so absorbed in each other . . . Well, cut a long story short, I had my camera with me, and I took a quick shot. It just struck me, how you were looking at each other. It was . . . I don't know how to explain it. Rare.

I feel my heart fragment inside my chest.

> Sorry. Hope you don't think it was creepy of me. I just have this weird instinct to document stuff. Anyway, I was actually going to send you the photo if you got in touch, but . . . well. It's attached. I'm hoping it might bring you some comfort. There was a reason I snapped it. You two look like you were meant to be.
> All my best, Caleb

I open the photo. It is shot at an angle, reportage-style, and centre stage are Max and me, the whitewashed frontage of The Smugglers in the background, its trademark line of lights looping from the thatched roof. I gasp out loud – it is like seeing him all over again, in that black woollen coat he loved and the pinstriped suit, which are both still hanging in his side of our wardrobe, because I will never get rid of his clothes. I am wearing a black dress – the same one I wore to his funeral – and my long blond hair is glimmering. I remember worrying I looked ropey that evening, but I needn't have. I looked good. We both did. Like we were posing for a slightly kooky office-wear advert.

I touch the screen with my fingertips, willing the picture to spring to life so I can be back there, just for a second, and revisit the joy in his eyes, smell the scent of his skin, reach out and touch his hand. Kiss him. Tell him I love him.

We might have been married ourselves by now. But in the absence of that, maybe this can be our substitute wedding photo. A day on which we looked at each other in wonder, like the world had stopped turning just for us.

I raise the screen so Hope can see. She blinks at it, and then at me, wriggling a little.

'That's your daddy,' I whisper, so she knows. 'He loved me so much. And he would have loved you so much, too.'

Three years ago, I took a chance on Max. And though it didn't pay off with the lifetime of happiness I'd hoped for – or our beach wedding, or four children – I know I have a different lifetime of happiness waiting for me now, with our beautiful daughter.

Tears are spilling from my eyes, so I press Hope to me and let them fall. She doesn't stir as I shudder. Perhaps she's used to my ever-changing tide of emotions. *I need to do something about that*, I think. I don't want my baby to grow up sad.

As the night deepens and Hope sleeps, I reflect on Caleb's email. And I think perhaps – lovely as the sentiment was – that he wasn't quite right. Max and I weren't meant to be. We *chose* to be.

I used to believe in soulmates. In fate, and destiny. Now? Being with Max has taught me we're actually the sum of our choices. Loving Max, and Max dying, and Hope arriving – weren't all those things down to the decisions we made? Paths we took, or ignored? Nothing is pre-determined, I'm pretty convinced of that now.

I wouldn't have it any other way, of course. I'd choose Max again in a heartbeat. But as for the future? I really have no idea. All I can do is work hard, and be the best mum that I can to Hope, and everything else should fall into place.

I open my email, and write Caleb a heartfelt thank-you. I feel sure – I'm not exactly sure why – that Jools will choose him to be her wedding photographer next spring.

And then, when I see him, I can thank him again in person.

Acknowledgements

I'd like to thank my agent Rebecca Ritchie, for your stellar support and guidance, as always. And my editors Kimberley Atkins and Tara Singh Carlson, for your endless effort and expertise in helping to shape and coax this book through its many iterations. Thanks also to Amy Batley and Ashley Di Dio. A big thank you as well to everyone at Hodder & Stoughton and Putnam Books: writing fiction for a living never fails to feel like a privilege, and I'm so grateful for everything you've done and continue to do. To all the amazing bloggers who champion books so tirelessly and passionately. To my friends and family, with a special mention to Mark. And finally, to our rescue dog Meg, who was by my side during every word of writing this novel. I miss you.